RUN AND HIDE

RUN AND HIDE

Pankaj Mishra

FARRAR, STRAUS AND GIROUX

NEW YORK

Farrar, Straus and Giroux
120 Broadway, New York 10271

Printed in the United States of America
Originally published in 2022 by Hutchinson Heinemann, Great Britain
Published in the United States by Farrar, Straus and Giroux
First American edition, 2022

Lines quoted from *A Bend in the River* by V. S. Naipaul.
Lyrics referenced on pages 10 and 56 from *Waqt Ne Kiya Kya Haseen Sitam*,
sung by Geeta Dutt and written by Kaifi Azmi.
Lines quoted on page 74 from *Rig Veda*, translated by Wendy Doniger.
Lines quoted on page 100 from the introduction by Jean Paul Sartre to *Wretched of
the Earth* by Frantz Fanon (translated by Constance Farrington).

Library of Congress Cataloging-in-Publication Data
Names: Mishra, Pankaj, author.
Title: Run and hide / Pankaj Mishra.
Description: First American edition. | New York : Farrar, Straus and Giroux, 2022.
Identifiers: LCCN 2021047317 | ISBN 9780374607524 (hardcover)
Subjects: LCGFT: Fiction.
Classification: LCC PR9499.3.M538 R86 2022 | DDC 823/.914—dc23/eng/20211014
LC record available at https://lccn.loc.gov/2021047317

Our books may be purchased in bulk for promotional, educational,
or business use. Please contact your local bookseller or the Macmillan Corporate
and Premium Sales Department at 1-800-221-7945, extension 5442, or by email
at MacmillanSpecialMarkets@macmillan.com.

www.fsgbooks.com
www.twitter.com/fsgbooks • www.facebook.com/fsgbooks

1   3   5   7   9   10   8   6   4   2

For J. H. B.

PART ONE

One

During Aseem's first days in prison, I lull myself into sleep every night with a vision: I am swimming across the clear calm surface of the sea until I am far from the shore, and then, turning and lying on the water, my face to the sky, I let myself sink.

The trail of breath-bubbles fading, the water penetrates my nostrils and mouth and gradually fills my body until I am heavy and falling soundlessly, deeper into the endless blue.

I am asleep before my body comes to rest on the messy floor of the sea.

That's how I used to lull myself to sleep as a child; and if I feel compelled to speak to you of those times, and to pick out of the past those scraps you overlooked in your own book, and unearth memories that I long suppressed, it is because they foreshadowed everything that happened between us.

I am sure I'll fall into the wrong tone, and risk provoking your disgust and anger; but I must speak, too, of Aseem. My first friend and early protector, he not only introduced me to you; he also encouraged me to pursue you, before so violently and inextricably knotting all our destinies together.

Aseem, who saw himself as a mascot of triumphant self-invention, loved initiating his friends into his dream of power and glory. He presented it, in fact, as an existential imperative, ceaselessly quoting V. S. Naipaul: 'The world is what it is; men who are nothing, who allow themselves to become nothing, have no place in it.'

It won't be easy, he would say, for self-made men of our lowly social backgrounds. He would cite Chekhov – how the son of a slave has to squeeze, drop by drop, the slave's blood out of himself until he wakes one day to find the blood of a real man coursing through his veins. He would become very emotional speaking of the struggle to take ourselves seriously – which he said came before the struggle to persuade others to take us seriously, and was more exacting.

He always seemed so fluent and so certain; I couldn't argue with him. It is only in retrospect that I can see the danger Aseem never reckoned with: that in our attempts to remake ourselves, to become 'real men' simply by pursuing our strongest desires and impulses, with no guidance from family, religion or philosophy, our self-awareness would narrow, the distortions in our characters would go unnoticed, until the day we awaken with horror to the people we had become.

The warning signs were there the very first time I met Aseem. I never told you about it during all the conversations we had about him, Virendra and the others when you were researching your book: how on our first night at IIT we were awakened by hollering men long past midnight from the deep sleep that follows nervous exhaustion and herded into a crowded seniors' room, where the blast of cigarette smoke was strong enough to knock you down, and where a student wearing a lungi that exposed his thick hairy legs shouted *'Behenchod'* with a Tamil accent, and asked us to strip and get down on the floor on our hands and knees.

This was Siva; heavy-set, his big round shaven head seemed to sit necklessly on his shoulders. He was furious, or feigned great fury, because the three of us had somehow missed a broader corralling of freshers that night.

'You sister-fuckers,' he shouted from his bed, where several of his friends lounged, their bespectacled eyes looking on us with malign inquisitiveness. 'You think you don't have to give us your introduction! Tell me, who the fuck are you? And I want you to bark like the good little dogs you are!'

From our canine posture, we intoned, simultaneously:

'I am Arun Dwivedi, Mechanical Engineering, All India Rank 62.'

'I am Virendra Das, Computer Science, All India Rank 487.'

'I am Aseem Thakur, Mechanical Engineering, All India Rank 187.'

We barked as Siva's cronies dissolved into giggles, and Siva himself emitted that booming laugh that you would hear many years later, when gathering material for your book, in those conversations taped by the FBI and leaked by his defence team to journalists.

Virendra, Aseem and I had met earlier that day in the student hostel assigned to us. So much already bound us together. At some point in our early teens, when our school grades started to show promise, our parents had decided that they would go into debt, skimp on clothes and food, and deny education to our siblings, in order to put their sons in the Indian Institute of Technology and on the path to redemption from scarcity and indignity.

For years afterwards, they told us that they were slaving from morning to night to give us the chance in life they themselves had never had. Our gifts of memory and concentration turned out to be a curse; the immense effort to enter the country's most prestigious engineering institution destroyed our childhoods, stuffing it with joyless tasks and obligations, and the dread of failure.

Now, our long wait, after passing the world's toughest and most competitive examinations, was finally over. On our first meeting, however, we barely exchanged a word. Overwhelmed initially by our achievement of fulfilling our early promise, we had been quickly demoralised into silence by seeing our ideal in the harsh light of day.

Peeling paint, naked light bulbs, croaking fans and the rainwater in the puddles jumping with mosquito larvae seemed to suggest that we had barely made it out of our dire lower-middle-class straits (I hadn't known, in those days before Google Images, what to expect of the portal to the world's richness.) The walls of our room were distempered sallow, with marks where oiled heads had rested, and smudges where mosquitoes had been squashed; the concrete floor of a pebbly roughness was encrusted with irremovable dirt, and in the darkness below our cots the layers of dust looked like velvet rags.

The dining hall with its dangerously swaying ceiling fans was on that first day a swirl of fathers in broad-lapelled blazers with brass buttons and thickly padded shoulders that left their hands lolling uneasily by their sides, and mothers unsteady on their feet in Kanjivaram and Benares silk saris and heavy gold jewellery, wearing smudged lipstick in the inexpert way of those who never wear it – people finally trying on self-satisfaction after subjecting themselves and their children to years of brutal fear and anxiety.

The air was full of the chemical tang of Old Spice aftershave and the flowery scent of Pond's talcum powder, suggesting, together with the dressed-up men and women, an attempt at celebration.

A staleness still lay over the hall, with chipped Formica tables and sooty blue walls, where flies escaping the fans bided their time.

Virendra, Aseem and I were among the very few newcomers unaccompanied by parents that evening. Our fathers and mothers knew better than to betray our origins at this crucial first step in their sons' ascent to respectability. On examination day, my mother had held a day-long Satyanarayan puja at home; and my father had paid for me to send him a telegram from Delhi when the results of the Joint Entrance Exams came out.

On receiving it, my mother told me, he had run around the railway station he worked at, distributing besan laddoos from an open box – to people probably as bemused by his extravagant elation as I was to hear of his transformation from sullen brute to deliriously proud father.

When the train taking me to my first semester at IIT Delhi pulled away, he waved. His lips moved, perhaps to say something, something that could not easily be put into words, then or ever: that I now belonged to a world that had scorned him. He would never dare come to Delhi while I was there; my mother could not even dream of the prospect; and I felt grateful for their psychic fetters every time I imagined them at the IIT's gates, asking in their dehati Hindi for me.

Many students would be ruthless in this regard. I remember the fair-skinned Bengali who boasted of his ancestral links to Rabindranath Tagore and a long familial connection to Oxford. Betrayed into ordinariness by the sudden appearance of his mother, a dumpy and dark-skinned little figure, who squatted on the ground on her haunches as she waited outside his room, he tried to present her as his housemaid.

Aseem kept his own parents at a distance, to maintain his fiction that his father was a very important railway official when he was only a junior engineer, and, perhaps, also to hide the fact that his parents, whom he ardently disliked, were bigots, determined to never allow Dalits and Muslims to enter their home.

I was nervous on that first day for a reason I could not dare reveal to anyone then. I had seen Virendra's surname next to mine on the bulletin board, denoting his ancestry among the pariahs who skinned the hides off dead cows, and were strictly untouchable, even unapproachable, for upper-caste Hindus.

A few minutes later, he stumbled into my room, weighed down by an olive-green bedroll and a tin trunk, on which his name was painted in Hindi in white, with curlicues aiming at a 3D effect.

Thin and small-boned, he wore polyester bell-bottoms and a blue nylon bush shirt. His shoes had been rubbed to a shiny black; and the buckle of his very broad belt, also black, showed two brass snakes in a headlock. In his small eyes above a snub nose and tidily trimmed thin moustache from Raaj Kumar films in the 1950s there was a startled blankness, and he filled the tiny listless room with a smell of coconut oil as he stacked his books and magazines – general knowledge guides and old issues of the *Competition Success Review* – on his desk and carefully placed a brush and tin of Cherry Blossom black shoe polish underneath his bed.

As he unpacked, the small golden watch on his slender wrist softly clinking, he revealed some more familiar emblems of a low-caste, semi-rural existence: a diamond-shaped hand mirror; a coarse-textured blanket; a framed portrait of Hanuman on one knee, ripping his chest open to reveal Ram and Sita enthroned inside; packets of Maggi noodles and a tin of desi ghee to garnish the thalis of the hostel mess.

I had made it to IIT, as they say, on 'merit'. I had an unimpeachably Brahmin surname, thanks to my father's efforts, and much fairer skin, attesting to birth among the highest born, and could even wear the janeu on any occasion that required me to bare my torso. But with Virendra in proximity, the hardwon security of my Brahmin lineage began to seem fragile.

*

Naked in Siva's room that night, amid a squalor of cigarette smoke, discarded chicken legs and empty bottles of Old Monk rum, and jeering men in dirty white vests and thick glasses, I felt completely exposed.

There had been a power cut and several streams of perspiration slowly coursed down my bare back before dropping on to the floor; the sweat rolled down my forehead, too, and from time to time I had to shake it off.

I became aware of a strange eye looking up at me; Virendra had taken off the watch that hung like a loose bracelet on his wrist – a HMT woman's watch, I noticed, on a thin fake-gold strip – and kept it on the very top of his pile of clothes, shoes and belt. From there, the middle of a coiled serpent, the ticking circlet stared at me, as if alive.

Lying back on his bed, underneath a pin-up of Cindy Crawford cupping her breasts, Siva kneaded his calves (years later, he would lavish a hundred thousand dollars at a charity gala in New York to sit next to the supermodel), as he shouted, 'Look at your shoes, as black and shiny as your face.'

There was a pause, in which I wondered why Virendra had worn his formal shoes to Siva's room in the middle of the night.

Siva shouted again, 'Where are you from, kaalu haramzada, blackie bastard?'

The question was aimed at only one of us.

'Mirpur, sir,' Virendra said in a reedy voice that made Siva and his friends dissolve into laughter.

'Where is Mirpur, saala chamar?'

'Basti in Gorakhpur district, sir.'

'Where is Gorakhpur, kaalu . . .'

I could see the halting place on the way to nowhere, shacks of tin and rags around a bus stop, a sugarcane crushing factory exhaling foul-smelling smoke in the near distance, and an artificial tank with bright green water choked by floating hyacinths, in which emaciated black-grey buffaloes stand perfectly still.

'OK, OK, enough geography,' Siva said. 'Gaana gao, saala chamar.'

After the briefest of pauses, Virendra started to jubilantly sing, '*Waqt ne kiya kya haseen sitam . . .*'

There was an explosion of laughter, and smaller bursts of mirth followed as a dauntless Virendra went on.

I heard Siva say, 'Panditji, please provide English translation.'

How little could he have known of the relief the honorific for Brahmins brought me.

'Sir,' I said, looking down at the floor, 'it means, "What a beautiful revenge time has taken, I am not who I once was, nor are you."'

My voice came out far too loudly. A couple of men cackled.

'What a fucking depressing song,' Siva said, eliciting more laughter. 'OK, OK, enough singing, Kaalu chamar. Ab chalo, Panditji ki gaand saaf karo.'

In his accent, his vicious command sounded as though he was asking a waiter for extra chillies with his thali.

His friends fell about, and it occurred to me that they might have also been laughing at his Hindi, sounding as he did like the comical South Indians found in Bollywood movies.

There was a pause as Siva took out from his pocket a folded white handkerchief and mopped his rotund face, polishing, at the very end, the tip of his nose.

I was wondering about that gesture when he said that Virendra could only enhance his karma, and avoid rebirth as a Dalit, by licking clean a Brahmin's anus while Aseem could aim at promotion from Kshatriya to Brahmin by jerking off at the spectacle.

*

You would have done more with this scene in your book than Aseem, who put it in his most recent novel. I noticed the spiral-bound manuscript remained unread in the pile of books on your side of our bed in London. I opened it one day, and then quickly buried it at the bottom of the stack; the character providing the novel's love interest – a young journalist from an upper-class Muslim background, educated at an Ivy League university, who won't drink water that hasn't been boiled or filtered, and smokes when she is nervous – was at least partly based on you.

Aseem was more inventive with his male lead, a Dalit student based on Virendra. He wished to show, in gritty social-realist style, the degradation of low-caste Hindus; and, accordingly, in his version of our first day at IIT, he turned all of us into Dalits, transposing the scene from IIT Delhi to a medical college in Ranchi.

The Dalit student based on Virendra became a victim of rape; his persecutors, placed behind drifting veils of beedi smoke, were uniformly upper caste and unsmilingly vicious small-towners from Bihar. And Aseem, in deference to a left-leaning Geist, turned Virendra into a Maoist ideologue, a charismatic spokesperson for a guerrilla outfit fighting mining corporations and their mercenary armies in Central Indian forests.

Virendra, as you know, took a wholly dissimilar path after IIT. But Aseem's exaggerated description of the atrocity inflicted on him was no sin against verisimilitude.

You were too young then, and probably don't know how commonplace, much more than today, lynching, blinding and rape of Dalits were in the darkness of the villages and small towns we had emerged from.

Politicians promising greater affirmative action and self-respect to low-caste Hindus were yet to become prominent.

Until then, the well-born Hindus could torment their upstart competitors without fear of reprisal or backlash. And Siva could always claim, in the unlikely event of an inquiry by IIT's administrators, that he was merely indulging in a rite of initiation that all new students underwent.

'Let's go, let's go, kaalu chamar, aage bhado, Panditji is waiting!' he shouted.

'Hey, Sai baba,' he addressed Aseem, whom he had told to kneel naked behind Virendra. 'What are you waiting for? Please get working on your pride and joy.'

'And, Panditji' he abruptly turned to me, 'please drop that miserable expression. I want you to look happy at this purification of your essential organ.'

His friends laughed a bit more at this, and Siva again took out his white handkerchief and mopped his face and polished his nose.

There was no recalcitrant pause from Virendra. I felt him move crab-like into position behind me, and then his thin bristly moustache was imprinting itself on my buttocks, his furtive tongue was leaving moist trails across their soft skin, and, trying to follow Siva's command and feign elation, I didn't know where to look, down at the coarse-grained floor, where the merciless eye of Virendra's watch stared back at me, or up at the boisterous faces below Cindy Crawford's breasts, two of them frantically chewing bubble gum, as Siva shouted, 'Faster, faster, behenchod, kaalu bastard.'

After four hours of this, punctuated by deafening and spine-chilling screams from elsewhere in the hostel, where other freshers were being ritually humiliated, we returned to our room.

Siva turned out to be overly fond of the ritual he had conceived; and our ordeal continued in his room for a few more nights. I came to know well the poster of Cindy Crawford, how the drawing pins holding it in place had grown rusty, and how its edges curled inwards morosely, revealing the abraded plaster of the wall. I came to recognise Siva's handkerchiefs, all daintily lace-edged. I can recall today the smell of cheap rum, and the sight of a rusty electric hotplate with naked wires and a plastic tea-strainer languishing in a dented saucepan in one corner; and I could not forget for a long time the ant that once kept scurrying about my knees before Virendra, quietly hectic behind me, mashed it into the floor and flicked the corpse off his fingers.

The skin on my knees and elbows broke; my eyes stung with cigarette smoke and lack of sleep; and for weeks afterwards my buttocks kept clenching and unclenching at their memory of Virendra's tongue. Aseem complained that his penis was sore for weeks afterwards, and that his foreskin bled.

Much more damage was inflicted on Virendra's frail body.

Occasionally, I heard stifled sobs on the other side of the room. And I once heard Aseem say, referring to Siva, 'What a rakshas.' Any expressions of fellow feeling or sympathy would have been superfluous, and none ever passed between us.

This would shock you, but then nothing in our lives had made us expect kindness from strangers. In Aseem's novel, the atrocity inflicted on Dalit students catalyses their radical political consciousness. In reality, none of us wished to or could break out of our assigned positions in the pecking order.

After all, those in Virendra's caste cluster had their own untouchables, people to terrorise and quell. In a year's time, we would have the opportunity to sit where Siva and his friends had sat, supervising the abasement of a new batch of freshers.

And then we knew that what awaited us in the future, if we remained imperturbable while both suffering and inflicting atrocity, was membership of the most superior caste: that of people who never have to worry about money.

Our habits of self-preservation had been forged early in our childhood, soon after starting the long preparation for IIT. We knew that we had no choice but to conserve our efforts; remain indifferent to all personal suffering and dishonour until at least the summit of security seemed within reach; and we knew, too, that four years at IIT would be the most gruelling part of this ascent.

Still, for months after that first night – long after Siva had ceased to call us to his room and began to appear less a demon than a Computer Science student of genius and an extravagantly generous figure, free with his notes to all and sundry, and the blunt features on his large round head welded into one impression of solidity and warmth – I would open the door to my room, half-anticipating the sight of Virendra's thin body dangling limply from the ceiling fan.

Suicides were common at the engineering and medical college. Virendra proved to be among those for whom humiliation was an expensive luxury. Opening the door to his putative corpse, I would mostly find him at his desk, bent over his Manufacturing Process homework, GRE practice tests or a copy of *Competition Success Review*, underneath the garlanded portrait of open-chested Hanuman on the wall.

His face seemed tighter, even obstinate, as though the weight of his impersonal will to succeed had settled even deeper into it.

He had attended coaching classes for the IIT entrance exams for much longer than any of us. Having barely scraped through, he would continue to struggle to raise his grade point average each term; and he held his pen in a clenched fist and drilled it into paper as though it was a weapon in a war with no mercy for the loser, where failure meant expulsion to his home: the room in the basti where young pigs and mangy dogs nuzzle mounds of trash, and bony black sheep rub themselves against a rusty water pump.

It was with a resolute bearing that he sat cross-legged on the floor, whisking a brush over his shoes, rubbed coconut oil in his scalp, holding in one hand his diamond-shaped mirror (which cracked after a few months, cleaving his head into uneven halves), or scrubbed his torso with Lifebuoy soap in the shower; it was with the agonizing intentness of someone teetering on the edge of non-comprehension that he took notes in one class after another, and read, lying on his side, the *Manorama Yearbook*, while intermittently rubbing his chilblains in that damp room.

Indifferent to the small joys of most students – rock bands, carrom and ping-pong contests, debating and quiz competitions, girl-watching at SPIC MACAY concerts and at the Priya cinema – he was diverted only by the old copy of *Playboy* featuring Kim Basinger on the cover that, troubled by bedbugs one evening, he found Aseem had concealed under his mattress.

Two

A year passed. The hostel filled up in the new semester, first with freshers looking disquieted by the initial fruits of their toil, and then with the sounds of their initiation: howls of exaggerated abuse, choruses of self-mockery and shrieks of hilarity and pain.

Virendra and Aseem had been allotted different rooms, but we were all in the same wing; and one day, passing Virendra's, and that familiar whiff of coconut oil, I saw a tottering pyramid of naked young men. Virendra in his Sandoz baniyan sprawled on his bed, underneath the print of Hanuman, hands clasped behind his neck and twiddling his toes.

In all those months, I had never seen Virendra smile, and was now struck by the kind of abandon with which he expressed mirth. He threw his head back while the tips of his glossy black shoes peeped out from under his bed; and he cackled and giggled at every wobble of bare flesh.

When the lumbering stack of acrobats collapsed in a melee of arms and legs, a surge of glee seemed to choke his throat; holding his neck, he appeared to be gagging.

Later that afternoon I saw Virendra walk down the corridor, his eyes still glazed from the effort of studying, with *Playboy*, Kim Basinger rolled up on the inside. I was on my way back from the toilet, and knew that he would have to pursue and achieve rapture before being overwhelmed by the smell of phenyl and the sight of excrement – turds that other students used to the pit latrines of home had, while squatting, aimed at the toilet bowl, and missed.

I had wanted to separate myself from Virendra when he was a victim; I felt distaste for him when he discovered the will to power. To avoid it, I had to learn to ignore his laugh, which revealed in close-up that some of his teeth had been pulled at the back; I had to learn to look at his retro moustache and his oiled hair.

It wasn't easy. I was, after all, trying to suppress the self-recognition he stirred.

When you said last year in London, 'I am so touched by Virendra. Despite everything. He is the most sympathetic of all the IIT people I write about in my book,' I remember thinking to myself that, despite your best efforts, you had missed something crucial about our lives: how the degradations inflicted on us had worked themselves out invisibly in our characters, seeding varied passions: a dream of worldly glory as well as a desire to hide from the world.

You had just returned from interviewing Virendra at his correctional facility in Massachusetts. 'He told me,' you said, 'how horribly he was being treated by his jailors. Still, he was so kind, so patient, so generous with his time. He gave me all these small details that help build up a narrative.'

You mentioned some of these details you were using in your book, your 'secret history of globalisation', and I heard again after many years the name (Brilliant!) of the best correspondence tutorial course for IIT-JEE in the 1980s. After many years I recalled the tiny stationery shop with cracked glass cases in Delhi where most study materials were illegally photocopied by a stout man in a grimy baniyan, his arms slack and bare, and the coaching institute, Agrawal Study Circle, to which anxious parents from all over Bihar and Uttar Pradesh sent their teen-aged sons.

'Virendra even told me,' you said, 'about all these acronyms he grew up with, and he very patiently spelled out the ones I didn't know.'

I shivered inwardly to hear again the abbreviations that had tyrannised our youth: IIT-JEE, CGPA, DR, IIM, CAT, IMS, GRE, GMAT. And how strange it was to see S. L. Loney's *Plane Trignometry* and *The Elements of Coordinate Geometry*, and Igor Irodov's *Problems in General Physics*, the Bible and *Bhaga-vad Gita* of all IIT aspirants, emerge out of an Amazon box one morning in London.

You laughed when at another unboxing I said, 'Are you se-riously going to read Resnick, Halliday and Walker, Sears and Zemansky?'

You didn't, as it turned out, but you did read everything you could find about our god: Rajat Gupta, alumnus of IIT Delhi, first foreign-born MD of McKinsey & Company, and role model to many US-bound students. You interviewed all our teachers at IIT – those wonderful men and women, who, speaking amazingly to us with respect, had allowed us to feel blessed after those first few nights, among the country's chosen people. You read all the long transcriptions of exchanges between Siva, Virendra and other financial wizards of our gen-eration at IIT; you travelled to all their workplaces and playgrounds, from New York to Tuscany and Kalimantan. You interviewed almost everyone they came across in their pursuit of wealth and sex, filling up Evernote and Dropbox and several cardboard folders with notes of conversations, newspaper reports, scanned statements and downloaded videos.

Even Aseem, who was always self-regardingly severe while assessing fellow writers, once said, 'I have no idea if Alia can write, but she is a terrific researcher.'

You were also aware, from a Twitter feed full every day of ingenious threats of violation, of a larger breakdown. 'There is a whole generation, maybe two generations, of fucked-up men in India,' you used to say. 'People without a moral compass.'

I now think this is incontestable – freedom for too many men like us had meant profaning values and ideals that guide most human lives. There is so much I have learned since I met you about the cruelties and oppressions of what remains, more insidiously than before, a man's world.

But just as my unreflective malehood disallowed the recognition of some vital truths, so your suavely inherited advantages of breeding, class and wealth prevented you from seeing the peculiar panic and incoherence of self-made men; how they spend their lives fearing breakdown and exposure.

Exploring the conditions that moulded them could have filled out the story you wanted to tell in your book. You were not sure if our pre-IIT experiences had any explanatory value. 'It's so American,' you once said, 'this obsession with personal history, this idea that it can really explain who you are and what you have done, as though we are always denied the choice to break free of it.'

Given everything that happened and my own choices, I can't but share your ambivalence, your unwillingness to discard the principle of free will. I feel, in many ways, as culpable as Aseem and Virendra.

I must still write about the circumstances and the patterns of our lives today – circuitously, for it is the only way to arrive at the truth. In one sense, this is the memoir you once urged me to write, a continuation of your own struggle to understand men like Virendra. I owe many of its revelations to you, the things I could not see until I met you, and though it comes too late, and you may not want to read it, perhaps I'll learn, just as I did when I was with you, about the selves that I have ignored or repressed, the things buried deep down in me that I do not understand but have always feared.

You came into our lives long after we had managed to disguise ourselves. 'Never look back,' Aseem often said, 'always forward, and take charge of your life, don't let it be decided by your past.'

He would then quote from *A Bend in the River* on the need to 'trample on the past', and the relative ease with which this creative destruction could be accomplished: 'In the beginning,' he would recite Naipaul's lines from heart, 'it is like trampling on a garden. In the end you are just walking on ground.'

Very early, then, we became lost, refusing to face fully our experience; even, hiding ourselves from it. Virendra never referred to his early years, and for a long time Aseem avoided the subject for more or less the same reason: the burn marks inflicted then had never properly healed, and only a masochist would have willingly scratched them.

He started to proclaim his lowly origins only recently, after 2014 when Narendra Modi triumphantly set off his cruel handicaps and deprivations – and that of hundreds of millions of injured and insulted Indians – against the over-entitlements of the English-speaking elite. Aseem learned from Modi that the disgrace of being born weak and ignorant, and growing up ashamed, was now obsolete, and that, in the meritocratic society emerging in India, one could publicise one's semi-rural, low-caste and low-class beginnings just as profitably as self-made Americans had for their origins in log cabins, peanut farms and East European shtetls.

Looking back now at our deformities, however, I can identify at least one of their sources: the desperation to escape an ignominious past, which always seemed to wait menacingly at home to reclaim us.

For two years before I got into IIT and left my childhood home for good, I attended coaching classes in Delhi. Like Aseem and Virendra, I always returned home with a growing dread of what I would find there.

How agonisingly vivid are those scenes from the 1980s, in which I find some clues to our later conduct. The train from Old Delhi station, obstinately fuming and grinding across the plains of Punjab and Haryana, reaches Deoli at about five in the morning. Narrow, roofless platforms hurtle past the windows of my second-class unreserved carriage all night, the wind through the bars blowing coal dust in my hair. When the train stops, I see a dimly lit station platform where coolies prowl, always in twos, ready to rush the rare alighting passenger, ready to roll their scarves into a circular pad on their head and receive a metal trunk on this impromptu cushion before mincingly walking away into the night.

From somewhere comes the clatter of an iron cart, and the clank-clank and dong-dong of a hammer testing wheels. Shadowy people pass the window, never to be seen again. One of them turns halfway around, but only to squirt a tremendous spit of paan juice on to the floor.

Then, with several hisses, the coach lurches off, passing the signalman holding up a lantern, his face fiendish in the trembling green glow, and a small low building housing a row of levers. It rocks gently as it switches tracks; the few lights thin and the extensive night outside my window resumes its course – but not for long.

I sit on a straight-backed wooden bench, wedged in between several people, and facing a similarly tense row on the opposite side, with sinking heads jerking up, and then again starting to slowly sink. In the bunk above me the faint yellowish light of the lamps exposes a jumble of half-slumbering bodies, with mouths agape like fish.

Sometimes I doze off, but the train whistles with piercing melancholy, stutters over a level crossing, roars into a loud tunnel, the metal window shutter starts clattering in its frame, or the man next to me, sitting hunched over, his big strong nose snoring softly, and giving off a thick smell of sweat, suddenly slumps on to my lap.

My whole body goes tense. I want so badly to stretch my legs and put my feet up on something; and in that state of immobility I become convinced that happiness will always be beyond my reach.

Deoli has no railway yard worth speaking of, only a few condemned carriages and wagons and locomotives of crumpled iron on a couple of sidings. There is one platform with a small roof, under which stands a stone building, painted with stripes of white and brown; it accommodates the stationmaster's office and a stall from which my father sells tea, samosas, sliced white bread, biscuits, hard-boiled eggs, paan and cigarettes.

At daybreak, men and women are sleeping everywhere on the paan-stained floor, draped head to toe in white, the white always shocking, the colour of death and mourning, under urgently spinning low fans.

Imagine me alighting into this haven for the destitute, walking through the anonymous white bundles, past the dogs that are beginning to wake and moan, through a muddy forecourt of two-wheeled tongas, cycle rickshaws and bullock carts, and an open refuse-heap which stray cows timidly pillage, shifting a hoof now and then, their skin twitching.

In a narrow dirt lane stands the barracks for railway workers, their walls plastered with drying cow-dung cakes, and broken furniture spilled across the small yards before every room. Underneath clothes lines laden with washing – crucifixes of shirts with waterlogged sleeves, pythons of crooked, wrung-out saris – scrawny chickens scratch the earth; and only the occasional row of tulsi in old Dalda tins speak of a feeling for order and the vanity of ownership.

At this time in the morning, cooking fires from angeethis rise in fine columns to the blue sky. In our own little yard, a cow stands nibbling under a rough lean-to roofed with thatch, over fresh ordure humming with garnet-green flies. She is tightly leashed to an iron stake so that she can't reach either our small cabbage and tomato patch or the black pot over the brazier in which my mother cooks every morning and afternoon, squatting on the tiny veranda made by the overhang of the roof, the aanchal of her sari spilling over into the ground.

Our home is a small kothri with beige-coloured walls and two high and narrow windows that lashlessly squint out at the yard. There is no furniture apart from an iron chest in one corner and a pile of mattresses of coarse coconut fibre on the red concrete floor. One wall has inset shelves, painted green, and enamel tumblers, steel plates and four china cups.

The white crockery is monogrammed with a steam engine that proclaims India's national motto, Satyamev Jayate (Truth alone triumphs); the only item of luxury in the room, it is carefully preserved for it was stolen, early in my father's career, from Indian Railways.

Next to the shelves, from a nail, a woven bag hangs against the wall. A copper sink stands in one corner, above a short-handled broom. Dust adheres to all the mouldings of the doors; it has turned stringy the cobwebs dangling from the corners of the naked galvanised roof, and stained grey the blades of the ceiling fan. The walls grow a greener shade of mould after every monsoon season; and the room is as chilly and damp in the winter as it is warm and humid in the summer.

In that kothri, where I seem to have lived for an eternity, it is impossible to imagine a future for myself that might be different. After dinner every evening three mattresses are spread out on the floor for all four of us to sleep on; and you can't then move around the room without stepping on or tripping over a recumbent figure. You have to look carefully for an empty space, and, having put one foot down, a place has to be found for the other.

The topography of my neighbourhood feels equally constricting. At the end of the lane is a white Shiva temple against a dusty neem tree, a small shrine with a lingam set in the centre of a concrete lotus, and draped by yellow silk that is always damp and black with flies and ants. Here lives an ambiguous figure of my childhood, a pujari with a grey-stubbled face, clad from top to toe in saffron, including on his head, which is covered by what seems like a jester's cap, with flaps over the ears.

This priest invited me into the shrine once when I was twelve to accept a sugary prasad of batashas and I discovered then that he looks more menacing with his head uncovered. He took off his cap as he knelt and started rubbing my penis, and I could, while smelling the sandalwood paste on his forehead, see his ostentatious caste badge, the Brahminical chutki, a long, uncut tuft of hair, moist with oil, at the back of his shiny pate.

He owns a donkey in his side business as a transporter of heavy luggage, and beats the animal mercilessly with a lathi when it refuses to move. The blows on bare ribs and shins sound hard and dry; the lathi bounces off the donkey's bones, and the beast often bends itself double under the beating. The priest pants loudly in-between the blows that he lands rhythmically with clenched teeth; and at the end, when the donkey dully straightens itself with an indifferent snort or two, he appears almost defeated by the coarse solidity and resilience of his animal.

It is his duty, he often tells me, scratching his grizzled beard, to steadily grow my lingam as big as Shiva's. I usually escape after the perplexingly ecstatic and vaguely tainting act in the clammy shadow of the lingam to a nullah; and I come to know by heart the narrow, rutted path to the ditch, which runs alongside black rails, through patches of scorched tall grass and ferns swaying silently, neat little pyramids of tracklaying white stone, and telegraph poles whose wood peels in greyish strips.

I can still recall that faintness in my chest as I warily descend to the water, skipping over faded lumps of excrement, down to the shingly, narrow bank, where the eddies hint at dark depths.

The only paved road in the vicinity, a thin asphalt strip between two lanes of earth that have been ground to fine, thick dust by the wheels of bullock carts, leads to my old primary school. In this small three-room naked-brick building, two teachers in spotless khadi check every morning the hair of pupils for lice, using rulers rather than fingernails for this purpose with the two Dalits among us, before allowing them to sit on the red clay holding their black slates and chalk.

A few hundred metres down the same road, that irregular black path through dust, past wooden barrows bearing freshly cut sugarcane and a machine to extract its juice into thick dirty grey glasses, is a white-and-ochre town of narrow lanes, black, open drains and many more pariah dogs – those who get kicked and stoned so often that, putting their tails between their legs, they run away from even the rare person who offers them food.

The town has shops, a cinema, several temples and even a mosque, its marble inlay gouged out by pillagers, its pink sandstone dome stained by the excreta of pigeons. From this shapeless agglomerate come, occasionally, the nasal calls of the maulvi, tinny, derisory bursts of trumpets at wedding processions, and the sound of a loudspeaker: a tongawallah announcing the attractions of the town's lone cinema.

The clop of hooves grows nearer, I hear the sound of a whip on hide, and I go out to see the gaudily painted posters draped across the tonga: images of men with long sideburns gnashing their teeth and pointing outsized guns at each other against a backdrop of exploding skyscrapers, and women, clad in sleeveless dresses and slit skirts or the sheerest of white saris, under waterfalls, showing bare shoulders and arms and, sometimes more daringly, legs.

We, only a generation away from the long agrarian centuries, live close to the earth, forced by meagre income into ways that would be hailed as ecologically sound today. Vegetables not grown in the yard are bought from the local mandi, in bags made out of Hindi newspapers whose creases I would smooth before reading, holding it this way and that to make out the words of the smudged print. The cows in the yard provide milk, cheese, butter, ghee, curd and manure; they consume vegetable peelings and leftovers.

Food is always organic, since fertilisers are unaffordable; and freshly cooked, for there is no fridge. I have moved on to Vicco Vajradanti in Delhi, but toothbrushes at home are still made of neem, hibiscus twigs that you break, crush one end and rub your teeth with; you then split the twig and scrape your tongue with the halves. The angeethi is stuffed with charcoal stolen from the railway yard; utensils and crockery are scrubbed afterwards with their ash. Water, fetched in copper buckets from a nearby handpump, is strictly rationed; nevertheless, the open-air bucket baths and washing-up turn the yard into a squelchy, grey-black mess.

I have to bathe in order to scrub the very fine coal dust and smell of burned coal out of my hair and skin. But I am glad that I used the lavatory on the train, picking my way through the crammed carriage to squat over a filthy roaring hole in the floor. For the shared latrine in the sentry-box building at the back of the barracks is too gruesome and comprehensive an assault on the senses; and we have to relieve ourselves in the open air on the bank of the nullah, next to the small eddies where the black water comes alive, when you look uninterruptedly, with wriggling schools of tiny fish.

Early in the mornings we approach the nullah through the shortest way, walking with stolen Thums Up cola bottles in our hands between the tracks, through a litter of excrement, discarded leaf-plates and broken clay cups, startling rats, pink depilated creatures, who have been fighting over them, and who hobble down the wooden sleepers at the first sound of our feet, to where the black strips of the rail narrow into the eyes of a distant bridge.

Just below this bridge over the nullah is a dirt path and the spot where we squat dutifully between 5.30 and 6 a.m., when no trains pass. Unless they are late, in which case, we brace ourselves as the train flies upon us with a hollow clattering and a strong breeze, crouching and burying our faces in our chests as the passing carriages gently blow dust at our exposed genitals.

Early in the morning, my home smells of agarbatti – a whiff of sandalwood was enough for decades afterwards to transport me soundlessly back to the depths of my past. My mother has been, as usual, up since four in the morning, bowing and bowing before bright framed postcard prints of Rama, Krishna, Hanuman in one corner of the room, her prematurely grey hair covered with the end of her sari, a figure of sorrowful submission rather than piety.

Later that morning, after lighting the angeethi, she would read aloud from *Ram Charit Manas*, a Gita Press hardcover wrapped in dark brown khadi, and though there is much she does not understand, Tulsi's praise of Rama's virtue, Sita's fidelity and Hanuman's devotion move her to tears and her half-hidden face becomes radiant with tenderness.

Meena, my young sister, sits with her, reeling from side to side, wearing a red ribbon in her long plaited hair and a faded shalwar-kameez. Meena is ten years old, but very short for her age, and thin: she doesn't look more than seven, at the very most, and she would stop growing at twelve. Like her mother, she is rarely unoccupied.

Soon, she will go down to the handpump at the station, gently swinging a bucket in each hand, to jostle there with foul-mouthed men and women; she'll return, water sploshing in the buckets, her thin arms stiffly elongated by her side. She will scrub and scour the cooking pots with ash, ramming them against the ground; milk the cow, tugging with, again, surprising fierceness at her udders; she'll ask me if I have any laundry for her, and will vigorously scrub the unremovable ring of dirt inside my shirt collars (a battle that I know results only in their fraying) and she will rise from her squatting position each time with tendrils of hair clinging to her forehead.

In her spare time, she'll sew burlap sacks for my father's shop, her hands swiftly moving up her lap and down, but her bent neck, her eyes, eyebrows and lips completely stilled by the monotonous work. Very occasionally she will raise her head to rest her neck, glance blankly at nothing in particular, blink, and then bend again over the sack.

She is beginning to resemble my mother. She has the same white and pinched fingers that come from endless washing and cleaning. Afraid of everything, she is seized with abrupt and irresistible urges to hide and cry.

You once said, 'The difference between the way men and women experience the world is the difference between day and night,' and the words immediately appeared to me to be expressing an incontrovertible truth. It turned out, however, that you meant something different from what I had supposed.

You were speaking of the way women in the public sphere live with the fear of men, the apprehension that their mere presence on the streets and in shops and offices would incite lascivious interest. This hadn't ever occurred to me, and my obliviousness to an everyday experience for women readily illustrated your point.

Yet I had been thinking of the women who stayed at home, and spent the day literally in the dark, in lightless kitchens, while their husbands went out to make a living. I had been thinking of how unchangeably our grandmothers and mothers lived and died in the shadows of other lives; how unbroken was the trance of servitude in which they transmitted their own feeling of smallness in a big, indifferent world to their daughters.

My mother had started to dwindle with the death of her father in an accident when she was nine; new terrors enfeebled her with her marriage at sixteen to my father. My sister's career in misery began even earlier, with her awareness that she has a father; it would become impossible to escape after her early marriage to a man who rapidly forces four children on her while turning into an incorrigible drunk – a nikamma and muft khor, wastrel and parasite, in Baba's favourite words.

As I arrive, Baba is brushing his teeth. The twig still in his mouth, he nods imperceptibly. What is there to say? My mother and sister barely look up from their tray of naked potatoes and spirals of peeled skin. We actually don't speak much to each other, and weeks go by with little conversation between my father and mother.

In this silent home, the sounds come from elsewhere: the thoughtful lowing of cows, the steady plop-plop when they drop their dung, loud male voices shouting abuse, the screams and sobs of children being flogged and wives beaten, corrugated-iron doors grating on concrete sills before being slammed shut, muffled thuds of passing freight trains, the blowing of noses or the diddling of transistor radios, strangled squeaks and creaks, until they are tuned, all to the same station: All India Radio in the morning, Vividh Bharati in the afternoon, and Radio Ceylon in the evenings, switching from sombre baritone to jaunty song.

The voices from next door always sound ominous. The neighbour is an old woman, the mother of a labourer who is often away, pushing the trolleys of Permanent Way Inspectors, his bare feet nimble on scorching-hot black rail. She mutters all the time, imagining scenarios in which she is being cheated or robbed.

The most common of these in her mind is our cow straying into her vegetable patch, whereupon she dashes out with a long stick and stands, bony and toothless, her short grey hair fluttering in the wind, swearing obscenely for half an hour on end – loudly enough to attract the attention of passers-by.

Once Baba came out of our room and shouted back at her: 'Kya bol rahi hai, beizzat aurat, yeh kaisi bhasha hai? What are you saying, you shameless woman? What kind of language is that?'

She suddenly looked puzzled, as though not understanding why her language was objectionable. The look seemed to deflate my father, who was ready to tell her off a bit more. He stood there for a while and then, exasperatedly waving his arm, retreated.

'What can you do with such barbarous people?' he would say. 'This is why you have to work hard at your studies and get out of here.'

My father – handsome, with glowering brown eyes, absurdly long lashes that I have inherited and expertly trimmed and combed beard, his only physical vanity, which he indulges before a rusty handheld mirror each morning – thinks he has already given us a good start.

Fleeing his origins in Rajasthan, where he was a mere Kurmi, he has turned me into an upper-caste Hindu by the stroke of the schoolmaster's pen: a Brahmin surname on my school certificate, a commonplace subterfuge that makes me less prone to condescension from the high-born while saddling me with a lifelong fear of being found out.

He sent me to a local primary, saving money for my education by pulling my sister out of school. He then enrolled me at a Christian-run secondary school five miles out of town, where I join Hindu boys as they mutinously mutter the Lord's Prayer every morning, mock the pampered Anglo-Indians, lust after their skirt-wearing mothers, carve obscenities about them with dividers and razor blades on wooden desks, fantasise about cricketing glory, and ransack the small library full of Enid Blyton's books about English schoolchildren, marvelling at their summer holidays on islands and villages with, astonishingly, benign policemen.

Topping his efforts, Baba borrowed money to send me to

coaching classes in Delhi. The local moneylender's terms are outrageous. But Baba is confident in the knowledge that my success is guaranteed to elevate me into the ranks of those who do not have to worry about money.

His own reputation, as he plots his son's ascent, has been in freefall. He once worked at the refreshment room of a major railway junction, dressed in a turban and a starched white jacket with brass buttons and a diagonal red sash. But a vigilance commissioner caught him selling railway stocks of flour and kerosene to a local merchant. He was transferred to a smaller station, where they did not serve hot meals, reducing the scope for private enterprise.

After another demotion, caused by the discovery that he was still misappropriating government supplies, he ended up, without his uniform, at Deoli, a station on a narrow-gauge branch line in an under-populated region. Here, the only cooked food he sells is samosas, fried in murky peanut oil (ruinous for the intestines, it is forbidden to us); and his only other source of income is a small commission made from card-players, mostly firemen after work, who use his stall to gamble and drink tharra illegally.

He returns home late in the evening, having sold off his samosas to the last of the trains, and carefully notes the day's takings in a notebook of ruled paper. The station, desolate for most of the day, is transformed by mini explosions of energy when the trains emerge breathily roaring and coughing around the bend at a level crossing, the black engines with cow-catchers that appear demonic with splayed metal teeth, but turn out to trail some tame wooden carriages, and, with a short, desperate shriek and grinding of brakes, shudder to a standstill.

The platform suddenly starts to seethe, with people scurrying like bewildered ants about the unmoving millipede of the train: and Baba needs several arms to meet the hands proffering coins and sweat-soiled notes across the counter. Grabbing biscuits, samosas and paan, while speedily counting cash and then throwing it into a greasy drawer below his shelves, he seems, briefly, to dance.

The long-stalked fans circling overhead seem more helpless, great billowing whorls of steam shroud one part of the platform in white, grey mail bags heaved out of the guard van land with loud thuds, and the dogs start to howl. Business is conducted mostly during these interludes of extreme disorder, which is abruptly heightened to a frenzy by the thin keen blast of the stationmaster's silver whistle and the waving of the guard's tattered green flag.

Silence descends rapidly after the trains take their bad temper to the countryside; the rhythmic creak and whine of the handpump can be heard again on the platform. But my father is fuming as he distributes his unsold samosas to the station's perennially hungry residents. Suddenly tired of the recipients of his charity shoving and swearing at each other, his arm leaps out into the crowd of ragged faces, and cuffs someone on the ear or cheek.

Back home, he likes to complain about the weather ('Kaisa mausam hai yeh! What kind of weather is this!'), the sweepers who fail to show up for work ('Nikammey Bhangi, muft ki kamayi hain, yeh Harijan karamchari ki. They are all freeloaders, these Harijan employees'), the occasional peasant who dares to hawk roasted corncobs and sliced cucumbers at the station (he hates any reminders of his own peasant past) and Muslims in general ('Yeh Mohammedan log bahut kattar hai. These Mohammedans are such fanatics').

His most favoured target is corruption, and it is true that

hardly a day passes without some kind of swindle. The merchants who sell him weevil-infested flour and withered betel leaves, the chokra vendors of his chai who hide their true earnings as nimbly as they balance rows of nesting clay cups on their arms; the stealthy gamblers in black overalls who leave smudges of coal on his playing cards and don't pay him the right commission, and even customers passing on torn currency – they all try it on. The engine drivers and linesmen and signalmen steal coal; the contractor for railway labourers inflates his invoices.

But he, a swindler himself, underpaying the under-age boys he employs, is really complaining about his own life and the lives of so many men like him: being shoved around by the stationmaster, who incessantly berates him for dirtying the platform; the local thanedar who demands his own share of the tiny commission from the gamblers; the junior staff at the government hospital miles away who keep him waiting for hours for a blood test; the Brahmin teachers at primary school who openly condescend to him, as though guessing at his low-caste origins from his obsequiousness before them, and even the clerk at the post office, who, while gently tearing along the perforated edge of the Gandhi-faced stamps behind a dusty grille, snaps at him.

He is angered, too, by customers who haggle or ask for credit. In his opinion this behaviour is just as indecorous at his tea stall as at the pharmacy.

And I am often left to guess at the ways his hatred – of crooks and sharks, and also of his own impotence and servility – explodes. I remember the evening in 1984 when he came home from the railway platform, his kurta-pyjama creased and speckled with blood, his eyes peculiarly aglow. I was twelve at the time and had never seen him like this before.

The following day, two days after Indira Gandhi's assassination, boys in the schoolyard described how brave Hindus had boarded every train that pulled into the railway station and lynched the Sikh passengers with nothing more than their bare hands and a few lathis. Schoolboys imagined themselves at the head of such a band of patriotic Hindus, barking out orders to exterminate every man and child in a turban.

I wondered for months afterwards, until other childhood fears emerged, if my father had been one of the mob leaders; I couldn't look at his hands, large with hairy knuckles and veins swollen on the back, without imagining them wrapped around the hapless neck of a turbaned head.

Dinner is the biggest meal of the day, as we eat leftovers for lunch, and, instead of breakfast, drink fresh warm milk, from enamel tumblers that Baba has also stolen from his employers. Food is served on aluminium food trays with crevasses, of the kind served to first-class passengers. My father stole them before I was born, and they are now dented.

And each evening we sit on the floor, the heaped trays before us, waiting for him to finish his ablutions.

On this evening of my brief return from Delhi, his white kurta has damp half-moons at each armpit, and his face is stained with sweat, though his eyes are as alert as ever, as though still monitoring the outside world for signs of swindling.

I can see him, framed by the doorway, as he stands in the yard with a plastic mug in his hand. His legs in white pyjamas are set wide apart, and his torso bent forward, as he douses his face. Still leaning, he snorts as he rubs his cheeks and forehead; pressing each nostril in turn, he furiously relieves his nose, and hawks and spits.

After mopping his face and hands with a gamcha, he throws

it over his shoulder, and walks back to the room, a few pearls of water still on his beard.

In the absence of running water, cleanliness for us is an arduous achievement. Some part of the body tends to be neglected, and as Baba settles cross-legged on the floor before his shiny tray, his bare feet, never washed, are dark and thickened and cracked at the soles.

Outside, the cow lows. The temple bells ring out, followed by a conch shell – this evening aarti is when the temple has the most worshippers. I imagine the priest in his jester's cap drawing big swooping arcs in the air with his diya; then, going around with the diya on a thali. The devout drop a coin into the brass plate, warm their fingertips over the camphor flame before taking them to their forehead and then rearrange their hands quickly to receive an offering of a cracked white batasha on their right palms.

I hear a dull rumble; it's one of the long freight trains that pass the station in the evening and at night. They tend to amble past, wagon after wagon, with a lot of rattling and shaking, but are brisk enough to cut in two the cows and buffalo that stray on to the tracks, or are pushed there, according to my father, by Dalits and Muslims eager to skin them.

Some lowering thoughts have been floating around my mind all day – anxieties about coaching class fees, the higher price of thalis in Delhi. I have been meaning to speak several times, but I glance at my father and go back to eating.

His family in Rajasthan had been peasants in a semi-arable part of the desert state, and I knew, for he declaimed this bitterness often, that he had only just managed to read and write when they pulled him out of school and put him to work in their fields.

I once overheard him as he described to a customer a life of nearly continuous hardship and worry. You had to fear so many things all the time, he said. For if too much rain rotted the seed, hail and thunderstorm broke the wheat stalks, drought stopped the ears from filling out, weeds spread like a canker over the soil and the frosts added to the perpetual threat of ruination.

He concluded with: 'Itni mehnat roti ke liye janam se maut tak. So much backbreaking labour for roti from birth to death.'

And then he added, 'Khair, apni zameen thi vahan, purvajo ki, apna paseena aur khoon khaad mein jaata tha, jin ped-paudhon ko paani karthey the, unme apna kuch astitva tha. Yahan to hum kutton jaise rahte hai. Anyway, that was still our own land there, it belonged to our ancestors, our sweat and blood went into the soil, the trees we watered had something of us in them. Here, we live like dogs.'

After the discovery of this past, I often examined his big face, and those chewing jaws, trying to see in them clues to his early life. Then one evening he suddenly looked up from jabbing at his dal-chawal, caught my watching eyes, and said, 'Yeh ghoor kyon raha hai, haramzada? Why are you staring, you bastard?'

Since then I would try not to meet his eyes for more than a second, even when he would lean forward and, holding his face very close to mine, bellow out his mantra. 'Bhikari banega tu agar padhega nahin, aur gutter mein mareyga. If you don't study, you will become a beggar and die in a gutter.'

After my mother and sister have taken away the dented trays, I clear my throat and say: 'I ought to go back to Delhi tomorrow evening. I shouldn't have come at all. The coaching classes begin on the first of September.'

'Jao, jao, kaun roak raha hai? Go, go, who is stopping you?'

'Raju ko paisa chaiye, coaching class ke liye. Raju must have money for the coaching class.' My mother speaks up in her low voice, using my nickname.

I do not expect this from her. Though she is still in her thirties, her face has broken out in wrinkles; and it will never occur to her to nurture the good looks that allowed her mother to marry her off so early.

She is always working, knitting, when not cooking or cleaning, thick woollen jumpers for her children, or embroidering hankies for me to take to school, my initials in one corner, her lips moving as she counts stitches.

Baba looks a bit startled. I notice a crumb of roti on his beard.

'Paisa? Bilkul. Paisa ke bina kaam kaisa chalega? Money? Absolutely. How can things work without it?'

I glance with relief at my mother's face. Deliberately, searching deep in his kurta pockets, and stretching out his leg to do so, Baba takes out some soiled notes. 'Kitna chaiye? How much do you want?' he asks.

I can tell from the way he clutches the rupees that they won't be enough.

'Ah, paisa, paisa! Money, money!' Baba sighs. He always sighed when he saw money, even when he was receiving it, though he treated the banknotes with disrespect, stuffing them into his kurta pocket as though they were used tissue paper.

'Yeh, do sau rupai lo. Take these two hundred rupees.'

I wait a little. I want to tell him that I was not allowed into classes last month because I hadn't paid my fees, and my landlord threatened to evict me from the room I share with two other students of coaching classes in Karol Bagh.

But my mother cannot restrain herself. She says, 'Aur paisa do usko, Dilli mai kaise phadega? You should give him more. How can he live and study in Delhi otherwise?'

She adds, gratuitously, 'Aur nayi pant-kameez bhi honi chaiye. Kitna kharab lag raha hai. He must have new pants and a bush shirt. He is a disgrace to look at.'

Baba shifts uneasily. He has never physically assaulted my mother, not in my presence at least, but there is always a first time.

I hold my breath. My mother, oblivious to her husband's oncoming mood, goes on: 'Chotta bachcha nahin raha. He is not a little boy now, you know.'

A silence of suspended munching falls; little bulges of food are abruptly thrust into cheeks.

I am wondering if I shouldn't reach out, take whatever money is on offer, and end this scene, when Baba suddenly stands up, and flings down his soiled notes right in the middle of the dented tray.

'Paisa, paisa, paisa, yeh lo paisa! Money, money, money, take this money!' he shouts in an unnatural voice. 'Gala ghot lo mera. Squeeze my neck.'

He clutches at his neck, and I think about his hands around a turbaned head.

'Nanga kar do mujhe. Strip me naked.'

On the faces of my sister and mother, their cheeks bloated with unchewed food, I see an expression of dull terror.

'Le jao note, aur nanga kar do mujhe! Take them, and strip me naked!' Baba is shouting, shaking all over. 'Kar le ayyashi bade shahar mein! Go carousing in the big city!'

I notice the crumb of roti jumping off his beard and don't know why I say, 'Baba—'

'Jubaan pe rakm laga. Yeh randi-khana nahin hai. Hold your tongue. This is not a brothel!' he shouts even more loudly.

I suddenly remember how when he gave me a proper beating (ostensibly for failing to study hard in English and Maths, but really for acquiring skills denied to him, as I was always an assiduous student) I had to stand at attention, hands pressed to my sides and look him straight in the face, as he struck my face from side to side. My mother watched, her face full of

39

horror at what I used to think must be the scarlet print of my father's hand on my cheeks; and once I became so transfixed by a smear of soot above his left eyebrow, and so full of pity for him, that I almost forgot he was beating me.

I wonder if I would still have to stand at attention in case he decides to beat me, and my face starts to tingle hotly.

I hear grumbling voices next door.

My father shouts even louder. 'Teri umra mein naukri kar raha tha . . . Nikal bahar kar doonga, muft khor, nikamma. At your age I was making a living . . . I'll turn you out! Wastrel! Parasite!'

Meena, who has been gazing fixedly at our mother with her mouth open, moves her vacant eyes to the floor, and begins to produce from her chest slow but extraordinarily loud sobs. Baba looks at her, as tears spurt from her eyes, and waves his hand.

'Band kar yeh drama-baazi. Stop this melodrama.'

Professor Sir at IIT used to say that for the weak and the ineffectual, who cannot rise to the dignity and nobility of tragedy, or the luxury of irony, for whom even ordinary acts of will are impossible, melodrama is a substitute. People deprived of the capacity to change their fate can only repetitively lament this fact, and since they belong to the vast majority of the world's population, melodrama should be taken seriously for its world-historical impact.

Perhaps you will understand why melodrama suffused most domestic scenes in my childhood. My usual response is to run into the yard, and then run away from the room, and the startled cow with the large eyes, and to keep walking fast. I take the road that goes to my old primary school, past the dim lights leaking through closed doors and the temple, substantial without its tinselly string of bulbs, where an old sadhu with grey dreadlocks squats at night, pulling at a chillum that smells of ganja.

I walk along the dusty road and think of suicide, and of Baba devastated by his repentant suffering. I picture all kinds of escapades on the road: I am recognised by a sadhu as a wise man whose true home is among the eternal snows of the Himalayas; a car stops to give me a lift, and inside there is a great beauty, wearing the sleeveless dresses of the women on the film posters, who identifies my innate brilliance and sponsors my study at MIT, where I join one of the scientific geniuses from India in charting a new path forward for humankind.

Absorbed in these contradictory fantasies, I walk on and on until, finally exhausted, I turn homewards, and, careful not to trip over anyone, join the sleeping bodies on the floor.

My sister is gently snoring, as always, with one knee pulled up to her stomach, and there is moonlight coming through the high window. I lie awake for a long time, feeling not anger towards my father but pain about my mother, before lulling myself into sleep with a vision of my body slowly sinking into the sea.

Three

I did not want to tell you all this when you first interviewed me for your book – the melodrama, the *squalor* of melodrama that outlined our adult lives for us well before we started living them. Even afterwards, I gave you the broadest details about my relatives, my home and its surroundings. I think you assumed, with the anxious but brusque sympathy of the very rich for the non-rich, that I and Virendra and Aseem had been the victims of great poverty.

In retrospect, this was one of the imprecisions in your book that I failed to correct, even though I read many drafts of it. I grant you that a life shadowed by debt, in which new clothes and other avoidable expenses are forgone, postponed to an imagined future of financial ease, may be, in its self-imposed deprivations and continual wanting, more soul-crushing than the life in which there isn't enough to eat.

There is too much shame in it, too many raw nerves about how one speaks and dresses. And then there is the gnawing fear that our pretensions to bourgeois respectability could be exploded any minute. Still, the utterly wretched and the truly destitute do not have our advantage: faith in a future windfall.

Even back then, we did not consider ourselves poor. The word was reserved for those tenants of the railway platform at night, some of whom escaped their lives of shiftless futility by prostrating on the tracks before the couple of diesel-engined trains that whooshed past the station; the sight of rats nibbling on a mangled and coal-blackened corpse one murky dawn haunted me for months.

When it rained heavily, the power went out, and much of the town was flooded, trapping its residents in knee-deep water. The sound of the rain was comforting within our solid walls; the paraffin lamp cast a soft and yellow light on everything; and the full and muddy gutters outside always gurgled with a thrilling possibility: that school would be closed.

We had at home two sets of clothes each. I also had a pair of shoes as defence against the hookworms and leeches that frequently tormented my chappals-clad sister; and, though we slept on the floor, our pillowcases were exquisitely embroidered by my mother, with bright red roses and green stems. Every morning before school until I was twelve or thirteen my mother put one of her embroidered hankies in my shorts pocket, then sat me down and carefully parted and combed my hair, finishing off with a kiss on my forehead.

I remember you speaking once of your own mother: how she had divorced your father soon after an Islamic fundamentalist shot a bullet into his spine, incapacitating him for life. 'She took legal custody of us,' you said, 'but then sent both me and my brother to boarding school in England. And while we were struggling there, trying to cope, and my father was in a wheelchair, she married this corporate honcho in Mumbai. I was lucky to have a wonderful aunt and uncle. They basically brought us up, came to see us in England, took us on holidays in Europe and America.'

You showed me a photograph of you with them in Disney World, and I told you how moved I was by this disclosure, one of the very few you made about your past. Yet there was another feeling I didn't confess to.

A holiday, when I was growing up, was a day when I did not have to go to school. Holidays of the kind you took were beyond ambition; and to see you in that photo with yellow-brown tints and a white crease, all of fourteen and extremely sad under a big straw hat next to Mickey Mouse in Orlando, Florida, was to see, with a little shock, emotional deprivation right in the heart of unthinkable privilege.

It was naïve of me to be so shocked. And, perhaps, it would be naïve, too, to make too much of the material deprivations and the moral shabbiness I grew up with.

I suffered them together with Aseem and Virendra, and our desire to escape them determined much of our lives, especially Aseem's, who developed a strong dislike for his parents' regressive politics and social illiberalism, and, like many self-made people, edited them out of his life.

Still, I recognise my childhood setting as a place that spoke to me intimately; and it provides, receding into my increasingly unshareable past, many moments that detach themselves from the noise of time to whisper of enchanting and irretrievable things: like the one rocket we buy at Diwali that flares into life with a gratifying *hissss* and then soars up and up, and then when green and red sparks tumble down, all our smiling upward faces briefly glow.

Long after our IIT stint, Aseem would remind me of growing up near lonely railway stations on branch lines; this nostalgia was the only romance about the past he allowed himself. 'Remember, boss, the most exciting event of the day was the passing of the trains. I wonder, now, how I managed to pass so much time. But we did, and happily.'

Yes, with nothing to do we found in everything an outsize significance – the quality of the air, slight changes in temperature, distant sounds, patches of sunlight, patterns on flagstones, and even torn scraps of *Navbharat Times* and *Hindustan* hopping absent-mindedly on the platform.

One reason I felt close to Aseem is that I knew he had once possessed the same alertness to a landscape cleansed by a downpour, the train carriages shining like new, the white clouds of smoke from the steam engine especially soft; to the breathing and purr of the paraffin lamp, glowing in one corner like a warm golden animal; the heady scent of sharpened pencils and new rubbers; to the kirana shop, actually a gloomy grotto, smelling damply of kerosene and Lifebuoy soap where a smooth-jowled lala sat as a deity in the dark; to the rumbling and jangling of donkey carts and bullock carts, their iron-rimmed wooden wheels wobbling over the potholed road; the whistling and cracking of long whips with knotted ends; to the perennial wetness of the ox's muzzle and the halo of flies around the mare's head; and the soapy water slowly eddying in the shadow of the nullah's bank.

How enticing were the sheet of gauze paper that covered the flamboyant frontispiece in many English books at the school library, the multi-hued balloons billowing and rubbing against each other high above their vendor, the transistor radio with the perforated leather case that my family finally acquired in a rare fit of keeping up with the Joneses, the thela of soft drinks that ragged hawkers trundled down the lane, bottles filled with syrups in dazzling floral colours, or the soft foil and intoxicating smell of a Gold Flake packet that I would pick up from the ground and crush to my nose.

Such useless possession brought the ecstasy of treasure-hunting to those who had so little. Still, lives driven by want cannot be reduced to it; they will still contain a range of human emotions. How much joy I extracted, for instance, from drawing houses on a slate and building a railway out of matchsticks. How scary were the nightmares about churails with feet turned backwards blazing through the thick blackness – an apparition that for years represented pure terror before being tamed into nights without electricity.

And what a great dream of tranquillity I used to coax out of the only decorative item in our home: the calendar with a picture of the Himalayas, white cones above a green valley, straining against a radiant blue.

I longed to be nestled somewhere within that vast Himalayan landscape. Many more years passed in Delhi before I found, miraculously, my sanctuary in Ranipur, a small village in Himachal Pradesh. We finally saw the last of Deoli when I moved to Ranipur, bringing my elderly mother with me. Yet, leaving our home, the setting of so much anguish, I was overcome by an immense sadness.

Claiming that I had left something behind, I ran away from my mother as she perched on the back seat of a tonga, clutching a bedroll, surrounded by bits of lumpy luggage fastened with rope, rigid with apprehension at the thought of travel, and now terrified that she would be abandoned by her son just as pitilessly as she had been by her husband.

The emptied room had an unfamiliar hushed air. I stood looking this way and that, at the signs of our old life that at this moment of parting suddenly seemed enigmatic and suggestive: a familiar dark shadow created by my sister's oiled hair on the wall, a vacant rectangle left by the calendar of the Himalayas, a perfect fingernail of peeling paint I was careful never to touch, the wavering indentation on the abrasive stone floor that I always avoided stepping on.

In a small pile of discarded things in one corner was a child's shoe on its side, its strap torn. Was it mine? The knife scratches in the frame of the door with which my mother had once recorded my growth in height had grown faint. And how had

I never noticed the scuffed wall near the door, rubbed by years of passing hands and elbows?

All this, whether known or unseen, would soon be irretrievable. I wondered if I could bear to part with the only reusable thing not packed by my mother: an unstoppered Thums Up bottle which I took to the open-air latrine near the nullah and which now stood in one shadowed and silent corner of the room.

I left the bottle behind, in that place where I had known myself to be unconditionally loved by my mother, and where other lives would now assume their distinct shape, leave their own marks, and be betrayed in turn.

Aseem used to say that to be modern is to trample on the past; it is to take charge, to decide being something rather than nothing, active rather than passive, a decision-maker rather than a drifter, in a world which, he never tried of repeating, is what it is.

You had your own, much less masculine take on this: you were never homesick, you used to say, because you never had familiar things during a life constantly improvised in unfamiliar landscapes.

But, sliding away from the barracks, seated backwards on the tonga, and helplessly confronted with what we were leaving behind till a bend in the lane, I felt my mother's hand on mine. She was looking at our receding home. Tears were streaming down her face, from high on the curve of her cheeks, where I saw for the first time a net of fine delicate wrinkles.

Going past the temple, where a new pujari with no known depravities sat under the neem tree, past herds of sluggish buffaloes and bullock carts on the dusty road, further away from the rutted path that led to the nullah, I felt fear rather than relief – what now seems a chilly breath from the future, a premonition of a world growing ever stranger, demanding constant treason against the past.

On the subsiding bank of the nullah, where I have my earliest experience of solitude, I also have my first clear visions of beauty – something that substantiates the strange sensation I have at school while reading a line of nature poetry in a textbook, the emotion that comes over me when I come across a stray sentence about a still lake mirroring the sky, the emotion I then hunger for.

Our outdoor latrine, where I look up from my ablutions at a late passing train at dawn, enchanted by the golden ribbon of lighted windows, was also the place where the local dhobis wash clothes, next to where the current runs swiftest over smooth stones, bending tall slender grasses together into a flowing watery mane.

Bringing down the twisted wet hanks on black rocks with a deep grunt, they seemed to be trying to beat the cheap clothes of the indigent to death; they then seemed bizarrely solicitous of the battered garments as they spread them out to dry.

These lengths of white dhotis, kurta-pyjamas and multicoloured saris lay spreadeagled all day. I would go back there in the early evenings to watch the dhobis raise their fallen adversaries from the rocks and fold them respectfully into a pile. By this time the heat of the day had burned away the reek of excrement, a dense silence had settled on the dust-stiffened, discoloured bushes, broken only by the one-note whining of mosquitoes, and far in the distance, thin mirages shimmered above the black steel of the tracks.

A train would pass through, the engine furiously expelling red-hot embers as it ground past, and I'd wait for the stray blue sparks, as sudden as flashes of lightning, spat by the retreating wheels of the forlorn guard's van.

There I would stand, until the dust set whirling by the train settled down, and pink-tinted clouds turned to copper-grey, and listen – to what exactly? Everything – the big-bellied clouds, the clacking of dry reeds, the coils of black smoke abandoned by the train, and even the licorice smell of cinders – seems so solidly *present*, unlike my liquid self, and to speak so eloquently and urgently of something, but the language in which everything speaks is unknown to me.

Four

Perhaps, you can see why I felt attracted to Aseem immediately while recoiling from Virendra. After years of isolation, of unanswered questions and inadequate words, I was struck by Aseem's power to order an experience that mostly baffled me, and to master a world that seemed opaque to me.

I remember you asking in London, not long after he had brought us together, 'How did you guys become friends? You are so unlike each other!' I felt too liberated then from Aseem's company, and gratified by yours, to answer your question truthfully or with nuance.

I told you that we had shared, growing up, a small-town meanness, and the wish to overcome it. I didn't add that I had also felt a degree of awe at his confident progress through an unaccommodating world. I didn't want to encourage any latent admiration you might have had for his success.

And for that reason I did not say anything about the consoling affirmation he gave to my uncertain choices in the beginning: how, for instance, I was completely disarmed when returning to my room from the IIT library one day he saw a volume of Tolstoy's stories in my hand and said, 'Boss, I love the fact that you read books for pleasure.'

He was wearing a white chikan kurti with paisley embroidery – he sported that Lucknowi look long before Fab India made indigenous garb chic. His legs were up on his desk, where a table fan blew hot air around the room with a rotating rattle, and as he spoke his sneakers jiggled with a tremendous eager energy, shedding thin dust on an oilcloth table cover marked with overlapping whitish rings of chai tumblers.

He had lost much of his looks by the time you met him. In his twenties, however, he was easier on the eye than those flabby-cheeked dynasts of Bollywood, with a body that was well proportioned and well developed without being grossly muscular. Even late in his life, he went to a boxing gym on weekends and played volleyball, that profoundly un-Indian sport with its requisites of height, speed and agility; he continued to possess, unlike almost all desi men of his age and class, a flat belly and held his tall and lean frame gracefully straight.

And then there were the oddly unblinking, piercing dark eyes which, framed and accentuated by a beard and a mop of thick curly hair, made him appear a man whose vocation keeps him focused every instant of his life.

'He has charm,' you once said, 'but it hides a basic coldness.' What you thought was coldness came across to me as self-possession, an enviable inability to be unhappy or tormented, and a sharp resolve to achieve in adult life everything his excessive, hungry soul had longed for, and been denied, in a childhood heartlessly sacrificed to his parents' ambition.

A deep loathing of his parents had further vivified his desires and dreams of fulfilment. Growing up as a Punjabi in small railway towns, safely remote from the pressures and constrictions of joint families and crowded mohallas, he had been able to conceive, unlike most Indians of his class, of the world outside as an opportunity.

Much more astutely than I ever did, though he had gone to the same mediocre kind of missionary school, called St Jude's, Sacred Heart or Christ the King, with other Hindu boys who merrily mangled the Lord's Prayer every morning.

Defying his parents' curfew, he had managed to see the late-night shows of films luridly advertised by small-town tongas, guffawing with desperate joy in smoky cinema halls at the machine-gunning of politicians and the humiliation of upstart 'modern' women. He knew by heart the film songs, which, leaking out of transistor radios, had filled the long afternoons of my childhood; he could sing, with a gravitas deeper than Bhupendra's, the Bollywood version of Ghalib's ghazal, '*Dil dhoondta hai phir wahi phursat ke raat-din*'; and he brought melody even to the rough English translation – My heart pursues once again those nights and days of leisure – he provided for the South Indians and Bengalis in his audience.

His English, like mine, was self-taught. But he had learned it by listening to *Just a Minute* and Dave Lee Travis on the BBC World Service; and, while I always spoke the language like a child, hesitatingly and shyly, he blurted it out with the autodidact's bluster, and a variety of accents: British, American and Punjabi. His pronunciation of his favourite word, 'career' as carrier, was just one of its many winsome idiosyncrasies.

While I read through a small school library full of books about English children in idyllic boarding schools and villages, he acquired cheap hardbacks of Dostoevsky, Sholokhov and Tolstoy on visits to Soviet-subsidised bookshops in bigger towns. While I settled for tattered old copies from the kabadiwallah of *Parag, Nandan, Chandamama, Kadambini, Dharmyug, Indrajal Comics* and Hindi jasoosi novels held together with rusty metal staples, and pounced on the rare discarded copy of *Manohar Kahaniyan* or *Satya Katha* in train compartments, he managed to steal the glamorous paperbacks of the Hardy Boys, Alistair MacLean, James Hadley Chase and Sidney Sheldon on sale at A. H. Wheeler bookstalls.

He had brought with him to the IIT a couple of Reader's Digest Condensed Books and four or five books by Hemingway, Faulkner and Mailer. Pilfered from a railway library in Jabalpur, the Penguin and Bantam paperbacks with bleached covers, and the hardbacks with gilt-edged pages, elicited the same quality of reverence as Virendra's portrait of open-chested Hanuman.

During his uncoordinated lunge towards modernity, Aseem had also come to possess pirated cassette tapes of Led Zeppelin, Deep Purple, Pink Floyd and the Eagles. Tinny on his Akai two-in-one, the opening riff of 'Smoke on the Water' nevertheless imposed a reverential hush on him, something probably comparable with the effect the four opening bars of Beethoven's Fifth had on listeners in nineteenth-century Europe.

At the American Center in Connaught Place, he sought not study materials for GRE, or information about MIT, but old issues of *Esquire*, *Paris Review*, *Time* and the *New Yorker*. He had already made up his mind (and would soon help me make up mine): the stint at IIT was meant only to establish his bona fides in a credentials-obsessed society.

Unlike every other student, he was not interested in escaping to the United States or the Indian Institute of Management. He was going to be a writer, a novelist, an *artist*, no less, rather than an engineer, scientist, banker, consultant, businessman or management executive.

He also claimed to have sampled the incomparable bliss presumably awaiting us in the future. Seduced in his early teens by his hockey coach at school, he had conducted a rambunctious affair.

Unlike my encounter with the priest, the experience had left an unambiguous memory of pleasure. 'He was twenty years older. But it was completely consensual and great fun and sad when it ended,' he liked to say. 'People make too much of sex between old men and boys. But we were just getting our rocks off. At least, I wasn't screwing my cousins and sister-in-law like many boys I knew, or trying to rub my palm lines on to my dick.'

Amazingly, Aseem already had a girlfriend at IIT: his wife-to-be Mrinal, whose periodic appearance with her luxuriant straight hair and sunglasses gave us all a frisson, and with whom, he seemed to suggest, he had already done the deed, not once, but many times, and with earthshaking power.

The two of us were fortunate to meet a humanities professor who told us about the international film festivals at Siri Fort and Alliance Française and the book fair at Pragati Maidan and who gave focus and depth to our love of reading.

I remember today how expressively Professor Sir, as we used to call him, spoke, in sentences of great beauty, with words that sounded new-minted, unheard before; how in his dusty office, the smallest gesture he made – picking up and setting down a copy of the *TLS*, taking off his glasses, extricating a Modern Library edition of *Ulysses* from a cascade of books, amusing his hands with a pen as he talked – appeared both momentous and perfectly natural.

It was Professor Sir, with his gift of imparting knowledge together with its excitement, who helped us move on from Bollywood movies to Wim Wenders, from Enid Blyton, Soviet translations and Western sex-and-spies fiction to Balzac and Stendhal; more importantly, he helped us move from thinking of books as only entertainment to regarding them as guides to existence, a way of finding oneself in the world with others.

Fortuitously, too, our reading was dictated by the books at the IIT library, which leaned heavily to classics that described the spiritual condition of parvenus like ourselves: people from nowhere, compelled to create a place for themselves, and find dignity, stability and love.

I was immediately drawn to these young men on the cusp of

society, struggling with contradictory desires, in *The Red and the Black*, *Lost Illusions*, *Sentimental Education*, *Rudin* and *Fathers and Children*, trying to resolve their inner conflict between idealism and cynicism. How many hours I spent reading about them at that deserted library, where the brass pendulum in the old long-case clock went from side to side with regal slowness, suggesting a majestic order in the life of the mind.

I can still remember that feeling after finishing a book and walking back to my hostel: that heightened sense of perception, and expectancy, soon to be broken by someone playing Deep Purple, or a bathroom singer attempting 'Hotel California'. Those fictions about young men, romantics and daydreamers, in which I could see myself, seemed to hold some fundamental truths in their tensions between ambition and repose, desire and indifference, their whispered truth that withdrawal into stillness or aesthetic and intellectual contemplation was superior to the pursuit of social and political ambition.

Aseem, I remember, was gripped in a different way by this literature, finding in it affirmations of his developing world-view. An early role model was Julien Sorel, the provincial who regards the world as a conspiracy against talented and energetic young men like himself, and hero-worships Napoleon. I was shocked by Maupassant's explicit anatomising of Bel-Ami's cravings for sex and fame. Aseem concluded, persuasively to me, that this journalist's cynicism had been necessitated by an unscrupulous bourgeois society.

'This is what the modern world is about, boss,' he said, 'whether journalism, literature, politics or love. You lose sight of your interests; you lose altogether.'

Virendra listened to our book talk with that same blank look that had become so familiar. He had read no fiction, apart from the pornographic reveries of Mastram and *Asli Kokshas-*

tra; and he brought a bizarre male jolliness to the one song he belted out on demand, *'Waqt ne kiya kya haseen sitam. Tum rahe na tum, hum rahe na hum'*, making Geeta Dutt's doleful classic from the 1950s seem a drunkard's chant.

A rumour about female nudity would motivate him, in his second year at IIT, to see his first foreign film at Siri Fort: *Kings of the Road* (and, disappointed, not bother with foreign films again). The only Western names he seemed to know, and mangled in pronunciation, were Wharton, Sloan, Stanford and Kellogg.

But I can recall him, sitting on his bed under Hanuman, munching sprouted beans, and listening closely, over the noise of the table fan, when Aseem read out to me that exhortation from a rich Parisian woman to her friendless relative from the provinces in *Old Goriot*: 'The world is loathsome and wicked . . . Treat this world as it deserves to be treated. You want to succeed, and I will help you. You will plumb the depths of female depravity, you will gauge the breadth of the contemptible vanity of men . . . The more coldly calculating you are, the further you will go. Strike ruthlessly and you'll be respected.'

Five

'If you are going to be in charge of your life, then you have got to be ruthless,' Aseem often said during discussions of our post-IIT future. And when I objected, he would say, 'OK, maybe not all the time, but sometimes, the right times.'

It was in this period – memorable because he moved from Lifebuoy to Liril soap then and always left a heady scent of lime behind him in the bathroom – that he borrowed a hardback of *A Bend in the River* from Professor Sir's personal library and started to quote from it about the existential imperative to trample the past into the ground.

I remember you saying when I first told you about the novel's opening lines: 'This notion that the world is what it is and those who are nothing, and allow themselves to become nothing, have no place in it – this is a pretty chilling sentiment. Isn't it a kind of manifesto for people who are already privileged? Isn't this the sort of idea Reagan and Thatcher were promoting? That it is all down to the individual and if you fail then it is your own fault?'

I wish you had elaborated this insight while writing of Virendra and Siva. I wish, too, I had grasped, long before events forced me to write my own secret history of an inner crumbling and collapse, this crucial fact: that our generation was the first to be exposed to the ideologies of self-cherishing that, emanating in Britain and America, arrived, fully articulated, in India in the late 1980s.

The old feudal elite to which you belonged managed to hold on to its assets; and there was a very small group of industrialists. But even this tiny minority of the wealthy had been constricted for decades by a national culture of austerity – a legacy of the pious ascetics and socialistic celibates who helped liberate India from British imperialists and saw self-denial as a way of accruing political as well as religious merit.

Moneymaking, in this vitally Brahmanical hierarchy of values, was looked down upon as a vulgar passion, best indulged by the merchant castes and the trading communities of Punjab, Sindh, Rajasthan and Gujarat. Foreign travel was unheard of; imported goods were either banned or discouraged.

It helped that we could afford very few of them, if at all. Private cars were rarely seen in our small towns. The luxury awaiting those moving on from Hercules, Atlas and Hero bicycles was a scooter, a second-hand Lambretta, with a cane basket hooked to its handlebar; and the absurdly long wait for it – curtailed only if you had US dollars in cash – lent glamour to the Bajaj Chetak, a reliable Indian-made Vespa, and to its ineradicable smell of petrol.

The India you grew up in, where private wealth creation and hectic consumption seemed patriotic duties, and petrol fumes were seen as polluting by a growing minority of the environmentally conscious, came into being only around the late 1980s, when the country started to open itself to global flows of goods, media, ideas and capital. And we emerged, I can now see, from IIT just in time, in the 1990s, to claim a share of the world's richness long withheld from our ancestors.

Looking back, no claim seems more insistent than Aseem's, and no individualism more uncompromising than his, even though he always made less money than Virendra and scaled much more slowly than him the mountain of prejudice and privation.

Aseem and I did nothing with our training in rigorous quantitative thinking at IIT. But Virendra – who boosted his CGPA from 5 to 9 by his fourth year, and moved from IIT Delhi to IIM Ahmedabad and then Harvard Law School, which he left halfway through for Wall Street – deployed it lucratively in American firms that had embraced innovations such as junk bonds and derivatives.

Despite all his close reading of American authors and magazines, Aseem did not seek to profit from propitious circumstances in the US. There, by the late 1990s, the opening of capital markets, new technology and a rallying stock market had created a fresh demand for brokers, bankers and traders, forcing America's old white-shoe aristocracy to accommodate women and South Asians in their companies.

Compared to Virendra, who eventually worked at Siva's hedge fund, and became a billionaire within a few years, Aseem did not seem ruthless at all when he became, after leaving IIT, a low-paid reporter for a news agency in Kashmir.

Covering the anti-Indian insurgency there, he came to be known only very gradually, and then to a small group of readers, for his descriptions of the massacres of civilians by terrorists – and Indian soldiers or mercenaries dressed up as terrorists. In a space where the most sensational news was drowsily recorded, he flexed a muscular prose: 'After years of shoot-outs between terrorists and soldiers, buildings in Srinagar are poxed with the acne of gunfire,' and that kind of thing. I recall a memorable image of a post-massacre scene from his agency reports: he was once walking down the aisle of a rickety bus, the floor made slippery by the profuse blood of the murdered, when he saw a harmonium, abandoned on a vacant seat, a clean bullet hole gaping from its burnished wood.

I now wonder if he really saw this. Was it possible for those slatted floors of buses to become slippery with blood?

Anyway, he resigned his job after two years – out of boredom with the routine carnage, he used to say – and went to Delhi one day to become an editor at a high-circulation features and lifestyle monthly; his pugilistic prose had caught the eye of the magazine's owner.

I often saw him during those years, drawn by that post-college dread of impending change, of attempting something that none of my America-bound classmates would have considered seriously. I had chosen, as Aseem himself often pointed out, the strangest 'carrier' of all. I spent a few more years at IIT, doing a pointless postgraduate degree. I then worked as an editor at a small literary review Professor Sir had introduced me to, and freelanced as a translator in Delhi for eight years.

'Why didn't you do,' you once asked me and Aseem, 'what most people do after IIT? Didn't you want to make it big in the West like your friends from IIT?'

Aseem said, 'It seemed too easy to scuttle off to a rich country and find your little niche there. I was pretty clear in my mind that India, Asia, the East, was where the real action was, the scope for improving people's lives, for writing and journalism, was immense, and I knew all along that I wanted to contribute, to make a difference in my own country. Now there is a fierce battle going on between liberal democracy and populism, and I want to be on the right side.'

I didn't actually say anything; and you might have taken my silence to signify agreement with this quasi-political sentiment. I found it impossible to explain that, by imperceptible degrees, I had reached the age when I knew that I could never become the person I was meant to be. The desire to escape generations of wretchedness, reared obsessively long before my birth by my father and then implanted in me, had failed to become focused ambition. The prospect of working even harder to fulfil material desires – those I was supposed to have but never truly made my own – fatigued me.

I felt mostly dread when I thought of faraway rich lands, and of becoming one of the innumerable millions from our part of the world that waited impatiently to crowd into them, and then waited much longer to be treated with dignity by their new neighbours.

I remembered my mother clutching me fiercely, my father on the railway platform, speaking inaudibly, and the hollow in my heart, as the train taking me to my first semester in IIT pulled away. I had already gone so far away from where they were, what to them was the world; the journey to a foreign land would have been beyond their comprehension. How much further did I have to run for a life free of everyday humiliation?

Nor could I enter Aseem's dream of India's imminent apotheosis. Rather, inferiority, which spurred fantasies of power in Aseem and Virendra, had worked away inside me into a kind of guilt at wanting too much from the world.

You once raised your head from a Virago Modern Classic to read out a similar sentiment: how even many well-educated women are trained to see fulfilment as an extravagant and unworthy ambition. I think you will understand why I was held by Aseem, and his ability to transmute inherited feelings of worthlessness.

While still at IIT, I could never believe in the big city's promise of self-expansion – certainly not while saving on meals to buy books and sleeping on mattresses stained by the semen of many desperate students.

Working at the literary review in Delhi, I was no longer so financially vulnerable, but I still lacked his gift, which you also have, of sensing a hidden excitement in the impersonal metropolis.

Having moved out of IIT networks, I hardly knew anyone

in the city apart from Aseem. And I had no idea how, nor the confidence, to reach out to the sons and daughters of the old elite, who moved through Doon School and St Stephen's College to Oxford and Cambridge, and returned from abroad to occupy senior positions in publishing and the media.

The literary review was one of their playthings: a rich Bengali's indulgence, with a small and unchanging subscription list, and staffed by Anglophilic scions of establishment families, who reflexively rejected someone with a Mechanical Engineering degree and hybrid English accent straying into a turf tended by Oxbridge graduates.

In their company, I couldn't get rid of the feeling that I had usurped someone else's place, and that I was being tolerated until a pretext was found for my sacking. At the couple of parties of theirs I went to – held in a vast bungalow off Aurangzeb Marg, with white-uniformed waiters scurrying under Souza's paintings – everyone present apart from myself provoked recognition and pleasure in somebody, and their eyes slid round me as easily as they did at the sight of the office chai-wallah.

The idea of a social life, let alone cocktail parties, was still new to me. Understanding little of my colleagues' banter, jokes and nicknames, and exhausted by the effort of inserting myself in conversational groups, chomping at any old bone thrown my way, all the while trying to appear natural and sophisticated, I stayed away from their gatherings after that. Far from encouraging me to join them, and to break my shyness, they simply did not notice my absence.

Nor did they have much time for Aseem, though almost all of them showed up at his parties.

'It's the old liberal elite of Delhi,' you once said of an acquaintance who had managed to drench you with condescension in two minutes of casual conversation at Chennai airport. 'They even look down on people like myself, who went to New York University rather than Oxford or Cambridge or the Ivies. It doesn't matter that my grandfather was a major figure in the freedom movement or that my family has a long record of public service. The wrong school or education is enough to condemn you.'

I remember how my co-workers, still disposed to exclaim 'By Jove!', mocked Aseem's accent, his pronunciation of 'career' as 'carrier' and 'ancien régime' as 'ancient regime'; these aficionados of P. G. Wodehouse and authors of D.Phil. theses on Kingsley Amis and Iris Murdoch sneered at his writing, claiming that he had 'no ear for English prose'.

I once overheard one of them say, with a soft laugh, 'Look at his shirts, that shaggy chest, the jeans bulging really tight at the crotch, that beard and Sai Baba bouffant, and those bedroom eyes – he really is a Punjabi avatar of Barry White.'

Looking up Barry White on Yahoo, I could see what she meant. But such scorn – and there was a lot of it – made me feel closer to Aseem.

I often wondered if I, too, provoked behind my back much mirthful derision; and the suspicion compounded my perennial anxiety that my low-caste origins were on the brink of shameful exposure, as much as the ring of dirt, smudged by futile scrubbings, inside my frayed shirt collars.

During those years in Delhi, I discovered, like countless bruised provincials before me, that the advantages of birth and ancestry didn't make for generosity to those who didn't have them. On the contrary, the small world of the Anglicised elite, perhaps because it was small, and desperate for recognition from London and New York, was governed by absolute egotism, its members capable of an unscrupulous hostility to each other as much as to outsiders.

*

The only letter Baba ever sent me arrived shortly after my graduation from IIT; its few brusque sentences, strangely written in more than two kinds of ink, on yellow paper bordered with pink roses, complained about how the marriage of my sister had exposed him to inhuman moneylenders and ended with: 'All our hopes are now on you. Only with more money can we regain our honour and self-respect.'

Baba could hardly bear to talk to me on the increasingly rare occasions I went home; and he never mentioned the small amounts of money I pressed into my mother's hands while leaving to go back to Delhi.

First in the family to receive an education, for which he claimed to have sacrificed much, I was expected to become a breadwinner. And yet in his eyes I was another nikamma and muft khor, a wastrel and parasite, frittering away my expensive education in a lowly occupation.

There were some days when I wondered if he was right.

My dream, fiercely nurtured in that kothri in Deoli, had been of freedom, of vast mountains and valleys that are unpeopled and mute and mine. In Delhi, I lived in a barsaati in Mukherjee Nagar, an exposed rooftop cube of cement that baked during the day, with windows made opaque by dust, a cupboard whose doors sagged on their rusty hinges and could never be locked, a kitchen with a blackened kerosene stove atop a wooden table, and a 'bathroom' open to the sky where the tap, after dripping all night, would on most mornings sputter into silence.

The large desert-cooler growled at night, throwing blasts of mildew-smelling air around the room, but the water stagnated, breeding mosquitoes, rather than circulating through the straw pads; and the early-morning autorickshaw commute to work in Old Delhi was very long, past street sweepers with great brooms desultorily swiping, their mouths covered with a strip of turban or sari against the tranquil white clouds they raised.

Each day at lunchtime I would leave my cubicle where a thin layer of dust perennially lay on the apparatus of editorial work – floppy disks, cardboard folders, photostats, Filofax, dot-matrix printer – and queue for rajma-chawal from the little dhaba on the street corner. I would work late into the evening, long after my colleagues had left in their private cars for their homes in New Delhi, the bow-fronted pseudo-classical bungalows behind smooth hedges, closed gates and armed guards in sentry boxes.

I longed to escape the warrens of Old Delhi, their battalions of stray dogs, smells of drains and rotting rubbish, and the frequent public brawls – the sudden explosions of blows and curses between men that spoke of the great fury and despair trapped inside the city's guts. British travel writers and upper-class Indian tourists found this part of Delhi charmingly awash with kebab dives and Sufi shrines and Urdu storytellers; I feared being permanently absorbed into the privations and strife of those narrow houses pressing their scabbed façades together, the balconies festooned with exposed cables, and choked with clothes lines, boxes, brooms, pots and buckets.

Aseem's company was sustaining not just to me but to many other young people, who sought escape from lower-middle-class depression but didn't know how to achieve it. For previous generations, progress in life so far would have meant going through the motions prescribed by caste and class: together, the imperatives of education (inevitably vocational), marriage (nearly always arranged, with love regarded as a folly of callow youth), parenthood and professional career (with the government) imposed order, without too many troubling questions about their purpose and meaning.

Regional and caste background dictated culinary and sartorial habits: kurta-pyjamas and saris or shalwar-kameezes at home, drab Western-style clothes outside; an unchanging menu of dal, vegetables, rotis and rice leavened in some households with non-alcoholic drinks (Aseem's first publication in the IIT literary magazine was Neruda-style odes to Rooh Afza and Kissan's orange squash, Complan, Ovaltine and Elaichi Horlicks).

We belonged to a relatively daring generation whose members took on the responsibility of crafting their own lives: working in private jobs, marrying for love, eating pasta, pizza and chow mein as well as parathas, and drinking cola and beer, at home, taking beach vacations rather than going on pilgrimages, and wearing jeans and T-shirts rather than the safari suits that had come to denote style to the preceding generation of middle-class Indians. Our choices were expanded far beyond what my parents or Aseem's could even imagine.

And for those making this rapid and confusing transition, Aseem's small rented flat in Saket, where he lived with his wife Mrinal, opened up a tantalising window on a possible new life.

The literary festivals, friendships with plutocrats, travel in private jets and other signs of his protean transformation came later. For now, there was this flat, furnished and decorated with the help of Anokhi and Crafts Museum shop, with many bookshelves and piles of *Esquire* and *Time* magazine in-between Warli terracotta pots and brass figurines from Bastar, a poster of Muhammad Ali ('Boss, he is my God,' Aseem told me, 'I learn the rules from him') and hot parathas coming in from the kitchen, where a full-time maid – an easy marker of middle-class success – slaved over the stove while he opened endless bottles of Jameson whiskey in a large living room.

*

The Indian media was breaking free of its staid past; some of the most established print journalists were mutating into television personalities, and they were all there at Aseem's parties, along with colleagues from his magazine. Another regular, I remember, was a police officer, T. C. S. Sood, a former head of Jammu and Kashmir police celebrated in the media for his methods of extra-judicial killing and torture, but known in Aseem's circles for his stupendous recall of Faiz's poetry.

Far below the rest in social status were young journalists from small towns, with scruffy and fringed khadi jholas hanging from one shoulder. Aseem had told these children of *Kalyan*-reading government officials, teachers and doctors to rid themselves of the third-rate worldviews of their parents and aspire for something higher than a government job, a Maruti van and honeymoon in Mussoorie.

He told them that a new hyper-connected world of unprecedented possibility was emerging; the internet was facilitating a broad emancipation that would dissolve old frontiers and enlarge horizons. It was from Aseem in the mid-1990s that I first heard the words 'globalisation' and 'information superhighway', and he was also the first person I knew to own a mobile phone, a laptop and a smartphone.

He urged the small-town strivers to follow his example and aspire to an adventure of the mind, spirit and body on the lines laid down by Oscar Wilde: 'To cure the soul by means of the senses, and the senses by means of the soul.'

Whether or not the inheritors of petit-bourgeois aspirations followed these instructions, they saw Aseem as their hero. He had energetically opened up whole new possibilities of growth and fun in a city still dominated by dour upper-class Anglophiles. Many of them consented to work for his later ventures without a regular salary. Initially bound to him, like me, with admiration, they developed over time an envious desire to move with him, and like him, unsurprised and buoyant, through a globalised world.

Gliding through his parties, taller than most people in the room in the long white kurta and churidars he had exchanged with chikan kurtis, Aseem seemed to love the moment of contact, the handshake, the hug, and, unlike the hosts at the parties of my colleagues, he radiated the same charm and liveliness to all.

His eyes, however, remained watchful even as he smiled and laughed – quite like those of his cat that would crouch throughout his parties under a planter's armchair, her gaze from green flashing eyes unbroken even when the swirl of a sari or shawl swept a glass of wine from a side table on to the floor.

I now wonder: was there even then, underneath the brio and poise, the amused and knowing air, a lack of certainty and an unassuageable desire for self-affirmation? Were these hours of triumphant vivacity followed by dissatisfaction, a sense of inadequacy? Was his damaged childhood still playing on the man with the ebullient personality?

I realised at one point that Aseem, still pursuing his IIT ambition to be known as an artist, had become obsessed with writing a novel. *A Suitable Boy* had just been published. Aseem's own magazine put the novel on its cover; and he wrote a flattering profile of the author, comparing him to Homer and Tolstoy. Privately, he rubbished the novel as a soap opera, and declared his own literary ambition.

'I promised Mrinal before we got married,' he often said, 'that I would write a novel by the age of thirty. I don't have the time now, boss. But I know you can't jerk out a novel just because your father is a big bureaucrat or judge, and you have been to Oxford and know how to make India look like the "in thing" to publishers in London and New York. When you write a novel, you are competing with the greatest in the business!'

He claimed that the novel was being reduced by a socially ambitious Indian bourgeoisie to a showpiece, quite like the degree-crammed nameplates and glass-cased gee-gaws in middle-class homes.

He seemed curiously bitter about it all. 'It's such a subversive artistic form, potentially,' he would say. 'Look at what the Latin Americans from small-town backgrounds like Garcia Marquez did with it. I never expect much from American and British writers, especially the whiteys. Their imaginations are limited by their first-world privileges; they can escape only into ironical self-regard and New York and London have the cultural clout to pass off their second-rate stuff as first-rate. But there is no reason for our desi bourgeois writers to infect the novel with their bad conscience, narcissism and fundamental unseriousness. Indian writers have so much rich material and yet these pampered kids are playing with art and making it flabby.'

One of these kids worked at my office; she was, in fact, a co-editor of the literary review. The daughter of a pipe-smoking, lushly side-burned eminence in the British-built civil services, she had gone to Cambridge on a fellowship arranged by her father. Regarded there as brilliantly beautiful, her pale skin, dusky hair and light hazel eyes inspiring some light undergraduate verse, she had made it known that she was working on a novel titled *The Sherry Drinkers*, an account, both satirical and melancholy, of Indians like herself who find themselves spiritually marooned in India after returning from an exhilarating stint at Cambridge.

'Faber and Faber have taken it on; they are thrilled with it,' she told me, not long after I started working at the review, and then added, 'Do you know it? It's T. S. Eliot's old firm.'

A couple of years later, she brought it up again: 'Knopf are looking at it; they are very excited about it.'

After another couple of years, she said: 'Faber are really thrilled with it.'

I reported all this to Aseem without telling him that she rejoiced most in the cooler-talk comparison of him to Barry White. 'Boss, that's *crazy!*' Aseem said, his voice going up again rapidly. 'I know that every pampered Indian who has been to Oxford and Harvard wants to write a novel these days. But I can't believe that chick can write a two-thousand-word piece that is readable, let alone a novel.'

The 'perennially aspiring novelist', as he dubbed her, was a representative member of what Narendra Modi later denounced, to an electoral windfall, as the 'Lutyens elite', and what his army of trolls took to calling 'libtards'. In many ways, Aseem anticipated this cultish, heady detestation of the Anglophilic occupants of New Delhi's British-built bungalows.

He loved quoting Bazarov's lines from Turgenev's *Fathers and Children*, which we had read and reread at IIT: 'You are nothing but a soft, beautifully bred, liberal boy.' His own words 'chikna' and 'raja beta/beti' expressed a similar disdain for India's cossetted ruling class.

One of his diligently formulated sentences in this regard was: 'These smooth-cheeked liberals, these chiknas, these raja betas and betis want to convert the surplus of their posh upbringing into the immortality of art.'

Modi would come at the Lutyens elite with an ersatz nativism, claiming to be a son of a humble chai-vendor who doesn't know English, and sees no reason why he should. Aseem faulted the sherry drinkers in precisely the realm that they claimed superior skill.

The small insults they aimed at me swelled into bruises in his company, and I often found myself confiding in Aseem the everyday transgressions I observed at the literary review: while books by prominent people were carefully assigned to their friends, the much superior work of socially invisible and inconsequential authors was slighted with either lack of acknowledgement or coarse hostility by dilettantish reviewers.

'Please don't let those second-rate chiknas in your office boss you around, Arun,' he would say. 'I would arrange a job for you in a minute if you weren't so hell-bent on serving literature. You are a genuinely talented person, and they are an incredibly hollow people. They thrive because there is no talent to challenge them, and they will crush anyone who dares to. This is the problem not only with your office but with India at large, and it has to be tackled: mediocrity is bolder and better connected than talent.'

I can't deny that it was invigorating to see the people I knew then through Aseem's bright hauteur. It seemed to energise him, too, and I can see now that it strengthened the inescapable bond between us: two class fugitives breaking free of shameful origins by acquiring the language and deportment of the elite, but never less than uneasy in their adopted skins, haunted by a sense of fraudulence, and the anxiety that something or other – the way, for instance, Aseem pronounced career as 'carrier' – would betray us.

Aseem did not write his novel, not even after the publication of *The God of Small Things*, about which, too, he grumbled privately while ballyhooing it in his magazine. He rode the dotcom wave instead to start, with the help of Virendra and some venture capitalist money, his own magazine. Insolently named *The People's Tribune*, and devoted opportunely to raising environmental awareness (a niche concern then), it was launched with a secret investigation of a taboo subject: corrupt senior army officers who had deforested large parts of Kashmir during India's military occupation of the valley.

His face, solemn at this moment of triumph, instantly appeared on dozens of magazine covers; and all the new television talk shows seemed to alternate between featuring him and his exposé.

Around this time, he rented the spacious new house in Golf Links you saw him in, where an unusually cheerful chowkidar slouched inside the plywood box at the bamboo-topped gate; and a new kind of guest started to appear at his parties: young women with shining hair and jutting cheekbones.

Social and economic liberalisation had brought many of them out of conservative families, and into the emerging professions of media, design and NGO advocacy. You can spot them on the internet now, revolving through the global circuits of literary festivals, conferences and TED talks, all mysteriously trained to have the bodily poise, and the polite but opaque demeanour, of a fashion model before the cameras.

Aseem seemed to have handpicked them for his parties; his manner with them was free and unceremonious, ostensibly bohemian. He stood very close to them, briskly cutting the tension-wire between man and woman, not touching but giving off the certainty that he would, eventually.

I recall, too, the time when he inaugurated 'Great Minds United', the festival of books and ideas that is now indelibly connected to all our lives.

I remember you saying, 'I wish I hadn't said yes to his festival. It gets these international thought leaders like Joe Stiglitz and Vandana Shiva, but I heard that the rest of the crowd consists of groupies and lecherous journos.'

This wasn't how I first heard of it, in an email that Aseem's secretary forwarded me, where the festival, sponsored by Shell as well as Prada, was described as the 'Aspen-cum-Davos of the Global South' and *Time* and *Forbes* were quoted as hailing Aseem as the quintessential icon of an intellectually resourceful, economically resurgent and generally assertive and vibrant 'New India'.

Moving quickly from environmental activism to international wonkfests, Aseem himself, I can see now, was perennially seeking fresh ways to embody that assertiveness and vibrancy. He had become keen on a theory: that sexual appetite grows livelier during national aggrandisement of the kind India is undergoing and finds franker expression.

He was fond of saying at his parties, 'Look at Miller, Mailer, Vidal, Roth and Updike in the United States of the nineteen fifties and sixties; they became pretty bold – much bolder than, say, Hemingway, the original priapic genius – about tracing the arc of their penises as these rose in tandem with the wealth and power of their country.

'The most randy among them,' he would add, 'were writers from humble backgrounds, fucking their way up through society.' And he would then quote (verbatim, I realised, when I checked) from *Portnoy's Complaint*: 'I don't seem to stick my dick up these girls, as much as I stick it up their backgrounds.'

He had obviously started to put this theory into practice. I remember the evening at his new home, one of the many fuelled by duty-free Johnnie Walker Blue Label rather than the Jameson whiskey bootlegged by the embassy of Sierra Leone, when he boasted about his collection of pornography – books and videocassette tapes and DVDs – and his sexual prowess.

'Ten thousand fucks, boss!' Aseem said.

He claimed to have reached the record figure just the other day. I stole a glance at Mrinal. The number seemed very high; it invited an audit. He had known Mrinal for twenty years. Had the two maintained an average of one and a half fucks a day?

The maths did not work out in his wife's favour. But Aseem's wife looked at him with detached amusement. So did many of the young women present there, and I remember thinking to myself how easily, within a few years, sexual frankness had possessed long-puritanical minds.

Aseem also had a little speech: 'We middle-class Indians are the world's biggest hypocrites about sex. Why can't we understand that the erotic has always been an intrinsic part of our lives? This is something the classical Indians who wrote the *Kamasutra* and built the temples of Khajuraho knew. We worship the phallus, for God's sake.

'Those ancient Hindus had it all figured out. Either you live in the world or you renounce it. And, mind you, the renouncer is revered; he is central to Hindu culture; people still hold the sadhus and swamis in great regard. But this doesn't turn into scorn for the guy who fucks extensively, marries, procreates, gets rich. The guy who embraces life in all its material and erotic excess has his own place in the cosmos.'

He liked to quote a line of verse from the *Rig Veda* to support his point about the amoral sensuality of classical Hindus: 'He achieves not – he whose penis hangs limp between his thighs; Achieves he alone whose hairy thing swells up when he lies.'

'It's a goddess, a woman, and not some horny man,' he would insist, 'who says that in the most ancient text of Hinduism.'

(I checked the Penguin Classics translation once: he had again got the quote right.)

'Compare that total acceptance of sex to St Augustine inventing original sin because his dick was rising without his consent. Indians in the past accommodated everything – homosexuality, androgyny, transgenderism, you name it. It is the Christians, the missionaries, the Victorians and the Americans who screwed us up with their puritanism. I am glad we are getting over it now.'

Aseem would then offer as evidence a story about a student journalist from Miranda House who had interviewed him for her college magazine, and afterwards gone for a drink with him at one of those dives in Defence Colony that serve underage drinkers. After only her first glass of wine, she had said, 'What's the point of hanging around here, killing mosquitoes, why don't you come back to my barsaati and we'll fuck.'

Aseem laughed and drummed the ground with his feet as he finished this story, and he seemed to deliberately not say if he had taken up the invitation of an undergraduate at a posh college.

'Even many smart men,' you once remarked, 'talk about women in overly sexualised ways and objectify them because they are too damaged in their inner lives and cannot connect with their deepest emotions.' It is one of the things you said that I now recall with guilt.

Back then, however, Aseem's utterances seemed like harmless boasting, inflating his claim to personify an Indian spirit untainted by sanctimony and hypocrisy.

He acquired, too, as part of his new forceful persona, a left-wing politics aimed at not only despoilers of the environment but also corruption, religious extremism, authoritarianism and patriarchy. To those Western journalists, think-tankers, and multinational executives beguiled by the New India, he was never less than reassuring with his precis of the country's untapped potential: 'Hundreds of millions of young eager beavers from the lower middle class,' he would say, caressing their clichés, 'the demographic dividend is going to be mammoth.' In his public appearances, however, on television and in press interviews, he appeared with his rising, cracking voice, in a state of permanent mobilisation against fearsome enemies.

I remember you saying that you had first heard of him because of his political outspokenness. 'I really came to admire his mojo, his chutzpah,' you said. 'And so did many people in my generation. To us, Westernised, privileged Indians, he showed just how dark our world was underneath glossy surfaces.'

I didn't say that, though I felt grateful for Aseem's emphatic solidarity with me, and other people from our class, I could follow his political denunciations only part of the way.

A passion for the environment, or social and gender justice, could not have been reasonably expected from those anxiously striving since childhood for high marks and a gateway to the United States. To the extent I became periodically aware of them, the victims of gang rape in Nagaland, colossal dams on Himalayan faultlines, and collapsing water tables across North Indian plains roused outrage and sympathy. Yet, my interest in the gaudy mural of wickedness and misery daubed weekly by Aseem's magazine remained limited.

I was unconvinced by Aseem, and not only because his social conscience had been too belatedly aroused, and had come to coexist too placidly with a trite boosterism about India.

He seemed to me to be exaggerating; to be disregarding the lessons of our own lives as well as of the books we had so eagerly read and reread at IIT. Hyper-masculine bigots, unscrupulous journalists and venal businessmen did not represent an unprecedented demonic reality to me. From what I knew of my father and of society as described by Balzac and Maupassant, they seemed perfectly normal.

Moreover, and I can see this now more clearly, Aseem did not wish, like you and many others, to rearrange this mean world. His indignation over climate change or injustice remained disconnected from any larger political cause or project: T. C. S. Sood, the executioner of Kashmiris, and role model to killers in uniform elsewhere, continued to book-chat at Aseem's parties.

It was as though Aseem was seeking some kind of personal distinction by appearing to stand with the wretched of the earth. Perhaps he had calculated that victimhood would become more glamorous and fruitful than the collective quest for a just society.

In Delhi, Aseem avidly sought and consumed ideas and pleasures, constantly enriching his original lode of high feeling. I started to move, after a few years, in a different direction. Having ended in Delhi that early scramble for food and a room of my own, I dreamed of escape to a more spacious life, of leaving my cramped environs and living in the Himalayan landscape of the calendar at home; and my dreams became more colourful after I discovered a calendar-village called Ranipur while on a trip to Shimla.

I had started to translate, while still working at the literary review, for a hardbound series of classic Hindi literature sponsored by a corporate philanthropist in the United States. The pay, in US dollars, was generous by Indian standards, and escape to Ranipur had begun to seem financially practical, when one evening I came home from work to find a letter from my mother.

She had written me the same letter for years now – 'Aasha hai ki tum swasth ho. I hope you are keeping healthy. Aur padhai-likhai acchi chal rahi hai. And your studies are going well. Itne dinon se koi chitthi nahin aiyi tumhari. There has been no letter from you for ages. Thodi chinta ho jaati hai tumhare swasth ke baare main. I get a little anxious about your health' – solicitude only occasionally interspersed with confessions of chest pain and breathlessness, which I read through as cursorily as the rest.

The idiom had altered as little over the years as the design of the inland letter card, with its three flaps and Gandhi postmark, even as I moved from attending coaching classes in Delhi to IIT and my first job; and I opened the latest missive somewhat wearily to find that it was Meena, my sister, who had written it, informing me in two terse paragraphs that our father had left our mother for another woman, and urging me to return home as soon as possible since she could not leave her business for long.

A strange memory flitted through my mind as I stood there stunned, the flimsy blue sheet with the impatiently torn flaps in my hand: Baba bringing a chipped white tumbler of fresh warm milk to his mouth, half-closing his eyes; his thick, cracked lips rest on the brim to assess the temperature, and gently blow. Finally, he sips his breakfast with closed eyes, his broad, cruelly handsome face briefly at peace.

I had neither witnessed nor dared to imagine the other hungers that drove this man. My mother could never bring herself to disclose how he had tired of her submissive femininity. I learned later, from my sister, that he had conducted a long affair with the widowed daughter of a local shopkeeper, and moved in with her as soon as her father died. He now ran the shop with his new consort.

From Old Delhi railway station, where the rolling crowds over footbridges seemed always on the verge of stampede, I took the night train, sleeplessly reprising all my journeys home. A diesel engine pulled the train now, but the unreserved second-class carriages seethed with sweaty and drowsy men, the hole in the toilet floor dully growled while ceiling lamps burned as weakly as ever; and golden sparks still rushed backwards in the black night like the fiery churails of my childhood nightmares.

When I opened my eyes from a brief nap early in the

morning, the ground seemed, dizzyingly, to be rushing past in the opposite direction. In the dawn's ash-pale light, I disembarked from the train and walked, still disorientated, through the white-shrouded bodies on the platform floor to my mother in the house abandoned by her husband.

Exhausted, from grief and sleepless nights, her frail body heaved with sobs as she clung to me in that fleshy embrace of hers.

Everything around me in my relinquished home seemed the same as ever, only shabbier and smaller, more smeared and chipped. Yet, walking away from the bottle of Thums Up in the empty room, where I had known the helpless sensation of being trapped for ever, and where everything had long since grown old and outlived itself, I found myself grieving; I felt full of mourning for that time when I was beckoned and supported by the possibility of a bright expansive life.

I was now going to meet, my mother unexpectedly beside me, that open and mysterious future in a new place. But as the tonga lurched out of the rutted lane, the bells on the horse's neck emitting a hollow din, and the tarmac road below the flickering hooves began to flow, a past in which hope was abundant seemed to be sliding away from under me.

PART TWO

Six

'But this is ridiculous,' Aseem said when I told him of my move. 'Such a backward step. What are you going to do in a little village? Listen, if you need a new job away from those chiknas in your office, just let me know.'

I told him about the translation project. 'Wow,' he said, 'that's a lot of money. You'll be rolling in dollars in the Himalayas.'

I told him, too, about the fate of my mother. 'I can't do anything about my sister,' I said, a little righteously, 'but I can at least try to give my mother a better life.'

But he was thinking of something else. 'You realise, I hope, that living with your mother takes you out of circulation.'

The thought had occurred to me, but then, during all my years in Delhi, I hadn't been able to visualise myself *in* circulation.

A little later in the same telephone conversation, Aseem contradicted himself. 'I envy you,' he said. 'Actually, that's a good choice you have made to stay away from the noise of the world.'

I was briefly flattered. But Aseem's wistful tone was misleading. For he was only then realising, with a strenuous exertion of his will, what he had always wanted – escape from his small-town constraints, a new life with new attitudes, standards and habits, a bright new circle of friends and a sense of power.

After years of travelling in an Ambassador to work, he was driven to work in a Pajero – bought, like much else in his office, with Virendra's money. People stopped and stared at him in airports; some sought his autograph or photo. Stories about his porn collection, his theory tying Roth's and Updike's penises to post-war American enlargement, and his photos with tycoons and fashionable thinkers were filtering down, via IIT Delhi LISTSERV, to even my village.

I came across interviews in which he was starting to speak proudly of his origins. He would say, 'The lower middle class is the true maker of history. Historians and sociologists focus on the working class and the rich. And the chikna novelists write about other chiknas. But it's people like us, very poorly represented in literature since the nineteenth century, who make and remake the world with our hunger and ambition.'

I never gave you a full account of the summer when I left Ranipur for a small lecture tour of America, and Aseem drove me to a party in East Hampton, hosted by Virendra, then a freshly anointed billionaire and his magazine's main financier.

I saw Aseem at his suite at the Pierre Hotel. The venue was not surprising. I had last seen Aseem at a party in his Golf Links home held for his hero V. S. Naipaul on one of my rare visits to Delhi from Ranipur.

There was art on the walls – not the prints of Canaletto and Vermeer he had in Saket but paintings by modern Indian artists who had started to exhibit in European galleries. Whiskey, single malt as well as blended, was available if you asked for it, but the tall glasses on passing trays contained Marquise De Pompadour, the Indian version of champagne, and Sauvignon Blanc from vineyards in Maharashtra and Karnataka. Growing older, and more networked, the small-town journalists patronised by Aseem had replaced their jholas with knock-off JanSport backpacks and their Bata lace-ups and kolhapuri chappals with Timberland boat shoes and moccasins.

In a crowd of foreign correspondents, journalists, advertising men, aspiring writers, bureaucrats and glamorous young women, everyone seemed openly awed by and striving for proximity to Naipaul, who, entrenched in one corner of the room, appeared stout and surprisingly small, in thick tweed, large glasses and thinning hair and bristly white goatee (I was expecting the intense – and taller? – younger man in *A Bend in the River*'s jacket photograph).

Only Aseem, assured of easy access to his distinguished guest and new friend, held himself apart from Naipaul's aura – he and his cat, a strikingly uncommon pet in Delhi, and his wife Mrinal, who, as always, hovered near him, not saying much as her husband held forth on Rupert Murdoch and India's sexual revolution, but with a half-smile that suggested gentle scepticism.

At the Pierre, I arrived simultaneously with a silver-haired black waiter holding a tray of brioches, jam jars, napkins and hotel silver. Aseem, clad in the hotel's monogrammed silk robe, scribbled his name wildly on the check while bringing, napkin-less, a brioche to his mouth.

As the elderly waiter closed the door behind him (slightly disdainfully?), he said, 'Look at us. We have travelled on bullock carts and here we are, transported on the top deck of a Boeing 747 from Asia to the Pierre. Has anyone made such rapid progress in a single lifetime?'

When did he travel on a bullock cart? I never did. In any case, I hadn't flown to New York on a Boeing 747; I had taken a Soviet-built Ilyushin with the low-cost Ethiopian Air, and after a long stopover at Addis Ababa airport, accompanied in the low-roofed lounge by Sikhs with duct-taped cardboard boxes and cloth bundles enigmatically en route to the Congo, I had spent four hours at immigration at JFK in a little cell full of depressed-looking people of vaguely Middle Eastern appearance, next to a Pakistani woman muttering racist abuse in Urdu at her African-American captor from underneath her black burqa.

I was staying at a Days Inn in the Bronx, where, encountering an American toilet for the first time, I had worried that the flush that merrily whirled the contents of the bowl, leaving them floating disquietingly before a spasmic suck, was broken. I had travelled on the subway to 59th Street, clinging to a grimy pole, and marvelling at the kaleidoscope of very different, but uniformly emotion-free, faces of the passengers. I was planning to travel by train the next day to Hamilton College for a lecture on modernist Hindi fiction for which I would be paid $1,000 plus expenses – probably the rate for one night at the Pierre Hotel, but, given my likely audience of five to seven people, very generous.

I stared out of the window at the dark, steaming tops of the buildings. Watching the second plane drill into the tower, days after the actual event, my first response was that it was a bit unnatural to live or work suspended so high up in the sky. The same thought returned to me now, shorn of its callousness, as Aseem handed me a thin long glass, cold, roseate champagne creaming and foaming inside it.

'It's early, but what the hell, it is Dom Pérignon, free from the hotel, and Mrinal is not here to monitor my alcohol intake,' Aseem said.

The champagne tasted, to my uneducated palate, inferior to, or at least less sweet than, the Marquise de Pompadour Aseem had started to serve at his parties. But I didn't tell him this. Nor that I had cut, while he was in the loo, my finger on the shreds at the edges of the New York Times squatting bulkily on his desk, and wiped the tiny beads of blood bubbling out of the scratch on the sports pages.

In any case, he seemed intent upon enjoying the park-facing

suite on the thirty-second floor that the hotel manager, mindful of his guest's contacts among his Indian bosses, had upgraded him to.

He invited me, one hand playing with the tassels of his robe, another twirling the stem of his glass, to inspect it.

'Panditji, you must get tired of the rustic and celibate life sometimes. Well, this is what is on offer in the big bad world outside your little Himalayan asylum.'

The pillows on both sides of Aseem's hurriedly and inexpertly made bed were indented. Did he have company the previous night? He positively hummed with energy; and I wonder now if living in a world that so eagerly met his desires, sex had become for Aseem almost an offhand mode of gratification, something to add to his tally.

I was trying to find something to say, something to reconnect me with this more exalted and slightly swaggering Aseem, as I sauntered through his suite with my glass of champagne, reminded by the furnishings – of pale gold and cream, the decorative fireplace, and the silver glass chandelier – of the *Playboy* centrefold over which we spent so much of our limited leisure time at IIT.

I didn't think I could even lightheartedly refer to this resemblance to Aseem in his new mood. He said, apropos of nothing, 'The hotels of Shanghai and Mumbai never get it completely right. They have grander premises, but they don't offer the unique frisson of a place like this.

'J. P. Getty built the private residences in the building. This is really the right house for Mr Biswas. Uncompromisingly fashionable, boss, and reassuringly expensive,' he added, laughing.

He laughed because he knew I would recognise the phrase 'uncompromisingly fashionable', evidently uttered by V. S. Naipaul to Paul Theroux when he, the descendant of indentured labourers, bought a flat in South Kensington, London: the first landmark in his personal journey from indigence and obscurity to the place where he could cherish his new self-respect and imperviousness to humiliation.

That was in the 1970s. Now, many more from a 1.4 billion-strong population were trying to reach the summit of affluence and confidence occupied for so long by white men and women. On the flight over to New York, I had watched on BBC's *Hardtalk* an Indian novelist in English, declaiming in her euphonious convent-school English how it is time for Hindus to assert with pride that they are Hindus, and help fulfil India's destiny as a great civilisation and nation state.

In Aseem's case, these longings for world-historical redemption were secular rather than Hindu-nationalist; they were, nevertheless, extensively shared. Shamefully identified for long with a country of beggars and elephants, many well-educated, upper-caste Indians were now demanding respect and attention from the white rulers of the world. A corporate dynasty from Mumbai had recently bought the Pierre and was ostentatiously seeking to purchase the company that makes the Jaguar, two of many trophy acquisitions in what Indian newspapers hailed as the 'Global Indian Takeover'.

A small-town swindler from Uttar Pradesh would soon purchase the Plaza Hotel across the road from the Pierre. Already, the Indian tricolour flew on Central Park; the lobby reverberated with the Hinglish and Mandarin of crazy rich Asians. Some ancient American ladies still clung to their Getty-built cooperative apartments in the thin building. Entering the wood-panelled elevator with their pampered poodles, they stood with disdainful backs to the Chinese and Indian upstarts clutching their loot from Fifth Avenue's emporia as they were all slowly drawn upwards.

Aseem responded with his own contempt. 'It's all over for

America,' he said. 'The American dream has been uncovered as a fraud, Americans themselves know they have been fooled, and the elite that perpetrated this deception is finished.

'Suicide, depression, drug addiction, random gun violence, rioting on the streets, believe me, boss, that's this country's future. I mean, Philip Roth, who started to publish when America was rising, is now writing about how Zuckerman can't get it up any more. What more proof do you need? They have had it too easy for too long, boss. Exempted from the horrors of the twentieth century, windfall of global power after the Second World War, and they got away with a lot of mediocrity in the absence of rivals. And now the Yanks have gone globally rabid with their war on terror after their first real brush with adversity, and opened the door wide to China's global supremacy. The thing is, ultimately, the mad gringos will have to get over their wounded egos and rely on people like us to fix their broken country and the international liberal order.'

And people like us, or Aseem, were already floating, in that plush eyrie, far above the desis of another era who had left behind bullock carts in India to find themselves driving yellow cabs, penned in at newspaper kiosks around Manhattan, numb and dreary, their children now stomping down streets full of people with thrusting faces and rigid backs, vying zealously for rewards that seemed as dubious as they were elusive.

A better class of Indians had risen above this futile thudding traffic everywhere – in politics, tech, finance, media, publishing. Aseem reeled out the names and credentials of some prominent Indian Americans – Sonny Mehta, Fareed Zakaria, Vikram Pandit, Vinod Khosla – who had come to share the task of interfacing between American and Indian elites with the great Rajat Gupta of McKinsey & Company.

He informed me of simultaneous cover stories in *Newsweek*, *The Economist* and *Foreign Affairs* that confirmed India's unstoppable ascent; and seemed a bit put out when I confessed that I never read those magazines. Even *Vanity Fair*, he reported, was becoming interested in the new Asian power; he'd heard it straight from Graydon Carter.

'The editor,' he said, wagering that I would not know.

There was a pause and then he added, 'Those crazy Mozzie fundos got it all wrong, bringing down the World Trade Center. They should have tried buying up the whole place.'

From his own account, some white men and women at least were reconciled to their decline, and eager to welcome their swarthy replacements.

'Tina is throwing a party for me tomorrow evening,' Aseem said. 'Do you want to come? We can go straight there from Virendra's place in East Hampton. Salman might be there.'

'Boss,' he said en route to East Hampton the next day, 'this is a new world we are living in, where your upbringing in an Asian country is suddenly an asset. Virendra's firm is opening offices in places its WASP founders had barely heard of: Manila, Bogota, Lagos, Jakarta. They need people of cosmopolitan backgrounds, immune to Delhi belly, culture shocks and other traumas that these soft whiteys tend to suffer.'

Aseem was leaning forward in his seat, gazing down the highway as if trying to glimpse his own future. Gripping the steering wheel, his hands shook perpetually, though almost imperceptibly; and he had some trouble with his left eye and kept dabbing at it with a handkerchief.

He added, 'You know that I am committed to India, and you don't want to leave your village, but I can see why Virendra has a whole new life here, where he has the chance to travel, to see new countries, and build up his ego. He had always felt himself to be an eel, wriggling into the most unexpected places; he can now roam the world like a gazelle, and even return to India as a hero.'

The bit about the eel and the gazelle seemed like something Aseem had prepared, perhaps for use on BBC and CNN, where IIT-LISTSERV always jauntily noted his appearance, speaking of New India's promise. I know that he used it when you interviewed him for your book.

'You know, boss,' he now said, 'Virendra's true model in this regard is Naipaul, even though he hasn't read a word of his. Vidia was the original of the completely self-made modern Indian, someone who successfully pursued a higher idea of the self, the prototype of the early-twenty-first-century globalised man.'

I remember you expressing some bafflement over Aseem's literary tastes during one of our earliest meetings. 'I mean, he still goes in for these dick-waving writers like Roth and Mailer. And talks up a storm about Naipaul, that total Islamophobe and misogynist. I don't know anyone who reads these people any more.'

I was surprised to hear this. I didn't know then that while familiarising myself with an overwhelmingly male canon of twentieth-century literature I had remained mostly ignorant of a rich tradition of writing by women. Feebly represented in Indian bookshops, those books by Jane Bowles, Zora Neale Hurston and Annie Ernaux that I found you reading and then picked up afterwards alerted me to ways of thinking about the world that felt immediately congenial.

Aseem, too, had no idea about this whole different world of writers (and readers). And then for him, surrounded by formidably credentialled Indian authors, who made a stint at Oxbridge seem a prerequisite for writing, Naipaul, that grandson of indentured labourers, was too much a man in his own image: the man who comes out of nowhere and succeeds against great odds.

Whether or not Aseem knew his books, which I found too schematic or bitter and rarely finished reading, he zealously upheld the myth of Naipaul. He also embraced his diagnosis of India's 'wounded civilisation', perhaps because Naipaul's targets were those soft, beautifully bred liberals, who, obsessed with securing the esteem of white Westerners, hushed up the cruelties of caste and poverty they were complicit in.

By the time Aseem met and befriended him, Naipaul had drastically changed his mind. India, according to him, had finally experienced a mass intellectual and political awakening. Incredibly, he saw evidence of this in the Hindu fanatics who demolished the Babri mosque in 1992, and massacred hundreds of Muslims across India. Their violence apparently represented a surge of historical consciousness from below, from India's trampled-upon classes and castes.

Though appalled by the carnage, which consumed the life of a close friend in Mumbai, and openly antagonistic from that point onwards to Hindu supremacists, Aseem was quick to excuse Naipaul's misjudgement after he befriended the writer at one of his festivals.

'Boss, at the end of the day, he'll say what is on his mind. Without fear. What matters to me is his integrity.'

Integrity: it was the highest praise from Aseem. As with some other English words he used, I wasn't entirely sure what he meant by 'integrity'. I took it to mean a candour that is uninhibited and even unpleasant, and he used the same word when Naipaul confessed in an interview to disliking his mother, his recourse to prostitutes and his erotic bliss with a mistress as his wife lay dying of cancer; and then again when a feminist critic charged Naipaul with debasing depictions of women in his novels.

My own opinion of Naipaul abruptly froze when I over-heard him say at Aseem's party, 'The Booker Prize is now a charity for homosexuals. Yes, yes, yes, it's a charity for homosexuals.' He was referring to the author of a recent prize-winner, *The Line of Beauty*, a novel that I had read with some incredulity, scarcely able to believe that such subtle perceptions and attentive prose were possible, and I had been half-dreaming about rendering it into Hindi.

Aseem explained away this side of Naipaul as part of his entitlement as a great artist. It seems to me that Aseem had started to see Naipaul as one of the nineteenth-century fictional antagonists he came across at IIT: another exponent of talent and raw ambition in a hostile society. He saw the Jewish-American writers he idolised, Roth and Mailer, in much the same way.

I didn't know or care enough about Naipaul to contest these visions of an aestheticised amorality. In fact, nearness diminished the writer that Aseem revered, reducing him to a balding man with hooded eyes, sagging double chin, pelican belly and unexamined assumptions of a right to revile.

I have to wonder now what effect Naipaul had on Aseem, as he in his last years became obsessed with being feted, and, consequently, vulnerable to the rich, famous and powerful – precisely, the people he had once so severely assessed.

I did not go to Tina's party in New York, and so never found out what it meant, in declining America, to embody 'rising' India. But I can verify that all the more conspicuous makers and publicists of what was starting to be known as the 'New India' – from the authors of books titled *The Indian Idea*, *The Amazing Rise of India*, *The New Asian Tiger* and *Super-Fast Curry Nation* to the gay Bollywood director, soap-opera queen and the silver-tongued advertising agency executive, who became three of Modi's rowdiest cheerleaders – were present at Aseem's parties.

The few times I attended them on visits to Delhi from Ranipur, I never saw the real-estate tycoons, politicians and arms dealers that would later come to support his various projects. But then this sort of person who decisively set the aesthetic and ethical tone of the New India operated invisibly, behind the scenes.

I should have taken as a warning one account of Aseem's newfound influence that appeared in a gossip column in *Outlook*. He had directed the young, idealistic organisers of a literary festival to the farmhouse of an American-accented businessman in Mehrauli. Emerging from it with US dollars in tightly packed bundles, of the kind you see in *Narcos* today, the literary groupies had later discovered that their uncommonly benevolent patron worked as a lobbyist for Lockheed Martin.

A whole idiom was altering, and Aseem had placed himself at the avant-garde of this moral and cultural revolution, holding aloft New India's banner of entrepreneurial pluck and sparkle, with spotlights playing on it from all corners of the world.

By the late 2000s, his parties were reverberating with the vocabulary and accents of Indians educated in the United States rather than England. Whether writing literary fiction and journalism or employed with one of the international banks and management and risk consultancies, they threw out terms that glittered with expertise and profit – 'opportunity costs', 'core competencies', 'branding', 'process input' – and made you feel left behind; they also, equally disconcertingly, addressed one as 'dude'.

You became familiar with these cults of private and national aggrandisement in your early years in the West. I saw much later how emigration to, and education in, the West had unleashed a new kind of Indian upon the world: ambitious young men from ghettos smelling of their mothers' spice-heavy cooking in Freemont, California, and New Jersey, initiated into can-doism and wonkery at their business schools, and now wholly Americanised, untouched by the reserve a straitened Indian middle-class upbringing or a stint in cold clammy Oxbridge would have given them, men we would have taken for hustlers had we not realised by then that aggressive self-presentation rather than modesty was the American, and increasingly Indian and global, way.

For middle-class Indians who stayed back, their affluent relatives in America had become the source of goodies: toys, gadgets, comic books and *Cosmopolitan* and *Seventeen*. These went on to circumscribe the imaginative horizons of 'rising' India.

You had little interest in Bollywood and were mostly appalled by its products when you caught up with them on long flights. 'Some producer approached me with a role at a party,' you once told me. 'He wanted me to play the fun-loving Indian in a mini-skirt who is a Hindu traditionalist at heart and ends up teaching the Gayatri mantra to white Americans. I couldn't speak, I was so horrified.'

You probably didn't know that by the late 1990s, when you came of age, *Archie* comics, set in a hormonally charged American high school, were inspiring some of India's most successful films: those whose rich world-conquering Indian characters embraced fully the brassy ethos of the New India.

That summer when Aseem drove me from the Pierre to East Hampton, we discovered that Virendra, having missed out on Archie and Veronica during his bleak childhood, had taken to enacting Jay Gatsby at his mansion, newly acquired from a former luminary at Sullivan & Cromwell.

On that breezy day, despite the trembling hands and eye trouble, Aseem drove very fast. I remember how the long grass on the steep meadows alongside the highway seemed to be nodding its approval of the planes loud and low in the sky and the cars rushing to the countryside, their chrome flashing and glinting in the sun; and how even the dismal-looking trailers seemed invested with speed and urgency.

The sea glittered through densely leafed woods, and then suddenly exposed itself, flatly lapping against barnacled rocks. Turning off the highway, we plunged into farmland. After Manhattan, with its miserably purposeful summer crowds and smell of blistering tar, its oppressive immensity of anonymous frantic life, this was the landscape I liked: white fences around cropped green pastures, where black-and-white cattle, so much plumper than their Indian counterparts, wandered.

We passed white houses with porches, so shiny that they looked as if they had been iced with white sugar, a steepled church that looked like a large toy left outside in overgrown grass, and signs for fresh mackerel and lobster. Aseem slowed down as the car rumbled over a wooden bridge and then clanged over a couple of cattle guards. Then, passing a porte cochère we came on to a winding gravel driveway. At the end stood a Greek-revival mansion facing a wide round pond.

No one seemed to be around, but as we stood blinking in the bright sunshine, before a nasturtium-crowded urn on a stone plinth in the centre of the gravelled circle, a man emerged from the pond and began to walk towards us.

For some reason, the sight of Virendra's torso, bare and glistening in the sun, thick black hairs wetly flattened on his massive chest, reminded me of a picture I had once seen of Mao Zedong emerging from the Yangtze.

'Hello. Panditji. Hello, Mr Playboy!' he called out. 'So great to see my two big literary gurus.'

I hadn't seen him since he left IIT. Though he had the same reedy voice, it was now at odds with his increased bulk. On thin bones starved in his childhood of nutrition there now hung much slack flesh, and though his eyes retained their blankness, his face, its thin uncertain moustache replaced by a fuller growth, looked calmer and shrewder.

'Look at us, man, all grown up and shit, here in the US of A!' he shouted, and started to belt out, with as much joyous incomprehension as before, his old favourite, *'Waqt ne kiya kya haseen sitam.'*

We stood there for a while after he stopped singing, the sunlight rippling through the nasturtiums.

'But it's true, isn't it?' Virendra added, in a level tone. 'We could have been like our parents, totally without power, totally helpless and trapped. We had to escape. Who could have thought it possible? But we did it.'

He had ceased to smile now. 'What's happened to your eye?' he suddenly asked Aseem. 'It's a bit red.'

His own breathing sounded laboured, with some ancient phlegm behind it. Or was he just panting? I couldn't stop staring at him, at the bare wrists where he had once worn, loosely, an HMT woman's watch: nothing in the Virendra I knew at IIT had foreshadowed his unhealthy fleshiness and his conviction of having achieved complete liberation from the life of his parents.

The gravel at the foot of the stone plinth had been scored up by the wheels of Aseem's rented car. Virendra, noticing the spirals, started to rake them smooth with his sandal-shod feet; and, though moved by this tenderness for his new property, I felt greater awkwardness with him than with a stranger, the great barrier of unshared years and memories rising between us.

Looking up from the now even gravel, he waved his arm around, saying jauntily, 'Isn't this place wonderful?'

I nodded. He gave us big hugs that left damp patches on our shirts; releasing us, briefly, he hugged us again to plant kisses on our faces, pressing his wet, cold moustache on our cheeks.

'Let me give you a quick tour,' he said. He walked us, still panting slightly, and his cheeks flopping, to the pond fringed with weeping willows and white red-bordered peonies. Swans drifted on the still water. Pointing to the grassy island in the middle of the pond, he said, 'That's where I hope to spend most of my summers with a gorgeous babe.'

He spoke lightly, as though seeking to cleanse the statement of its implication.

Walking through a small grove of locust trees with white blossoms, he took us to an ancient-looking barn. Standing in its musty darkness, he pointed to spinning wheels, candle moulds and a gigantic pair of scales. 'These are what these first American guys were using. They were spinning their own cloth and making their own candles. Isn't that incredible?'

Returning to the house, he touched the fern-draped walls and said, 'They are a foot and a half deep!' We entered through the front door, which, adorned with a massive brass knocker, opened out into a vast hall with a carpeted staircase.

A sharp smell of beeswax hit my nostrils as we walked through well-proportioned rooms full of objects that I associated with polish-scented antique stores in Shimla – little mahogany tables with slender legs, high-backed and spiral-legged chairs, red Bohemian glass decanters, a mirror with the American eagle painted on top, and paintings of romantic landscapes everywhere in gilt frames, things that intimated not only the age of the house, its historic abundance, but also the plumpness of the lives that had been lived inside its walls.

Aseem wandered off with Virendra, still dabbing at his left

eye. I stayed back to look at the framed photographs left behind by the previous occupants of the house.

Many of the pictures looked old and faded, probably taken in the early years of the century. With one exception – a lady ancestor in a gold frame with a hooked chin and long neck – they were all of men, and suggested a self-sufficient all-male realm of power: the young schoolboys in their starched Eton collars, suits and pumps against the white Gothic chapel of Groton; athletically handsome young men against the spires and narrow English archways of Yale; older, more confident-looking men with gold watch chains peeping out from their suits, standing under a sign with the name of Sullivan & Cromwell; a white-haired gentleman who looked like Cromwell himself in striped trousers, a silk hat, morning coat and white shoes.

Only the youngest men in the pictures were smiling. I was struck by one of them, a boy holding an old-fashioned tennis racket of wood, whose large uncertain eyes betrayed vulnerability. Who was he? What had become of him?

The faces and postures of the rest of the men presented an imperturbable façade; alert, and united in purpose, they seemed to have already embraced a high awareness of their role in the world.

They were like the pictures of colonial hunters I saw in old almanacs about Shimla and Ranipur: the callow young officers in pith helmets and jodhpurs, Winchester rifles against their knees, their wives in perms and cloche hats, a tiger sprawled like a big soft toy before them, its legs stiff in death.

I often think now of what Aseem said about the modern world's oldest elites, and the new, unexpected beneficiaries of globalisation: how a Dalit from a roadside settlement near Gorakhpur came to supplant the clans of Groton and Yale;

how an eel crawling out of a cruel past was liberated to roam like a gazelle across the modern world.

Did you know that Aseem often went journeying with Virendra, as part-payment for the copious funds made available to his magazine by Virendra? On the way back from East Hampton, Aseem told me about their Kenyan safari, where Maasai tribesman at a small airport were startled to see a man as dark as themselves emerge from the private jet leading an entourage of women in silk saris and men and children in T-shirts and sneakers.

One birthday (whose? I wonder, but it could have been any-one's), Aseem flew in a private jet to Tuscany where Siva and Virendra had rented a villa formerly used by papal bankers for their extended families. By the swimming pool – its smallness a disappointment to those accustomed to Olympian sizes in East Hampton and Cape Cod – vintage Chiantis were opened and then quickly discarded; they didn't go with the spicy Mala-bar food the chefs imported from Kerala were preparing.

'It was just amazing,' Aseem said. 'These pampered kids were running screaming through the vineyards and the olive terraces.'

His voice started to rise and crack as he related how, under the antique cypresses, whose calligrapher brushes striped the lawn, the little brutes played football, and, after lunch, rinsed their oily fingers in the swimming pool.

I would have quoted to Aseem, had I known then, the lines from Sartre's introduction to *The Wretched of the Earth* that you recommended me to read. 'Europe is springing leaks every-where. In the past we made history and now it is being made of us.' Old Europe now plugged its leaks with coquetry before Oriental arrivistes; and though it seemed that, in her historical decline, leaky Europe had set too high a premium on her commodified heritage, it couldn't be high enough for budding masters of the universe like Siva and Virendra.

I was always struck by the unselfconscious ease with which you had inherited the wealth of your family, which made your multiple residences, often with salaried staff, in Delhi, Mumbai, Ranipur, London and New York appear an ageless and natural habitat. To be newly rich, however, seemed a more uneasy condition.

Virendra and his friends had to ceaselessly find opportunities to savour it, and to affirm their great good fortune. And the easiest way was through extravagant spending on holidays – long transatlantic trips, seven-star hotels and yachts.

A cavalcade of chauffeured BMWs took Aseem to famous cities in Italy, and he became the unofficial guide to a new batch of grand tourists who had no idea where they were.

'Aseem knows this shit; he has read all the books,' Siva claimed.

'I could have lied, you know,' Aseem said. 'These guys making loads of money have become totally philistine. I guess we were lucky, having Professor Sir to initiate us into great literature at IIT. These guys wouldn't even read my books – Virendra said he loved the bits about shagging, though. I did as much as I could. I had read up a Tim Parks book before arriving in Italy. I told them about the Medicis, and the Renaissance popes who were closer to money than to God.'

Aseem said that in a sea of glazed eyes, Virendra's were most alert, and he asked the most questions. He liked the idea that bankers could be ruthless rulers as well as indulgent patrons of the arts.

Virendra asked Aseem later for book recommendations. He said he was enthralled by the arrogance and cupidity of the Renaissance popes and fascinated by the story of papacy acquiring its political authority in the eighth century from a forged document.

Aseem said, 'I don't know whether he read any books at all, but he looked up "The Donation of Constantine" on Wikipedia, and then kept coming back to it, saying, "That's amazing. A great institution like that, built on fraud."'

Virendra, it occurs to me, might have been seeking private exculpation from medieval forgeries, or developing a higher idea of himself. I was moved to hear from Aseem that, in addition to sponsoring his magazine and festivals, he had set up scholarships for students from his basti, built new houses for all his close relatives, and donated thousands of dollars in his widowed mother's name to a charity for homeless widows in Varanasi.

'He had to escape from India to do all that,' Aseem said.

'But you know what, boss,' he added, 'the guy still has to squeeze the slave out of himself drop by drop – of semen.'

Aseem chortled. We were on our way back from East Hampton. His magazine's tenure ensured for another five years, Aseem's hands seemed steadier on the steering wheel, and he now told me that Virendra had become obsessed with fellatio, and that he paid exorbitant amounts of money to get the blondest Russian models to go down on him.

'He's the Leo DiCaprio of our IIT generation,' Aseem said. 'Will have sex only with young women. And only blow jobs from them. And why not? He's not being hypocritical or false with his desires. He doesn't believe in love or marriage; will acknowledge only the reality of the sexual urge. I wish more people were as honest as him.'

'Oh, come on,' I said, prompting Aseem to once again make light of my inexperience.

'Perhaps,' he said, 'Mr Celibate can still learn from our

exploits. I know you like to come on all shy and reserved but perhaps you are covering up a wild, lustful man inside.'

Aseem went on with his raillery, and I kept up my end and laughed, though uneasily. I had felt something shrink inside me, at the revelation of the gross desire of an old college mate whom I had first known as a timorous victim of brutality. But I recognised, too, in Aseem's voice and somewhere in my own heart – and, perhaps, every man in some licentious depths of his being responds with – a sense of awe at modes of pleasure so casually obtained, at sex so cleanly sundered from sentiment.

What strange, self-distorting journeys had we embarked on at IIT. It seems easy today for me to judge Aseem and Virendra and Siva as people, finally, too dazzled by their own hard-won freedom. Back then, I was haunted by a sense of the world's opacity and tongue-tied before people who seemed to have vigorously mapped it out, who had arrived early at an idea of who they were and what they could do.

Seven

During my years in Ranipur, Aseem finally wrote his novels. He never stopped relishing his success as an environmental activist, cultural impresario and intellectual entrepreneur of the Global South. But he still wanted to be known primarily as a writer of literary fiction, as an *artist*; and he sent drafts of his novels to me repeatedly by DHL (which refused to deliver to a village, necessitating him to resend by registered mail), and he spiritedly contested (and ultimately ignored) my editorial suggestions.

These were largely of a technical nature. I could never bring up with Aseem many other things about his fiction. I could not challenge his commitment to social realism, his resolve to unflinchingly document the most grotesque facts of Indian life, from the lynching and rape of Dalits to the routine pogroms against Muslims – things, he said, novelists in English, members of a self-satisfied ruling class, were oblivious to.

Nor did I question his stridently professed anger over injustice, though it had been clearly diluted into flamboyant gestures as he amassed his wealth and power.

It did strike me as a loss that, having secured the status of an uncompromising truth-teller about social and political realities, and thrown the light of rational intellect on some major issues of the day, he paid no attention to the shadows and half-shadows in which all lives are lived.

Invariably well researched, with an abundance of detail – whether about the manufacturing of country-made pistols in Gorakhpur, timber-smuggling in Kashmir or the infinitesimal gradations of caste in a Bihar hamlet – his novels simply refused to acknowledge that we continue to inhabit private discontent and anxiety, no matter how overpowering the chaos of public life, and how developed or undeveloped our societies.

Aseem's all-knowing first-person narrators briskly assigned rousing destinies to themselves and a range of characters. They reverently detailed fervid organs, thrusts and penetrations, raising the penis to the sanctity of religion. But they seemed wholly oblivious of the eternal questions: Who are we? What are we here for? Is there any reality beyond our ever-shifting desires, and their stubbornly unsatisfactory fulfilments? And isn't there something else beyond the most dark and brutish everyday reality – a promised, if unattainable, enchantment of another world and another life?

Aseem never suspected the existence of truths outside of literary and intellectual egoism, the things that might remain tragically unknowable. I, on the other hand, should have been more alert to certain personalities and events in his novels, especially when he described a nymphomaniac, in whose ear the main protagonist – clearly modelled on Aseem – mutters obscenities in Spanish as they make love standing up against a Sintex water tank on a roof in Nizamuddin East.

I risk the awkwardness of mentioning her only because this was another early warning that I missed.

'You have been alone all your life, Panditji,' Aseem used to say when I saw him in Delhi. 'Get over your reticence. Don't deprecate yourself. If you want to be a renouncer in the great Hindu tradition, and leave social life altogether, please be my guest. But stop being a pathetic little hand-job artist. There is a sexual revolution going on and you are still serving in the ancient regime of masturbators. Meet some girls. Mrinal knows some who are dying to get into your chaddhi with you, but think you have taken a Gandhian vow of celibacy and renounced the world.'

He repetitively quoted Mrinal saying that the 'girls' found me very 'cute', a dead ringer for Dharmendra, but unflirtatious, even a bit cold – 'Thanda Dharam rather than Garam Dharam,' he said, laughing hysterically.

'Well, at least,' he said, 'you haven't gone in for an arranged marriage. That's a relief.'

So it was. Neither of my parents ever mentioned it – why? I often wondered. Anyway, I couldn't stomach the idea. To agree to marry a woman I didn't know, to perch, as in the baraats of my childhood, on a horse, half-blinded by my veil of red roses, while a brass band in tattered and grimy white uniforms ineptly blows trumpets and crashes cymbals, and drunken men thrust their hips under a shower of very small and largely fake bills; then to occupy red velvet-draped thrones on a stage with my bride, receiving congratulations and white envelopes from wedding guests in silk saris and ill-tailored Western suits – all this struck me as deeply shameful.

I never told Aseem that I did once meet someone at his parties. She invited me to have coffee near her flat in South Extension, ostensibly to discuss a contribution to the literary review. She then changed the venue to her flat, claiming in her text that it was too hot to go out and she had some 'freshly roasted beans' at home.

I walked up two flights of filthy stairs, my heart thumping, and head unusually aching, to find her looming above me in shorts and a T-shirt. Closing the door behind me in short, gradual jerks, she pressed herself against me, and stuck one hand inside my kurta, circling my abdomen; the other softly stroked my forehead and hair.

Close by, her face looked weirdly distorted to me; I was relieved when she embraced me, and I didn't have to meet her eyes. As I scanned her untidy room with its leaking air-conditioner, coir sofa and crooked bookshelves of bamboo, I became aware of celebrities on glossy magazine covers grinning up from the floor.

That first visit set a pattern. We didn't talk much – her proposed contribution to the literary review never came up. In the months to come, I returned often to that room, finding in sex a balm to the injury of social exclusion. Thrilled to indulge reckless instincts without the fear of humiliation, I was always surprised, surprised and pleased by their novel fulfilments, and relieved, too, to find some release from the tedium at work.

One Sunday afternoon in June, she was lying on the unkempt mattress beside me, her body moist with sweat, when she said, 'You know, this thing is not going anywhere. I think we should end it before it gets too complicated.'

'Why do you think that?' I blurted out.

'You're just a bit intense,' she said.

Stunned, I could think of nothing to say. She disappeared into her bathroom. I heard the soft sizzle of her defective shower as I sat there, still naked, but with my socks on.

Dressing quickly, I left before she returned. I took an autorickshaw to my barsaati through a dust-storm, and for some reason the clear prints my shoes created on the floor made my heart even heavier.

Had she expected something more from me? And what could I have offered her anyway? Had she guessed that I was concealing my low-caste origins, or something equally dishonourable?

Reading Aseem's novel in Ranipur, I tormented myself with the likelihood that the sexual glutton he described, with her exquisite face, deep, dark eyes and sensitive mouth, and the touching air of injury that, Aseem wrote, 'invited virile redress', was modelled on the woman in South Extension.

I wondered about the mole that he placed on her pubic region rather than her navel, and I wasted much time scouring his prose for more telltale details. I felt relieved that I hadn't told Aseem about her, and had escaped his mockery, for being Thanda rather than Garam Dharam.

I was indeed overcome, at times, by a restlessness, the sense that I was missing out on the best things in life, and that an exhilarating dimension lay just outside my reach. After a long day's work, I would wonder, lying in bed, *Is this all? To look forward to, and to look back on?* By morning, when I was often woken up by the expectant whine of the tap or the clatter of a filling bucket in the next barsaati, the panic would have faded.

Looking back, I realise I should have recognised Aseem's dread of boredom, his immense need for stimulants, the desire to be perpetually infatuated, especially with youth and novelty. I should have recognised, in his chosen pose as an erotic prince, a deranging fear of worthlessness.

He couldn't really persist for long in the state of inner concentration that writers need. Not surprisingly, the international apotheosis he longed for – bestseller lists in London and New York, translations into multiple languages, monetarily negligible but prestigious prizes in Lisbon and Berlin – eluded him.

He tried to cover up his embittered hope with launch parties in five-star hotels across India. I saw the pictures in the *Delhi Times* of Aseem with politicians, businessmen, television anchors, fashion models, cricket stars and Bollywood starlets, if not writers. I was surprised one day to see that he had taken to wearing a rakish flat cap on what seemed a dramatically thinned bouffant; it did not go at all well with his kurtas, churidars and vests. I should have realised that, approaching middle age with a receding hairline, he was panicking.

I went to one of the celebrations at the Taj Palace Hotel in

Delhi, where Aseem was 'in conversation' with Soumak, one of the better-known liberal television anchors then. I spent almost all of my time either avoiding the woman from South Extension, now a television anchor herself, or addressing the puzzlement of a young Dalit writer in Hindi from Gorakhpur whom I had unthinkingly brought along to the party. On his first visit to a five-star hotel, he seemed both appalled and fascinated to find writing in English in such a luxurious setting.

He said, nibbling on a filo pastry (which the openly sneering waiter, raising himself with caste and colour prejudice above his present role, had described to him as a Greek samosa), 'Yeh angrezi-waley sahitya ko upabhog kee vastu mein badal rahe hain. These English-wallahs are turning literature into a consumption item.'

Aseem's secretary now routinely forwarded to those in his address book YouTube recordings of Aseem holding forth at literary festivals and panel discussions about the craft of the novel. And then Aseem announced that he was setting up the 'Metropolitan Grove': a private members club where, as he put it, 'highly successful and sophisticated Indians can meet each other and enjoy a curated menu of classy drinks and fine food'.

With the decline of his prose, Aseem's desire to write better than his peers had mutated into a wish to be more powerful, famous, important, wealthy and stylish than his peers.

It is strange to recall today that Aseem, helped by Virendra, had at the same time placed himself and his magazine on the correct – and losing – side of all contemporary political battles: against political and religious extremism and climate-change deniers and for democracy, justice, feminism and human rights.

His magazine didn't go after big businessmen supervising the Global Indian Takeover – the tricksters who would end up fighting extradition to India from townhouses in Mayfair and Park Avenue. But it was the only one to consistently cover environmental depredations and routine torture in Kashmir and the North-East. It exposed corrupt politicians, judges, and bureaucrats; it took the lead, after the atrocity in Delhi, in demanding swift justice for victims of rape.

So consistent, even predictable, this upholding of political virtue had become when Aseem called me three years ago with the news that Siva and Virendra and three other Indians had been arrested in New York for insider trading, money-laundering and tax evasion.

'It is a federal grand jury indictment,' he said. 'Virendra and Siva were profiting from confidential information they got from their Indian pals at Intel, IBM and Goldman Sachs. And they were putting their money in tax havens in the Caribbean and using shell companies in India to bring it back into the US.'

Aseem seemed breathless with excitement on the phone: 'It's a kind of hat-trick of Indian corruption abroad. First Vijay Mallya and Nirav Modi and now Siva and Virendra.

'It's just amazing, how much money Virendra was making when we met him in the US. That's why he was so jolly. Back then Google's stock was rising into the stratosphere. But Virendra heard about its poor financial results from a young Indian employee at an investor relations company that worked for Google. He promptly sold his Google stock and took a $15 million short position. Two weeks later when Google announced its results, Virendra had made a cool $7 million in profits.

'You will like this side-story,' he added. 'The employee who passed on the info is a beautiful young woman from a poor family in Murshidabad. You can imagine her journey from some madrasa with some bearded mullah bullying segregated boys and girls into the Koran, from all that to San Francisco, the single life of an attractive woman in the Bay Area. Virendra had paid for her tuition fees at some Texas college; and Siva got her a job. And she invited them to her wedding with an African-American guy – another act of rebellion.

'It's all such a great story, something so novelistic,' he said. 'But the feds had started to follow their every move, collecting evidence, waiting for the right moment to strike. And they are saddled with an Indian-American prosecutor who wants a big reputation before he himself enters New York politics. It's curtains for our friends, I am afraid. At least, a life in prison for them, and only if they plea-bargain.'

Aseem went on to give more details, savouring them as though they indeed were from a novel. Virendra had been caught in the early morning at his Chelsea townhouse; Siva, taken off a flight to Vancouver, together with his adopted son, a Tamil from Sri Lanka. Their lawyers had taken ages to arrive; and the feds had found cocaine on Virendra's bedside table, and a larger stash in his Bentley.

I had not encountered Siva after he left IIT and I had not seen or spoken to Virendra for more than a decade. I had tried half-heartedly to arrange a phone call once after a publisher in Hindi came to know of our IIT connection and asked me if he would underwrite a translation project. Much to my relief, the awkward conversation, endlessly postponed due to widely spaced time zones, did not occur.

In one sense, you were right to keep me, if not Aseem, out of your narrative. On occasionally googling the people I knew at IIT, I found them at HSBC in Hong Kong, Deutsche Bank in Munich and high-tech labs at Palo Alto and MIT. Some of these glimpses of alchemised lives and faces were irresistible, especially the images of Siva with Cindy Crawford and Elle Macpherson, and Virendra at the Met Gala with a lofty blonde whom further googling would reveal to be a Victoria's Secret or *Sports Illustrated* swimsuit model.

I was also fascinated by pictures of Siva, the persecuting demon of our first night at IIT, laughing uproariously at various social occasions. His smooth round face, once so terrifying, now seemed to showcase his unperplexed life; untouched by worry or doubt, it was lined only by humour.

But I didn't keep up with our IIT mates nearly as much as Aseem did; my knowledge of their lives in the United States, so remote from mine, gleaned from what I read in the press and on IIT-LISTSERV. I saw Aseem himself more often on Indian television than in the flesh during my years in Ranipur.

When he called, I had just emerged from a lengthy struggle with a particularly difficult bit in a book I was translating. So, I received Aseem's extraordinary news a bit coldly; and didn't know what to make of it.

But he did. 'That global party that started back in the nineties is over, boss,' he said. 'This is why Modi is becoming unchallengeable. And people like Donald Trump are emerging. History hasn't ended. The world isn't being flattened; it is growing more uneven. The aspiring lower middle classes feel too frustrated; they have had enough of a rigged system, and they are electing crazies who can bring the whole thing down.'

I recall seeing Aseem on the BBC a year before Modi's election, proclaiming an 'Indian Century' and arguing that the white nations must cede their political, cultural and moral leadership to great Asian civilisations like India and China. He was on CNN another night, going on about the moral superiority of India's 'founding fathers', Gandhi and Nehru, and making it seem, with his rising, cracking voice, that to be Indian was to bring a special gift to humanity.

India's imminent global leadership had become a constant theme at Aseem's conclaves of what his secretary's emails described as global 'thought leaders': Garry Kasparov, Hillary

Clinton, Tony Blair and Ayaan Hirsi Ali. But it seemed that a Hindu supremacist in power had forced Aseem to revise his faith in Indian exceptionalism.

'India: The Beginning of the End' his magazine cover had announced in the week after Modi's election. I remember it well since that same day I saw my father on Facebook welcoming the regime of a true 'son of India's soil'.

Aseem's troubles had multiplied since then. Two of his sponsors, the owners of New York's Plaza Hotel and Kingfisher Airlines, had finally attracted the malevolent attention of regulatory authorities. A vindictive new government was digging up old cases and sending him tax notices.

And Aseem had embraced the new interpretations offered by the thought leaders. He now said, 'Liberal democracy is in mortal danger everywhere from racists and populists.'

I was struck, as usual, by Aseem's fluency and also by the way he had so quickly distanced himself from his old friend and sponsor, subsuming him into a political abstraction.

I saw him on television – the news channels had pounced on the story of Indian-engineered turpitude on Wall Street – speaking of what he called a 'larger issue': whether the American system, which was built through slavery and genocide, taints everyone who becomes part of it. 'I mean, you have a total crook as a president,' he told a nodding young anchor. 'White liberals liked to pretend their country was a city on the hill. But their supposedly glorious history has the same quotient of crime and bestiality as the history of all mighty nations.

'Look, white men reserved the best positions for themselves in the world they ruled. They helped each other while holding down other races and peoples. Now, of course, these white masters of the universe are nervous, and are trying to hold on to their privilege with whatever means necessary. We used to envy and admire them from afar, used to credit their success to superior merit and hard work. But their success was due to their early breakthrough with racial capitalism and technology – they know it, too. Now the darkies and the Chinese have caught up and they have their own big claims.'

When questioned about his close relationship with Virendra Das, he seemed to have a practised retort: 'Look, I'll be frank. In India, where intellectual activity is still under-resourced and unsupported by the wider public, you need to hustle a bit for good causes, and you can find yourself in the company of people writers and artists should ideally avoid.

'This is nothing new if you know your cultural history,' he would say. 'The big museums in Europe and America were all built by crooks and hustlers. As Brecht said, the mansion of culture is built on dog shit.

'The world is a messy place,' he would add. 'I mean, we have far-right people at our festival of ideas that we violently disagree with. But we have to recognise that they also are entitled to a stall in the marketplace of ideas.'

Aseem's general manner in these public appearances suggested that, from the cool distance of his hard-won stature as writer, editor and cultural icon, questions about Virendra were a waste of his time, and that he would rather spend his time on air defending the recently deceased V. S. Naipaul, or 'Vidia', as he had started to call him, from the feminist critic who had again listed instances of sexual abuse of women in his novels.

'The world knows about Virendra's crimes,' he said, 'but please don't make the simple mistake of confusing a great artist like Vidia with his creations. My magazine and I stand in total solidarity with the Me Too movement and gender justice, but we don't want to encourage a cancel culture of random accusations and philistinism.'

The inability to extend fellow feeling to Virendra didn't surprise me because I shared it. For some reason, you thought of us as a close-knit group. But the more I learned about what Virendra had been up to, the more indifferent I became to his fate.

As a beneficiary of Virendra's largesse, Aseem felt compelled to moderate his callousness with some melancholy. I remember him saying, 'The terrible thing about the trampled-upon darkies like Virendra is that their claim upon the richness of the world came too late. Just before we entered the endgame of modernity all over the world. Every grand edifice of modernity – growing economies, political institutions, information ecosystems, trust between citizens – is collapsing today, and we all risk being buried alive by the flying debris.'

Perhaps it was out of some persistent unease that Aseem called me often to share the latest details to emerge from the trial of Virendra and Siva. Those details will be immortalised in your book, but I don't think I told you what Aseem said about one of them.

Virendra used to record his favourite carnal exploit on his iPhone, and then edit the film on Lightroom. The hard drive the FBI got from his computer revealed, among other things, that he sought not so much the moment of rapture as the sight of a bobbing blonde head below him, and the subsequent spraying of his semen across the histrionically avid face.

Reporting this to me, Aseem said, 'I guess there is something damaged about him.'

There was a pause. Then he added, 'About all of us.'

I was looking forward to putting the phone down and getting back to my work, and it is only in retrospect that Aseem's observation seems surprising. Like many of us, Aseem had become unpractised in introspection. Perhaps he had been pushed into it by the inkling of a comprehensive endgame.

'Maybe,' he said, 'the difference between us and the Hindu crazies is not so great after all. Ambition and vanity have probably made us more alike than we like to think.'

Eight

Aseem said in the same conversation that he envied my life in Ranipur. 'Boss, you have been fortunate to spend all these years in a remote village while the world was falling apart. I kept dreaming like Mirza Ghalib – Dil dhoondta hai. But you went ahead and did it. I really admire your decision.'

But I was not aware of making any such decision. You, too, seemed to imply with a mix of admiration and exasperation that, removing myself from the hothouse of metropolitan ambition, I had committed myself to a project of self-effacement.

The event that drove my decision was actually pretty crude – my father's desertion of his wife; and I was merely lucky, in that Ranipur, first visited as a day-tripping tourist from Delhi and quickly made central to my fantasy of living in the Himalayas, turned out to be the perfect refuge.

Aseem was right in one respect: he – and you – came to the village from an India where life was seething and hurrying on with a great roar through the early twenty-first century. In Ranipur, life flowed by inaudibly for much of this time. A great calm seemed to flow from either the sky or the earth – I wasn't sure. In any event, after those long years in Delhi, years squashed into such a colourless blob by drudgery and my outcast's nerves that they could not be separated, I felt childishly happy to be in Ranipur, seven and a half thousand feet high above the world.

Though only fifteen miles from Shimla, the village still felt very distant, allowing me to think that I was finally living my own life, private and unobserved, in a place of my choosing.

There were few motorised vehicles to be seen apart from a Jeep of Second World War vintage, its windscreen spider-webbed with cracks and a canvas hood that flapped in its metal frame. It brought the mail from Shimla to the local post office, a damp and drowsy room with a non-functional public telephone and a broken clock that seemed to signal the village's indifference to notions of linear progress and development: stilled at ten minutes to two, in the shape of a lushly curled Rajput moustache, its hands did not move for at least a decade after I arrived.

Small trucks delivered vegetables, flour, rice and cooking gas, and in late summer took away apple boxes from the local orchards. An irregular bus that ran to Shimla always seemed keen to hurtle past the village's lopsided little wooden buildings, depositing another layer of dust on the saffron ears of corn hung from their eaves and on the palimpsest of old and new advertisements – from Nirodh to Coca-Cola – on the solid panel shutters of the kirana shops.

When flagged down by a passenger or two, the ramshackle thing halted with an agonising racking of its tin panels, startling the stray dogs out of their slumber, and forcing them to get up and shake themselves violently.

The bus then waited, the radiator on its unbonneted engine cantankerously steaming, as the dogs, idle again, scratched behind their ears with their hind paws.

Life suddenly seemed what I had, unknowingly, always wanted it to be: free of the strain of ambition not my own and the fatigue of insecurities imposed by others; and happiness immediately began to feel something uncomplicated, something found in even the cool silence of a path through a deodar forest.

In Ranipur, everything – the pair of cows with big heads,

pink noses and sad eyes that lived underneath my cottage as well as the clouds parting to throw rays of light into the valley like the illustrated Bibles of my school – had the enchantment of something very familiar.

I marvelled at this immediate sympathy with a new place. It occurred to me later that, living with my mother, it was to a purified version of my past that I had returned: to my unhurried childhood, those afternoons at the nullah of isolation and solitude, where gross matter – the heavy masses of earth, sky, rocks and water – existed to impede the flow of time, and the world still felt whole and replete with mystery.

I felt for the first time in my life the year dividing clearly into seasons, each marked by distinctive changes in smell, temperature, colour and texture. The first monsoon rain, unruly elsewhere, moved in procession across the valley in tall stately pillars of grey, and, afterwards, the grass in the apple orchard was never as green and luxuriant, nor the crickets more exuberant. By early September, the scarves of mist that had malingered for two months in the valley whisked themselves away, revealing a fresh vista of moist green hills and glittering high snow.

Unlike in the plains, autumn was imaginative in Ranipur. Lavishly withering nature by reddening and yellowing the deodar trees, thickly carpeting mountain paths with crunchy leaves, and bruising the plums blue until their skin split, it gave a kind of sweetness to decay.

Hoopoes and bulbuls tore at the flesh of rotting apples and apricots, leaving them to slowly expire on the grass with their brown cores exposed. The chilly evenings of October, and something sad in the monotone of the last crickets, and the damp aroma of pine resin, portended a long sepia winter of snow and frost.

The earth thawed swiftly enough in spring to make the air

vaporous; and the smallest gust of wind made the cherry trees shake their heads and shed a flurry of blossoms, which then lay intensely pale on the dark damp ground for days.

The two cows were let out of their shed underneath my cottage. Warmed by the sun, they shook off flies while blinking their eyelashes, and snorted before lowing deep and long into the valley.

From the kitchen came the hiss-hiss and *hisssss* of the pressure cooker, and the static of garlic and onion frying in desi ghee – my mother preparing meals. I could hear, too, the footsteps of passing villagers on the narrow path through the orchard. But I could never hear Naazku, the grass-cutter, who lived in the fir and spruce forest that pressed against my cottage on the right, until she emerged from behind a thick cover of trees; trudging down a steep path with a sickle in one hand, she dislodged a few pebbles, and woke me up from my siesta.

There were family rituals and ceremonies – funeral, wedding, initiation – when a drum could be heard beating erratically somewhere in the village, accompanied by enthusiastic brass cymbals; but the sound, faced with incommensurable spaces, faded fast. Like most residents of Ranipur, I had no landline at home – the government's waiting list extended indefinitely into the future.

The only other sounds came from my landlord, Devdutt, a tall man with exaggeratedly gentle manners, who singlehandedly typeset and printed a monthly magazine in Sanskrit on an ancient treadle-operated printing press in a low-roofed shed adjacent to my cottage.

He looked after the apple orchard, and I often ran into him there, loosening and heaping up the soil, or standing on a ladder against a tree trunk, clicking his pruning shears, the leaves swaying close to his cheek. He also fed and milked the cows and cleaned their stalls in the evenings, filling my room with the mingled smells of hay, manure and fresh milk.

And when the racketing wheels of the press, the stuttering of my mother's sewing machine and the unhurried rustle of fresh straw in the cowshed ceased, and Devdutt walked back home through the orchard, the purest silence descended, in which I could hear the crackling of leaves and dry twigs, the soft thud of a shifting hoof below, and the gentle beating of my heart.

Darkness fell rapidly on the village with no streetlamps, and everyone seemed to go to bed by nine. Later at night, snatches of talk rose up from the valley; a dog barking indifferently, a baby crying. There was, occasionally, a wind-blown surge of singing voices, or, in September, the thump of an apple falling on the grass. But the sounds seemed to come from a void and affirmed our remoteness.

I suspect you would have looked down on my cottage. Its three rooms, and narrow balconies perched on thin wooden pillars had been built – rather, improvised – by Devdutt, who lived with his wife Pratima in a handsome many-roomed house at the other end of the orchard.

The story I heard was that some local materials of construction – mud, wood and corrugated iron – had been left over from repairs to their own house, and Devdutt had decided to erect a small library for his Sanskrit manuscripts above a cowshed and a room where he stored apples.

The wood had been planed and nailed together hurriedly at an ageing carpenter's hut, from which always emerged four or five separate sounds of sawing, chiselling, hammering and chipping as I walked past it to the bazaar. I had to hammer back the protruding rusty nails and their possibility of tetanus. The uneven floorboards rasped at the lightest step, and silky silverfish kept gracefully emerging from their cracks.

For my mother, however, the cottage represented luxury. For the first time in her life, she had a kitchen with a gas stove that flared instantly into life, and a tap that blurted out a stream of water, on demand. No foraging for coal in the rail yard, no painstaking lighting of the angeethi, or cumbersome disposal of ash. No more toiling over blackened pots and setting down meals in pilfered and dented aluminium trays to a sweaty brute.

Naazku, our neighbour, came to help her clean the house; and my mother's thin fingers, though more trembly than before, lost their white and pinched look. A sewing machine, bought second hand from a shop run by Tibetan refugees in Shimla, took the place of her knitting needles; and, as word of her – to me, mysteriously acquired – skill spread, it turned into a source of income.

The wooden handle, which resembled a thick tail, was cracked, and always seemed on the verge of breaking under my mother's fluttering hands; its chest, waist and rump, and the wooden stall on which it stood, were as black as the steam engines of my childhood, and smelled of machine oil.

By some miracle, the maniacally bobbing and chattering needle never once pricked my mother's fingers as she pushed the seam through it. The cloth came through unbloodied; and little girls came from across the village to be measured and then, shyly standing with outspread arms amid a litter of scraps and ravellings, to be fitted with school uniforms bristling with pins.

I often heard her remark, with disbelief in her voice, to Naazku, 'Yahan pahadon mein kitni kam dhool hoti hai. There is so little dust here in the mountains.'

Another revelation for her was the refrigerator, which in its early days she opened, her eyes glowing, and then closed just as gently, a dreamy expression on her face. To her, its

Styrofoam wrapping was no less captivating than the smooth white surface and the repeatable miracle of cold water and ice, and she kept it for years until I quietly threw it away.

She had packed some of our old monogrammed tableware into her tin trunk before leaving Deoli. One day, suddenly affronted by the motto Satyamev Jayate (Truth alone triumphs), I discarded this stolen property of Indian Railways, meeting my mother's surprisingly deep anguish with cheap ceramic crockery that she immediately adored.

She still read her *Ram Charit Manas*, rocking from side to side with devotion; she recreated her altar, with fancier figurines, in one corner of her room at the cottage, and bowed before it every morning and evening, moving her lips in silent fervent prayer. She was also gripped by Bollywood's versions of Rama and Krishna, watching old television episodes of *Ramayana* and *Mahabharata* that she had missed when they were first broadcast on an endless loop in the long afternoons, in-between meals and after dinner.

Passing my mother, and, very often, Naazku, agog on the floor beside her, I would invariably find the small screen ablaze with fiery arrows and whirling discs, and densely bearded sages dispensing wisdom about karma and dharma. Switching off the television, the two women then discussed the moral virtues and failings of Ram and Sita as though they had known them personally.

It was the kitchen, however, that gave her the greatest joy. She filled the small space with a regular hubbub, the whistle of the pressure cooker, and the clanging of pots and pans accidentally dropped. But from that cramped noisy room and those quivering hands emerged delectable meals every day of dal, chawal and sabji; and she would summon me in-between eating hours to taste freshly made mint and tamarind chutneys and lime and mango pickles.

She turned to making things she had never attempted back in Deoli: puris and kachoris, mathris, gajar halwas, til ka laddoos, and, nearing Holi, half-moons of gujiyas, sprinkled with powdered cardamom, just as in the mithai shops of my childhood.

She sang as she cooked, songs I could not recognise, and, watching her diminutive figure, which had asked so little of the world, and had received even less, I wondered what memories ran through her head – she, who had from the time she was five got up before everybody else, and then spent the day working with her hands – cooking, sweeping, scouring, milking, kneading, knitting, darning and sewing – before going to bed long after everyone else.

It was impossible when she was living in Deoli to get her to stop moving long enough for any retrospective conversation. In any case, I could never ask her about this – childhood shrunk, and old age lengthened, in a life made impersonal by grinding and incessant work. It didn't seem fair to her, to point to such extensive starkness, what she had kept out of sight by turning to God; I knew I was far from prepared if she, breaking out of habit, had discovered her helplessness, and succumbed to despair.

And though we talked a little more than we had in Deoli, often about small events – weddings, births, departures to big cities, new arrivals – in the village that Naazku and her girl customers reported to her, I could never bring up the continuous violation that had been her marriage to a man with whom she seemed to have shared nothing except the physical acts that had produced two children, and whom she seemed to have endured largely so that I could learn to read and write and add, and, eventually, rescue her from him.

Baba, in fact, had receded swiftly from our lives. News of him trickled in only from my sister. His business had expanded. He was building a new house. In recent years, he had acquired a smartphone and a laptop. Establishing a raucous presence on Facebook, he now excitedly forwarded WhatsApp theories about treasonous libtards, agents of the Vatican (Sonia and Rahul Gandhi), urban Naxals and sinisterly breeding Muslims.

For my mother, it was as though he had never existed, though she still wore sindoor in her hair – her only acknowledgement of the man who had abandoned her.

She occasionally corresponded with her daughter; and once, after a long gap between letters, she asked me to check on her. The trip back to the roadside settlement near Deoli where Meena lived revealed that her husband now spent most of his time at the local hooch shop, leaving his wife to bring up their four children and to run his dhaba.

The dhaba was a cluttered little room surrounded by tall sugarcane fields on three sides, with a single door that opened on to a pitted road and ruts of black slush imprinted with tyre treads. On the afternoon I visited it, the children were sniffling and bawling in the back room where they all slept, and flies buzzed over the glass shelves containing half-open packets of glucose and Krackjack biscuits while my sister ran back and forth, serving boiled chai to truck drivers.

The drivers, all with stubbly faces and dark circles under red eyes, sat with their knees apart on low charpoys. They lowered their heads to hawk and spit on the cement floor; they then dragged the dust on the floor over their spits with their big fluorescent sneakers. One of them walked, waddling a bit as he untied the drawstring of his wide-leg pyjamas, to the sugarcane field. Perhaps fearing snakes, he changed his mind and urinated against the wall of the dhaba.

Even before the drivers left in a fog of diesel exhaust,

cutting fresh treads on the black slush, my sister appeared with a red plastic bucket of water in one hand and a rag in another. Kneeling down, she twisted the rag into the water, brought it out, dripping, and started to wipe the floor, the red glass bangles on her arms softly chinking. The soapy water widened around her in a pool, and the soles of her bare feet were as hard and dark as hooves.

In-between her chores, she brought me tea, and implored me to stay for lunch. We had shared such an odd childhood, playing rarely and then only with each other. With her thinning and greying hair, clinging wetly as always to her forehead, she seemed the same overworked and harried girl I had known, now grown into an overworked and harried woman.

Sitting before the askew, empty charpoys with sagging strings, I found myself feeling not so much sympathy as a desire to leave as soon as I had arrived.

A convoy of four near-identical trucks thundered in, the black pompons on their front and rear bumpers swaying; the charpoys were occupied by hawking and spitting men again. I became more restless. I lied in order to expedite my departure, saying I had urgent work in Delhi. Meena, shaking out soggy tea leaves from a plastic strainer, didn't protest.

I gave her a wad of rupees, which she accepted without expressing surprise or gratitude. As I left, she clung to me and wept for so long that the truck drivers drinking chai in slow, noisy draughts started to stare at us with their bloodshot eyes, and I heard myself, to my shame, saying, 'Main phir aaonga, Meena, main phir aoonga. I'll come again, Meena, I'll come again.'

But I knew I wouldn't, and that the tie between us, never very strong, was now broken.

*

It is a moment of cold-heartedness that now seems significant, of a piece with my other betrayals. Back then, discomfited by a familiar squalor, I rationalised my feelings in the way Aseem would have approved of: one has to look forward, not back, especially when the past is full of useless and unredeemable pain.

I felt less guilty when my mother seemed unmoved to hear of my sister's plight. But then her daughter's fate was, I later realised, too much like hers.

She had spent her childhood in one of the hottest regions of Madhya Pradesh, and occasionally spoke about the suffocating dust-storms of those summers, and the long days in the parched countryside when there was nothing to be seen in the shimmering distance except tall laden carts, great bulks that came closer after an eternity, and then swayed past, scattering the white country road with bits of hay.

She, too, had gone to work as a child, and, watching Naazku cut the grass in the orchard with rapid, tireless strikes, I often imagined my mother in the vast fields, under a blazing sun, tying up bundle after bundle, sheaf after sheaf, for hours on end, without straightening her back, or putting her lips to her matki.

She had not always been unhappy, it seemed, despite everything; and she had not always been tormented by want. Her father had died when she was very young, but her extended family of rice farmers had owned a well, ploughing bullocks and a cow; they had saved from each harvest to store gunny sacks full of husked rice away in a small stone-lined granary.

Her strongest memory was of leaving, at the age of sixteen, this place of self-sufficiency (of her wedding she recalled little except the sharp pain of the thick ring being forced into her nose). Her wailing mother stands in the doorway. There are no tears in my mother's eyes, but her face is bloated with their weight. She does not know what to say or how to behave with her new husband. A stranger she has only just met, he is seated already on the bullock cart with a tin trunk full of cooking utensils and her saris next to him, and he looks a bit impatient. She is sick and often stumbles in her wedding sari of thick silk and new slippers that don't fit, the payal on her ankles tinkling loudly each time.

Somehow, she manages to sit in the cart next to him, knees drawn up to her chest. Eyes downcast in her long veil, all she can see are her heavily bangled arms, the hennaed hands, and fingernails that have been painted for the first time. The cart begins to move, lurching as the bullocks get awkwardly into rhythm, and she throws up on her lap, much to her husband's disgust.

Theirs was a marriage commonplace in my class and caste, between two people who did not know each other nor had any sexual knowledge. I once imagined what I shouldn't have: my mother's first days and nights with her husband, the novel act of passion, no doubt rendered brutal by him, and experienced by her as violation, crushing whatever private expectations she had.

Living in tiny rooms of railway barracks, did she ever grow accustomed to his touch, or did she submit to his relentless male desire only with distaste? And was it this experience of serial humiliation that stifled her mother's desire to see her son married and settled?

I imagined, too, her isolation in the small track-side settlements she lived in immediately after her marriage, cut off from her family and wholly dependent on her husband, the days when a passing goods train broke the silence, and a flock of frightened black crows rose out of the trees lining the rails – the long days and nights when she would have deepened her habit of trusting in God to see her through.

My birth, dangerously premature and attended by mishaps, had given her some protection from despair. My earliest memories are of her kneading my limbs with mustard oil, and painstakingly hunting for and squashing lice in my hair, both of us sitting on a gently rasping charpoy; and for some reason the mild sun of a North Indian winter always shines over these memories of a time of peace and security.

I remember, too, her proudly scratching the frame of our house's only door with a knife to record my height, and taking me to my school, her fingers interlocked with mine, and another hand holding a satchel that she had stitched for me out of burlap sacks. When I saw her again, waiting trustfully outside the school door a few hours later, she took out from my shorts pocket one of her embroidered handkerchiefs; and, shaking her head over my forgetfulness, carefully removed the wet tusks of snot hanging from my nostril.

As I set off in the late afternoons, homework done, for the nullah, she would always say, 'Dhoop se bachkar rahna, Raju beta. Aur gehrey paani mey mat jana. Be sure to protect yourself from the sun, Raju beta. And don't go deep into the water.'

On my return, she would hand me a glass of hot milk, and, as I blew at its gauzy surface, she would inspect, her eyebrows twitching, my legs, looking for signs that I had disobeyed her; and, finding nothing, run her pinched finger down the white scratches from stray twigs and over the swellings from mosquito bites.

A near-fatal bout of malaria once took her away to a railway hospital in another town for three weeks. In the days that followed, spent with my father and young sister in that kothri, where the Satyanarayan Katha was recited by the pujari one morning and an earthen lamp with a cotton wick was kept burning day and night on his instructions, I had my first experience of misery. And when she returned, thin with black circles under her eyes, and the earthen lamp was extinguished, I felt that my world had been miraculously made whole and given back to me again.

I write about my mother at length because we never spoke about her. 'So good-looking, especially your mother! Though your father looks dishy, too!' you said when I once showed you a tiny, creased black-and-white photo of my parents taken shortly after their wedding, my mother looking away from the camera, her hair pulled back in a low, tight bun; and I was so thrown by your response that I did not know what to say.

I did once describe to you a memory of my mother, which was of her soft voice in the next room, in the slightly bigger home we had before Baba was demoted, and the thud-thud of my father hitting the wall with his fist. Lying silently in dark suspense, next to my sleeping sister, I tormented myself with questions – what were they arguing about? Was he going to hit her?

Peace finally seemed to descend in the next room, but I lay wide awake for hours, my heart still tight with foreboding.

I suffered with my mother. But there were times I disliked her for suffering so much, and to see in her distress, and everything else, the will of God at work. At other times I wished for Baba's death before quickly rewishing that he, the sole breadwinner in the family, lived just long enough to put me through university. After that, I had decided, I was going to take care of my mother.

I sent, from the time I received my first salary in Delhi, a money order of 300 rupees every month to a post office account I had opened for her; and on the rare occasion I visited her in Deoli I alleviated my guilt by showering her with small presents.

It turned out that while I discarded all of the letters she wrote to me when I was in Delhi, she had kept all my replies in the green inlands with Gandhi on the postmark, carefully preserving them in an embroidered jute bag (I wonder now: where did she get that?).

I read them one afternoon, while she was sleeping, and was ashamed to discover that I had responded to her heartfelt notes with evasions, if not lies, which in their bland terseness owed something to a basic language-learning textbook. 'Yes, I am well. The weather is fine. I am eating well. My house is very comfortable. I have put on some weight.'

Her letters had been her strongest and most sustained claim as a parent on me. But I could never accept her in this role, since she was so clearly incapable of protecting me, or even herself, from her husband – the feeling of inadequacy against him that we sensed in each other was what had brought us closer together from the time she took me by the hand to my first school.

In Ranipur, the reversal of roles was concluded: I became her guardian from the world that had so ruthlessly pushed her down into herself.

Still, and I know this better now, she was not as simple as she seemed. Beneath her diffidence lay a delicate hardness, an unsparing lucidity born of long resistance to pain.

Every morning at eight, the doorbell would ring; I would open the door to find Vishal, my landlord's son, there, in his school uniform, holding a plate of steaming aloo or gobhi parathas and freshly boiled milk.

'We now realise we built the cottage for someone like you,' Devdutt said one day with a courteous smile; he and his father, Panditji, a sprightly octogenarian who lived in Shimla, had been talking about my quasi-literary work of translation at the old house. It seemed to redeem the failure of any members of their own family to take up the ancestral vocation, or even to possess a non-instrumental interest in books and scholarship.

The two men took this apostasy seriously. Panditji, who came from a line of priests, had given up well-paid service in the court of Rampur's maharaja to devote himself to the study of Sanskrit. He had set up, with his own money, the first Sanskrit college in the region. Indeed, Devdutt and his father had hung, in their only gesture to wall decoration, portraits of illustrious Sanskrit scholars and writers in the cottage's largest room.

All the paintings depicted white-bearded men sitting cross-legged before leaf manuscripts against a backdrop of the white-capped Himalayas. They were crude copies of devotional bazaar art, devoid of aesthetic merit, even ordinary skill. Nevertheless, they served as a link to an earlier era of noble endeavour and creativity. They preserved, in a materialist age, an ideal of intellectual and spiritual autonomy; they personified the ideals of renunciation and austerity that, even Aseem agreed, were once revered and are now mostly disparaged, if noticed at all.

I couldn't quite see myself in the distinguished lineage of Panini the grammarian, or Valmiki the author of the *Ramayana*, though I worked all morning in my room, my concentration broken only by the slap and thwack of my mother's rubber slippers going in and out of the kitchen (she still refused to wear shoes); and I read in the afternoon and late into the night.

I became very uncomfortable, gripped with old anxieties about my low-caste origins, when Devdutt, a tall man with intelligent eyes beneath overhanging brows, a reserved mien and measured speech, suddenly started ranting against low-caste Hindus, blaming them for India's failure to progress.

Still, I was happy to be adopted by him on the basis of a misunderstanding; it was preferable to be mistaken as a scholar than as a Brahmin. He was palpably delighted when, looking for a milch cow for a cousin, he came to know of me as a connoisseur of the genre from my childhood, and asked me to accompany him to the cattle market, where I made sure that the udders of the cow he bought were long, the teats supple and squarely placed, with good orifices.

Such unqualified warmth and goodwill, emerging from a people so palpably rooted in their environment, made up for the vagrancies in my past. I felt a new freedom among these men and women – freedom from scrutiny and judgement and impersonation. And, waking up every morning with the sunlight streaking through the crevices in windows and doors, I never ceased to marvel at my luck: that this is where I live.

My mother had her place in the local cosmos as a housemaker and seamstress. With no obvious job, I had initially caused some perplexity in the village. Frankly curious male eyes followed me whenever I walked through the bazaar; crooked windows in narrow houses often framed an inquisitive female face, pallid complexions outlined against pitch darkness. Bantering shopkeepers tried to figure out, as they wrapped my purchases in newspaper bags, just what I did.

It would have been hard to explain, and I never did try. I felt my own strangeness, walking through a remote Himalayan village with a paperback. Unlike you and Aseem, I couldn't claim to be a writer. I lacked the drive – the essential resolve to cut myself a figure in the world, and to regard the very existence of contemporaries as a standing threat. Nor did I have the confidence, outrageous at one level, that I have something vital to add to the colossal sum of published works out there. Unsure about what to think about the larger world, and unwilling to speculate, I lacked, too, the need, which drove Aseem to make other people see things as I do.

'You really should write a memoir,' you often said, stressing the word 'really'. I was touched by your attempt to bring out what you saw as my 'potential' and make me shine in the larger world. And you always thought I was being facetious when I said that my small and secluded life held little interest for anyone.

I had briefly wanted to write, encouraged by Professor Sir at IIT, who, on the slender evidence of a half-finished short story, said I had a 'literary mind' that I ought not to waste on mechanical engineering.

I started to scribble in a notebook a bit, to record this or that experience, and transcribe poems and prose that I had liked. I read all the books that Professor Sir recommended, but never actually finished writing the story. Occasionally, I would find something in one of the magazines I first read at the IIT library and later subscribed to in Ranipur, and think, *I can write better than this*, but the moment of vanity would soon pass.

I was meant to be a reader, to eavesdrop on the past, to know how people in faraway societies had felt and lived, to enter a state of receptiveness in which their joys and torments might touch my own soul and mind; and the same curiosity served me well as a translator, finding an ideal mode of expression for ready-made prose.

The arrival of an advance copy with my name on it was always a wonderful moment: the object taken out from Jiffy bags (marvellous in themselves for being so rare) was solid and very satisfying proof of nearly forgotten labour. Of course, finished copies disappeared, review-less, soon after publication, into American college libraries and remainder bookshops, leaving behind the sense that I had collaborated with my authors and publishers in a stillbirth.

Also, my work was unavoidably imperfect, because no amount of skilful meditation can bridge the abyss between the emotional domains of Hindi and English, let alone capture what lies beyond the boundaries of language.

But I consoled myself with the thought that what I did at least intimated an otherness that could not be fully assimilated. And the writers in North India's towns whose works I Englished were always gratified to see their names on brighter covers and sturdier spines, and to escape occasionally from the condescension of Indian writers in English and general neglect into visiting professorships in America and Europe.

Almost all the people I knew – running small shops, working in government jobs or in tourism – owned plots of land where they grew some food for themselves (mostly vegetables, cereals, plums, cherries and apples) and had enough left over to sell in the local markets.

Devdutt had long retired from his teaching jobs; his magazine, a labour of love, was meant to uphold, on a reduced scale, his family's commitment to the ancient language. The apple orchard, where Devdutt spent hours planting and budding and pruning, was a link to his ancestral occupation rather than a commercial enterprise.

My own contribution to his income through the monthly rent on my house was trifling. Panditji had been a guru to many local politicians, dispensing astrological advice about their careers. Devdutt retained his father's clients. Trained as a priest, he also officiated at weddings and Hindu rites, travelling to them dressed in a silk tunic and white dhoti, holding a brown leather valise containing his pandit's tools. Pratima, his wife, and Vishal's mother, worked in a clerical job for the state government. And from their pooled salaries they had enough to live on.

My other neighbour, Naazku, owned the steep forested hill to the right of my cottage. Her face was a pattern of branching wrinkles; yellowing eyes and bad teeth spoke of a lifetime of malnourishment, and a black head-kerchief that gave her rabbit ears on the top of her head released the frailest ringlets of her grey hair on her neck.

She had married while still an adolescent, Devdutt told me, and lost her husband and newborn son in the first two years of her marriage. She had brothers and nephews; but they were too poor to take her into their homes. She had started to make a living by cutting the abundant long grass that sprouted on her property after the monsoons, which she sold as fodder to cow-owners in the region.

The exacting work, which had to start early in the morning, when the dewy grass is tender, and undertaken with no tool more complex than a sickle, had bent her small body; she couldn't have been more than sixty but the wrinkles on her birdlike face, and the loose skin hanging from her neck, made her look ninety, and, though relatively healthy, the stick she leaned on as she walked, with the stubborn short steps of someone accustomed to a lifetime of ankle-cracking mountain paths, suggested great and perpetual infirmity.

She lived in a hut of mud and grass in a clearing in the middle of her pine forest. On my only visit to her home, the yard in front, paved with cow dung, looked well swept, scarred by the deep whorls of her broom. A plastic bucket of water, which she must have carried from the public tap near my house, stood next to gleaming enamel and brass pots. A calf was tethered to a picket and in the corner of the yard was a pile of pine cones.

Smoke wriggled out from under the thatched eaves, and through the half-open door of thin and curling tin. Crouching before a chulha fire, which glowed on her cheeks as she blew at it, she would make her evening meal: chapatis on a thick iron griddle that seemed to need a more intense heat than that of pine cones to rise.

In one corner was a string cot with a shrunken mattress and an uncovered quilt on top. I recognised our small transistor radio in the perforated leather case that my mother had passed on to her. Everything in her hut had the same worn look, of time and overuse, and of the pity of her benefactors; and the only decoration was an old calendar of Shiva, showing the year 1979.

She was overwhelmed to see me; she rarely had any visitors, she said, and she could never have expected the Brahmin man from the big house to knock on her door. She covered her head and the rabbit ears with the end of her sari, insisted on dusting her bed, and making me sit while she squatted on the floor and, abandoning the chapatis, made me milky chai. She then watched me sip it as the fire faded, and blue smoke curled up against the thatched roof.

'Aaapki maata ji aapke baare me chinta karti hai. Your mother worries about you,' she said.

'Kyon? Why?'

'Unkey baad aapki kaun dekh-bhal karega? After her who will look after you?'

'Koi chinta ki baat nahi hai. There is nothing to worry about.'

We went on in this vein for a while, Naazku outlining fears I had no inkling of; and me dismissing them.

I felt more and more uneasy. I had been proud initially to have broken a taboo by visiting her, but I was now assailed by the pettiness and absurdity of my pride and the exasperation of speaking in a much louder voice than usual – she turned out to be a bit deaf.

I was relieved when she abandoned the subject of my mother's fears about my future and started to talk about her property. Her husband had died, leaving her to look after it; she had a few relatives, cousins and nephews, but she never saw them. Her ownership of a hill made her potentially a dollar millionaire several times over in a national economy driven by real estate speculation.

Property developers from the plains constantly knocked on her door, I had heard. I was incredulous at first. Who would pay to live in Ranipur, or even own property there? It was hard to believe anyone could see monetary value in the village, the few houses and shops scattered around a ridge, a place that did not even have streetlamps.

It turned out that a realtor from Chandigarh called Mathur, who visited Devdutt to have his horoscope freshly cast every few months, was persistent. I often ran into him. A very polite stout paan-addict in his late forties, he stood with his hands interlocked behind him and back half inclined, as though ready to bow – though really to eject red betel juice from his mouth. Wearing two identical Mont Blanc fountain pens in his safari shirt pocket, he peeled his plastic business card out of a rubber-banded stack; he then held the stack in his left palm, a thumb caressing the rubber, and chewing paan even faster, as you looked down at his logo and degrees – a double MA in English literature from Punjab University – on the card.

Mathur already owned the Hotel Kipling, trading in on the

name of an old colonial establishment to attract empire-hunting British tourists and upper-class Indians. There were rumours that he had bribed the local forest ranger and that his men brazenly set fires in the pine forests below the hotel in order to kill trees and clear space for construction.

After that I could not see any of the remote forest fires in the valley at night, silently and swiftly spilling down slopes, beautifully radiant as though in a dream, or catch a cindery smell in the wind, without thinking of Mathur, and the way a little worm of red betel-stained spit crawled slowly down his chin when he talked.

He had offered to build Naazku a 'penthouse apartment' in one of his proposed buildings on her property.

She did not know what the words meant; only that they denoted inconceivable luxury. I asked her why she didn't sell.

She was quick to reply: 'Mujhe shahar ke log mein koi vishvas nahin hai. Agar kagazaat ke baat dhakka maar ke nikaal diya, to? Main kya karoongi phir? Kahan jaongi? I have no faith in these city folk. What if after the paperwork is done he kicks me out of my land? What will I do then? Where will I go?'

She had come to her hut on the hill as a young married girl. Her small hope from life had faded with the death of her husband and son. She wanted nothing more than to continue her work and die in the same place.

'Daant nikal gaye, peeth mein hamesha dard rahta hai, lekin zinda hoon, sar ke upar chhat hai, bhagwan se zyada nahin maangna chaiye, yahin itne saal beet gaye, yahin se ab arthi uthegi, and karta-dharta se milne jaongi. I lost my teeth, my back aches all the time but I am alive, and have a roof over my head. One should not ask too much from God. So many years have passed on this hill, and I will leave it on my bier to meet my maker.'

★

I imagined her flower-decked bier departing her empty hut amid chants of Ram Naam Satya Hai, the tin door squeakily hanging open to reveal the calendar from 1979, and the transistor radio from my past.

Aseem would have laughed at this confession of fatalism, this resignation to a life of hardship, this contentment with God's design. He recoiled from anything that smelled of the past and appeared to constrain the many possibilities of knowledge and pleasure in the present and future.

The more time I spent in Ranipur, however, the greater my respect grew for the necessity that drove people to tenaciously cling to their narrow but strong lives. I came to understand better the fierce mistrust with which they regarded the unknown and the desire for improvement.

It had become impossible for educated people like us to rest in a worldview that continues unchanged from generation to generation. That life eternal of humility and prayer, in which nothing was felt as too frightening or shocking, since it was all divinely ordained, and the pageantry of religion offered both drama and mystery, had come to an end with the generation of our parents. But who were we to scorn it?

Brought up into a life with little meaning, we had convinced ourselves that meaningful ways of being existed, and we would find them. In reality, this amounted to running this way and that, uncertain of our destination, and looking back enquiringly all the time.

I suppose it had always been different for Aseem, who early on reached such exceptionally good terms with the future. For him, the feeling he had right from IIT – that somewhere deep within his life germinates his true vocation, and the day is not far when he would turn to coaxing it into reality – had turned out to be no idle fantasy.

Still, I dared not imagine what we would be like, when we

were in our seventies and eighties, when meaning leaks away from sex, beauty, art, family and nation; when we grow dull, old and sour, tormenting and boring everyone around us, with no connection to our long religious past, and no future to look forward to.

Nine

Shortly after I arrived in Ranipur, I started to go on long treks in the high mountains and valleys bordering Tibet. It is hard for me to compress the details of those trips into a moral or a formula, or to define precisely what they meant to me. Perhaps the most truthful thing, if also somewhat strange, I can say is that those landscapes, which I had never previously visited, made me think I was returning to a familiar spot. Triggering memories, and awakening the notion of some previous existence, they certainly crowded me out of a sterile self-absorption.

As I walked, I felt taken more and more out of myself, far away from the person I had been earlier that morning, and that feeling would deepen when, after a daylong ride on potholed roads, during which the plunging and bucking bus seemed determined to oust me, and my palms became pink with grasping the rusted metal of a seat back, I would step out into a village clinging to sheer cliffs and customs like polyandry.

From its twilight murk, massive sheepdogs with glossy black coats would emerge, their tongues hanging out, followed by ruddy-faced children.

At night, in the darkness unbroken by electricity, fireflies floated, shining with a topaz light. From somewhere would come a muted and irregular drumbeat and the throaty wailing of what always seemed to be the same endless song. I would look out to see bonfires blazing in the distance, surrounded by stirring, swaying shadows; and, oddly comforted by the sight, I would go to sleep and then be jolted awake by one of those

142

enigmatic nocturnal sounds high in the mountains: someone crying out, far away, and being quickly answered. You listen carefully; there is nothing there, but the sound you think you heard continues to resonate long afterwards.

Early next morning I would start my trek. I would ascend a valley lost in thickets of rhododendrons, fording hoarse streams of cold silvery water, quietly exulting at my narrowing distance from the gleaming peaks that I saw from my balcony in Ranipur, which seemed cleaner and whiter and bigger with every step.

I would sleep in the open, muffled in my sleeping bag, or, when they were available, in mildewed rooms at PWD rest houses, built by the British, and still with terraced gardens planted with apples and plums, an ageless chowkidar, iron bedsteads and 'bedding' that smelled of the brackish soapy water in which it had been repeatedly washed into the texture of a mosquito net.

After two days of walking, which would always scrape off a round of skin on my fourth toe, I would finally arrive at the base camp for climbers, to see the mountains standing even more defiant with their jagged snow-layered summits.

Here I would linger for a few days, tending to my sores and drying my dampish clothes, and trying to somehow feel and absorb and pickle the stern majesty of my surroundings: the massifs presiding all day long over a slow dance of snow and mist, light and shadow: long towers of cloud spiralling out of icy holes, obscuring and revealing expanses of rock, until settling late in the evening into a long and broad apron of mist.

I read during the day, but nothing among my books, carefully selected for such journeys, seems to match my craving – I don't know for what, probably to unravel the cipher in which the boundless sky and earth first spoke to me during those evenings at the nullah in my childhood.

Here, high in this bare and radiant landscape, everything seemed disposed in such a way as to yield meaning: a blue-and-white prayer flag's tatter in the wind, the murmur of a hidden brook, the howl of a wolf at night.

The nights, in particular, a spectacle of light and space, had the crystalline certainty of some great truth. Lying in my sleeping bag, I would gaze for a long time at stars that were startlingly near, profuse, and prone to fall dramatically, and a strange exhilaration coursing through my body and mind would keep me for hours from the deep dreamless sleep of high altitudes.

In Ranipur itself, there were long walks to take. One of them took me past what is now your remodelled villa, on a partly metalled path to Salerno, a nineteenth-century hilltop retreat built by an Italian pastry chef, which the government had turned into a forest rest house.

I urged you to explore it once, but you never did. Lined by the abandoned villas of the British, the path went on to sleepy settlements, or to solitary houses, and a lone jeep or bus often lurched across the potholes, enclosing pedestrians in a thin grey cloud of dust.

I preferred the other trail that Vishal and a friend of his took every day to their school near the old Viceroy's Lodge. It went through Naazku's forest, and showed no sign of human presence, apart from an occasional shepherd with a tinkling flock. The paths were not always clearly marked on the rising ground thickly paved with pine needles and tangled roots. I often got lost in the dense dark green clumps of cedar and oak trees, where brown woodpeckers kept running up gnarled and bronze-lichened tree trunks to sunny tops.

Pausing to get my bearings, I would become aware of my quickening heart, and the fragrance of resin and damp earth.

On trails with a thinner canopy, the sun sprinkled bright patterns of light and dark over the ground; the russet pine needles glistened uncannily; and on still spring mornings, you could hear the rustle of last year's oak leaves stirred by the thawing ground.

One of these tree-lined paths led to a sunlit clearing near the Viceroy's Lodge. From here Ranipur appeared like one of those villages I saw from my balcony: peaceably and humbly self-sufficient. The sun was warm on my back, and everything I felt and heard – the trees whispering softly, the chirring of insects, the unhurried flapping of a hawk's wings and the clouds silent over the valley – seemed to confirm my heart's freedom to pursue once again those days and nights of leisure.

I wanted Ranipur to go on just as I had found it: secluded, becalmed and healing, perfectly fulfilling a child's yearning for a safe home deep in the mountains. And, magically, time there seemed to stretch and stretch.

Light filled the valley each dawn, the stars in the sky were clear and fixed, and the moonlit nights seemed to steep us in privilege and mystery. The seasons repeated themselves, as clearly and sharply as when I first noticed them. Opening my eyes at dawn, I often felt my spine tingle with familiarity, and walking out again and again to the view from the balcony I was half-amazed every time by how exactly my mornings, afternoons and evenings in Ranipur resembled each other over the years, their configuration of the sun, the valley, and the presiding mountains forever remaining the same, innocent of all our doings, despite all the time that passed.

Looking back, however, my early years there seem to represent a lull in the life of the village, a pause before time began to race forward and the place that had sheltered and consoled me became full of a craving for change.

Ranipur couldn't remain immune to the explosion of energy and ambition on the plains, though it could only be modest in its courting of worldliness.

For years, there had been rarely more than three or four travellers at the bus stop, anxiously clutching battered suitcases or gunny sacks of vegetables and fruits, next to the stray dogs sleeping in the dust. It took some courage for Sood, a driver with one of the tourist businesses in Shimla, to take a bank loan and start a local taxi service.

Sood lived with his family in one of the tumbledown houses at the northern end of the village. Tall and wiry, he walked with stooped shoulders, as though permanently marked by the effort he had to make to squeeze himself through his tiny front door and into his low-ceilinged home, or by the tense long journeys on broken, precariously perched roads into high mountains.

Ownership of a Tata Sumo, which stood gleaming white at the crossroads, seemed to transform Sood; he seemed taller, his shoulders seemed broader, and within a few years he added an Innova and a Scorpio to his fleet.

By then there were many other taxis lining the crossroads: the government was pushing roads deeper into the mountains; and, with buses yet to start running on them, Sood turned out to be a pioneering entrepreneur. Raju, another red-cheeked local, but with intense green eyes and a booming voice, opened a teashop overlooking the crossroads. He even put some eggs, bread and dry rusks in his glass cases, though customers for his omelettes were few in this strictly vegetarian village; the rest of his shelves remained empty.

Other businesses opened, a 'gift shop' and a children's

ready-made clothes store, both over-supplied with products from China; their shiny glass window displays remained blank, as though advertising the uncertainty of their owners, their misgiving that most villagers and tourists would prefer to shop in Shimla. Very soon they failed, and their shutters began to show rust below their new paint.

A cable television operator did much better by sharing, illegally, his expensive satellite television dish. The village came to be festooned with white co-axial cables, all emanating from a dusty shop crammed with broken and probably irreparable black-and-white television sets. The low houses, previously silent, now rumbled with made-in-Mumbai soaps and cricket matches in Australia, South Africa and England; the old people in the village, in particular, seemed to sit at home all day and watch television.

Other electronic sounds came to be heard more often as a communications revolution swept India. My application for a landline phone was finally approved; and Devdutt, who had then started to officiate as a priest at weddings and funerals, became one of my Bakelite's regular users along with young men looking for jobs outside the village.

The telephone did little for me. I came to hate the way it crouched petulantly in my mother's room, waiting to detonate, its shrapnel ricocheting off the wall and ceiling; lifting the receiver, I would encounter the smell of its last user's breath and, often, a hollow silence. The prohibitive cost of national and international calls meant that I had to monitor the length of the conversations and put the phone in a padlocked wooden case lest a reckless talker plunge me into penury.

I liberated the phone from its case when cheap prepaid connections became widely available. Suddenly, everyone seemed to have a mobile phone, and even two or three, with jaunty ringtones, though the signal was still very weak, and extended only sporadically to my own cottage.

Another shop opened in a now rapidly developing village square around the bus stop, offering, in addition to passport photos, access to a computer, dot-matrix printer and Xerox machine. I began to see a few young men hover there, typing out applications to private universities, whose ugly squat buildings had begun to disfigure mountaintops in the state.

Neeraj, the cherubic son of a dhaba-owner, announced his intention to do computer and English-speaking courses, since that was what everyone he knew was doing. It could, he said, be his springboard for life in a big city like Delhi.

Somehow word got around that I was interested in advancing the careers of young villagers. It was only a couple of shy young men at first, thin, with shoulder blades sticking out from under their shirts. Many more turned up at my cottage after they learned that I had studied at IIT, their curiosity tinged with naïve hope.

Most said they were poor and wanted money to continue their studies in Delhi and Chandigarh. Others had more specific goals: a computer course, a degree in Business Management or Medical Science.

I remembered them as obedient schoolboys with plump red cheeks that were randomly pinched by passing elders; the dragging chorus of them cramming multiplication tables at the local government school often reached my cottage. Lengthening into young men in leather jackets from China, they didn't seem to have lost their mountain air of indolence, and that talent for slow living almost everyone in Ranipur seemed to possess from birth.

But, unlike Aseem, Virendra and me, they had grown much faster, largely due to the internet, which had spread not only knowledge and ideas, but new, bolder attitudes.

The people I had known at my small-town schools had

disappeared without a digital trace, as I discovered when I googled their names; it was as though they had settled uncomplainingly, after their never-very-high expectations, with a low-level destiny in the analogue. Many of the 'aspirers' in Ranipur, on the other hand, confessed to ambitions of starting businesses and becoming super-rich. India was rising, they said; it would be a superpower soon, and they wanted to avail of the new opportunities for prosperity.

I often thought at such moments of the parties in Aseem's home, and the many such gatherings of the elite in New Delhi, where eager foreigners and go-getting Indians acted and reacted on one another, and a fantasy of an irresistibly 'rising' India hardened into conviction. Travelling to Ranipur, that mood of exaltation could only appear a state of delusion.

I listened to these aspirers, many of whom were very bright, and even encouraged them with small gifts of money, suggestions and contacts. It seemed cruel not to, though the new universities and computer courses were gruesomely expensive, often malevolently designed to con the poor out of their meagre savings. The kind of coaching class I had gone to in Delhi had turned into a pan-Indian racket.

I don't think you knew that Mohit, whom you employed at your villa, was one of its victims. His parents, resting their ambition on some fly-by-night operation in Ludhiana, had lost three lakhs. They had then, resting their hopes on a younger son, fallen prey to a recruiting agent for an immigrant-smuggling operation based in Amritsar, which promised to take young men to Italy via Afghanistan, Turkey and Greece.

I even sent a couple of young men to Aseem, hoping that they would at least find employment in one of the call centres in Gurgaon, mimicking the idioms of Atlanta and Newcastle. I was not pleased when a friend of his in online retail hired them as peons and office boys, and I was distraught when I heard about another Delhi-bound aspirer working as an errand boy at a massage parlour. I came to despair of their chances of progressing beyond menial jobs.

Ignorant of lifestyles elsewhere, they had been resilient for long amidst their relative poverty. The aspirers now nursed an extravagant hope of inclusion in an evidently prospering world. The main result was that they lost the immunity to soul-crushing humiliation that remoteness had guaranteed them.

Some of those I tried to help returned from their forays into the big cities with bitterness in their faces. For a while they avoided me, and, encountered in the village, their eyes looked away in sudden and frank embarrassment, especially Mohit's younger brother, who had got as far as Greece before he was arrested and deported.

The only valuable asset most villagers had was their land, tilled or owned by their forefathers: potato fields, a terrace or two of apple, plum and cherry trees, pine forests and tumble-down houses with a couple of cows swishing about in the backyard. Remarkably, the Rajput moustache in Ranipur's post office drooped, and the clock started to tick again, if joltingly, after every minute – about the same time that real estate speculators – the major contributors to India's economic growth – reached Himachal.

One day Naazku told me that Mathur had helped plug the leaks in her thatched roof, replaced her tin door with a wooden one, and bought some new clothes for her. I tried to warn her to hold off, or at least to drive a hard bargain.

I had read in Aseem's magazine about the new phenomenon of farmers across North India, tempted by amounts of cash they had barely imagined, much less seen, selling off cultivable lands to property developers, and then squandering their capital in either ill-advised business ventures or extravagant consumption, often of heroin and alcohol.

Some had already succumbed to the lure of easy money in Ranipur. Concrete apartment buildings, neat and blank, were beginning to rise on hillsides denuded, with methodical malevolence, of their tree cover. Judges, politicians and businessmen owned these new summer homes, all parking their untaxed income in real estate, and, indirectly, in Mathur's construction company.

You, I found out only much later, had also contracted out your villa's renovation to Mathur.

I heard complaints. On their occasional visits to Ranipur, mostly during the summer, the village's new property owners denied local stores even a small bit of business by bringing their own groceries, as well as servants, from the plains. As for the locals, tormented by rising food prices, most of them could barely afford their only consumerist indulgence: smartphones.

With property values going up, Raju, the teashop owner, tried to turn himself into a broker. Every time I passed his shop, he came out from behind his glass-fronted counter, through a litter of crated hens, and told me about new deals on offer, coolly mentioning astounding sums of money that he had never seen.

Migrant labourers, from places as far as Bihar and Jharkhand, trickled in to help clear and level the land, and build more unused playgrounds of the rich. As more summer homes came up, the village seemed to be going back to its original colonial hierarchy: the masters above, and the servants somewhere below.

The wage slaves, almost all from forest-dwelling tribes, huddled, shivering, under tarpaulin shacks beside construction sites in the evening, after a day spent hacking, digging, sifting and carting. Unattended, and roaming free across the village, their children, dressed in scarecrow clothes with patches, shreds and tears, their hair stringy with dirt, brought to Ranipur some of the bleakness of extreme destitution on the plains.

At the small post office, I would invariably be requested by a labourer or two to write brief messages on postcards and money-order forms to their parents.

'How is your health now?' 'Did my last money-order reach you?' 'It is very cold here.' 'I'll try to come home for Diwali.' I wrote in Hindi, in a steadily deteriorating hand.

Occasionally, I was also asked to read out letters the labourers had received. These, too, were about long and anxious separation between parents and sons, wives and husbands: 'I think of the days you were here and hope you'll be back again soon, you haven't written for a long time, the money didn't arrive, it was late last month.' I read the barely legible lines haltingly, trying not to think of my own and my mother's letters, and was relieved on days when I could ask Devdutt to pick up my mail.

I should not be sentimental, however. You might remember, if you were in India then, those Modi masks that in early 2014 made their way from assembly lines in Shenzhen to the smallest Indian towns and villages. I saw them on sale one spring morning at a kirana shop that clung to the ridge towards Salerno, having survived the depredations of real-estate agents in its neighbourhood.

The masks lay next to the open sacks of rice, kidney beans, soybean nuggets, and weevil-ridden flour. I picked one up: the man's fleshy lips distended by the rubber and painted bright red, with black grime firmly settled into the folds of the white beard.

The shopkeeper, sitting cross-legged amid his wares, did not look up from his mobile phone as I put the thing back. In more than a decade, while he moved swiftly from youth to premature old age, I had only once bought something from him: a Maggi noodles packet, in the days when I did not worry about the high content of monosodium glutamate in my food.

Back home that afternoon, I came out on the balcony to scare the monkeys away and saw another Modi. This time the face loomed up above the slight frame of a very short man in jeans and sneakers. Walking up the winding path to the house, he must have seen the monkeys pounding my roof, and also noticed me.

He took the mask off as he came closer.

I had expected a coarsened adult face, unafraid to proclaim his faith in an unrepentant killer, like that of Mumbai's corporate chieftains, American-accented economists from Columbia and Princeton, and Delhi's Oxbridge-educated television anchors. But here was a ten-year-old tribal boy, with a narrow face, thin arms, eczema-scarred legs, hard, dilated belly, and hair that had gone nearly blond with malnutrition, smiling weakly.

Ten

When Aseem telephoned last year, I braced myself for another conversation that mixed salacious gossip about Virendra with detached insights and observations. He had recently phoned me to disclose he had finished writing a novel featuring a version of Virendra and our early days at IIT. I was taken aback when he announced, 'I am finally going to be in your Himalayan sanctuary this weekend.'

Finally: more than a decade after I moved to Ranipur, the life I had left behind on the plains had come looking for me. How little I knew of the upheavals ahead as I spoke to Aseem on the phone.

He said, 'This chick called Alia wants to interview me about our IIT friends. I met her at JLF and asked her to moderate a panel at Great Minds United next year. She told me she has been commissioned to write a book by HarperCollins India. I told her that she should also talk to you. She said she has a house near where you live. Something she inherited from her family and has been doing up.'

Aseem didn't give me more specifics. The landline crackled, as usual; it was hard to make out what he was saying – something about you being the ex-girlfriend of Soumak . . . I nevertheless recognised the villa he mentioned.

It was easy to, because this villa stood on the highest part of the ridge, claiming supremacy over it. I would often trespass through its grounds while returning home from my walk to Salerno, walking past a white stone gateway, next to an unconnected telegraph pole, down two rows of very tall silver fir trees that, closely planted, stood like two solid walls.

I first wandered into it during my mother's illness, when the vacant afternoons combined with reminders of her infirmity everywhere in the house drove me out. At the end of the avenue of firs stood a white villa with a portico, its pillars crumbling, its roof red-brown with rust, and the black voids of the windows indifferently looking on an overgrown garden.

From the time I moved there, I had associated Ranipur with such heartwarming images of decay and ruin, these reminders of ephemeral and dubious achievement and transitory influence.

The village had been a summer retreat for India's British rulers, the grandest of whom built villas for themselves along a steep ridge, facing the abyss of a teacup-shaped valley. Imperfectly imagining long-abandoned homes in England and Scotland, they created gardens of rose and honeysuckle and dahlia and hung pots of fuchsias and geraniums on their verandas; they drank tea and ate watercress sandwiches on their lawns and went riding through the forests of cedar, oak, silver fir, spruce and birch, assisted by loyal Indian servants, who, barred from the paths frequented by their masters, huddled in a settlement on the lower end of the ridge.

Sold by the departing British after 1947 to Indian royalty and businessmen, who neglected them, these mansions had long sunk into the quiet repose of places liberated from perennially fidgety humans. After every monsoon, the estates ran wild with lilies of the valley and peonies, the ancient apple and cherry trees failed to bloom, and the rust on the iron lace of broken greenhouses and the mailboxes hanging aslant from gates turned a deeper shade of brown.

I preferred these villas in their state of slow perishing, the dead leaves amassing in broken fountains, and owls flying in and out of porticos where wisteria silently strangle columns. So customarily did they fulfil their promise of eternal peace that I was a bit dismayed when one late afternoon I walked through the abandoned estate to find a tall woman standing at the end of the row of fir trees, incongruously dressed in the cold weather in a knee-length skirt (though, and it was too far to see, you may have been wearing your thick tweed skirt and tights).

You seemed to be supervising a construction crew; and you towered over the diminutive tribal men and women from Bihar and Jharkhand scurrying around with loads of bricks on their heads, and buckets of water balanced like a pair of scales at the ends of their arms.

I waved embarrassedly and immediately turned back.

I kept away from the house as over the next several months it underwent swift transformation, with only the high solar-power panels glinting in the sun as its visible sign. And when I next went there it was at Aseem's invitation.

How strange it was to find myself after the familiar walks between the firs, and the unfamiliar sight of the renovated villa coldly staring down at a mud-flecked Pajero with 'D' Delhi plates, in a very large living room, its largeness accentuated by the high ceilings, the removal of a loft and several pillars and partitions, the relative absence of furnishings, the white-painted, bare walls, and a view through great panes of plate glass of the teacup valley and the mountain ranges beyond it.

Light flooded in from the glassed walls and a skylight. It was unusually warm inside.

The fantasy of home for British colonials, that overly uphol-stered realm of chintz sofa covers, quilted coverlets, thick carpets and mounted heads of leopards and nilgai, had been streamlined into a spartan 'studio' with gleaming surfaces and Turkish kilims and acute-angled lamps.

Only the fireplace and a mantelpiece had remained of the old congested and dark interior. And the leather-bound volumes of Trollope, Thackeray and Dickens in walnut bookcases with carved tops and glass doors had been usurped by multi-hued paperbacks of *Everything Is Illuminated*, *Norwegian Wood* and *The Tipping Point*, brashly rising against the pale walls on open shelves.

I didn't know then that this freedom from clutter, and the careful arrangement of space and light rather than of objects – the artful bareness I would later find in Shoreditch and Hackney, and in the weekend supplements of the *Financial Times*, which for some reason you bought every Saturday in London – were the surest manifestations of twenty-first-century wealth and taste.

I felt myself shrinking, suddenly aware of my kurta from Shimla's Khadi Ashram, an indigenous garb rendered shabby by the advent of Fab India, and though of course neither Aseem nor you had seen it, of my own tumbledown house, more solid than most other dwellings in the village, lopsided buildings of rotten wood, mud and naked brick, where the servants of the Raj had once lived, but still devoid of clear design or planning, and replete with signs of hasty construction: mud walls that sagged and leaned, windows that didn't close and needed cloth wedged around the frame to keep out draughts, and a corrugated-iron roof that leaked during the monsoons, the water dripping through fissures in the ceiling boards, and keeping a row of steel pans and plastic buckets occupied.

Aseem, on the other hand, had swiftly made himself at home in this up-to-date setting. He had just finished recording an interview with you; and while I briefly hesitated, as I sat in a low chair, lower than any I had ever known, as to what to do with my hands, placing them successively on my thighs and knees and then on the chair's arms, he seemed comfortably sunk in the abyss of a brown leather armchair, fingers locked over his chest.

His legs were widely spread in a way that abashed me; his jeans were tight around his crotch, and two of his shirt buttons were open. He was chewing something – almonds, I saw, from a bowl beside him on the floor, where a spear of sunlight, seething with dust motes, was perfectly aimed. And, despite his slack posture, Aseem seemed tall, athletic and alert, especially to you, as you reclined on a low sofa, yogically cross-legged, a MacBook Air perched on your lap.

'Listen, boss,' Aseem had said on the phone earlier that day, 'you should check out this new neighbour of yours. She's a sort of Indian that didn't exist when we were growing up, from a conservative Muslim background but very much in tune with the global progressive zeitgeist, at home every-where in the world without belonging anywhere. A gypsy, but a very modern gypsy, densely wired into the metropolitan nodes of London and New York.

'Moreover,' he added, 'she's really hot. Rich, but with some brain cells, and very engaged, politically, unlike these dumb rich kids I meet all the time at Delhi parties who just want to burn up daddy-mummy's ill-gotten cash partying in Mykonos, and tell you that Modi is the most dedicated nationalist and best manager since Hitler.'

He had emailed me your book proposal, and now shared with me the fruits of his own research on you: the tweets on LGBT rights in Indonesia and Indian repression in Kashmir, the retweets of Me Too campaigners in the United States, the Instagram posts about the crackdown on Uighurs.

'There is some worm in the apple there,' Aseem said. 'I guess it comes from being financially secure and not having to work. Anyway, it's all a bit touching. She is trying to find a way of being noticed in the world, like many young people today. 'But why single her out?' he added. 'Actually, even those of us in our forties and fifties are doing that. The most celebrated writers of our time are trying to catch Barack Obama's eye and get their books on the bestseller charts through his reading list. Basically, social media forces everyone to become an operator; everyone is a hustler in the neo-liberal marketplace. We all have to learn how to blend aggressive self-promotion with sincere activism – apart from you, of course!'

I think Aseem could speak this way to me because unlike his other acquaintances and friends, or you, I was not in any danger of surpassing him in the quest for glory – a competitor to silently resent and, whenever possible, to undermine. Rather, he was baffled and even a bit exasperated by my failure.

We had both turned our backs, after IIT, on the career of easy moneymaking open to us. In his eyes, however, I ought to have done more: taken charge, realised my 'true potential'. I had remained a mere translator, locked into sterile intimacy with a few obscure authors and uninfluential university presses.

He never ceased to bring up the fact that I did nothing with my erotic opportunities. On the phone from his hotel, he ad-libbed an *LRB* personal advert for me: 'Arun Dwivedi, Lonely 1970s heartthrob-lookalike living in the Himalayas seeks companion. Age, caste and class no bar. Ability to converse about Hindi literature and nature is not essential. But eagerness for erotic play is.'

I laughed. He could be funny; and I was gratified by his interest in my life, which no one else shared, though I didn't always like the way he ran his fingers around its edges, feeling for some secret compartment that might disclose a sexual vigour just as unsubdued as his.

He concluded I was held back by something, and I was relieved that he was too delicate to press this issue further. I couldn't have explained to him the complexes that precluded a genuine relationship, a true exchange of tenderness.

My renunciations did mean that he never brought to my existence the vigilant envy with which he researched you and followed the lives and careers of his more successful contemporaries.

Aseem, still semi-horizontal, scratching up almonds with his fingernails, introduced us: 'Alia, meet one of my closest friends and now your neighbour.'

You stood up to shake my hand and I saw that your internet images had downplayed your height – you were an inch taller than me, and very straight-backed in your black T-shirt and tracksuit pants.

My first impression was of indifference. Your hand felt small and cool, and your eyes, so clear and calm, conducted a quick survey, as though to discover if there was anything in it for you personally, and then turned away. Your longer and more expressive gaze was for Aseem; and I wonder now if he knew this as I retrieve his words and gestures from that crucial first meeting.

Aseem was saying, 'I guess I should move here, too, and become your neighbour. Sorry, boss, I should have visited you earlier. It felt like a long way to come just to look at some mountains and smell the apples. But I really admire the way you and Alia have chosen to live your lives. That's my own fantasy – to live in seclusion in the Himalayas and spend the days reading and writing.'

Is that what you had done? The information surprised me.

Aseem said, 'Jii dhoondta hai phir wahi phursat ke raat-din.' And when you looked nonplussed, he added, 'My heart pursues once again those days and nights of leisure. The anthem of our frantic generation.'

You smoothed the sofa's deep blue satin coverlet before you sat down again on it and swept up your hair on top of your head; the casual gesture left the nape of your neck covered in wisps of downy curls.

I sat diagonally to the view through the French window. I kept looking at it. It had been breezy outside, and the plum trees below shook, sending shadows indoors. A pattern of criss-crossed leaves shivered on the empty white walls.

In the soundproofed hush, a sound, something between a rattle and a gallop, came from somewhere inside the house. I must have looked a bit startled because you said softly, with a smile, 'That's just the electric kettle.'

I asked you about your book. 'When did you start writing it?' I said, feeling as I spoke, slowly, the awkwardness of English words on my tongue. I almost never spoke the language in Ranipur, and months would pass before I had occasion to use it.

You said you had been researching your book for more than a year now, and had interviewed Siva and Virendra and many of their associates in the United States.

There was a pause, and then you added, 'I don't have a US or UK publisher yet.'

I wondered what to say. In the silence, Aseem started to talk again, slightly tactlessly, I thought, about how the Indian market for serious fiction and non-fiction is shrinking.

Some birds flew close by the French window, casting shadows on the walls, and disappeared. When I looked after them, I saw leaves floating smoothly through the air, settling on the grass below the trees.

Presently, a young man I had known since he was a school-boy, his face glazed pink with sunburn, appeared with teacups and sugar bowl arranged on a tray. I knew him to be, like many young men in the village, agreeably unemployed in Chinese-made leather jackets bought from the Tibetan market in Shimla. He and his friends were often found hunched over a chessboard beside a road at the edge of the village, overlooking a precipitous and scenic drop where tourists would often stop their cars to take photographs.

Mohit noticed me; he grew very sheepish. Covering his stomach with the tray, he retreated sideways into the kitchen as though shielding himself from reproach.

The milky tea sat there for a while, exhaling cardamom-scented fumes, as Aseem began to complain.

'This country is going to the dogs,' he started. 'We have lost our idealism – the ideals that our founding fathers Gandhi and Nehru fought for. Hundreds of millions of young people are looking for decent jobs. But you have a hopelessly inept prime minister who changes his clothes three-four times in a day while pretending to be the son of a humble chai-wallah.

'These chikna journos, these fake sherry-drinking liberals, like to pretend they are leading a resistance to Modi. But they are only helping him become more popular with their British-accented English.'

I recognised this as one of Aseem's heartfelt declamations, which though uttered from a barely open mouth, always seemed forever to be racing towards warning and exhortation. His voice would crack and rapidly rise until he sounded near hysterical.

'I tell my nephews and nieces every day, "Baby, get out of here, go to America, and stay there." There is no future here for them, so don't come back, just stay there! Trump's America has its problems, but none on the scale of India. It is still a functional society, whereas in India we are looking down double gun barrels. It's all over for liberal democracy here: the crazy populists have won.'

Those very dark eyes of Aseem's flashed as he spoke. His hands traced the arcs and bridges of his argument; and his shoes jiggled even faster. By the end of his outburst, he was running fingers through his mop of hair, and laughing, shoulders shaking, and shoes pounding the floor.

'I tell them every day – every day, boss! "Yes, go away and don't come back! Just stay there!"'

Every day? Aseem always dared me to believe his exaggerations. And I mostly did.

I noticed a small ashtray full of red-stained cigarette ends on the floor below your sofa. Had you been smoking them? What social occasion in the middle of nowhere, apart from Aseem's arrival, might have prompted you to put on lipstick? That ashtray was oddly vexing.

Meanwhile, you had started to speak of a Delhi-based correspondent for the *Financial Times* whom you had recently met at one of Aseem's parties in Delhi. You thought he was 'nice'. Aseem had another opinion.

'Listen, Alia,' he now said, 'I have known Gordon since he first came as a journo for some British tabloid in the 1990s. Back then, India denoted beggars and maharajas to Westerners, so he retailed those Orientalist clichés then. Now he has got some book out about India modernising and leaving the West behind, etc. The East is a career, as Robert Clive of the East India Company used to say. But, at the end of the day, boss, we are to blame. These white guys start wearing juttis and Fab India churidars and throw Bollywood-themed parties and the brown sahibs just fall to the ground. Compare the sycophantic and insecure Indians to the Chinese who have always kept whiteys at a distance . . .'

You let Aseem go on, smiling as he talked. I couldn't tell if you were in awe of him. Or perhaps you were finding that, for some reason, Aseem's audience always let him rave on, find fault with someone or something at length; he was gifted at eliciting our indulgence.

'Look, Gordon is a sweet guy, but I can't take these over-promoted public-school boys from the *FT* and *Economist* seriously on India. I run a magazine and we know what a mindboggling country this is, how hard it is to get to grips with it, and of course you can get away with telling white people whatever you want about India and they'll believe it.'

I went to the bathroom, directed by you down a white corridor. In that spacious and serenely ordered alcove with tidy rows of bottles and thick clean towels, I sat on the lavatory rather than risk missing my aim and wetting the carpeted beige floor. A series of small farts broke free, and I began to fret that they could be heard in the living room.

It was a relief when I returned and Aseem immediately turned to me to mock a young new novelist in English from Delhi.

'These smooth-cheeked liberals, these chiknas, want to convert the surplus of their posh upbringing into the immortality of art.'

Was Aseem repeating himself for your sake?

An email announced its arrival with a ping, and I wondered if you had wi-fi; no plastic gadget with winking lights and clumsy cables marred the clean surfaces of the room. I had googled you cumbersomely that morning – disconnecting the cable from my rotary-dial Bakelite, connecting it to an old laptop with a dial-up modem, only to find that the number in

Chandigarh was as usual busy – and had wished, not for the first time, for broadband in the village.

Aseem said to you, 'You should talk more to Arun about Virendra. He knew him well at IIT where we all shared some unforgettable experiences.'

You looked up at me, and smiled vaguely. It seemed to me then a polite gesture to a guest. Was I wrong? You then moved to pick up a pink cardboard folder that lay next to the ashtray on the floor.

'I would really so love to,' you said as you settled back into your seat. 'Perhaps we can meet soon.'

'Yes, yes, I would like to,' I said, again struck by the English words blurting out of my mouth and worried if they were the right ones.

You and Aseem went back to the conversation about your book.

Aseem had developed some fresh insights into the matter. 'People in my generation,' he said, 'grew up believing what my hero Naipaul once wrote: that if you allow yourself to become nothing, you have no place in the world. If you are a black or brown person, there is no point in complaining about racism and claiming victimhood and hoping for some Damascene moral conversion among the whiteys on top. You have to get to the top yourself, and then make the world safe for your own people, and for the generations to come. That's what those WASPs and then the Jews in America had done in the white-shoe firms of Boston and New York before the Indians arrived. That's what the people who voted for Trump are doing. That's also what Virendra and those other Indians abroad were trying to do, but I guess they went too far.'

There was a pause; and then he said, 'But the thing you have to keep in mind about Virendra is that he was a Dalit, and more than anything he wanted to squeeze out the blood of the untouchables flowing through his veins. Poor Barack Obama – he arrived at Harvard Law School a few years before Virendra and left with the blood of slaves still flowing through his veins. No wonder it left him in awe to bullies like Larry Summers, so much beholden to rich white men on Wall Street, and made him a weak protector of his own people.'

'Fascinating,' you said, looking up from the screen. 'That's really fascinating.'

While you talked to Aseem, I couldn't stop looking at the view from the plate-glass wall. It was the same, from a slightly higher elevation, as from my balcony: a deep valley with forested slopes presided over by an expansive range of white-topped mountains.

It was a bit faded in the late-afternoon haze; and I knew that the setting sun would soon fall red on the snow of the peaks, the mountains just after sunset would become a faint amethyst outline, cooking smokes would veil the hillsides in a transparent blue-grey, and the lights in the humble homes scattered at random across the valley would start to come on.

An everyday sight from my open-air balcony, but the frame of double-glazed glass, perfectly symmetrical, charged it with a chilly aloofness, the sharp geometry of that dustless room extending outward, deep into the wildest nature.

Aseem and you were still talking, barely cognisant of my presence, and I started to remember that it had been early spring when I came to live in Ranipur with my mother. The air was still cold, the grass stiff with frost in the mornings, and the floor of the empty cottage encrusted with dead bees whose withered corpses cracked underfoot.

The lights weren't working, and at night shadows from candles danced around the bare walls, up to the spiderwebs in the roof timbers. The animals in the cowshed below filled the two bedrooms with the smell and the damp warmth of their bodies and of their litter; the tiny kitchen, built of concrete rather than wood, with a window that didn't close properly, remained bitterly cold. One morning I walked into it to find that a frozen jug of water had burst, creating a large icy puddle on the counter.

There were rainstorms: the trees in the rising wind seemed to grow taller and dark, white snakes of lightning stood over the valley, followed by enraged claps of thunder. The frightened bulbs hanging from the ceiling began to buzz and flicker.

There was a long gap broken by a roll of thunder that seemed to begin somewhere very far, and it came up and down many mountains and valleys before passing over the village, leaving ears cocked, hearts beating louder.

During a series of flashes and remote crashes, rain tapped on the roof a few times, as though politely seeking permission to begin, before it burst into a rage.

Amid a hard, vengeful drumming, water flooded down the roof's corrugations, leaking through its holes to plop straight into the pots and pans on the floor. The electric bulbs, having survived the worst, suddenly expired, leaving prickly ghosts of yellow filament in the dark.

'Kya toofan bhagwan ne bheja hai. What a storm God has sent us,' my mother said as she took lit candles to each room, her face thinner and more anxious behind the wavering flames shielded by her hands. She had not seen much of me over the years since I left home for IIT, where we had slept on the floor in the same small room, where I awakened to find her next to me but far away, her face with its eyes closed looking small and tranquil, as if she were walking some place without pain.

The vastness of the space around our house in Ranipur gave us pangs of loneliness. We had so little to communicate when I was growing up in Deoli, and even less after I moved to Delhi. Slowly moving towards each other now in a new place, we were both shy, and worried, too, about the life together to come; and I would watch, long after she left my room and the rain stopped, the drops of water on the windowpanes as they traced their descent on the glass, wriggling to avoid other drops, before swiftly darting into them to together perish out of sight.

Suddenly one gusty evening there was a rattle of gunfire, a shower of bullets lashing the tin roof and rebounding on to the wooden balcony. Within a couple of minutes, the hailstones piled up until they covered the ground with a gleaming layer of white.

Then one night, while I slept, wearing a jumper and woolly hat under two quilts, fine, teeming rain turned into snowflakes, turned into a mini storm that swooped and rattled the roof, before dying down with a soporific drone.

Entombed under the double quilts, the night seemed endless and joyful. I woke up to the warm breath of cows chewing the cud below my room, and I parted my curtains to see the valley white and steamy with mist, the bare apple trees bright against the hopeful spring sun, the crows cawing and dogs barking somewhere far below.

It was not my first snow; I had already witnessed, in Mussoorie one winter, the miracle that brought hordes of awestruck plains-dwellers to the hills during Christmas and New Year. Yet I stood amazed on my balcony at the hushed valley, half-wondering if I was entitled to such beauty and peace.

I persuaded my mother to emerge from under her multiple layers of quilts and join me on my balcony, where we noticed, for the first time, breath coming out of each other's mouths.

We had gone to Shimla soon after arriving to fit ourselves out with overcoats, mitts, mufflers and woollen socks. She still refused to wear shoes: she had never worn shoes, and she claimed that they did not fit her feet. Instead, she wore sandals with thick socks.

None of her new clothes fitted her, and as we both stood, eyes half-shut, before the blinding whiteness, resembling two sturdy bears in stiff new duffel coats that slightly lifted our arms from their sides, heads almost invisible under the wrappings of woollen mufflers, a smile of joyous complicity began at the corners of her mouth, wrinkling the flesh of her cheeks and lighting up her eyes.

The snow crumbled fast after the sun emerged, falling from the roof and the pine and cherry trees with startlingly loud thumps. Water ran from under its white shroud, and within a couple of hours streams were rushing down the valley, churning up a haze wherever they were impeded. The stereophonic gurgle of falling water reigned over all other sounds by the evening, when the white sickle of the moon hung in the grey sky as the final emblem of a magical day.

It was dark when I left your villa, the lights motionless in the grey-blue haze of the valley, the row of firs suddenly terrible in their blue-black height, and the thickets of forest ahead already withdrawn into their mysterious nocturnal life.

A fleeting moon between the clouds suddenly sharpened the lines of the gravel path that led to the iron gate.

Something kept me from looking back. Was it Aseem's reluctance to leave his seat as I left? When he did rise, it was slowly and grudgingly, and I felt, for the first time, a stab of irritation at his compulsion to dominate the conversation, to conduct it on his own terms.

But I looked back, anyway; and then couldn't turn my gaze

away from the pale sheen that lightened the villa's façade, and the dark windows that blankly returned my stare.

I now think about all those things on my first visit to your villa that I found alien: those electronic sounds, suggestive of a busy metropolitan life; those mysterious birds and that lipstick-smeared cigarette; the lightness and capaciousness of that room; Aseem's ease in it, and even that something lapping between you and him, which I didn't know then would one day rear up and overturn all our lives.

PART THREE

Eleven

'That Soumak was on to a good thing with her,' I remember Aseem saying after that first meeting with you in Ranipur. This was the boyfriend he had mentioned on the phone – the Oxford-educated Bengali with a prize-winning D.Phil. thesis on Locke, who had recently mutated into yet another Hindu nationalist hysteric on his talk show.

We were having a quick coffee before Aseem's departure for Delhi at Mathur's flagship property in Ranipur: Hotel Kipling. We sat in the vast panelled lobby, surrounded by giant paintings of Anglo-Afghan wars, and an excess of waiters, familiar locals all, even more sheepish than Mohit in their Raj-style cummerbunds and tunics.

Aseem had had a bad night; he hadn't got much sleep, he said, though he normally slept like a log. 'I am not at ease in the natural world,' he said. 'I can't really tell the difference between a bee and bumblebee.'

He wouldn't confess this, but, like many first-time visitors, the peace and silence, the aimless and, therefore, incomprehensible beauty of the valley during daytime, and the sky at night, had unnerved him.

It made him sourly censorious about both Ranipur and you; and, as always, I let him rave on.

'The problem in countries with Western-educated and socially ambitious bourgeois like India is that they produce more aspiring writers than readers. She has done her research, but I am not sure if this chick can write,' he said. 'She might be just another one of these over-entitled types. A pushy self-promoter, like the kids today, more into images than words, more into self-branding than producing content. As I keep saying, everyone is an operator now. No one, not even the most rich and beautiful and famous, are sure of who they are, and everyone is jostling for recognition in the attention economy of social media. Have you seen her Instagram? Also, did you see how clueless she looked when I quoted Ghalib? Even our Hindu fanatic friends know those lines by heart. She probably knows Stormzy better than Urdu poetry.

'But she is definitely smoking hot. Great hair, and what a sexy shrug. I bet she'll be the biggest eye-candy at the festival next year,' he continued.

'She is probably a tigress in bed. Some of these Mozzies are pretty wild, I guess, because their mullahs are so priggish. I hear that the scene in Pakistan is crazy, orgies right and left, cocaine everywhere, and Imran Khan can only get it up when he is doing threesomes.

'But, you know,' and Aseem's voice started to rise and crack, 'the Prophet himself was a perfectly normal horny guy, like the folks who came up with *Kamasutra*, so it's good that some Hindus and Mozzies are going back to the fundaments of their faith. Hey, you know what? This is the kind of fundamentalism I like.'

I glanced around to see if anyone was listening. I was growing uneasy, but it would be dishonest of me to claim now that I was immediately offended by the way Aseem spoke of you. I was too accustomed to IIT banter about women from him.

He soon went back to talking about you: 'She's got the right politics. Actually, it's pretty annoying how right-on her Twitter is about everything – Kashmir, Palestine, climate change, corporate capitalism, Me Too . . . You name it. Forget about meritocracy, Black Lives Matter, Dalit assertion, LGTBQ rights, anti-imperialism, feminism, social justice, and all these noisy slogans of our time. It is this kind of black or brown princess with her elite networks, social conscience and social media who is looting the bonanza of fashionable progressive politics.'

I noticed, for the first time since I had known him, something discontented about his face, a frown in his usually unagitated eyes, and a slight twitching at the corners of his mouth. It was as though, having picked himself out early for fame and glory, he felt, in middle age, he was lagging behind the young; as though, unable to admit that the sheer scale of his ambition was defeating him, he increasingly found satisfaction in belittling his competitors.

I tried to take him back to one of our pointless but enjoyable arguments. We had been wrangling over Ranipur before he started to talk about you. He had noticed on his walk through the village some women grinding grain in a stone mortar, and presented the sight to me as evidence that geographical isolation and underdevelopment make for a mix of extreme poverty and backward customs.

In his own fiction, villages were sinks of iniquity where Dalits were lynched for marrying or romancing outside their caste, or simply for belonging to a low caste; women were burned for bringing insufficient dowry, and police stations were settings of torture and custodial murder. He claimed that the same benighted people voted Modi into power, though it was clear that the latter was supported by the country's richest businessmen and much of its middle class.

I don't know why I sought to claim Ranipur as exceptional; perhaps, to keep Aseem away from subjects that tormented him.

But Aseem wanted to say more about you, and his voice was starting to rise and crack: 'You should look her up! She's right on your doorstep! What is the point of being single and a Dharmendra lookalike if all you are going to do is live in a

village, translate Hindi writing, and look after your mother?!
When will you realise your true potential, man?'

I knew he looked down on Hindi writing mostly because its
practitioners seemed to be either portly old men or unphoto-
genic women, and because it had never been reviewed in the
magazines – *Esquire, Time* and the *New Yorker* – he used to care
about.

I was privately elated by his encouragement. Something
about you – that calculated undoing of the colonial villa, the
large territorial Pajero on the driveway, or those red-stained
cigarette ends – had stayed with me.

One sign of that interest was that by the end of our conversation I had started to dislike Aseem's derogatory references
to you, and I had started to feel a long-repressed exasperation
with his domineering ways.

Also, I resented the way he, who had summarily discarded
his own obligations to his parents, referred to my ailing
mother. It made me feel righteous, briefly at least, before the
sense of virtue faded, leaving behind a faint embarrassment.

But then Aseem couldn't have known that it was in a compromised idyll that he had arrived and introduced me to you.

One late afternoon I returned from my walk to find Naazku's pink slippers aligned on the doormat. It was odd: she
never visited during that hour. Simultaneously I took out my
phone from my pocket to see six missed calls from Devdutt.

Naazku said, 'Ek ghantey se zameen par bechaari baithi thi.
She had been sitting helplessly on the floor for an hour.'

My mother had slipped on the kitchen floor. Devdutt, coming to deliver my mail, had seen her through the window,
slumped against the refrigerator door, crying silently, and
unable to get up by herself.

In the days that followed, she slipped again. I bought a walker for her from Shimla. But she panicked while using it: 'Mein gir rahi hoon, Beta, main gir rahi. I am falling, Beta,' she would say, 'I am falling.'

Naazku made it worse by screaming, 'Hey bhagwan. Kya karenge, kya karenge, hey bhagwan, bachao hamey!' Oh my God, what should we do, what should we do? Oh my God, please save us!

The next time she slipped, it was in the bathroom, next to the squatter toilet, and she let out a wail that startled the cows below; their bellows echoed loud and deep in the valley.

And then, very soon, she became, after a couple of visits to a doctor in Sood's latest Scorpio, a certifiably sick person, a whole shelf in her room colonised by pills and tonics – to mitigate her arthritis, to cope with her blood pressure, to regulate her bowel movements and, after a while, to keep her heart beating.

There were some humiliating experiences with the enema, which left her frightened and helpless. After many years, she again cried easily, shrivelling up on her bed; fear lurked in her eyes in the way it had when I was growing up in Deoli. She seemed to have lost her ability to tie her sari, and wore it high, showing her petticoat, and white socks and slippers.

One morning she forgot to change from her nightie, and from then on wore only nighties day and night; they were all with fluted collars, ballooning out in ample folds, with wide cuffs that hid her hands, and she seemed to shrink further in them.

One of the girls who wore shalwar-kameezes stitched by my mother became the first in a long series of her paid and untrained helpers – young women with immobile faces that expressed little except timidity and uneasiness and who in my presence always sat awkwardly on the edge of their chairs, legs jostling, their palms gripping their knees.

Pouring vitamin, magnesium, zinc and calcium supplements and fresh fruit juices down her throat, and carefully setting her out in the sun every morning, the helpers made my mother resemble a desiccated plant.

Naazku came to cook; I was disturbed by how meekly my mother took the ruin of her most important and enjoyable preoccupation.

I left the house only after ensuring that she had gone to the toilet, and was seated, pillows piled up under her back, a blanket covering her swollen legs; I returned to find her in that same position, like a stiff corpse.

At the dining table, she'd say nothing, cough a bit, without raising her eyes from her plate, into which, unnoticed by her helper, a thread of clear saliva dropped from her lips. And if she did suddenly start talking, it was so unexpected and loud that it gave me a start.

Her teeth had long been replaced by dentures, and she ate more slowly now, and with great effort, exposing, disconcertingly, a mouth with rolls of fat, that parted, closed and stretched to reveal chewed-up food scattered across small pale bones.

Her face slumped; there were little pouches under her eyes; her eyelids were finely wrinkled; the skin over her elegant, high-bridged nose thinned.

A strange sensation came over me when looking at her face, as if I had never seen her before – until I realised one day with a little shock that it was the face she would wear on her funeral pyre.

Twelve

On the day I first saw you, looming over a construction crew, the most shameful evidence yet of my mother's rapidly deepening physical incapacity had come to light. And, on the day I saw you and Aseem, another inept helper had announced, while standing over the meanly snarled blankets on my mother's bed, her resolve to leave.

Your villa became a place of possibility; I started to walk past it every afternoon, hoping to catch sight of you, my twitching hands impregnated with a quick wave, my lips ready to issue a warm greeting. Even on the dark forest paths I kept on my face a look of friendly expectancy just in case I ran into you, though I always emerged with a slackening pulse into anticlimactic sunshine.

One day, when your mud-flecked Pajero was parked at the gate rather than under the covered portico, I walked down the driveway. My shoes crunched the gravel, my heart beat faster, and, feeling myself watched by invisible eyes, I wondered if I should have shaved my two-day stubble.

I knocked on the heavy wooden door. Someone moved inside; but it was Mohit who appeared, red in the face, as usual, a Himachal cap on his head.

'Madam Shimla gayi hain, aati hoongi. Madam has gone to Shimla but she will be back soon.'

He was looking at me curiously from head to toe.

'Intezar karenge? Would you like to wait?'

Waiting for my reply, he removed his cap; he stroked his

forehead, ran his hand over his flattened hair and then replaced the cap.

It seemed like a challenge I could not refuse.

Your living room seemed larger than in my memory, and the view of the valley from the double-glazed window chillier than before.

Mohit disappeared into the kitchen. I wondered if he was spying on me from a chink in the door; and I worried if I had vaguely snubbed him at some point.

Not knowing what to do, and thinking that I should leave, I stood before the bookshelves, looking at their spines in the dark. I noticed a stylish Penguin Modern Classics edition of *Delta of Venus*. It reminded me of Siva's pirated Indian copy with a lurid cover; scuffed and stained, it was widely 'used' in our IIT hostel.

There were no books in translation in Hindi, or any Indian language.

Suddenly discouraged, I slumped into the armchair Aseem had so insolently occupied on my previous visit. There was something hard in its folds: an almond, it turned out (did Aseem drop it there?). Holding it in one hand, I sank down again, watching, since I had nothing else to do, the blue satin sofa where you had sat, cross-legged, typing in Aseem's opinions, and which now looked sullenly back at me.

Your voice down the crackling phone line later that day was apologetic. 'I am so sorry to miss you. I had to go shopping in Shimla; the little shops here are charming but sell nothing useful. Can we meet later today? Would you like to have dinner?'

It was overwhelming, the promise of this unfussy invitation. Still, feeling a bit embarrassed after a long and fruitless wait, I said no; I had errands to run for my mother. Some other time, perhaps?

I spoke stiffly, I felt, like a formal old man. In the days that followed, days haunted by self-reproach over my refusal, my curiosity about you turned into a craving.

Living in Delhi and then Ranipur, I had hardly met any Muslim women, let alone one as beautiful and well educated as you. And when we first met, I could not quell the whisper in my brain that you ought to be somehow handicapped by your religion in the regime of Hindu supremacists and Islamophobia in general.

I expected you to have the anxious countenance of someone in a state of siege; and I couldn't get over how uncommonly self-possessed you were, scarcely conscious of being a Muslim (and, months after we met, I would still be surprised to discover that you had been inside a mosque only twice, at Jama Masjid in Delhi and Suleymaniye in Istanbul, both times as a tourist).

The facts Aseem gave me – slanted by, I now recognise, his fear of being left behind by the young – were mostly confusing. 'She did a lot of different things,' he said, 'like working at an online literary magazine in Brooklyn, in Sri Lanka for Amnesty, modelling for a moisturising cream, some television books show, before deciding to write a book. I kind of have her number. My magazine gets a lot of this half-firang, half-Indian type of person working as interns. They can be a bit difficult to deal with – they have the pride of rich people wasting their precious time for a good cause.'

Unlike Aseem, I had never known someone like you before, not really, and I wanted to know more. Discovering that broadband connections had indeed become available in Ranipur, I acquired one, bribing the BSNL engineer to expedite its installation. Forced by the cottage's layout to put the modem and router in my mother's room, I had to wait until she was asleep or out of the room to feverishly track your apparitions from one website to another.

And so, while the helper massaged my mother's useless legs on the balcony, or laboriously wiped out traces of her incontinence, I reconstructed different stages of your life as student, television anchor, model and aspiring writer.

There were pictures of your father, elegant in a sherwani and achkan, a 'leader' of Muslims in a polite and reserved way that seems quaint and impossible today; pictures of you as a little girl, uncommonly sweet with dark ringlets down your cheeks, and of your teenaged self at your beloved uncle's funeral, doing the salat-al-janazah, tear-stained face gazing at the upturned palms of your hands; pictures of your mother, youthful in thick-framed, bejewelled sunglasses, sitting with Begum-like poise in her new husband's corporate box at an IPL match in Mumbai; pictures from your political and literary associations at NYU, one among many international students playing at being responsible adults.

It turned out, on eBay, that old issues of those Bombay glossies titled *Society*, *Savvy*, *Verve* and *Gentleman* had frequently featured your family on the cover, relaxing on wide green lawns, elegant mansions in the background, ferocious dogs at their feet.

I looked closely at the faded pictures, in which your family seemed to be conducting a romance with itself in public; and I found myself more and more curious about its pampered and protected world, so different from, and even opposed to, mine that it seemed a chimera, hardly the milieu of a woman I had met and talked to.

I was intrigued, too, by the fact that, though born among those who were or could become powerful by dint of their family connections, you had improvised a separate personality for yourself. In the musty darkness of my mother's old room, just above her altar of miniature gods and goddesses, where marigolds sweetly rotted, and next to a mess of half-used jars and tubes, I clicked through the images of you as a model for a toothpaste, your face under your jet-black hair lit up by the brilliance of your teeth.

A stalker-ish fan had saved videos of you as a television anchor on YouTube, which, my aged laptop loudly panting now, I opened, and saw you, with spiky eyelashes, arched eyebrows and rosy lips, interview Riz Ahmed, Mohsin Hamid and Nassim Nicholas Taleb with a mix of earnestness and good cheer.

I realise I am sounding like a stalker myself. Maybe that isn't an inaccurate description. I found pictures of you and Aseem at the same venue in the society pages of the *Delhi Times*, you, elegant in a Rajasthani lehenga, next to a ferociously mustachioed regional potentate, and Aseem, reverently captioned and as athletically buoyant as ever in blue jeans and white shirt, at the annual Amber Palace party of the Jaipur Literary Festival.

Facebook demanded that I befriend you in order to read your posts, and Twitter, where your profile picture was an old photo from your modelling days, and your self-description read 'writer, feminist and activist', urged me to become one of your million-plus followers, among those scribbling such messages on your timeline as 'Hey Hottie! DM me. I have a great offer for you'.

But your Instagram account, opened a few years ago, freely proclaimed your political and aesthetic preferences, using book covers, black-ink drawings of Audre Lorde, and pictures of political demonstrations from Hong Kong to La Paz.

Your most liked post was one where, next to a picture of a Uighur girl in handcuffs, you confessed that you had turned down offers to advertise some Indian fashion brands on Instagram. I AM NOT AN INFLUENCER, the post was titled, in capital letters, and went on to argue that social media, though terribly compromised by brand capitalism and the right wing, could still be an agent of positive change.

No boyfriends seemed to lurk anywhere, though the first autosuggestion for you on Google search was 'Alia Omar boyfriend', but who was the untagged man with a trunk-ish neck and muscular legs in shorts, climbing a cliff face? As I relearned during those days of rapt looking and swelling desire, a 'true' story needs to be unfaithful to reality in order to seduce.

I learned for the first time that the internet's glut of representations can heighten the mystery of the represented. Escaping from a house of illness, and into those funhouse mirrors of your social media, I felt myself both more restless and more fulfilled than I had been in years.

When one has missed something utterly vital from one's life, the hardest part is not being able to identify what's missing. Perhaps, this is the true definition of a damaged life: not knowing what can make it whole, and thinking that ten thousand fucks, expensive fellatio, a suite at the Pierre, a Greek-revival mansion in East Hampton, or intellectual and literary glory could be permanent modes of self-fulfilment.

My own illusions in this regard came later than Aseem's and Virendra's. They developed in your company; and claimed, unconscionably, an innocent victim in you. If I write today in detail about our time together, of which you would have different memories, it is because I hope to understand the nature of my malady, my incapacity for the different, healthier life that you gave me a glimpse of.

When we met again, it was at Hotel Kipling. The lobby seemed abandoned, as usual, to giant paintings of indomitable Pathan tribesmen and their resilient British foes. Walking through it in your knee-high boots, you, too, conveyed an impression of vitality and endurance.

I saw one of my mother's ex-helpers, and the question – what is she doing here? – was answered as she came to our table with a bottle of mineral water and filled up our glasses, smiling shyly at me.

I caught myself staring at your soft, elegant hand on the table. It was all a bit strange: a very beautiful woman was sitting before me, in Ranipur of all places, and I couldn't quite remember how it had come about.

Your abundant images on Google may have over-stimulated me; I noticed for the first time that, turning your head with its coiled weight of hair to one side, querying our nervous waitress, or looking straight ahead at me, your looks constantly reconfigured themselves.

I had, however, been misinformed about your plans. You had not moved to Ranipur, and were there only briefly, long enough to complete your villa's renovation. You were going back to London soon.

I remember how you said, 'London is really nice. It's *the* place for a writer. By the way, any time you go there you can stay at my family's flat. It's vacant when I am away and available for friends; we never Airbnb it.'

I was unexpectedly wounded to hear you were leaving soon for London; but then surprised and moved by your quick assumption of friendship – and flattered to be attached, however lightly, to a life of such enigmatic plenitude.

Your openness provoked indiscretion. We began to talk of Aseem.

You said, 'He tends to exaggerate, doesn't he? I mean, none of Obama's ancestors were slaves.' And I wondered why you hadn't contradicted him at the time, and had even said 'fascinating' to him.

We talked, too, about Aseem's novels.

They were sexy, you said, with a shrug.

'I mean, they actually feature sex, so unlike the priggish Indian novels I have read.'

You added: 'Although, the novel I read had a very male gaze, wanting a woman to submit to the narrator, to be under his physical spell. Very pre Me Too. You can't write about women like that any more.'

I wasn't listening. I had looked for references to Aseem on your Instagram, going deep back into the years, the quality of the images steadily deteriorating, and had been relieved to find none. I now found the word 'sexy' so disconcerting, especially for being accompanied by the shrug Aseem had remarked on, that I launched, disloyally, into a critique that I never offered to him.

The previous day the postman, plodding slowly down the orchard, had brought a thick parcel containing the manuscript of his new novel, about a Dalit student based on Virendra and his radicalisation, and I had wondered if I could somehow avoid that predictable encounter with one of his garrulous narrators of sex, politics and crime.

I now contrasted the soft-spoken apprentices of Beckett, Walser and Kafka, those connoisseurs of failure I translated, to his noisily flamboyant storytellers. I compared the Indian storyteller in English, more specifically Aseem and his publicity networks, with my experimental Hindi writers with their tiny but loyal and respectful readership.

I was unwilling for us to have Aseem in common, and I suspect that all that I said about him in my hesitant English came out somewhat pompously, tainted with resentment.

Nevertheless, you leaned forward to catch my words, one hand cradling your chin.

'Yeah,' you said, leaning back in your chair, 'he's very, very smart, and politically totally spot on but, as I said, a bit old-school, even when it comes to literature.'

You rolled your eyes when I told you that Aseem referred to women as 'chicks'.

'Is he for real? But that's exactly, what I mean! That's so nineteen sixties!'

We started to talk about London. I had been there only once, on a month-long translation fellowship, when I would take the bus every day from my B&B in Kentish Town to Bloomsbury, and I started to expand on my love for something I had only experienced briefly: London buses.

I said I preferred the solitude and spaciousness of buses over the underground trains foraging through the topsoil. I was being utterly sincere. To me, an alien city had suddenly become attractive after I clambered up the twisting staircase to the top deck, and saw from there London's glossy green cover, the weeping elms, the flaking plane trees, the crows streaking across the sky, and the roses in private gardens.

Cautious, careful in every word and movement, when we first met at your villa, I seemed to have become verbose over-night; and I worried, as I spoke, that I was boring you. I learned later that you did not much use public transport in London – the Tube occasionally, buses, never.

You seemed to always have a slightly aloof, preoccupied look. And then you smiled a little lopsided smile, leaning back in your chair.

Someone near the reception asked in a booming voice, 'What is the wi-fi password?' And then immediately: '*Stop* that, stop that *now*.'

We talked of our setting, and again I may have been seeking too much to impress, too eager to pour into you the mass of unshared thoughts and feelings I accumulated during my solitude in the village.

We talked about the future of the village. Did you sense how keen I was for you to see what I saw?

Small places like Ranipur, I said, had to find their own equilibrium; maybe get better with the help of new technologies at what they have always done well: small-scale industries, agriculture, horticulture. I brought up Devdutt. I told you about Naazku.

You hadn't heard it in your villa, but the evening before, the village had erupted into noise, the barking and yelping of dogs followed by human cries. I learned from Naazku later that a wolf had attacked a calf in one of the backyards on the edge of the village, while its owners were having supper a few feet away, and had all but carried it off. At the cowardly din from the dogs, some men had leapt out of their homes with lathis and had won the calf back, dead, its side ripped open.

We talked about the environment, how deforestation and overdevelopment were making the animal population desperate for food and water.

'You should tell all this to my brother,' you said. 'He is one of these bankers who think of India as a goldmine with its young urbanising and modernising population. He said he would walk past Occupy protestors and quietly gather up spit in his mouth. He said the fools had no idea how capitalism was bringing hundreds of millions of people out of poverty.'

I found myself lapsing into a tirade against Mathur, who had recently made one of the aspirers I sent him wait for two hours outside his office, before dismissing him in less than a minute. I identified him as the main despoiler of Ranipur with his property development, whose sub-contractors, furthermore, worked tribal peoples into the ground while paying them a pittance, including those who helped rebuild your villa.

Your face scrunched up, and you spread your fingers across your mouth.

'Oh my God,' you said. 'I wish I knew that. That's just horrific.'

You started to grope in your bag. 'I am googling Mathur right away,' you said.

I dimly realised that I was being gauche as I went on about India's massive internal migration, the indigenous peoples expelled from their ancestral homes, and forced to seek work elsewhere, by the nexus of mining corporations, politicians and the police.

When I leaned forward to pick up my teacup I noticed that you had finished your research on Mathur and were looking at your Twitter feed.

Hastily putting away the phone, you said, 'What you were saying is so, so interesting and original. We never have a view from the village in all that we talk about politics and economics. People complain about the growing divide between the urban and rural areas, but the dominant viewpoints are that of the metropolitan elite. I wish you would write about this somewhere.'

Your response encouraged me. I imagined your brother on Wall Street and in East Hampton. I felt conscious of advancing a globally resonant argument, and I became more righteous.

You spoke about your brother with a satisfying frankness. 'He is really embarrassing in his views. He is a Muslim, of course, and yet he is convinced that Modi is the right leader for India. I wouldn't be surprised if he went to one of those huge rallies for Indian Americans that Modi does in the US.'

You also spoke very grippingly about your work with Amnesty in Sri Lanka.

You said, 'It was very stressful, banging your head against walls to get some basic facts about the treatment of Tamils.

I got so tired; I had to get away from the frustrated foreign NGO crowd to Galle every weekend to lie on the beach and get a massage.'

And when, towards the end – the bill settled by me without argument, another, more awkward smile exchanged with my mother's ex-helper, and a vague plan to meet again aired – you said, in your slightly bored manner, 'Hey, Arun, I meant to ask you for a huge favour. Aseem said you are such a brilliant reader, and I wondered if you would mind taking a look at a draft of my book? It's still very rough, but the main ideas are all there, I think. I would really love it if you could' – a vision emerged of us sitting on the blue sofa in your villa.

Mohit arrived, oddly capless, at my cottage later that same day with a printout of your draft. I read it intently over two days, annotating nearly every paragraph, and writing a long memo.

You had written in your proposal that you wanted your book to be a 'secret history' of globalisation, an 'intimate account' of the New India. I remember I told you that it hadn't yet found its internal rhythm, something that I looked for in all the books I chose to translate, and that your focus on the minute particulars of Virendra's and Siva's venality in the United States had been achieved at the cost of omitting their specifically Indian torments, especially the complex injuries of caste and class inflicted early on many successful men of their generation.

Those complicated facts about how Virendra and Siva defrauded the American system always struck me as the least interesting part of your narrative. Yet you had spent most of your time and energy on it, wishing to describe the inferno of greed and lawlessness that you said had existed on Wall Street since the 1980s.

The book needed to be radically reorientated, I felt; it

needed the details of our class backgrounds and moral and emotional lives I try to offer here. But you weren't curious about them, and I was too ashamed of those early humiliations, the small acts of violence at home and at IIT, to volunteer them to you. And so, while always keen to meet you for editorial discussions, I never made anything more than minor suggestions.

We met at Hotel Kipling one more time, awkwardly as I became aware, walking out of the hotel with you, of the underemployed young men slouching by the roadside; their eyes hovered around us as we approached, and pierced our backs as we went past, occasionally with a muttered remark I was happy not to catch.

I was relieved when you suggested your villa for our next meeting. Many dinners and drinks followed – occasions where Mohit, silently setting the table, clearing it, appearing and reappearing with gin and tonics on a tray, gingerly picking up ice cubes with silver pincers and dropping them into tall glasses where they splintered and smoked, seemed finally as neutered as a servant, and, sitting close to you on the blue sofa, in that living room where the sunlight pressing in from above magnified your skin, I smelled, every time you moved, a tiny cloud of what I would later recognise as Molton Brown shower gel.

On a visit to the toilet, I noticed your bedroom, bright and high-ceilinged, its view through plate glass of the valley as coldly elegant as the one from your living room; and, observing these routine luxuries (even water served with the small attentions of ice and a slice of lemon), that so exceeded anything in my own life, I marvelled again at the sureness of taste and indifference to money with which you had transformed the villa.

And, very quickly, I became so accustomed to the comforts

of your well-conducted villa that on certain nights, sitting on that blue sofa, I used to wonder how I could manage to tear myself away, to plunge into the darkness and walk down the long dead street of the village, back to the bachelor meanness of my cottage above a cowshed.

I was no longer nervous speaking in English. After years of my mother's inarticulate company, and brief instrumental exchanges with Devdutt and others, I was discovering the satisfaction of asserting ideas and opinions, of starting sentences with, 'I think', 'I believe' and 'I feel'; and I often caught myself listening to the sound of my own voice.

I was savouring, too, the pleasure of listening to you, those insights from your reading and travels, so different from mine, and often illuminating about a reality grown over-familiar to me. I remember one late evening on your lawn before a view of the serrated peaks, gin and tonics glowing in our hands in the failing light, when you turned to me and said, 'Don't you think it is wonderful that a single mountain is like a whole world in itself? It has so many different levels, all kinds of hidden places and unexpected sights and smells.'

There was a pause during which you went back to gazing at the silvery cones in the distance. You then added, 'Also, isn't it wonderful that there are many places in these mountains where no one has ever set foot? Right from the beginning of time, things have gone on, I mean, the sun has shone, and snow and rain have fallen, all very quietly, without anyone's knowledge.'

There was something entrancing about such perceptions, giving solidity to a self that on the internet seemed weightlessly radiant. Your eloquence, unlike Aseem's, cast its spell by being carefully rationed; and then there was the way you spoke, calmly and gently, as though confiding a long-cherished secret to an intimate.

So protective I became of my new alternative life that once I almost asked you to keep my visits between us. But I could not find the words, and it occurred to me later that the request would have been superfluous: we knew no one in common apart from Aseem, who lived hundreds of miles away. I could never bring myself to tell my mother about you. I was the son who had chosen to stay by her side, and, no matter how unselfish her affections, or unprejudiced her mind, it did not seem fair to suddenly confront her, while she lay ill, with a rival from another religion and class. And the secrecy gave the glow of the forbidden and sinful to our meetings, something I found myself exulting in.

FaceTime? you texted one day. And when I said I did not have an iPhone or MacBook, you texted back: *Skype?* And I Skyped for the first time from my cottage, sitting on the balcony with a view of the valley, marvelling at how what belonged to me could be shared instantaneously with everyone.

When your phone would ring in the middle of a conversation, and you excused yourself and walked away with it, I would begin to speculate, and then pity myself for assuming that a woman like yourself would remain single.

And then you called one evening while I was helping Naazku move my mother from the balcony to her room. 'I've been thinking about you all day,' you said in a warm voice, and I had to tuck the phone between my shoulder and my head. 'You have really helped me figure out what I am doing.'

By the time you hung up, I had finished my chore, and I stood for a while in my mother's room, staring at the thinning top of her head.

A text arrived the next day: *I love watching how your brain works. I can actually hear the crackle of the circuits.* Texts from you arrived nearly every hour after that, some longer than others; my eyes swam over them before they focused, and then I read and reread them many times, especially the one that said, *Sorry to be so keen! I feel like a hungry person who suddenly has a full meal in front of her.*

I agonised a long time over how I should respond, what I should say to avoid looking staid and cautious, before, still uncertain, I finally texted back, *That's really very kind of you. Please believe me, it's a great pleasure to engage with your book.*

When my screen remained blank, I walked all the way to the village bazaar, closer to the mobile phone tower, to check if I had missed any texts. I was not in the least tired by these uphill treks, buoyed by the feeling that something new, unusual and important had entered my life.

There were annoying interruptions: another trip to the doctor in Shimla with my mother in Sood's Scorpio, during which, negotiating a high step, her walker broke. Her latest helper, always reluctant, became more insistent on leaving.

I rang Aseem to ask for help in finding a source of trained helpers or nurses in Delhi. I shouldn't have expected him to understand my urgency: he had defused any potential anxiety about his own mother by reconfiguring her as a monster, vain, greedy and hypocritically religious.

He said he would look into it. He asked me if I had got around to reading his new novel. I said I had been a bit busy.

He said, 'It's my best, I think. Everything I know about the novel and the world is in it. I also sent it to Alia – I think it might give her some sense of where we all came from . . .'

He went on and I half-listened as I peeled off a yellow thread, probably from my mother's sewing machine, sticking to my fly, wondering if you had noticed it on our last meeting.

As though divining my thoughts, he asked if I had seen you; he said you had called him to get my telephone number.

I admitted that I had.

'Good work,' he said. 'I have a feeling she is looking for a man like you: sensitive and intellectual. She has had her flings with randy men her age. Now in her mid-thirties she needs a mature lover.'

Despite the sombreness of the moment, the deathless adolescent in Aseem re-emerged. 'And please score on my behalf. What are the hills and forests for if not some shagging under the trees and in the bushes?'

He went on in this tiresome vein, and I wonder now if his paeans to limitless erotic possibility came from the ageing Lothario in him, pursued and maddened by the fear of missing out; if, unnoticed by me, his inner climate had long been darkening.

I started to protest, but then had to stop. My heart was pounding as ridiculously hard as it had when you asked, earlier that afternoon, while discussing your book over WhatsApp, if I would like to 'get away for a few days to someplace warm'.

'Yes, yes, that would be lovely,' I mumbled, though in the bathroom to which I retreated to ponder your words in privacy, leaning both hands on the sink, I looked at the mirror and found myself suddenly voluptuously at peace.

I hadn't simply invented the significance of our relationship, and that the small signs of reciprocity I had started to see from you had been no deranged fantasy of mine.

I was not only calmer when I rang Aseem a few days later; I felt a delicious tingling – erotic, but mixed in with an expectation of discovery, almost a spiritual enlargement – as I gave him the same shaky lie that I had given my mother: that I was going to a conference in Chennai on translation and émigré writing. And, oh, did he know of a nice place on the coast nearby I could visit for the weekend?

Uneasy memories now stir: of my mother, molar-less, masticating strenuously and audibly, her scalp showing between a wilderness of grey hair. And I am feeling more and more annoyed: her unconditional love for me, sustained through her infirmity, has begun to repulse me slightly.

It strikes me that she has always shown towards me the same docility she showed towards my father. She never sat opposite me at the dining table and I am now irritated by how, despite her inability to cook, she still insists on waiting on me, instructing Naazku from her bed to put some more sabji on my plate. Why had she so meekly accepted her subservience to men, her husband and then her son, cooking for them, making sure they ate well and before her?

I am also irritated by small things that had never bothered me in the past, such as the beads of sweat on her upper lip, and the noises – groans and sighs and grunts – she makes when she moves. The sight of women's undergarments – huge, fawn-coloured – spread across a neglected small chair in my mother's room makes me scold Naazku with a severity that shocks her.

She has been busy, she says, quite reasonably: I only have to look out of the window to see the unbroken sea of grass of late summer, some of it mowed and raked, but much still there, heaving in the gentlest of breezes, awaiting her humble sickle.

I catch Naazku later looking at me with a sad, wondering expression, and I feel my irritation rise.

One afternoon I see my mother lying face downward on her bed, her little shoulders gently shaking. When I come back late at night from your villa, tipsy from the gin and tonics, my shoes all wet from the dew in the grass, my mother is still awake; I hear her softly sobbing as soon as I step inside.

I lie on my bed visualising the moment when, slowly walking down the avenue of firs to your villa's iron gate, my arm touched yours, touched and separated until we stopped, and you said goodnight. I compile an inventory of scenes in which you sit or stand close to me, seeking confirmation that you are no longer indifferent to me.

I try to read concealed meanings in your most trivial words; embellish perfectly innocuous things you have said; imagine conversations in which I shine.

But it is a long time before my mother settles down, and I so want to linger in my state of hopeless longing – more seductive for seeming unquenchable – that I almost yell at her.

The whole time I feel as though I am watching the scene from afar, watching and disgusted by my own heartlessness. Sometimes, I even grow resentful at how your presence in Ranipur extorts constant and exhausting attention from me; at how much work I do to dispose you favourably towards me. Is all this really fitting for a man in his late forties? And what is it leading to anyway?

One morning, I continue examining my face from different angles in the rust-edged mirror in the bathroom, wondering if Aseem's comparison of my looks to Dharmendra's still holds, even as my mother's helper keeps knocking loudly on the door – she tells me when I finally open it that my mother has lost control of her bladder.

But I can't help myself. Images of you keep returning to me; and that only deepens my self-disgust.

The thought of your life before you met me, and the life you lead far away from Ranipur, the thought of my total exclusion from them, is peculiarly piercing. And I flinch inwardly when I remember your casual mention that you are heading soon to London, *the* place for a writer, as you called it, to work on your book.

I mock myself for assuming even briefly that someone as young and vital and worldly as you would bury herself in a remote Himalayan village. Still, that you are leaving and would soon be gone is my first thought every morning. I imagine you driving away in your Pajero, for some reason at night, the tyres crunching the gravel, scattering small stones, and huge head-lights sweeping across the avenue, taunting the sleeping trees.

Strange new thoughts assail me: I have lost my twenties and thirties; I have been waiting all the time on the outskirts of life – for what?

I still read and write, but with difficulty, as there is some-thing suddenly unpleasant about passively following other people's lives. I want too much to live myself.

The days on which I don't see you seem particularly bereft of promise. The cottage suddenly feels too small, its ceiling too low; my room, unchanged in more than a decade, seems like a prison. There is faint reproach now in the warmth and tang of cow dung. I worry that it lingers on my clothes when I am in proximity to you; and I am seized more and more by the desire to break free.

But I don't know how until you suggest, with staggering simplicity, a trip 'someplace warm'.

Thirteen

There are so many things I could not confide in you when we first came together and must now rehearse: my mother's illness, my growing urge to escape my responsibilities, and the relief compromised by guilt that I knew during so much of our time together. I also never told you that it was Aseem who, when asked to suggest someplace warm, recommended Pondicherry.

He had visited it after seeing a beautified version of the town in *Life of Pi*, and was still enchanted by its feel of a small French colony in the tropics, the clean, calm boulevards, the high walls green-shuttered and blank against the intense sun. He even recommended the yoga retreat on the beach we stayed at.

Do you remember the receptionist with severely pulled-back grey hair and large disappointed eyes? She looked intently into our faces and I suddenly became conscious of performing in a scene that many people had enacted before – a man with a younger woman of a higher caste or different religion checking in as a married couple.

'You are not married?' the receptionist said as she abruptly turned her back to us, and, without waiting for my reply, started to Xerox, the flesh on her forearms wobbling, my Aadhaar card and your American passport.

'Do you think she is a Hindu fanatic?' you whispered in my ear. 'And wasn't this a hangout for hippies and free love once?' I felt a promising pressure of your fingers on my hand; and the gleam of something elegantly wild in your eyes as you smiled at me seemed to link us in some wonderful delinquency.

I had felt a similar flare of illicit excitement on the concourse outside Delhi airport when you suddenly placed two fingers on my shoulder as you glanced backward and downward. It was a dead spruce needle that your heel had transfixed in Ranipur and carried all the way to Delhi; you scraped it off with the tip of your car key, while pressing tighter on my shoulder, and a dark ringlet fell from your mass of hair.

Intermittently touching forearms on the flight from Delhi to Chennai made me more nervy than expectant; my eyes grazed a paragraph in the book I was reading a dozen absent times. And there was something displeasing about the heads that swivelled to check you out as you walked down the aisle to the toilet in your tank top and jeans, and kept turning at the carousel until that intriguing suitcase of yours – retro-modern with metal edges and snappy silver locks, covered with traces of luggage labels – came around.

But, driving from Chennai airport to Pondicherry, watching egrets hop in the rice terraces, I had felt my heart kick.

For weeks in Ranipur, we seemed to have been moving towards each other. There was no turning back, not after you booked the room at the retreat in our names; and, though I had kept wondering how inadequate against your ample and recent erotic experience would be my memory of ardent but long past encounters with the woman in South Extension, or whether habits of private make-believe and gratification had unfitted me for reciprocity in love, in that new landscape of gently sloping hills and young rice and banana, the clean light a prodigal change after smoggy Delhi, I had started to relish the feeling that the last of my anxieties – of leaving home, of travel – lay behind, and that a long-awaited adventure was imminent.

Alighting from the chilled air of the car at the beachside, the backs of our hands brushed for a moment; and in my state of excitement, the luxurious feeling, almost, of an elopement, I seemed to register everything: the sky and sea babyishly blue, the white gulls chasing one another, and the gardener with the leaking watering can tracing a zigzag moistness on the red clay.

As it turned out, the receptionist told us to wait; our room was one of the few being photographed for the retreat's updated website.

Leaving the chairless lobby, and the garden, where inmates from the care home next door sat in their wheelchairs, quiet and morose, we walked to the beach, and settled down on the sand. Arms around our knees, we watched the sea tug impatiently at the golden sand, suddenly shy with one another under the high and open sky.

A very tanned French lady behind us glacially smeared her flesh with suntan lotion. A piebald dog with a dirty tail stood before her and watched, its tongue hanging out. From somewhere to the east came the irritating sputtering of a two-stroke boat engine being started; and the pigeons cowering in some plastic trash under a cement bench surged into the sun.

A skinny little boy in a sleeveless vest brought out a tray of filter coffee from a shack behind us to a horde of young men, day-trippers from Chennai, who were taking turns to glance, ferret-like, at you.

As the brass tumblers were eased from hand to hand, and coffee poured into davaras, the boy said something in Tamil that made all of the men cackle and turn towards us with bold mocking grins.

Their hateful mirth was typical of everything that was making me tense; and in the coffee boy's sidelong sneer as he walked away there was something of the rudeness that the low-born reserve for those they recognise as their peers.

Determined to stare him down, I watched him return,

jauntily swinging his shiny steel tray between thumb and fore-finger, to the shack of rusty tin and rotting wood and faded Pepsi Cola signs; he then suddenly reeled and the tray fell to the ground with a prolonged clatter: some unseen man, the shop-owner probably, had slapped him.

'Which do you like most,' you were asking, 'the mountains or the sea?'

'The mountains, no question,' I replied, adding falsely, 'that's where I have spent most of my life.'

When you turned away, I thought about the less banal and more truthful things I could have said. My shirt felt sticky on my back. The dog suddenly barked. I looked around for the coffee boy. Why had I become fixated with him? I felt a bit ashamed of the twinge of gratification I had felt as his cheeki-ness was brutally punctured.

I began to think of Sarita, my mother's new helper, whom I had left untrained and jittery in Ranipur. A teenage girl from a nearby village, she broke or dropped nearly everything she touched. She trembled if asked to do anything; and her fright-ened eyes seemed to say, 'Do you think I can cope?'

I went back to worrying about how I would appear to you, in my swim shorts or unclothed, bearing an unfamiliar body under a familiar head, a well-made but unexercised body that, more than my face, would make me seem blandly avuncular to a younger woman; how you would regard this concealed self, shorn of its wrappings.

After a while, you took out your phone. Your sunglasses kept slipping as you looked down at it; and you would push them up with a knuckle.

You had only recently told me about your thousands of Twitter trolls, the mildest of whom called you a 'jihadi bitch', and though you seemed blasé about this routine barrage of slurs – 'You have to take this stuff in your stride,' you said, 'if you are a Muslim woman and politically engaged. I am suspicious of people who make too much drama out of this; there are much worse victims out there' – I braced myself inwardly every time you looked at your phone.

But something on your screen was making you smile, repeatedly, and the curve of your nostril alternately stretched and tightened.

You suddenly turned and aimed the camera at me.

'Smile, please!'

In the photo, which caught me halfway to a smile, the French sunbather, the stray dog and the day-trippers were a blur.

You finally put the phone back in your bag, and stretched out on the sand, your hands beneath your head, your feet extending to the sea in delicate white sandals, the toenails painted pink.

A kite kept rustling overhead. Swooping down at us once, it abruptly rose again to frighten the drifting gulls. A man in broad fluttering pyjamas and Hawaii chappals of pink plastic crossed the horizon trailed by a small monkey. The man paused briefly to look at the sea; his enchained animal immediately started to catch fleas on himself, twisting his head to bite at them.

How slowly time moves when you are waiting for something to begin.

I thought of your insight about mountains and tried to say something equally interesting: 'You know, I was thinking of what you said the other day about those secret places in the mountains. It's strange to think that thousands more years will pass and billions of people will live and die, and those places will still exist and no one will learn their secret.'

'Yes, that's so true,' you said, looking up at the sky.

I don't know what I was trying to convey, yet carried on.

'So true,' you said again.

Some more time passed. The sun went behind a thick grey cloud. The seaweed-laden waves that came creeping up the sand looked sullen; and I felt that we were reaching that point when the momentum to something long prepared fizzles out, and you are left wondering what to do and how to restart.

'I feel a bit thirsty,' you said, and I wondered if I had it in me to ask the coffee boy for a bottle of Bisleri.

A few minutes later, you brought out your phone again.

You scrolled through something for a while, still smiling secretly, your sunglasses slowly slipping down your face.

'KashmiriMuslimTraitors is trending, I have to tweet about this,' you said. As you typed with your thumbs, your feet curved into each other to form a fan, the pink-nailed toes all tensed up.

Afterwards, you took off your sunglasses and turned your intelligent, clear eyes towards me. 'It's so horrible,' you said, 'what this country is doing to Kashmiris. Much, much worse than what Israel does to the Palestinians, and nobody cares.'

You spoke in a note that was weary and aggrieved and I found myself saying, 'It really is,' even as I felt dread of this unpromising and lowering subject and wished it to go away.

I knew you looked at the news obsessively, several times an hour, as though knowing what was getting worse all the time could forestall the worst, and you assumed that I did the same. I did not, and in fact felt churlishly your political concerns to be depriving me of something important – your full attention and interest.

You began to relay, now with an accusing look, the news from Kashmir and its analysis that had so upset you, and I found myself uttering the usual commonplaces about remote atrocities while avoiding your eyes, and worrying, again, that you would one day discover and judge me for my lack of political passion.

It was after an hour of stop-start conversation and quizzical half-smiles that we staggered into our room with our luggage and some fine sand, to find inside two narrow single beds meant for celibate yogis.

Pillowless, they looked, with their tucked thin white spreads, as smooth and forlorn as marble sepulchre.

The humid heat that had been trapped inside all afternoon – and, perhaps, the expectancy in the air now – made sweat roll down our faces. Opening the stiff door on to the balcony, admiring the view, reading the list of instructions on what to do in case of a fire, scrutinising the framed photo of the 'Mother', the retreat's founder, or even finding the missing pillows in the wardrobe, we looked anywhere except at the two downcast beds.

Later that afternoon I watched as you lay smoking on one of them, wearing a gingham bikini, below a long-stalked, furiously spinning ceiling fan. You were looking at the photo of the 'Mother' on the wall.

An elderly Frenchwoman with large, slightly protruding teeth, darkened eyes, and an embroidered scarf over her head, she called us to a life of earnestness and probity from every corner; her angular face was engraved on all things, from towels to writing paper and coffee mugs and the flypaper that hung from a solitary nail and twirled slowly under the draught from the frenzied fan.

Defying her summons to virtue, you blew perfect smoke rings, and, still holding up your tanned arm, watched the smoke eddy and thin in the sunbeam that cut the room in two while your other arm lay still on the bed, the hand open and upturned, as though to a fortune-teller.

It occurred to me that I had found something to replace my

earlier visions of happiness: standing as a boy at dusk, amid sounds of crickets and the muted barks of dogs, at the nullah near my home, or the afternoon in a remote Himalayan valley, where peaks of snow and ice stretched for miles under pure light, and crows with their guttural exclamations emphasised the silence everywhere.

Life had yielded another flawless moment, unexpectedly in the midst of anxieties about my mother. Lightheaded with the sense of having got away with it, I resolved to remember everything in it: the heat and light of the late afternoon, the sea lazily shuddering, as though there was all the time in the world, and behind me the room with red-brick walls, the twitchy flypaper, the velvety brown of your skin, and the heart-shaped tattoo on the untanned flesh below your belly.

I resolved never to forget how I woke up from a post-shower nap to find the bathroom door open, you bent over the basin, in a kimono, rinsing your mouth; how you, meeting my reflection in your mirror, shouted, 'You can't come in here!' but then had turned and walked over to my single bed, leaned down, and embraced me as though you were my wife, as though you had held me, both softly and fiercely, many times before, one hand pressing into the small of my back; and how I had embraced you, too, with the same long-established intimacy, while first smelling on your cool body the shower gel you always carried with you.

During this initial intimacy, made clumsy by my disbelief that it was happening at all, we almost lost our balance. You giggled and said you had to go to the bathroom quickly. The toilet flushed with a growl, and when you finally came out, your kimono seemed more tightly belted than before.

There was more embarrassed giggling when we slid off my single bed and had to push ourselves back on. I became aware of a trembling in my legs and was livid with myself. Then, neither of us had any condoms; and the nearest pharmacy turned out to be on the Indian side of the town, reminiscent, as I trudged through its narrow lanes in the heat, of my childhood bazaar setting.

In one barber stall of rough packing-case wood tottering over an exposed gutter, a stubbly chin was being deliciously rubbed with a crystal of alum. A stray dog that lay on its side, its ginger coat wetly black, lifted its head and turned its humid eyes at me.

The unhealthily obese teenager at the open-fronted pharmacy, who wore a Hawaiian shirt and multiple fat rings on his fingers, leered as he gave back my change (or had I imagined it?); and an impatient autorickshaw trip back to the yoga retreat managed to achieve precisely what it was intended to avoid: it made me perspire all over again.

After another shower back at the room, I spent some time scraping up with my fingernail a long hair stuck to the tiny bar of Cinthol soap supplied by the retreat. The tendril, assuming a different curve each time I tried to claw it free, refused to come off. Green, dry soap collected under my fingernails, and tiny drops of sweat beaded my forehead.

But I remember, too, how the air in the room was thick with heat and earthen smells that late afternoon when you turned around on the bed, pushed your thick hair away from your eyes and took my face in your hands. With gentle fingers and thumbs you seemed to measure my features; and the gesture was so startling – nobody had touched my face in years – that I almost prised away your fingers.

Out in the still, somnolent heat, fishing boats hovered at the rim of the glittering sea. Later that afternoon, however, I woke up to a steady soft incessant noise from beyond the open door to the balcony: rain.

Everything had darkened and grown lonely. Your severely

made-up bed had gone back to resembling a tomb. Where had you gone?

From the balcony, now gloomily damp, I saw a small crowd on the beach, men huddled under black umbrellas, some squatting on the sand, gazing attentively at something.

It was the corpse of a drowned man, as I discovered, when, after futilely waiting for you to return, I decided to go out in the now very thin drizzle. Seaweed trailed across the back of his white shirt and khaki trousers, and a miniature dead silvery fish clung to his shoeless but soggily socked feet. A young fisherman in a white lungi poked tentatively at the sock with a stick before two gendarmes in French-style kepis who had silently arrived among us told him to desist.

It was high tide, and the white surf crashed and hissed a few feet away. Shells peeped up from the thongs of seaweed on the sand. The sea was grey, with a blurred horizon. A strong breeze blew; the coconut palms swayed and rustled and crackled; and the piebald dog ran this way and that, soaking wet, as though deciding whether to bark.

At the coffee shack, some men on scooters and mopeds had stopped by the police jeep to gawk, huddled under anoraks dripping with water. I recognised the coffee boy with the steel tray, still and sombre now under a leaking roof.

A local bus from Chennai slowed down as it passed; passengers at the windows craned their necks to spot the action, and then recoiled from the spray. A police jeep arrived, with more gendarmes, and the gawkers started their scooters and quickly scattered as the men in kepis started asking around for witnesses.

An ambulance ablaze with red and blue appeared, together with the gloomy truck from the morgue, and stood agitatedly for a few seconds, before, sirens still blaring, it disappeared into the mist.

A man, someone shouted unexpectedly in Hindi, had been seen wading into the sea an hour ago, carrying a beer bottle in his hand.

The police ordered the spectators to disperse, though the fishermen among them were already shuffling back, holding up their lungis, to their homes: shacks of unplastered hollow clay bricks and unpainted timber, which jostled right up to the sea, and to which – it was four p.m. now – uniformed school-children with canvas satchels and ribbon-tied hair began to trickle back across the sand.

Back at the room, you barely looked up from your computer as I came in, my hair damp from the drizzle, my shoes crunchy with wet sand. I was full of what I had seen and was about to tell you all about it in a rush when I heard Aseem's baritone.

You were transcribing the video recording of the interview you had done with him in Ranipur a few weeks earlier, on the day he introduced me to you. There was Aseem on your iPad's screen, sunk in a leather armchair, looking at ease, completely indifferent to the camera focused on him.

'My young relations,' Aseem was saying, 'love to ask me about life way back when. They have grown up living in five-star comfort. They can barely believe me when I say that we had no gas and no running water. We had coal stoves in our kitchen – *angeethi*, we used to call them. The kids had to fan the fires, and then duck to avoid the flying embers. One of us had to collect the ash, which was then used to clean the brass utensils.'

He never worried, as I did, that reminiscences of scarcity might bore or disconcert you.

'But you know what?' Aseem continued. 'Life was simpler – and richer. I am homesick for that simplicity. Life is too full of distractions and anxieties now. The world is too much with us, as the poet said.'

I can't say I wanted Aseem in my line of vision just then. In fact, I realised I resented his presence on that momentous day. Earlier that afternoon, we had both been too nervous, too unaccustomed to the new selves the act required, to make love well. It didn't seem to matter, for we had made a start, and we seemed together in unsatiated desire.

But you were no longer the woman I had known just a while ago. Bent over your MacBook, a serious expression on your face, you had entered what you called your 'work mode'.

'People like us have to be very careful,' you had told me not long after Aseem introduced us. 'We really need to have a project in hand at all times and work hard. I know I am one of them, but I hate the rich Indian kids who spend all their time on Twitter and Instagram. The rich should work hard like everyone else whether or not they are interested in political change.'

I had found the sentiment fresh and admirable like so much else about you. Yet as I stood rooted behind the waves and curlicues of your hair as you typed, I kept flexing my big left toe in that space in my damp shoe where I had found a snug thistleball the day before.

You typed fast and hard; your keyboard – you said it was one of Apple's worst ever – approximated the urgent and assertive noise of a typewriter; and you paused only to push your hair back from your face.

'Aseem speaks like a book, in clear long sentences,' you said, without looking up, 'which is great for a researcher.'

I stood and tried to listen, but while Aseem was speaking of the New India my mind wandered to a humid police station, where a policeman sitting under framed portraits of a toothlessly grinning Mahatma Gandhi and a sternly grey-bearded Narendra Modi is writing up a report in triplicate. He finishes with a sigh and slides one copy along with badly printed photo-graphs of the seaweed-smudged corpse and the autopsy report into a manila envelope marked 'unidentified dead bodies' and then pushes it into a metal filing cabinet overflowing with envelopes.

On the iPad's screen, you started to arrive at your main questions by asking Aseem about corporate sponsorship of his festival of ideas, especially his relationship with Virendra Das and Siva.

Aseem is primed to say what I heard from him on television soon after our IIT friends were arrested. I am sure the unvary-ing reply always left Aseem a bit uneasy – he knew how much he and his magazine owed to our rich friend Virendra, and you might know even more. Also, his connection with a convicted felon was likely to expose him more to Modi's wrath.

He seems to have the niggling awareness of survivors – of having behaved imperfectly to the dead and the disgraced. Trying to appear sincere as well as truthful, he retreats into platitude – strange, and revealing, how much of platitude makes up our public utterances.

He mentions the length of our friendships, he speaks of a grossly neglected human condition, which consists of a basic struggle for humanity – he is warming up for some of his favourite locutions. He quotes Chekhov, and goes on to Naipaul.

I think again of the man with the beer bottle, pushing out into the ocean, the subcontinent receding behind him, and then suddenly going under a big breaker, and I have a moment of lucid panic: the whole world is being slowly washed away and he was among the first to be washed away with it.

I see on the edge of the screen that you are groping for a pack of cigarettes on the floor. Aseem rises from his armchair – to offer you a light he doesn't have? You get to your feet, too, and I then see you both in the frame.

Aseem stands very close to you, looking keenly at your face with his dark eyes, as though inspecting your bones; you sway back a bit, move towards the camera with one hand out-stretched, and the screen goes blank.

Fourteen

Aseem was fond of saying (or quoting – not sure where this was from): 'We all live inside stories, and when one story ends, another begins. The trick is to find what constitutes that story and have the power to confront your fate.'

But how does one story end and another begin? What made me abandon my mother in Ranipur and follow you to Pondicherry, that setting of white sand, sunlit breakers and blue sky beyond criss-crossed coconut trunks, which seemed as stylised as an Instagram post, and in which I, too, appeared, in the beach photos you took on your new Pixel, as characterlessly smooth, while the drowned man, the urchin with the steel tea tray, the French lady and the voyeuristic day-trippers from Chennai blurred into the background?

We may all live inside stories, but it seems better to exit them while we still can.

The helper Sarita was one sign that I was failing. Aseem had said he could get me a trained nurse from Delhi. But no one from the big metropolis really wanted to work in a Himalayan village. And Sarita had a very different idea of the work she was supposed to do.

Devdutt had said, an unexpected tone of anger in his voice, 'Yeh Dalit log kaam nahin karna chahtey hai. Unke badey dimaag hain. These Dalits don't want to work. They have high ideas about themselves.'

I hadn't wanted to deal with his prejudice just then. It had not been a good year for apples, and the slight frown of doubt that appeared on Devdutt's face in late spring had kept intensifying.

I emerged from the third afternoon in Pondicherry with you to find seven missed calls on my silenced phone.

When I finally reached Sarita, after a few 'the number you have dialled is not in service' messages, she was near-hysterical.

Why had I not picked up the phone? she wanted to know.

What could I say? That I had yet again spent the morning in one of the little coves that indented the coast near our yoga retreat. In that air thick with the smell of hot conifer needles, and silence broken only by the sawing and scraping cicadas, I had watched you swim.

At midday, we had walked along steep, stony paths, through an air still and thick with the smell of pine, back to our room at the retreat. It was cool and shady after the hot glare, and three more euphoric hours had passed there before I picked up my phone and noticed the missed calls.

'Main nahin kar sakti hoon,' Sarita said, 'yeh kaam mere liye nahin hai. I can't do this. This work is not for me.'

She had washed the rug three times already but could not get rid of the stain. Nor had the sandalwood incense sticks, taken from my mother's altar, worked against the smell. The chair would have to be thrown away.

The worst aspect was that my mother had sat in the evidence of her loss of control for a couple of hours, while Naazku went shopping in the bazaar for vegetables, and Sarita waited for the new gas cylinder to arrive.

'Unhone kuch bhi nahin kiya, kewal baithi rahin, gandh main. She did nothing about it. She just kept sitting there in the stench.'

I thought of my mother, trapped in her low-bottomed, armless cane chair, unable to rise to her feet, and waiting to describe what had happened.

I was aware of you behind me in the room. Naked, you were doing stretches on your single bed, long legs drawn up to your breasts, and then slowly released.

That afternoon had started on the balcony with you asking me to massage your shoulders; and then, feeling my erection beat softly against your hips, we had moved inside.

In that room with the portrait of the Mother, on a bed that creaked a bit, you had seemed to derive a special rapture from the innocent sound of footsteps in the whitewashed corridor, and the voice, it turned out, of the receptionist in the garden speaking to a wheel-chaired elderly man.

Pacing restlessly the small balcony, I tried to point out the obvious to Sarita: that her ward's knees did not allow her to stand.

She seemed adamant.

'Aap koi aur intezam kijeye, Main nahin karoongi yeh kaam. Dalit hain to kya hua, hamari asmita bhi hai, ganda kaam thode karoongi. Please make some other arrangement. I can't do this. So what if I am a Dalit? I have my dignity. It doesn't mean that I can do such filthy work.'

You came up behind me silently. As if wishing to heighten your blasphemy, you pinched the slight layer of flab at my waist and whispered in my ear, 'How do you think that Hindu fanatic receptionist will react if she sees a nude Muslim woman molesting a sexy Brahmin?'

Absurdly and shamefully, I found myself whispering into the phone, 'Itni jaldi decide mat kijeye. Is kaam ke liye main aapko aur bahut paise doonga. Please don't decide in haste. I'll give you lots more money for this work.'

Fifteen

When the call came one afternoon in Pondicherry, I picked it up right away; I had forgotten to put the phone on airplane mode.

The number on my screen was of my landline in Ranipur. I assumed that it was Sarita. It was my mother.

Promising to be back in three days, I had stayed on a week, going over the unaccommodating receptionist's head, when she told us there was no room, to the North Indian manager, a sympathetic Brahmin, who found a cancellation.

And everything by then – the room with the ochre-red walls, the heat and glare of the afternoons, the sea invisibly thumping against the beach at night, caking the wrought-iron chairs in the balcony with salt, our nakedness, the way you so perfectly fitted in my arms – had started to feel natural, a continuation of a life I had long been living, something flowing directly and smoothly from your first texts to me in Ranipur.

So much so that a little before my phone started to vibrate, I had been researching, huddled around your MacBook on my bed, airline fares from Delhi to London, and screen-capturing them. I had checked my passport to see if my UK and Schengen visas, acquired a year before for a lecture trip my mother's health forced me to cancel at the last minute, were still valid, if I could accompany you to London on the same flight from Chennai via Frankfurt that you were taking.

Leaving Ranipur – my mother raised her head from her pillow in an effort to embrace me, her breath unfresh, and her hands gripped me hard on my arm, nails pinching through my jumper's heavy wool to my flesh – I had left a piece of paper with my number pinned under the telephone.

I did not expect her to call, for the simple reason that she never initiated a call, though the Bakelite sat on a cane stand right next to her bed.

When I called, she rarely picked up the phone, and, when she did, seemed eager to get away. I think she may have been afraid to admit that she was a little deaf.

'Beta, kaisa hai wahan par? What is it like there?' she now said.

'Yahan to bahut oley padey,' she added, running through her sentences.

There had been a hailstorm in Ranipur.

'Conference ho gayi?' she was asking.

What conference?!

With a start I realised she was referring to the lie I had told Aseem and her while planning my trip to Pondicherry with you.

I remembered how I had lain in bed late at night, slightly drunk, and thinking of you, while she sobbed in the room next to mine.

'Haan, achchi rahi. Yes, it was good,' I said.

Then, panicking, I asked, 'Sarita kaam pe aa rahi hai? Maine usko bataya ki main double paise doonga. Is Sarita coming to work regularly? I told her that I will pay her double.'

But she wasn't listening to me.

'Kya kar rahe ho? What are you up to?' she was asking, in that artificially high and fast voice of a rare telephone user running out of things to say.

My mind ran through very recent scenes with you, rejecting them all.

I suddenly felt guilty that my mother did not even know of

your existence and, even while telling myself to rectify this, knew that I couldn't and wouldn't.

'View ka anand le rahe hain, sundar hai, samudra aur akash and suraj ek saath. I am enjoying the view, it's very beautiful, the sea and sun and sky all together,' I finally said.

I remembered as I spoke that she had never seen the sea.

There was a pause. I imagined her silently straightening the small pictures of Hindu gods and goddesses and little books compiled from *Ram Charita Manas* that were crammed next to the phone beside her. She often passed entire afternoons lying on her side, with a hand under her cheek, gazing at a gaudy picture-card of Krishna or Gayatri, as it shook in the bones of her fingers.

'Naazku ne bataya . . . Naazku told me . . .' Her voice trailed off. What did Naazku tell her?

I felt she was waiting for me to say something, though she herself did not know exactly what.

Did she know something? We had left Ranipur separately in order to avoid speculation and gossip. Only Mohit had routinely seen you and me together. Had he told someone in the village, and had the information reached my mother?

And then I heard her say, 'Dhoop se bachkar rahna, Raju beta. Aur gehrey paani mein mat jana. Be sure to protect yourself from the sun, Raju beta. And don't go deep into the water.'

The gentle exhortation, rearing up from the depths of my childhood, from those idle afternoons when I set out for the nullah in my only pair of shorts and bush shirt, and returned to a tender scrutiny of my legs by my mother, went through me like a knife.

I heard a click. She had put the phone down.

My guilt quickly turned into a feeling quite like anger – ludicrously at her, as though she was to blame for not knowing what I was incapable of telling her.

And the impossible anger, feeding on itself, refusing to be placated, gushed inside me when, a minute later in the bathroom, I knocked my temple against the washbasin while recovering the top of a toothpaste tube that had fallen to the floor.

Two days later, I was hunched again over your MacBook after a hedonistic afternoon. We had spent another morning at the cove. I was always mesmerised by the way you set off over the pebbles towards the sea, your head aslant as you untied your hair, releasing it thickly over your bare long brown back: how you then stood, your ankles tensing, for a moment beside the calm water, tentatively splashing about in it with your feet, before wading ahead and, when immersed up to your hips, suddenly throwing back your black head, and falling forward decisively.

I marvelled at such moments, as you swam far out, at how a clean boyhood vision of beauty, smeared by solitary gratifications and cracked in a short-lived affair, a vision that seemed to belong to the past, had come to be embodied by a flesh-and-blood person before me – someone who now held out a possibility of companionship, of tenderness and passion, of living together, understanding and caring for one another, the possibility of what I was still too terrified to call 'love'.

Lying on my back, my eyes closed against the burning sun and the prickly silver of the sea, I recalled details of my sudden good fortune, until a lost ant scrambling nervously through my feet made me sit up, or you returned, dripping and glittering and squinting, to the rocky cosiness of the cove; and, shaking your hands free of water, gingerly picked up your Pixel to check what you had missed.

Back in our room, a few hours had passed that afternoon before I noticed that I hadn't switched off the airplane mode on my phone.

I did so now to find four missed calls from Devdutt.

A man of aloof dignity, he seemed to be strangely gasping as he came online.

Sarita had not shown up for days; Naazku was down with flu, and earlier that morning he had discovered my mother's body.

'Cottage bahut thanda tha, toh decomposition nahin hua. Lekin shareer ekdum sakht ho gaya tha, dhaini aankh badi mushkil se band hui, Shimla se jauhri bulakar unki sone ki ear-ring nikal wayi, Antim sanskar turant karne pada. The body had not decomposed due to extreme chill in the cottage. But it had gone totally stiff. I shut her right eye with great diffi-culty and had to call a jeweller from Shimla to snip off her gold earrings. We had to cremate her right away.'

There was something in his tone, though it was really the horror of the revelation, and the memory, sudden and lan-cing, of my mother's telephone call, that made me want to close my eyes and look away.

'Ant main unko zyada peeda nahi hui. She didn't suffer much in the end,' Devdutt said.

I barely heard him.

Devdutt said, again, as though wishing to console me, 'She didn't suffer much in the end.'

How did he know that? But I had to control my surge of irritation. He, after all, had made the horrific discovery.

Devdutt said he would perform the chautha. Would I be able to make it? He had saved the ashes, he added, now openly sobbing. Perhaps I would like to go to Benares to immerse them in the Ganges?

For some reason, an image came to me from my only visit to Benares decades ago: the boat on the calm river on a misty morning, ghostly shapes of temples along the banks, and a marigold garland that had snagged on the stern rippling softly through the long silver rim of the wake behind me.

I heard a raised voice in my ear: Devdutt had started to blame the Dalit helper.

'In logon par bharosa nahi karna chaiye. Itihaas ke shahid bankar bade jurm karte hain. You cannot trust these people. They pose as martyrs of history while committing gross deeds.'

He was trying to work himself up, and also provoke anger in me. But I had ceased to listen to him.

Calendar pictures of Himalayan peaks, and images of nullahs, steam engines and Thums Up bottles, were streaming before my eyes: a whole world, unsung and long outlived, was passing with my mother.

The past, that solid ground on which I had tried to stand for so long, had finally slid from under my feet, and I was swinging free.

Devdutt uttered words, in-between longer snuffles, that I intermittently followed, something about how soon I could return, Baba being informed, and the cottage having to be fumigated.

'What happened?' I heard you ask behind me.

You were scrolling through Twitter on your single bed, waiting for me to finish my airfare research and give you back your MacBook.

'Nothing,' I said, pressing the end button on my phone. 'Nothing.'

It scarcely seemed like my own voice, so muffled and strange. You didn't notice, and I felt relieved that I had my back to you, and that no eyes would search my face for information.

I sat up spine-straight on my bed, my head high, as though doing so would relieve the warm mounting pressure behind my eyelids. And then I noticed the MacBook before me. Through teary eyes, a blurry picture clarified itself: my screenshots of flights to London.

Sixteen

Devdutt was puzzled when I told him that I wouldn't be attending either the chautha or the tehravi. He had just told me that Naazku and the girls my mother knew in the village were inconsolable. He seemed only slightly more understanding when I said that my father should not be invited, and that my sister was too burdened by work to travel to Ranipur.

You were sympathetic, despite the fact that you hadn't met my mother and I hadn't brought her up at all in our conversations. You claimed to understand, too, my decision to not make a painful return to Ranipur for the post-funeral ceremonies, and to go instead to London with you.

'I can only imagine your grief,' you said. And when you repeated this in the midst of the pensive silence – and abstinence – that I felt obliged to observe for a few days, I felt like raising my hand and telling you that I did not deserve such solicitude.

The sobbing and wailing mourners in Ranipur Devdutt told me about had found a way to express their grief. But I was discovering, whether in that room with the ochre-red brick walls and the framed photo of the Mother, where your fingers on the keyboard chattered away, or walking by myself on the empty beach after sunset, the sky still gashed with lurid vermilion and yellow, that I didn't really know how to mourn.

The mirror in the bathroom, which showed a middle-aged man with stubble and dark hollows under his eyes, insisted that this was what grief looked like. And you assumed I was feeling it intensely as you went to sleep at night with your hand lying lightly on my shoulder. More tortured emotions, however, kept assailing me.

I knew self-reproach, for being a bystander, increasingly remote, even repelled by her feebleness, as my mother faded. I felt, and resisted, an obscure sense deep within myself that I had betrayed her, had betrayed and dishonoured all her years of devotion to me. I felt I owed her something for all the sacrifices she had made in her life, and I was bewildered by my failure to give her even a pitifully belated tribute of grief.

But there was a new part of myself created by our intimacy, in addition to that deeper and older part that cares for nothing more than itself; and a voice kept insisting that I had done my duty to the woman who had died, and that it was time for me to live my own life.

Just when the glow of my time in Ranipur had dimmed, you had come along and brought me a kind of second youth – a recompense for my anxiety-ravaged first youth. How could I turn my back upon this miraculously retrieved moment of carefree vitality, this time out of time dictated by my own desires? After a life in which so much had been ordered externally by duties and responsibilities, how could I spurn the freedom to shape it to my satisfaction?

It seems crazy now: to embark upon a journey to the West, with only a few clothes, and many unmet responsibilities awaiting me at home, including books essential to my work. But, in the mood I found myself in, not examined, never revealed, the mood created by my exhilarating new life with you, which felt as though it could last for ever, no obstacle before me felt insurmountable: after all, the shops in Pondicherry and Chennai sold clothes, my visa was still valid, my credit and debit cards worked outside India, I could wire money to Devdutt instead of paying him rent by cash, and I could have the books I needed sent to me in London.

I felt weirdly committed to, even liberated by, this extreme course of action; and oblivious, at the same time, to what now seems an immense break with the past. Though when I thought of all the years that had slipped by changelessly, and the new beginning I would have to take up in a foreign country, I felt twinges of my old fear of change.

Devdutt had said that he would perform the chautha with Naazku and assorted villagers. On the appointed hour one morning, I sat beside the swimming pool at the airport hotel in Chennai, deserted apart from two sunbathing French couples, and imagined the mourners, all in sparkling white, cross-legged on a grey dhurrie under a shamiana with red and black stripes in the small clearing beside my cottage.

I hadn't been able to imagine my mother's funeral, always stopping after the first scene of a straggling procession up the hill from my cottage to the road; it was in a dream that I saw her white-shrouded cadaver lying on a stack of fired wood. I now saw Devdutt vividly in the midst of a sombre throng, sitting in his pandit's costume, silk tunic and dhoti, before a miniature pyre, reciting shlokas from the Upanishads about the immortality of the soul, interrupting himself to say *swa-ha* as he released ghee into the sacred fire, thin sweet-smelling smoke curling above all the bowed heads.

These images of an immemorial and well-attended funeral rite were oddly consoling; they seemed to purge me, temporarily at least, of grief and guilt. What could my own presence, I told myself, have added to the event? My mother's life, I felt, had been honoured, and it was time to move on.

I kept all this – the rationalising and self-persuasion – invisible to you. How strange it now appears: distantly sanctifying my mother at a five-star hotel's swimming pool, next to European tourists who lay like offerings to the dwindling sun, through an invented scene in the Himalayas where people wear white cotton on chilly mornings.

From living life, with all its infirmities and bereavements, I had escaped, with Aseem's help, into good-looking representations of it.

I shouldn't be too surprised or appalled at the ease with which I made myself at home in them. My life, after all, had been a series of impersonations – believable performances, with hardly any slips and fluffs, as an upper-caste Hindu, diligent student, fanatical reader, loyal son, and so on.

With you, I had cast myself in another role: I became your lover. And moving on from loss and its emotions came to mean resuming, after a decent interval, the rituals initiated in that room in Pondicherry in other locales, more self-consciously, but also more powerfully.

Making love to you those first times had made me aware of the great deprivation I had lived with for years. I had discovered in myself during our days there an avidity, a profound need for physical fulfilment, which you seemed to fully match. Your response became a new source of my identity; and now, as desire refined itself, becoming less furtive and headlong, my early nerves about my performance gave way to tenderness and gratitude.

Though he had encouraged me to try out this character, and continually insisted on trampling on a useless past, I didn't want to think about Aseem any more. I had not responded to his new novel. I did not even tell him about my mother and my departure from India.

For one reason or other, however, I couldn't avoid his memory during our intimacies.

On our second night in London, when I was still emerging from jet lag, and trying to find some footing in a place in which I felt a stranger, even an impostor – your apartment of lofty ceilings with fresh flowers in polished vases, a pantry stocked with nuts and olives, a bathroom with unfamiliar, tricky fittings, a cast-iron claw-foot bathtub in the bedroom and honey-hued wooden floors that seemed to creak unsympathetically – you suddenly asked how Aseem and I came to be friends.

I was taken aback. We had just finished making love, for the first time since my mother's death, and with a great intensity by that part of my self you had awakened, a self that I had missed for some days and then regained from the moment I, embracing you that night in London as you stepped out from the bathtub, felt the humid flesh on your back between my spread fingers.

I blurted out something vague about our shared past, though as I lay there, naked and luxuriating in my new-found sexual ease, I couldn't help but remember the occasional envy I had felt at Aseem's uncomplicated attitudes, the way he probably had of whistling soundlessly while taking off his clothes at an assignation.

As though explaining your question, you said, 'Women are always interested in knowing what brings men together, what makes for male solidarity, often against women.'

I should have said then that I felt no such solidarity with Aseem – not any more, if I ever did. In fact, your question prompted me to consider for the first time just what had kept me attached to Aseem years after he first offered me, in Delhi, protection against the pain of individuality and the condescension of the privileged.

It hadn't been, I could see, a relationship between equals. He had become my protector, having divined in me a need to be protected; and I had continued to accept him in this role the same way I had lived much of my life: passively, letting things drift rather than forcing them into any kind of shape.

I now made light of Aseem's attitudes, unwilling to confess my own weakness. I started to speak of how in his novels he tried to present sex as the sole truth in the world – an affirmation not only of our biological nature but of some kind of cosmic order.

You laughed, and I grew more certain in my new-found view of Aseem. Brief annoyances from the past resurfaced: Aseem in Ranipur, directing the conversation at every turn and then running down village life.

A part of me, however, kept wondering what you really thought of him. I knew you planned to go to his festival of ideas in the New Year despite your misgivings about its high concentration of lecherous men. You had told me in Ranipur that you saw cold calculation behind his charm. You now said, 'I can see why women are attracted to him. He radiates this great passion . . . for ideas, books, the world.'

You then added, 'Of course, if you are an aspiring female writer in a man's world, you find yourself immediately gravitating to intellectually confident men, especially those on the left.'

I worried occasionally that you were one of these women, though I could find no evidence, and I remembered, too, with relief, how you had dismissed as pre-Me Too his fictional depictions of women mesmerised by male erotic prowess.

Nevertheless, I could not get rid of images from Aseem's novels, of their male narrators tirelessly responding to the plea 'fuck me hard' from their sexual partners.

I thought of my own father thrusting himself into his young bride, his face distorted with the same bliss with which he drank warm milk or strangled a turbaned Sikh; I couldn't help but think of the diminished woman in my cottage.

And when we made love, something mysterious seemed to linger in your eyes, and there would always come a moment when I felt you withdraw. Though holding me close, you seemed somewhere else, your face twisted to the side, your eyes closed as if you were seeking behind them something of greater fascination. After the moment of release, I would feel you slowly return to me, but in your open eyes, fiercely triumphant, I would now see an unshared and unshareable thought.

There remained something rushed and incomplete about our intimacy, as much as my departure from Ranipur and farewell to my mother. To be with you was to be alone in a different way; and after weeks in London I felt I still didn't know you well enough to know if you felt the same.

Neither of us seemed to want to reveal much about ourselves, even when you talked about your boyfriends, with the forceful candour of someone who wants to give the impression of revealing herself without really doing so. I could not cease prying about them but eventually found more curious your casualness about these failed men; they seemed like the clothes you relegated to the back of your wardrobe, deeming them to be 'not a success'.

It was only after the charged atmosphere of sex dwindled that our deeper needs floated to the surface, just where we could see them in close-up, in our eyes.

I knew, then, that sexual passion wasn't what tied me to you. Rather, it was a feeling I had never known, that mixture of leisure, openness and protectedness children in stable families must enjoy. Lying next to you, hearing your breath rise and fall, your even, hollow heartbeat, your lashes tangled together at the corner of your eyes as always, I felt liberated from the fears and inhibitions, the sense of humiliation that had settled in me when I was a child.

Sometimes, we didn't have sex at all and just talked disjointedly about this or that – your book, the things you regretted, such as your brief modelling career – you restlessly ruffling my hair all the time, touching the small of my back or tracing the knobs of my spine, your fingers speaking of uncertainty, and I, running my fingertips around your lips and eyes, tucking your ringlets behind your soft ears, or gently caressing the skin on your suntanned shoulders that peeled in brown flecks weeks after Pondicherry.

The imperfection excited in me a tenderness I could not explain to myself. Perhaps, it reminded me of that moment in Pondicherry when you touched my face with your hands. Or, because it was only during such caresses that both of us openly craved affection, and betrayed vulnerability.

I talked and listened, as we spoke about your book, my work, London, your plans for India in the New Year, your voice gentler than usual, and all the while I thought about your unconfessed life, the pain and loss that were moving through you even as you lay still against me.

You otherwise remained abstract and remote for me: undetachable from your chosen postures of intelligent and aloof composure on Instagram and Twitter. To me they were as intriguing as when I first encountered them in Ranipur, still offering not so much a likeness, what ordinary photographs used to offer, as a self that was perennially becoming – that always promised something more.

Having long settled myself in a changeless present, I was fascinated by how you were constantly propelled towards the future; and you seemed to need the virtual new world in the same way immigrants needed the original new world: as a limitless expanse in which to start a new life, and realise your true potential.

In London, we found ourselves revolving, soon after arriving there, with some young expatriates, mainly Indian and Pakistani, with Arabs, Iranians, Nigerians and South Africans, a couple of Europeans and an occasional American. I wonder now why from all of us you had kept hidden the scope and drama of the tragedies you had suffered: the incapacitating assault on your father, which had trapped him in a wheelchair, unable to even talk or eat without assistance, or the abandonment by your socialite mother, who often appeared in Instagram posts of her relatives and friends, as glamorously inscrutable behind her oversized sunglasses in Monte Carlo as in Mumbai.

There might have been political reasons for this reticence. 'I am a bit embarrassed by my family,' you once said. 'I know they were freedom-fighters and all that, and sincere in their politics, but wealth and privilege like theirs is always built out of other people's suffering.'

I was still surprised by the tinge of puzzlement in your voice when you recalled being summoned to the principal's office to be told about your father, as though what had happened had happened to someone else. You met with boredom my occasional enquiry about the aunt and uncle who had effectively raised you. They were good-natured, benevolent godparents – what else was there to say?

The story of your past, like mine, seemed undeveloped, with entire years missing, though it had been populated far more variously and densely.

I discovered in London, among other curious things, that, though friendly to everyone you met, you had no close friends there, or anywhere, and that, though people from your school and university now lived across the world, in Hangzhou and Osaka, Melbourne and Oslo, Cape Town and Lima, you were, like me: a loner.

With white Westerners, or the rare olive-skinned Israeli who strayed into our orbit, you claimed to be never at ease, though they were far more forthcoming than desis with tributes to something you valued, your beauty, with self-confident men in particular eager to partake of it, pestering you for dates, one of them, a rising poet from Montreal with glorious hair, frequently drunk dialling you to ask if you would like to look up his work on Instagram.

The reason was, you said, that white people expected you to be grateful for their accommodating you, a Muslim woman, in their exclusive domain; they wished you to become their pet, to help burnish their credentials as cosmopolitan liberals.

I wondered whether this was true for the couple of white men you told me you dated at college in New York. One of them, a fitness freak, now a twice-married hedge-funder with children, still appeared in his Facebook profile picture with his Superman-ish jaw and glisteningly oiled pecs.

You spoke of your liaison with him as disparagingly as you did of your fling with the Oxbridge fop turned Hindu supremacist: you were young and lonely in New York, had effectively lost your parents not so long ago, and were looking to feel safe with someone who was literally strong.

Nathan, one of your other early boyfriends, whom we saw occasionally in London, did not fit the profile of the condescending white liberal either. He seemed too self-absorbed for that. The son of a Connecticut stockbroker and a great-grandson of Holocaust victims, Nathan rented a vast panelled studio in an old house overlooking Hampstead Heath, pursuing an elaborate if outdated fantasy of England.

First incited during an undergraduate year in Oxford, and pursued through multiple viewings of *Brideshead Revisited*, the make-believe now involved subscriptions to *The Times*, *The Economist* and the *Spectator*, membership of the London Library and the Royal Academy of Art, lunch below horsey pictures at the Athenaeum, tea at cafés where the newspapers hung from wooden holders, cocktails at Soho House – strange, that for his tweeds and cords, Nathan still relied on Brooks Brothers, and wore wraparounds that made him look more Australian than English.

I was curious about him, and slightly insecure in his presence. It seemed that, meeting you in New York, Nathan, geekily handsome and benignly exercising some power as editor of a small journal of ideas, had fallen for your accent, a mix of imperious convent-school headgirl and dulcet British, as you yourself described it laughingly, and certainly posher than anything he had heard at Harvard and Oxford.

In London, Nathan's Anglophilia must have turned exasperating. In Hampstead's cosy lanes and York-stone pavements, it avoided collisions with the bleak reality of modern England: mendacious newspapers and race-baiting politicians. How could, you once said, an intelligent well-read man allow himself such illusions about a former colonialist power whose downfall had been so extensively catalogued? There was no question of such intimacy now with a people so deeply complicit in, and yet so blithely unaware of, 'structural injustice'.

From what I had seen of non-white people, starting with my libtard-obsessed father, it seemed prudent to fear that, whatever their skin colour, the poor and oppressed today were very likely to be persecutors tomorrow – even, sooner.

I remember arguing with you about this: how phrases such as 'intersectionality' and 'broader struggle against patriarchy' that you used in your tweets didn't quite account for the fact that some brave protestors against tyranny in Tahrir Square could turn, given the chance, into rapists.

I also remember your exasperation when I remained silent

in a tetchy argument you had about Islam and democracy with Oliver, the blond American banker. I recall he was a friend of someone you had known at NYU, a new arrival in London, and you had imagined yourself making a friendly gesture when you invited him to a bar in Hoxton. Then, drinking cocktails out of marmalade jars with stripy paper straws, we had somehow drifted into a conversation about the failure of the Arab Spring.

Oliver's indolent manner and Ralph Lauren costume spoke of an ancestral summer house in East Hampton quite like the one Virendra had bought for his Gatsby fantasy, where black or Hispanic servants still slice off the crusty bits from toast in the morning and at sundown splash martinis out of cocktail shakers into crystal glasses.

'This is on me,' he had grandly announced as we surveyed the drinks menu (and I, shocked as ever by the prices, had been relieved). He had an obvious crush on you, and mostly muttered out his conviction that democracy had shallow roots in Muslim countries. I had nothing to say to this. But you were tough with him.

'God, these rich white men are just hopeless,' you said afterwards, 'they can't get rid of the idea even now that the West is best.'

You often hosted the children of people you knew or someone in your family had asked you to meet. Some of them were from Pakistan, members of your extended family, objects of great curiosity, even fascination, to me. You would complain good-humouredly that I spoke even less to them than to other people you knew. I could not say this to you, but I found these desis, as you called them, more self-absorbed than the rich white people you shunned – self-absorbed and indifferent, particularly to anyone they deemed outside their circle.

I waited for a flicker of curiosity from them; as always with well-off Indians, I braced myself for doubt, distrust and condescension; and I became self-conscious of my English. But in their eyes I was your boyfriend, and had been nothing else before.

Though Muslim (nominally at least; like you, none of them seemed to have ever stepped inside a mosque to pray) they had that useful upper-caste trait: an instant blindness in the face of potentially uncomfortable realities. Even Olga, our astonishingly beautiful Polish cleaner, whose look of subjection as her hoover drearily howled around the apartment made me break out into loud humming – perhaps, I was not used to a white person as a menial in my house – even Olga was rendered invisible in their presence.

I often remembered in their company the slight, stooped figure of my sister, moving like a crab between the feet of the customers at her dhaba as she swept the gritty floor clean of pan masala sachets, cigarette butts and gobs of mucus.

They would have disregarded my sister, who had been degraded, despite her father's best attempts, to the menial castes she belonged to, as calmly as they ignored Olga. Listening to them, I could not stop thinking, back home, *I would have never met people like these*, except, perhaps, at the literary review's office, and Aseem's parties.

The Indians among them seemed a bit ruffled only when they brought up the state of their country, and of Muslims specifically, under a Hindu supremacist regime. Something like political despair seemed to enter their voices then. One of them, a woman in her twenties from Bombay, even brought up, looking at us meaningfully, the campaign against 'love-jihad'.

You, leaning against bolsters on a low settee, a vape dangling from your right fingers, didn't take the bait. You never wanted to make much of those who called you 'jihadi bitch'.

Or perhaps it was absurd to imply that someone like you could ever be affected by a ban on romantic relationships between Hindus and Muslims.

Anyway, your visitors made it easy for me to think, righteously, that the state of Muslims was much worse than those privileged Indians Aseem called chiknas could ever know.

I once said this to you and afterwards you often tried to make clear that you neither respected nor trusted your visitors from South Asia. Unwilling to join even the big climate change protests down Oxford Street, they were kind of 'pathetic' – and you would say this with the same kind of cheery confidence with which you dismissed your ex-boyfriends.

'They don't really know me,' you said. 'They think I am just some rich kid.' And you thrust out your lower lip and blew a puff of air upwards.

But – and your life was as messy with contradiction as mine – it was evident that you still enjoyed their company. You left chirpy acronyms – OMG, WTF, LOL – below their Facebook and Instagram posts about birthdays and parties and cupcakes and running into minor celebrities ('Be still my beating heart' was a frequently deployed sentiment); you were infected by their naïve vivacity, largely fuelled by the 'fun' things they had been doing or were about to do – tennis weekends in Mallorca, beach vacations in the Algarve, baking classes in Borough Market – things that hinted at an almost negligent possession of wealth and always made me feel poor in a way I never did when I was living in Deoli with my parents and sister.

We had come to each other from such different worlds. In the early days of our relationship, I had tried to account for it, for what had mysteriously broken my isolation but not my solitude; and, resisting the words 'love', 'infatuation' and 'lust', failed.

At times, I searched for signs of decay, imagined the time when it would be all over, and worried about the sad nostalgia I was storing up for myself.

'I am so glad you guys are together. She is a very sweet person, but a bit lost,' Nathan said to me at the bar at Soho House once, while you were in the loo.

Just before you left us, I had been, as often before, watching you drink your wine. Ordering it nonchalantly from a long menu with French names that defeated me, you smelled and tasted it carefully and then sipped it with a palpable enjoyment that at once seemed sensual and meticulous.

I smiled vaguely at Nathan, hoping that my intense embarrassment over his unexpected declaration was not visible.

'She has had a tough life, though it might not seem that way. I am sure she has told you about her past, growing up without any parental care and affection. Her boyfriends were mostly losers, so she is a kind of emotional orphan and—'

He stopped midway, his mouth open, his eyeglasses glinting, and you appeared from behind me. I was suddenly very curious, and would have liked him to say more, though I found such heart-to-heart talks both agonising and petrifying, and I sensed some paternalist condescension behind the way he discussed you, suggesting that your immense material privileges had worked out in you as a kind of pathos.

A part of me was always made anxious by the thought of finding out something vital about your past, something that could jeopardise what I knew and was content with. I was still nagged later by the thought that you had spoken, evidently extensively, to Nathan and not me about your early youth, and your boyfriends.

What else had you confided? And in what aspect of your past lay the key to your personality, your easy way with money, your connoisseurship of clothes, cuisine, wine, writing and interior decor, and your passionate desire to be more original and successful than your peers? And what attracted you to a figure like Soumak – a question that often perplexed me.

In the end, however, it mattered more that you had met a wish, acutely felt if never formulated by me, for an end to loneliness; that you had opened up a conduit towards some kind of meaning in the closed and sterile circuit of self; that you had introduced me to an ease with material comfort, never more evident when you signed bills without reading them and stuffed receipts into a plain white envelope ('For the accountant,' you said).

And, after a while, I ceased to think of moving beyond the allure of your social media incarnations, your thick hair, the heart-shaped tattoo on your navel, and the long-legged stride with which you walked into crowded rooms, as if the world were watching and taking note.

When I first arrived in London, I loved to watch you as you meditatively ran your fingers across clothes, shoes, bags, purses and scarves of delicate colours; you moved languorously, flicking wooden hangers as you briefly chose and then rejected, your head often angled, frowning when it straightened; and you dressed and undressed, touching, adjusting, looking at the mirror, until you struck the right sartorial note.

I loved, too, the sight of you, after all that elegant indecision, stepping with uptilted chin and booted legs into heated, crowded rooms, and the swarm of bodies and voices and smells of hors d'oeuvres and perfumes. Darting from one circle to another, seeking and finding familiar faces, you recovered afterwards in the grand order and quiet of your apartment.

You would start running a bath before unzipping your boots, and slowly pulled off your clothes and earrings to the whine of the bath tap. You then lay sombrely for nearly an hour in the cast-iron claw-foot tub with scented lavender candles on the rim, finally sipping the glass of white wine you had scrupulously turned down all evening, one pink-nailed foot perched on the edge.

I would wait for you to finish, listening out for the soft splash of you standing up and reaching out for a towel, the sound of flushing water, the terminal choking and groaning, so that I could then prepare to occupy the tub.

I behaved as one to whom such self-cherishing was not novel. Indeed, I indulged in some of it myself. Having stepped into a new, ready-made way of life in London, I began to feel jauntily handsome in the bomber jackets and trousers with herringbone patterns you bought for me in the Massimo Dutti in Knightsbridge, and the eau de toilette you gently slapped on my face and neck before we went out.

I should confess that I liked what I saw of myself in the shiny, seductive surface of your projected self – even though the reflection was, incongruously, that of a middle-aged Indian man with a quasi-European appearance and deportment. My new appearance was improbably pleasing; for the first time, my sense of contentment was related to how I looked to others.

I knew I still didn't fit in. Often, I would retreat, from the midst of an amiable throng, to a lonely corner or rooftop with a view of the city's skyline, half-sensing the strangeness of my situation: free-floating in London, the wild, empty electricity-free nightscapes of my past supplanted with LED-draped structures of brick, glass and steel that always seemed, especially against a dingy sky, to be over-signifying the future.

Speaking English all the time, I felt an alien person springing loose inside me: another impersonator, using words from a past that was not his. Walking past the antiquarian retailers of Piccadilly, I would be detained by a print in a shop window of Shimla hills, and then grow frustrated by the refusal of that familiar scenery to yield a reminiscence, to arrange even a micro-second of access to a lost mood.

At other moments, memory would assail swiftly and sense-lessly, as when, in a city filled with simulacrums of cheap Bombay eateries, I recognised at Dishoom one day the knobby glass of a Thums Up cola: a decorative double of the bottle I had abandoned in our old home all those years ago.

Memories of my mother – unbidden from childhood: of my wrists holding a ream of wool that she slowly winds into a ball, the blood of squashed lice on her white fingertips – crowded me, sharp as splinters, together with images of her cold body in my cottage.

Her unfussy affection and kindness had for so long, until she fell ill, created a kind of comfort for me. I knew that if I had not left for Pondicherry with you, she would not have died like that, alone in an empty house, helpless, and recalling who knows what moments from her life; and the honest relief I knew – over the fact that I had been absent during her painful last days, missed the sight of her stiff corpse and its stubbornly open right eye, left the complications of her funeral to Devdutt and Naazku, and avoided the vicious custom of breaking the skull of the deceased on the burning pyre – was felt at other moments as mortifying guilt.

I had forgotten to pay her helper Sarita after promising her extravagant sums on the phone from Pondicherry; and the awful lapse, identified after four weeks in London, and recti-fied after an awkward phone call with Devdutt, made more acute my anxiety about what he and others were thinking now, and what conclusions they had reached about my clan-destine withdrawal from Ranipur and my failure to return.

One morning, a strange new thought occurred to me: did

they dread my reappearance as much as I did? Were they hoping I had left Ranipur for ever?

I found it agonising to imagine returning to my cottage, to the silence and indifference of a house emptied by desertion and death, the dead person's things scattered across it, each one of them – her postcard pictures of Gayatri, her knitting needles – threatening heartache.

Then, seeing in my mind the vacant kitchen, and the faint coating of dust on everything in it, I would move on to worrying about how I would feed myself, and I would be appalled the next moment by my selfishness.

I had changed my online passwords, which consisted of my mother's name and year of birth. But I would still find hankies hemmed and embroidered by her in the pockets of trousers or a sadri lurking at the bottom of my suitcase. A popular Hindi song of the 1980s played by a desi Uber driver – 'Tujhse Naraaz Nahin Zindagi, Hairan Hoon' – made tears roll down my cheeks, and I often lulled myself to sleep at night with visions of the nullah by the railway tracks, that first glimpse of a world I have seen too much of and not enough into, of a riddle that has remained unresolved.

I would dream of wandering in perpetuity along the rocks where the dhobis have spread many-hued saris, where everything stands still in sacred silence under an enormous sky, and I am on the brink of some absolute truth; and I would wake up in your dark, high-ceilinged bedroom to what sounded to me like the crickets and dogs on a late evening.

I felt the past rushing back at such moments, and I heard then that whispered question again: *What am I doing here?* And I felt fear – a simple fear of having lost a world.

Seventeen

We worked in the mornings and afternoon, in separate rooms, until you needed help with your book. We made love a lot, often during the afternoons, starting with the most fleeting of touches, and, though it was not the same, the early excitement and joy were gone, holding you closer still made me feel that my arms had been empty for too long.

In the evenings, we went to dinner parties and films; we attended book launches, and these outings were preceded by the spectacle I never ceased to relish: of you before wardrobe and mirror, dreamily fine-tuning your appearance.

After dinner somewhere (initially at some white-draped table with napkin pyramids in a restaurant freshly recommended by the *Evening Standard*, where waiters opened menus as gingerly as an antiquarian bookseller I knew in Shimla exhibited an over-priced edition of the *Illustrated London News* until, in an awkward but necessary conversation, I reminded you that I was comfortably off only by Indian standards), we would take an Uber back, suddenly mute now in its darkness as you checked your social media feeds, often the first reports of the events we had just attended, the loud colours from your screen flowing across your face, whose eager intent always made me a bit jealous.

To emerge from the car in your street, the private gardens with high railings on one side, and glowing French windows on another; to open the blue front door of your apartment and hear it shut behind us with the oiled click of an expensive lock; to then find ourselves, subtly lit in amber, in the tall gilt-framed hall mirror, and hear the grandfather clock ticking vigilantly, was to know security again.

At a time when so many of my thoughts and memories were shaded by sorrow and guilt, your old apartment in Kensington, home to several generations of your family, and still suggesting in its renovated state all the great many things said and done inside it, became a kind of reassurance, the space and order and light of its vast, high-ceilinged rooms suggesting a durable fastness against death and separation.

During those long London twilights, the windows of even the homes of strangers showcased a reality that seemed to have stood firm and eternal for centuries: a woman lying in an armchair holding a glass of white wine, children reading or playing or drawing, a man taking off his tie, and a cat crawling out between roped-back curtains to lounge fatly on a sill.

Coming from a society rent by anarchic poverty and cruelty, where you could never feel history to be on your side, or any institution of government and law working in your favour, coming from a society that had frightened and traumatised so many of us for life, I was learning how to appreciate, or at least not be afraid of, a rich and steadfast world.

Then, too, we avoided, living in that part of London, the journeys through terraces of brick, past boarded-up shops, cardboard dwellers and iPhone-snatchers – hints to me of a larger dereliction up north, the de-industrialised country about which I knew nothing except that it had sprung Brexit upon unsuspecting Londoners.

How much easier it was in that, yes, uncompromisingly fashionable and reassuringly expensive watering-hole of Russian and Asian oligarchs, where the destitute, unlike India's, slumped in doorways, nearly always out of sight, to enjoy the city's array of parks, restaurants and bookshops; to experience even things abandoned on the pavements – disembowelled sofas, collapsed hoovers, computer keyboards – as a kind of visual novelty.

How lightly our legs skipped over the devout row of shoes on the pavement outside a mosque in Southall, where we had ventured to get your 'fix' of desi khana at a restaurant serving authentically Gujarati food; and how great was the security of the rich tourist that I felt in the mithai shop with a garlanded portrait of Modi we repaired to afterwards for some ras malai – the security that those raving about kebab dives and Sufi shrines in seedy Old Delhi, my old workplace, always knew.

I didn't have to worry any more about the Indian toilet-cleaners at Heathrow; like Aseem in his suite at the Pierre in New York, I had been elevated above the meanness that was the fate of most immigrants to the city. And, unlike them, I had in my mind the comforting knowledge that I could go back, that I didn't have to, after all, be here.

I envied your intimacy with the city, the confident way you placed yourself in it, and professed metropolitan habits ('Let's meet at my regular: the LRB bookshop'). Unconsciously trying to imitate you, I often found myself making observations that struck my own ears as affected ('The best coffee roasters are in Shoreditch') and I suppressed the things that puzzled me: flat white coffee; orchids, rare and expensive in my mind, available at Tube station florists, and the numerous white young men with thick squarish beards and hats who seemed clones of Renoir and Manet.

I reignited my love of London buses that I had blurted out to you. Seen from the top deck, above its chaos of terraces, crescents and squares, the city revealed at last the 'order' that Naipaul relentlessly counterposed to the 'disorder' of India and the non-West in general: the solid edifices of brick and steel, the well-swept roads, the spiked iron railings, the clusters of chimney pots, the symmetrical spans of the bridges over the Thames and the long shopping streets, where, as though in a film, buildings, billboards and display windows floated by, and miniature figures dashed around on the pavements.

I discovered, too, the joys of wandering through the free museums, those oases of warmth and colour. On my first visit to London, there was so much that I had missed while trying to save money. I now availed myself of all the amenities denied to me in my rural retreat: from lingering at a café with a cappuccino and shopping at Whole Foods to watching a Satyajit Ray retrospective at the South Bank, listening to music in Wigmore Hall, and luxuriating later in your cast-iron bath.

It was in this restful state that I received one day the news from Ranipur, relayed by Devdutt on the phone, that Naazku had sold her hill to Mathur for a pittance, and that her forest was already being cleared and levelled for construction.

You seemed more shocked when I told you. I was in the bathroom, finishing a shave, and you stopped to rest your face against my back and to put your arms around my middle. 'I am so, so sorry!' you said. 'I don't know what Mathur will do to that poor woman. Whether or not she gets her penthouse apartment, the neighbourhood will go to the dogs, for sure.'

I looked at the freshly planed face in the mirror, feeling pleasantly hampered by your arms.

'Can you do something about it?' you asked.

I didn't even want to think about it, though I had often worried in the past about how my own time in the village could come to an abrupt end if Devdutt decided to cash in on the real-estate boom. I was in London, with you, and seemed to lack nothing. In Ranipur, I had felt desolate when you announced your intention to go to London: your imminent departure felt like a stark judgement on my world. Now, that great privilege of yours had become mine, in that apartment where the honeyed light from tall sash windows glowed on the dark red of Turkish kilims.

I had slipped easily into my public role with you, helped enormously by speaking a foreign language in a foreign city. Indeed, in my dramatically altered mode of being, I became pleasurably aware, as gazes followed us in restaurants and at parties, of being a strikingly good-looking, even glamorous, couple. When a picture of us appeared on the hectic Instagram of an acquaintance of yours, an event-organiser from Istanbul, commended by a stranger with a winking emoji and hashtag #couplegoals, I did not show it to you out of embarrassment, but I was actually more amused than embarrassed.

Indeed, we, Alia and Arun (the names often taken together, and falling like musical phrases on my ears), were continually in demand, the recognition swiftly giving reality to a relationship that felt so new. As people with a quasi-intellectual vocation, we were set apart from, even a bit above, our group of moneyed expatriates, credited with special qualities, and required to be thoughtful, if not provocative; and when, after playing ourselves in public, we got home and stood side by side brushing our teeth in the golden light of the small bulbs flanking the bathroom basin, I sometimes couldn't suppress a smile at our two unmasked faces in the mirror.

No one in London knew or cared enough about my past, the landscapes of want and the memories of underdevelopment locked in my head, to note my new 'character' in the city. I felt immeasurably more relaxed in their company than, fearing exposure of my low-caste origins, I had ever been in that of Delhi's Anglophiles, or, sensing condescension, in the presence of your South Asian visitors.

To be sure, as your older lover, I rarely had to perform in

my role. The assumption people in your class made about each other – that they shared a similar background and worldview – helped me become invisible.

With my background fading from view, I made it a pastime to observe what to me were true exotics: members of the racially and ethnically diverse but otherwise remarkably homogenous group I found myself in: the geography-dissolving people with hyphenated identities that I had started to become aware of while looking at a British Airways inflight magazine on my first trip to London.

I had never before seen the airline's flight paths on a map of the world, blithely swooping across national and geographical obstacles. The spectacularly creased map of India that the teacher at my primary school hung on a tree proclaimed nationhood to be eternally fixed, with a revanchist Mother India pressing even Pakistan-ruled Kashmir to her bosom. Even the more sophisticated atlases I came across enhanced that impression of something settled for ever, of a jigsaw that, however jagged its parts, finally fitted.

It was in this quasi-coherent world that the Anglo-Indians of our childhood briskly traded one identity for another. Boys with names such as Desmond and James suddenly announced they were emigrating to Britain, Australia, Canada and New Zealand.

Those they were leaving behind didn't take them seriously at first. Mediocre students, who performed well only with English writing and comprehension, the Anglo-Indians often failed to take advantage of the 'grace marks' bestowed on them by the Christian teachers. Everything about them – the Western-style skirts and suits of their parents, their Cliff Richard and Bing Crosby LPs, living rooms full of framed photos of relatives in Surrey and Sydney and books by A. J. Cronin and Daphne du Maurier, and kitchens which to fastidious

Hindu nostrils smelled strongly of beef – expressed an unvarnished craving for absorption by the white West.

Promising to write, and to send us goodies from their bountiful new homes, these last living embodiments of empire quickly disappeared into the white Commonwealth and were never heard from (though Aseem did once receive from one Adrian his much-used copy of *Playboy* with Kim Basinger on the cover).

I pictured the Anglo-Indians for years afterwards, walking in line across the tarmac to a waiting plane, and then walking straight out of it into the English village of Enid Blyton's books – with its grassy cricket ground, pub, dog lovers and cyclists in the mist quite like the rural idyll the Tories still invoke.

The British Airways route map came as an early intimation of how, while I was still trying to root myself in a little village, the world had come to be densely interconnected; and how, in this increasingly mixed and irregular realm, the catalogue of available identities had thickened.

Yugoslavs had ceased to be Yugoslavs, Anglo-Indians had become extinct, and Hindus from India had become the richest minority in the United States. It was my thinking, however, that had not caught up with a disassembled world and its splintered identities.

In middle age, my mind still languished in the small towns of the 1980s when after anti-minority pogroms even middle-class Sikhs shaved off their hair and went around with downcast faces, and the overwhelmingly destitute Muslims, though still defiantly long-bearded, retreated further into their ghettos.

You and your friends in London represented to me a completely new kind of confident, worldly person, able to quickly discard inherited identity, or wear it, when the need so arose. You would often say, 'White people think of me as a Muslim woman who needs to be rescued. They want me to write about Muslim subjects. They want me slotted into the role of the victim. But what if I don't give a shit about my Muslim identity?'

You would refer to your childhood trauma. 'My father was almost killed by another Muslim for daring to speak up for Muslim women. I am actually not into identity politics. I am interested in questions of social justice – for all, not just for Muslims or Indians.'

Until I met you and your friends and relatives, I hadn't been able to see your background of global nomadism clearly. Aseem had gone on about the early twenty-first-century globalised man (not woman: did women feature at all, I now wonder, in his vision of a larger emancipation?), but I hadn't myself noticed the fact that going *away* for a tiny minority of the world's population was not an undesirable but an unavoidable solution to an intolerable existence; it was a chosen way of life, a compulsive movement through a world made safe for them by class and education, in which the failings of no society clung to them for too long.

I found it remarkable that whatever their ancestral origins or profession, they had all studied in either European or American universities. It seemed very unusual to me, too, that, marrying out of their ancestral homelands, many of them had young mixed-race children.

But I was always more struck by how, placidly celebrating their good fortune in London, these beneficiaries of global capitalism seemed to have assumed multicultural existence to be the norm; how with such dreamy benevolence they had imagined the future to consist of enlarged freedoms for more and more people.

They lived in versions of the house I had first seen in your renovated villa in Ranipur: all high ceilings, skylights, white-painted walls, wooden floors and strategically placed lamps. Free from lumpy inherited furniture, and regularly vacuum-cleaned by East Europeans, these homes gleamed with ease and goodwill.

But with two or three passports and email addresses and several socials each, people in your circle always seemed to be living somewhere else, on Eurostar and Heathrow Express, hotel rooms and business-class lounges, moving walkways, escalators, taxis and planes (with constant low-level anxiety about carbon footprint, partly mitigated with environmentally responsible takeaway coffee mugs).

Their real homes often seemed, messy and badly lit, to be on Facebook, where inexpertly taken pictures of hummus, shaped like a volcano crater, with olive oil floating in the middle, and a plate of chocolate brownies would on any day alternate with photographs of babies, toddlers, birthday parties, destination weddings, weekend getaways, a Meera Sodha recipe and refugees behind barbed wire, attended by likes, emojis and such verbalised effusiveness as 'you look so gorgeous!' and 'aw, thanks, it was great to have you over' and 'Europe's shame'.

All along they seemed to be making a fortune, adding to their wealth. Yet this side of their lives remained hidden. Perhaps, it obsessed me because I often felt searingly my lack of disposable income in London. I watched my savings – built over long years of frugal living in an Indian village – leaking away, and, though you seemed oblivious to my repeated failure to pick up steep restaurant bills, carefully folding them, as always, for your accountant, I increasingly felt ashamed about my dependence on you.

I wondered what you made of these people in your social circles, or if I could talk frankly about them to you. You may have found me unusually silent in their company at times. We went to so many parties in those months in Kensington, more than in the rest of my life, that now they've run together in my mind, along with their varied settings: restaurants, Soho clubs, publishing offices in Bloomsbury and the Strand, private apartments in Ladbroke Grove and Islington, and, once, a houseboat in Chelsea. But I distinctly recall a brunch in Tower Hamlets one Sunday.

It is being hosted at a large apartment, one of the few converted out of a knitwear factory. There are For Sale signs in the streets we pass. The borough is gentrifying, but it still has enough rough parts to keep house prices sensible.

A window takes up most of the west-facing wall, framing the City's glittering edifices of glass, and the buildings of gloomy brick snuggling up to them. On a long table of scrubbed oak, big velvet-stamened lilies fan out from two cut-glass vases, over Ottolenghi salads sprinkled with pomegranate, chia and pumpkin seeds, butter beans with feta, courgette fritters with yoghurt-y sauce, hunks of sourdough, rows of crackers, and manifold dips and cheeses. For dessert, there is the gift of a pavlova from an Australian couple, a miniature EU paper flag flying over the strawberries and kiwi fruit.

There are children everywhere: babies in pushchairs, toddlers weaving unsupervised through the crowd; belligerently seeking fun, their zigzag steps make the parquetry squeak.

Aseem would know our host. She has been to one of his festivals: a fiery human rights lawyer, who had once tracked down victims of Modi's massacre in the United States, whose bright Cottage Emporium saris, big red bindi, densely bangled wrists and raspy voice on NDTV once held out a possibility of justice.

She now works for a human rights NGO; her froth of hair is now white; and her indignant left-wing politics have been tempered by the routines of professional advocacy, and by marriage to a divorced Iranian hedge-funder.

She is an enthusiast, by vocation. 'I love Simla,' she repetitively informs me every time I see her. (This small subterfuge makes me uneasy, but in London I tell anyone who asks that I live in Shimla. You overheard me once; I explained, 'Well, Shimla has a better chance of extending small talk than Ranipur.')

'We spent,' our host says, 'our summer holidays in Simla in this huge bungalow with just the best view in the world.'

She uses the British pronunciation: Simla. She also says, 'Bombay' and 'Madras' and 'Calcutta', and I can't then help but feel a pang of affection for her. With each passing year, there are fewer of us who use the old names of Indian cities.

Her husband, pot-bellied, tousle-haired and perpetually grinning below his hawk nose, is obsessed with gadgets, like many men of simple origins. He relentlessly urges me, among other things, to switch to Android from iOS, Samsung Galaxy from iPhone, though I have told him several times that I have never possessed an Apple product.

Today, I tell him that I don't need Google Home since you have Alexa in your apartment; and see no need to add Sonos speakers on top of your old hi-fi system.

He says (repetitively, again), 'What has happened to India? We in Iran used to look up to it. It was the land of Gandhi and Nehru, the only real democracy in the post-colonial world . . .'

This compatriotic solidarity usually leaves me restless, especially when it comes from members of supplanted elites, for whom the times in which they held power were always better. Today, however, the garrulous but kind Iranian unexpectedly adds, in his husky voice, 'I mean, as we speak, some poor

Muslim is being lynched in India,' and I feel a bitter pang – yes, why had the land of Gandhi and Nehru become so squalid?

In London, I increasingly find my homeland stuck like fine coal dust to my skin. I am forced to say something. An inane sentence comes out of my mouth: 'I think the rot started with Indira Gandhi.'

The hubbub suddenly rises, distracting the Iranian. There are laughs and shouts near the door: a new batch of guests have arrived.

As I use the opportunity to move away, I hear the lawyer say, 'I am so depressed about people like Priti Patel and Nikki Haley and Tulsi Gabbard and Kamala Harris. Is it our fate to be ruled by right-wing Indians outside India as well?'

'Harris?' Someone counters. 'As far as I know, she is on the left.'

'Not to people who have studied her record as prosecutor,' the lawyer retorts.

'You know,' someone else behind me pipes up, 'I know someone who was at school with Priti Patel; she was horribly bullied, called not-so-pretty Patel.'

'That doesn't justify anything, let alone her cruelty to immigrants.'

The guests today are typical of the people the Indian and the Iranian like to collect. I recognise a Bangladeshi food critic – uneasily, for when first introduced to her, she kissed me hard and wetly at once on both cheeks and continues to do so every time I see her. She maintains a blog post on ethical eating. A casual admission that I like coffee motivated her to send me several emails with links to fair trade roasters and farmers' markets.

She has recently announced her pregnancy in a long Facebook post. The baby was conceived with her Pakistani husband in Tangier, at a villa owned by a famous British photographer.

She and her husband, a surgeon, are going back there for Christmas. But weekend breaks in Crete are scheduled in-between.

She is saying, 'The sea is still warm until mid-November and it is a great way to use frequent-flyer miles. These European sectors are available on British Airways even when you book a day before, and you can avoid flying horrid Ryanair.'

You are upstaged a bit today by a writer from Morocco who has come with her model friend, one of the two white people in the room, a very tall woman with a babyish face whose glasses with extra-large frames make her look like a girl playing at being a grandmother.

In the past, the Moroccan used to pester you with requests to retweet her BuzzFeed articles about fundamentalists in North Africa. Success, unexpectedly in France with a book about how identity politics is undermining secular democracy, has now exalted her above mere tweeters; she has even mounted attacks from her new platform on Black Lives Matter for encouraging racial polarisation and inadvertently helping Trump.

You told me, 'She would be horrified if someone said this to her face, but she is a total right-winger now. The French love her. She thinks it is because of her secular principles. But it is because she is an Islamophobe.

'Though she is unusual in one way,' you added. 'The white establishment wants its favourite Oriental informants to look like babes.'

The Moroccan is also new to our group, provoking everyone to be extra nice to her.

'The trouble with Facebook,' she is saying, 'is that you can never really lose your exes – they keep popping up.'

Everyone around her smiles dutifully, but you can sense what they are thinking: *How many exes could she have had?*

I think, yet again, about how the world is made safe for good-looking people.

'I really look forward to reading your book,' she tells you.

'It will probably be a big flop.'

'Why do you say that?'

'Well, no one is interested in India and Indians any more. Everyone has their own issues at home to deal with.'

The Moroccan, unable to read the bold sign that says, 'Reassure me, please!' goes on: 'But isn't it true that Netflix and Amazon Prime are pouring billions of dollars into India?'

She digs into hummus with a cracker as she waits for you to respond.

I feel a bit tense. As it is, you tend to approach the riddle that is your future as a writer through the progress of your peers: why your proposal for a book on rich Indian Americans had been accepted for publication only in India while your college friend Sonia had sold her book on British attitudes to their empire in several territories and languages. You have lately seemed personally offended by HBO's decision to buy the rights to a crime quartet authored by an old acquaintance from your television days.

The situation is rescued by the arrival of the other white person in the room: the husband of the Vietnamese-Australian woman who brought the pavlova. William, a man with silvery, swept-back hair, has just spent two weeks in Sri Lanka touring tea estates to find a new source for his boutique delis in Sydney and Melbourne.

'Absolutely wonderful people,' he says. 'So gentle, so unspoiled.'

You contest this. You have worked in Sri Lanka for Amnesty International, cataloguing hate crimes against Tamils.

Your phone rings, and you snatch it up, and then flash the screen at me with a weary smile: it is a mildly lecherous journalist from a fashion-cum-literary magazine in Mumbai who wants you to write a piece about your days as a model. You let the phone ring out before slipping it back into your sling bag.

I overhear an academic of Indian origin from the United States complaining about racism at Oxford and Cambridge. A small man, he wears an uncertain smile underneath his bushy black moustache, and always seems half-embarrassed, though not on his Twitter feed, where he is dogged in his pursuit of moral infraction. He periodically announces a long and necessary break from Twitter to work on his book, only to sign back in a few days later, in order to, he claims, alert his followers to a new and important atrocity, usually of a racial nature: the latest one is the persecution of Meghan Markle by the British press.

I retreat, as always, after an hour or so. I have examined the bookshelves enough times to know by heart the paperback spines I will find there, and there is something vaguely unsettling about the parade of flash-lit grins and hugs on the mantelpiece photos of relatives and friends across the world.

I prefer now to stand in one corner, studying the silver-framed sepia pictures on the wall of the Iranian's family in Iran: wedding photos with serrated edges, heliotrope-stamped by the photographer, of lower-middle-class grandparents in the 1950s, the solemn couple standing on a Qashqai rug, a velvet curtain against their large staring eyes.

Behind me is a crescendo of claims and counterclaims, drowning out the Iranian rap playlist.

You are saying, 'Arun can't get over the number of bearded hipsters in London.'

'Aren't hipsters sort of over?'

'The news gets worse all the time.'

'She's so good. She just knew, just by looking at me, in one glance, that I was at that stage in my life when I needed highlights.'

'Anyway, if Harari is right, it's all over for humanity, so why . . .'

'And I am, like, "I will be far from beach-body ready after Christmas."'

'I mean, I don't recognise my country any more. Who are all these Tories who voted for Boris Johnson?'

'You're in Stoke Newington, aren't you? A cousin of mine just moved there. Great South Indian restaurants there.'

'I think it is pretty clear: populists are a mortal threat to liberal multicultural democracy.'

'Airbnb really should have a filter for smart TVs. I need my rubbish Netflix wherever I go.'

'Better way to put it: it is a battle between Cockney black cab drivers and those many Mohammeds of Uber, and the nativists are winning.'

'Maybe Rebecca Solnit is an exception, but white feminists are the enablers of neo-imperialism.'

'C'mon! Sonos is a sure sign of middle-age crisis!'

'She got one K retweets in five minutes.'

'But are you calling Michelle Obama a feminist because she is black?'

'This new site for villas has a smart TV filter.'

'I am sorry, but Michelle Obama is the wife of a man who made lists of people to kill by drones in his office every week. She is more like those book-club mafia wives in *The Sopranos*.'

'I just heard on the radio on the way here that the government is returning another group of people to the Caribbean.'

'Writers are way too overexposed now. They have lost their aura.'

'Brick Lane is no longer the place depicted in the novel.'

'These lit festivals are to blame. They turn everyone into performing monkeys.'

'If you are looking for grittiness, try Jakarta.'

'But isn't that what late capitalism does: turn novelists into beach-holiday content-providers?'

'And KL with its malls for different classes is the kind of experience you won't get in the West.'

'I like the fact that she exists, but Arundhati Roy is just too radical for me. I prefer Chimamanda.'

'It's kind of transitional. Like Crown Heights.'

'I realise I was wrong when I said that Meghan Markle is going to politicise the royal family.'

'These Incredible India ads on television are nauseating.'

The assertions, great or small – and those sentences beginning with 'I believe that, no, I don't agree with that, how can you believe that, actually, I think it is more that' – are a bit too aggressive or too defensive; the attitudes too well known, even to those who assume them.

I am reminded, by the homogeneity of the gathering, of the gentlemen's club in Covent Garden I briefly visited with you, where, while searching for your literary agent, we blundered into the smoking room, and saw old men unmoving in leather armchairs underneath a large crystal chandelier, some hidden behind the *Daily Telegraph* tremblingly raised, others murmuring or trying to listen to murmurs with cupped ears.

It was a brief glimpse, but long enough to reveal that here, in this immobile assembly of titled men, bank directors, retired corporate executives, civil servants and publishers, among people you termed 'a bunch of old duffers' as we walked down an august staircase, lay real power, which, accumulated over centuries and hoarded in institutions, made itself felt without audible speech.

In contrast, most of the expatriates present at this Tower Hamlets apartment seem to be working too hard, over-stressing their political and ideological commitments, and their meaningfulness. And it also seems that, away from such proc-lamations of liberal-left virtues, their energy is consumed by the struggle to make a good living and a name for themselves, and to fight off an inner suspicion of inauthenticity.

Aseem turned early in his life against the soft, beautifully bred liberals we read about in Turgenev; he forged his identity in opposition to them. But he then joined them in their mag-azines and their festivals of ideas and social media platforms, leaving others to report on the nihilistic backlash from those with inferior social and cultural capital.

In London I often logged on to Facebook under a pseudo-nym to read posts by Baba. You didn't seem interested when I told you, saying only that 'Facebook is for old people', and I didn't add that in his house-cum-shop, its wooden beams dark with soot and roof loaded with ferns and thick stone walls sodden enough to periodically turn the electrical wires into Diwali sparklers, he had managed to get a broadband connection through his phone line, and now, in his eighth decade, warmed his patriarchal heart over a laptop several times a day.

He said nothing about his first wife's demise, but since Modi's re-election his page had come to resemble a garish roadside shrine, fumblingly garlanded by passers-by. 'Modi is positive for India's greatness,' commented one. 'It is a victory for Hinduism,' suggested another, and Baba himself hailed, inaccurately, the 'first low-caste prime minister of India'.

The mass flogging of Kashmiris by Modi provoked fresh cele-brations. These were tinged by malevolence – the proposals 'kill the Muslims, libtards, urban Naxals, and all anti-nationals' and 'send Sonia Gandhi back to Vatican' received many 'likes' – but most commenters seemed overcome by a deeper ecstasy.

I could see my father – his big, heavily lined and bearded face expressionless in his profile photo – red-eyed with emotion, mostly against 'libtards'; he has never met any of them, is unlikely to pronounce the word correctly, but he blames them fully for letting the minorities get out of hand.

He now imagines himself, like so many lately bewitched by the internet, to be robustly participating in, not just passively living through, great events. Perhaps, this was another one of history's cruel tricks: to forge dreams of agency and self-empowerment, of making history, among people it has irrevocably unmade.

But it was possible to judge Baba's Modi-mania too harshly. Of all those millions fantasising about national glory, and frenziedly hounding enemies of the people, he was one of those to know over a long and unrelieved period what true individual degradation was.

Aseem and his magazine couldn't get over the fact that dirt-poor Dalits comprised the mobs that raped pregnant Muslim women in Gujarat in 2002, and then slashed open their wombs with trishuls. He went on about this moral catastrophe, organised and supervised by the prime minister, in his last novel. He couldn't see that a leader had given the lowest of the low-born a rare chance at social mobility, and they eagerly took it.

I hope you will understand why the deepest impression your friends in London made on me was of innocence. Finally jolted into political panic and news junkiedom by Brexit and the election of Trump, they became compulsive refreshers of the *Guardian* and *New York Times* online; they emailed each other comment pieces by Fintan O'Toole and news reports favouring the Remain cause, seeding long conversation threads that artificially inflated my email count each morning.

Their novel political passions had not yet hardened into victimhood – the weird victimhood of the elite – and were still indistinguishable from the thrills of virtual activism. I felt more sympathetic to their conceit than I had been to my father's: that following live news blogs and posting pungently worded opinions on social media against either libtards or ethnic-racial supremacists was a way of remaking history.

They had, after all, morally impeccable demands, unlike my father: that the full and pleasant life they had known ought to not only continue but also be widely shared. Their parents and grandparents had made private escapes from the history long convulsing their ancestral continents by migrating to the West. Two decades of unhindered upward mobility there had convinced them that history, still destructively raging in parts of Asia and Africa, had ended at least in their comfortable new home. They couldn't but be confounded by its volcanic re-eruption in the heart of the modern West.

Perhaps, having quickly become something rather than nothing, to paraphrase Aseem's favourite line, they hadn't had the time to see how the world came to be what it is: how people could have good reason to be attached to blatant injustice or be convinced by transparent falsehoods.

They rarely enquired into my background, or my work. The few who bothered saw the vague presence in my past – an idea floated, perhaps, by you – of material scarcity, and may have been slightly unsettled.

You would occasionally present me as a translator, bringing vital literary news from an India that most novelists and journalists ignored. Writing about crooked global elites, you saw me, too, as engaged in an arduous but necessary endeavour to *expose*, to bring to light a suppressed or unheeded reality, before a world that didn't seem to care much.

You looked at me slightly encouragingly, hoping, perhaps, that I would say something and establish myself as someone you can be proud of. I did say something like, 'Yes, it is fascinating how much undiscovered richness there is in literature in Indian languages; we give too much attention to writing in English,' but I squirmed inwardly at your noble-sounding description of my work.

It misrepresented the non-mimetic nature of the fiction I translated, and reminded me of Aseem, who righteously claimed, slighting literature, a journalistic urgency for his own work.

I shrank, too, from your vision of us against an unaccommodating world because it clashed with my own desire, buried somewhere deep inside until I met you and came to know the exquisite orderliness of wealth, for a bit more *comfortable* and certainly a lot less tense life.

I could never confess my desire to cling to something that had been your destiny, a way of life created by your ancestors, which you had chosen to question. Nor could I remark to you, without appearing cynical, how it was the largesse born of 'other people's suffering' that sustained a protest against oppression and inequality.

In any case, I doubt if your presentation of me registered on any of your acquaintances in London.

You said, 'They really respect you for the different perspective you bring.' (You often quoted me on these sociable Sundays from our conversation about Ranipur's left-behinds at Hotel Kipling; it was a struggle then to assume the role of an expert from India on the rural-urban divide that had led to Brexit and Trump.)

I wasn't so sure. I worried as I said my thing if my listeners thought of me as one of the left-behinds; they did not seem to know anyone acquainted with failure and probably were inclined to regard it as a moral lapse.

Whether or not they respected me – you were always too generous – they all seem to have assumed, again probably helped by you, that I was another writer inflamed into activism by recent political outrages.

I may have even played up to this misunderstanding. It would have been too hard to draw a true picture of my life for them, or even for myself.

Eighteen

Towards the end, as my fear of the unreality in and around me grew and I started to panic, I puzzled a lot more over what you thought of me.

'Women can become deliberately naïve when they are with a man,' you once said, speaking of one of your boyfriends. 'They can put all their cognitive abilities to sleep.' I started to wonder if a similar naïvety underpinned our own relationship.

At social occasions, when you were invariably surrounded by men younger, more accomplished and better-looking than me, and eager to flirt with you, I felt a twinge of insecurity: that I was not performing to your expectations.

And I would goad myself into bitterness with the thought that my own role in your life was to give your self-image some sort of depth, that I was merely accompanying you through your enthusiasms like some personal assistant, and that our relationship was only one of the many episodes in the life of a rich and beautiful woman.

I would fret that you had never been much interested in my background, or, for that matter, in Virendra's – which you had been commissioned to explore. You hadn't even read Aseem's new novel, I would tell myself, though I had actually tried to conceal it. In this testy mood, I would persuade myself that you were too preoccupied with becoming what you wished to see of yourself in other eyes.

I would try to convince myself that your imagination was too broadly netted, capable of holding only big political causes: poverty, injustice, imperialism and neo-liberalism. Individual experiences or palpable things, like the tribals squatting in the dust at your villa, slipped through it.

I would even complain to myself that your looks matter to you more than ever, though you appeared younger than your thirty-four years, and that you seemed to spend more time on your appearance in London, pursing your lips a bit longer as you applied colour to them.

This secretive semi-hostility would dissipate as soon as you returned to me, your beaming face holding proof of affection. You once said, cupping my face with your hands just as you had that first time in Pondicherry, 'I have never felt so connected to anyone like I do to you. Really, Arun, it is as though I had been waiting for you all my life.'

It was so emphatic a sentiment, so complete an expression of faith, and I was both too moved and too scared by your capacity for love and trust to say something commensurate.

It seemed to me that we had found pleasure in living with each other, or living for the sight of ourselves in the other's eyes. And we liked making love, or had grown addicted to the passion that seemed to annihilate, every time, all the griefs, frustrations and uncertainties of the past and present. But I was never sure if what we had could be called 'love'.

'All the men I met before,' you said on another occasion, 'were so hollow, nothing inside them, no deeper consciousness at all.'

Reassured, I mumbled something about you being too kind; but it was never anything as affirmative as *our relations would never end, and one day we would marry and have children and raise a family.* At such moments, placed right at the centre of your life, I was still nagged by the feeling that I would never get close to you – more my fault, I know, than yours.

*

Life went on outwardly, the jolts and thumps from your tread-mill in the morning and the cries of the *Evening Standard* vendor in the afternoons and evenings providing a kind of audible frame to the comfortable inertia we had arrived at.

You said it was reassuring to be in the proximity of my quiet labour; I felt the same. The silence was broken sometimes when you read aloud your drafts, and I would hear something like, 'At IIT Virendra had striven hard to overcome his background of poverty and discrimination; in New York, he succumbed easily to the global elite's corruption.'

There was much more to this story. I remember one particular incident that Aseem had related to me. Virendra had decided to pay a senior Brahmin informant at McKinsey a commission of two million dollars after a stock-market bonanza. Since he wished to pay the large sum without inviting taxes and unwelcome scrutiny in America, he opened an account for the Brahmin's in-house maid at Credit Suisse in Switzerland.

Morgan Stanley, which was transferring the sum to Switzerland, wanted proof that the account holder was not resident in the United States: notarised passport copy, original utilities bills, bank statements. Virendra had to ask Aseem to activate his networks in India: emails and telephone calls to a banker at HDFC in Mumbai, a notary in Delhi and a Vodafone executive, all adept at living on the wrong side of the law. A bank account was opened in India, mobile phone connection acquired, and documents notarised within three days – all this international bustle on her behalf completely unknown to the account holder, the maid, an illiterate low-caste woman from eastern Uttar Pradesh, living in the outhouse of a Brahmin's mansion in Greenwich, Connecticut.

Such details seemed to securely anchor your book. But you kept changing your idea of it: a secret history of globalisation, of the New India, or an account of its 'Hollow Men'. Living in London and on social media, amid intense culture wars of race and gender, and crises of climate and environment, and feeding off a generational hostility to far-right villains in power, you were finally keener on shaping your book into a political tract, a reckoning of the moral left with the immoral right.

You wished it to speak 'truth to power', and I didn't think I could say that power probably already knows the truth and, in any case, may not be open to learning it.

You once asked, 'What if this book doesn't work out?' You used a flippant tone, possibly to mask fear. 'And even if it does, who will buy it?'

I remembered then what Aseem had said, 'It's a great subject. Basically, the general public forgives the super-rich most things except their failure to routinely supply scandal and drama.'

I wondered what to say, toyed with something like, 'Of course, it will,' and then decided in favour of: 'If you keep working, it will.'

How little I knew then that I would write something like the book you didn't want to write, the story about the hollow men.

You went to the United States to do more interviews. I worked harder on a translation I should never have undertaken, untying one knot after another, always feeling the solution to be beyond me. I didn't tell you that I took up French again with the help of Duolingo all those years after a brief attempt at IIT? And found the acquisition of a language more precise than both English and Hindi oddly soothing.

I found some ready-made dal at Whole Foods that, microwaved right, came delectably close to the one my mother cooked. I went to the optometrist and discovered I needed reading glasses. You said, when we Skyped, that I look distinguished in them, and rotated your head – your neck, you said, was stiff with all the rapid notetaking.

I told you that I had finally read *A Bend in the River*, in a sunbleached Picador paperback I found on your shelves, with your father's name inside in ornate handwriting, and realised that the sentiment about trampling the past so often quoted by Aseem, and credited by him to Naipaul, is uttered by a character who ends badly in the novel.

You said, 'You are always making these discoveries in London.' You had decided that London had brought out another side of my personality, in which, you once said, 'worldliness' and 'naïvety' were charmingly combined.

I started to say that I should have read *A Bend in the River* earlier, and that Naipaul struck me as less a prototype of the globalised man than an elegist of defeated and damaged men, but then stopped, out of fear of meeting your political objections to him.

You now said, changing the subject, 'You know, talking to Virendra, I felt again that you should write a memoir.'

'I can't think of anyone who will be interested in my life,' I said.

'But you have so much to say about other people, India, everything.'

We talked in this vein for a bit, about books that were best left unwritten. Your head froze when I mentioned I had run into your literary agent on Oxford Street, and she had blanked me.

I became more alert in your absence to the various electronic sounds in your apartment: the washing machine completing its cycle, the boiler going *whoosh*, and Alexa suddenly piping up, unasked, in the miraculous stillness. And though Alexa always said, '*Sorry, I can't help you with that,*' I marvelled at how easeful the world had become for me.

You returned from the US with news about Siva and Virendra. The latter recounted stories of being viciously abused at his correctional facility in Massachusetts. Though he had known that law enforcement in America is institutionally racist, its actual experience had shocked him; he had vowed to devote his life after prison to fighting racism in American life. He was also determined to battle senior upper-caste Hindus at Cisco, Apple, Google and Facebook who discriminated against low-caste employees.

He had spoken emotionally of the central folly of his life – taking men like Rajat Gupta, recently released from prison, and other go-getting Indian Americans as role models. Siva had turned philosophical in custody, asking for translations of the *Bhagavad Gita* and the *Upanishads*. You also reported that your brother was finally turning against Trump.

It rained unrelentingly in London, adding to the gloom of the news about Brexit and the likely elevation of a Churchillian delusion with crazed hair to 10 Downing Street – developments that you seemed to take as a personal blow.

Sunlit places across the English Channel beckoned. 'Let's go to Venice,' you suggested in the midst of transcribing your interviews.

And we did, still partaking of the attitude to experience you and your fellow expatriates had, that prodigal conviction that one reality can be swiftly exchanged for another, more comfortable one: a drizzly grey morning in Kensington for incandescent San Marco where two sunglassed teenagers in very short shorts were being vivaciously indecisive over strawberry and pistachio while a beggar with a headscarf knotted under her chin squatted in a sunless side alley.

From the usurious Hotel Danieli, which you had insisted on paying for, and where I uncomfortably watched you bleed money, to the demure tunes of that trio in the lobby, we took a gondola to the Lido.

I remember well that afternoon on a white strip of beach under a beaten-tin sky scraped and ripped by the echoless loud Italian of children on tricycles, shouts of young volleyball players, and laughter from spectators perched on the promenade above the beach, their bare brown legs hanging down in a fringe over the sand.

A flag behind me kept flapping mournfully, though there was no breeze. You went for a walk; I lay on a towel over the fine white sand and watched the very short masseuses from Guangdong sidestep their way through rows of pink-hued sunbathers, nearly poking them with their plastic-sheathed bilingual menus in contrast to the tall, robed Somalis who stood near the water, offering their knock-off Louis Vuitton bags with stylish gestures that fully admitted their lack of hope.

Both vendors were met by the raptly recumbent figures with a half-raised head and dismissive flip of the hand. Oddly wounded by the sight, I imagined the local dwellings of the Chinese and the Africans, from where they had set out each morning of that fading summer, arms and shoulders laden with bags and backpacks, making their last futile attempts of the year.

The chorus of delight from the children and teenagers rose and fell, and then faded; the flag kept crackling and ripping. I started to think for some reason of those first expectant hours in Pondicherry with you: the many small hurdles thrown in our way by the surly receptionist, the leering teenaged cashier at the pharmacy and even the accommodating North Indian manager who asked us why we had not joined any of the yoga and meditation courses on offer at the retreat.

As if transported on a time machine, a contingent of fully dressed young men from India crossed and recrossed the horizon.

They seemed a bit lost, to be searching for something or someone. Their Punjabi voices were calming and in my dreamy haze I stood shoulder to shoulder with them: fellow desis, residents of Ludhiana and Amritsar, wrenched out of place, and looking for a familiar landmark to guide them home.

And then I noticed two of them surreptitiously filming you on their phones as you strolled across the beach, hugging the waterline, with movements out of swimwear and beach resort advertisements: promising and rich.

As you turned back, and started, with a wave, to walk over to where I lay, they shot me curiously mixed looks, contemptuous and lewd and knowing.

Back in Venice, after a trip through a fierce late-summer thunderstorm, the vaporetto struck the dimly lit landing with a harsh clunk; the boat rushed backward, and I nearly fell into the noisily churning water. The thought came to me, more loudly than ever – *What am I doing here?* – as we walked back to the hotel through crowds of people – people I would, it abruptly became clear to me, never understand, and I ached with a longing to go home – not to the hotel with the trio playing in the lobby, but home, to all that I had once known and understood.

Then came the news of Virendra's death. You saw it on your Twitter feed as we landed at Heathrow, after a delayed flight, during which you fell asleep against my shoulder. He had hanged himself using a trash bag – a common method of suicide, I later learned from Google. A will – evidently prepared even as you were interviewing him in Massachusetts – left millions of dollars to a charity for homeless widows in Benares, a campaign for prison reform in Texas and an advocacy group fighting against upper-caste bias in Silicon Valley.

He had also set aside some money for Aseem's magazine, and for a Dalit publishing house in Chennai – heartfelt but empty gestures to a world he was leaving, for the will, I later read in one of the articles, could not be observed.

Did Aseem also know that all of Virendra's assets would be seized by the government? 'A fascinatingly complex and flawed human being,' you read out the title of his obituary while we were still at immigration in Heathrow. When you resumed in the Uber to Kensington, the sentence that nagged at me in the moving car was: 'Virendra's suicide note was his extraordinarily munificent will, which showed the deep sincerity of his late feeling for social justice.'

I don't know why I found the word 'munificent' grating. Why couldn't Aseem have said 'generous' instead? You read aloud a couple of other notices as the London of wet light and frigid buildings flickered past the windows, and I found in myself not sadness but a cold curiosity about the details of Virendra's last moments.

At home, I surfed through your Indian satellite TV channels while you unpacked, moving quickly through the hyper-nationalist ones to linger on the only non-hysterical broadcaster left on television, to see if there was any news about Virendra.

There was nothing; the New India had long disowned its first Dalit magnate.

I kept watching, marvelling, yet again, at how the unfolding calamity of my homeland – the fiendish rulers, the brutal para-militaries in Kashmir, the lynch mobs, the poor everywhere, starving in droughts, and drowned by unseasonable floods – became manageable when described in the smartly modulated tones of the Oxbridge-educated anchors.

I muted the TV and sat hunched on a beanbag without moving. I thought of what Virendra had told you about his sense of futility about a life spent conforming to conventional images of success and fame.

Did he have a choice in his long climb out of destitution and indignity? I wondered if I should have tried to be in touch with Virendra while he was in prison. We may have drifted apart ages ago, but hadn't we come, via different routes, to inhabit a similar state? Hadn't we allowed our early experience of humiliation to dictate too much of our lives, by first enduring it dumbly and then refusing to put words to it?

'Do you want to talk about it now or later?'

I looked up to see you standing in the doorway, a coffee mug in one hand. You wore the burnished burgundy boots you had collected that morning at an on-site workshop near the Rialto, and an aromatic whiff of leather and polish reached me.

I don't know why, but the boots made up my mind: I didn't want to talk about it.

You walked away and started to run a bath. I moved to my study, to its tomb-like gloom of closed curtains, where the chill in the air seemed like something from my past. I sat on my chair in the dark, and, to the churning and gushing of water, again tried to feel grief over Virendra's death.

But the memories I summoned, perhaps too deliberately, from our shared years at IIT and that afternoon at East Hampton were lifeless, except when I remembered the scene of our ritual degradation and the fear I lived with for months: that one day I would open the door to our room and find Virendra hanging from the ceiling.

When you turned off the bath, the flow of my feelings also subsided; and I began to look through my pile of mail, and to unpack and undress.

The tears came later that night, you asleep beside me, and they flowed in such a torrent that I stopped wiping them away and let them trickle down my temples and fall on the pillow. But they came out of other griefs, and returned me to them.

Of course, what I began to feel especially acutely after that trip to the Lido – the veils of unreality coming down, muzzling my deepest thoughts and impulses – had long been silently ripening within me.

In the midst of a near-perfect sensuous existence, I had begun to feel horrified by myself, by my near-total inability to connect and reconcile my past to the present, my failure to retrace how I entered another life, almost an entirely new mode of being.

Seized with fright of all that had changed and was changing, I became desperate to hold on to a time when the rules were clear, the feelings simple, and no impersonations were necessary.

Over the years, I had recreated some certainties in Ranipur, finding in my life there the dignity and stability I had so painfully lacked as a child and student. In Pondicherry and then London, I had abruptly freed myself of them. I had abandoned the place and people that had once welcomed and comforted me. I had started to resemble Aseem: floating through the world, using up its opportunities of power and pleasure.

Aseem upheld this kind of improvised life powered by ambition and endless self-invention as a noble human adventure – one that had been providentially made available to us after many bleak centuries of zero choice. But I increasingly felt – and perhaps this was the most crucial of the discoveries you said I made in London – that, starting with nothing from Deoli, I had succeeded with my improvisations too well, and that they had saddled me with a self-consciousness when I was content not being noticed at all.

★

I remember, in this connection, our last evening out in London at the second anniversary of a left-wing literary magazine at the LSE. As often in the afternoons before going out, you had warmed up on the treadmill, done squats and lunges with a kettle bell and showered before inspecting, wearing a kimono, your walk-in wardrobe. You had dressed carefully: a high-necked blouse, short skirt, sparkling earrings, eyeshadow and lips made up big and full. Leaving the flat in your new Venice boots, you put on a red beret, took it off, and then put it back on.

The speeches at the event had been unusually long, intensifying the Gadarene rush to wine and cheese. Holding a glass of sparkling water, you towered in your beret over the crowd, and that curious London party chatter, both vehement and measured.

I looked at your face, as desirably regal as ever, but bruised, the swollen lips that so thrillingly suggested poised defiance thinned into a half-smile.

You started to rage against one of the speakers, a New Labour functionary, and chief exponent of its 'tough on immigration' policy, who proclaimed his love for literary fiction, connecting it nebulously, with some jokes that we could not hear, to the need for Britain to remain in the European Union.

I kept looking at your face. How often I had looked at it with amazement and joy, close up in bed or from across a crowded room. But today it seemed a stranger's face; and a frightening realisation came to me: that you belonged to a world that could never be mine.

You said, 'Do we really need to hear about literature from such discredited Blairites and Obama-ites any more? Is it enough that they read literary novels?'

We left the LSE and walked down an already Christmassy Strand to the Wagamama in Covent Garden. Crossing a street, we nearly collided with a bicyclist. You looked over your shoulder to glare at him, quickened your stride, and resumed your complaint. In addition to the New Labour apparatchik, you had been provoked that evening by the presence of a Somali-British woman in a green turban and ankle boots, who had used her much-retweeted arguments against social media to secure a book contract and a feature article on *Vogue* online.

'Come on!' you started, thrusting out your lower lip and blowing a puff of air upwards. 'This is just another mode of self-branding on social media. You attack Twitter on Twitter, Instagram on Instagram, shout to the skies how they are all awful to women, LGBTQ people, people of colour, but you are never ever not online. If you were truly honest, you would leave your socials, delete your accounts. Like so many people who found it noxious. But publishers fall for it. They are looking to fill their very few slots for people from minority backgrounds . . .'

Your bad temper always seemed a bit exaggerated for my benefit. Battling on in that city against discouragement, you had only me as witness to your private moods, if millions more to your chosen posture on social media.

I would often say, 'You can't let yourself be distracted by what other people are doing.' I would bring up the example of the Hindi writers I translated, who did their best work in isolation, burdened with day jobs, often on the edge of penury but unperturbed by rumours of large publishing advances to rivals, and immune to temptations of 'likes' and retweets.

Today, I listened to you, but trapped in my own thoughts and afterthoughts, and anxieties about travel, I did not say anything.

I had been failing lately to meet your tone of complaint; had even begun to begrudge the tame way I fell in line with it. It reminded me of a larger loss of will: the way you had remoulded my life until I fitted into yours while remaining utterly indifferent to my past.

I could still play myself at those Sunday brunches. I even went to a political demonstration for the first time in my life, against Brexit, for the environment, my own face carrying the slightly foolish expression of nervous participation as I marched and ambled with you and your acquaintances amid a sea of tense eyes and jaws resolute with virtue. And, as always, we returned at the end of the day to the apartment steeped in silence and discretion and took off our make-up before the bathroom mirror flanked by small golden bulbs.

But I couldn't avoid the feeling that I was performing in a troupe with better actors. The artificial bond between us of coupledom – Arun and Alia against an unaccommodating world – had started to come loose.

I had cherished, from the time your fingers touched my face in Pondicherry, making something inside me come open, the reassuring feeling of skin against skin, and outside it, the animal ease with which you, naked or half-naked, went about your routine. I had come to need your presence, from the time you calmly walked up to me from the open bathroom and embraced me in Pondicherry, as pure intimacy; it summed up everything I had shied away from for much of my life.

In bed this last night, you held me just as self-confidently and affectionately as you had, emerging from that bathroom in Pondicherry. I felt again that peculiar innocence in acting out desires under a foreign sky with nothing from my past in attendance. In repose, your face filled up again with its promise of clarity and trust; and, seeing again those tangled lashes at the corners of your eyes, I felt that I was solely responsible for my unhappiness, that all my judgements of you were an attempt to shift the blame, and that I had deceived both myself and you in playing a role I was never cut out for.

And when on this cold night you suddenly got up, and with one large gesture, pulled the Kantha duvet cover off the bed, wrapped it about yourself, and walked hurriedly to the bathroom, slamming the door shut, the bedroom suddenly felt desolate.

'What is meant by emptiness?' you had asked, casually, when you saw me reading in bed a book by a scholar of Buddhist philosophy with the word in the title. We talked about this for a bit. To you the word denoted lack, something missing or absent, such as love and attention.

You had noticed it in the men you dated, whom you had found lightweight, not in their credentials or commitment but in their self. Emptiness was a space that could be filled, leading to happiness.

This is broadly what I thought, too, until I met Sonam a few days after returning from Venice. A Tibetan monk, who had been living in exile in Himachal, a day's drive from Ranipur, actually, Sonam was speaking at a Buddhist centre just a few stops away on the Underground.

I wonder now what made me seek out a man of irreproachable virtue: perhaps the close reflection I found of myself in fallen men.

The dingy squat building on the Caledonian Road was almost full when I arrived, the small lecture hall packed with people who had clearly come straight from work. Listening to middle-class men and women solemnly describe their lives and struggles, Sonam picked his nose, and, more scandalously, laughed; he seemed continuously driven to mirth by the neuroses of the West. 'Too much self, self, self! Too much fake drama!'

He interrupted a woman who said that she had 'spent years in psychotherapy, struggling with feelings of guilt and narcissism' with: 'What is achieved by becoming a spectator of your own fake drama?'

Someone behind me gasped; I think I also heard the rustling and scraping sounds of an early exit. Sonam carried on, 'Please understand! This is very, very important. Very, very important . . . very . . .' His English waning, he turned to his interpreter, a saffron-robed Irish nun, speaking to her in Tibetan.

She began to speak: 'This Western psychologising is a cheap way to make you feel you have a unique self with enigmatic depths. The fact is that there is no self that is separate from your state of desiring and anger and fear and guilt and anxiety. The self itself is empty. It has no existence by itself. It is empty.'

Delivered in her melodious accent, Sonam's thoughts had something piercing in them.

When a man, probably American by his accent, started to say, 'I wanted to find myself, so I . . .' Sonam retorted in English: 'Why? When did you misplace yourself?'

He then turned to the Irish nun with rapid-fire Tibetan. She translated, 'Don't get entangled in emotions, views, concepts and theories, and start identifying your self with them. Stay away from what the Buddha called the "jungle of opinions". Just observe, just observe the nature of your mind, the constant flux in it, observe the true nature of things. And that nature is empty.

'I am not asking you to get rid of the self: that's not possible, because there never was a self. I am not asking you to get rid of the sense of your self that your state of desiring and anger and fear and anxiety creates. How can you function without it? It is a reflex. I am asking you to work towards a sense of self that is more aware of, more comfortable with, its constructed nature. I am asking you to mediate and to observe your mind, the way thoughts and emotions and desires arise in it and fade away. I am asking you to calmly watch this self that you so desperately cling to, how it crumbles, how it vanishes.'

The interpreter didn't tone down Sonam's tactless questions to those who confessed their unhappiness to him: 'What is this happiness you are pursuing or lacking? Show me someone who has achieved it, and I will show you an evil or absolutely ignorant person.'

Clapping began somewhere at the back, and then spluttered out in lonely embarrassment, like the applause of tourists between movements at Wigmore Hall.

To people who had tried to raise vegetables in allotments, joined gyms and tennis clubs, and promised themselves to read all the top 100 fiction and non-fiction books compiled by the BBC, Sonam generally offered reproach rather than release. He demanded a confrontation with suffering, claiming it was the only key to contentment – never, happiness. He urged us to come to terms with death, our mortality, and 'embrace the void within'.

I couldn't help staring at the stubby white space on Sonam's hands where his fingernails once had been. The Chinese police in Lhasa, who arrested him at his rural monastery for possessing a picture of the Dalai Lama, had taken pliers to his fingers and nipples, and an electric cattle prod to his genitals, during the seven years they kept him captive.

During the Q&A, I raised my right hand awkwardly, and kept it up briefly even after the roving mic was in my left hand.

I asked him: 'What is the difference between the feeling of inner emptiness and the Buddhist notion of the void?'

He answered tersely, speaking through the Irish nun, that there was none, except that there was no fear and anxiety in the latter.

No other words passed between us on this first meeting; he seemed not to notice my existence any more.

Still, I was entranced by him, by his indifference to people and events, by a presence so stark and dense, and insights so apt to my long imposture: they suddenly dispelled the swarm of disjointed and impotent thoughts that had invaded my mind since Virendra's death, and started to crystallise a radical decision.

You asked why I was suddenly delving into Tibetan history and philosophy, setting aside my bedside mini-tower of fiction and literary periodicals. I said, 'I just find them fascinating.'

Assailed by guilt, over the plan germinating inside my head, I couldn't add why I had become fascinated by Sonam and figures like him – 'renouncers', Aseem used to call them, whose acceptance of limitation gave them a quality of eternity, a substantiality and strength such as we no longer encounter in our circles, or confuse with intellectual fluency.

I also couldn't say to you how cold my usual reading had lately left me. Neither the individual fates detailed in literature nor the ideological chatter of the periodicals, reproduced and annotated in countless emails and social media posts, seemed to give me the frisson that indicates the presence of a liberating truth.

I had never thought of myself as religious or even spiritual. I think I left it all behind at the temple near my home with the bidi-smoking priest with caked sandalwood paste on his forehead. It was with pity that I watched in subsequent years my doomed mother prostrate herself every morning before a litter of religious pictures and figurines in her altar.

I had read about Sonam in a *New Scientist* article, which, tweeted by a Tibetan activist, had been, you might remember, retweeted by you. I immediately recognised the name, though it was misspelled in the article, of his monastery – I had visited it once during my early treks.

The article cited neurologists and clinical psychiatrists as saying that torture victims from Tibet were remarkably undamaged by their ordeal. Campaigners for Tibetan independence had flown him out from his monastery in Himachal, to which he had escaped from Tibet, and wheeled him out in London; they were hoping to revive their failing campaign to prick the world's conscience about Chinese atrocities in Tibet. But they miscalculated.

Sonam turned out to be as indifferent to political passion as to bourgeois tactfulness. During his long trauma, which he endured in the Tibetan way by meditating on a mental image of a corpse, he had been primarily afraid, he told us, of hating the Chinese; this loathing and the craving for revenge would have destroyed him more quickly than the electric cattle prod of his torturers. He also had no interest in his personal drama of arrest, torture, imprisonment, escape to India, and might have also dismissed it as fake.

For an aspirant to nirvana, such an experience was more evidence of the calamity of being reborn and dying again. He had none of our desperate attachment to the drama of history, nothing of our lunatic aspiration to direct it, and cast ourselves as lead actors.

I envied him his indifference and serenity. I had approached Sonam with the conventional respect due to an extraordinary survivor and a rare saint in our times. As I listened to him, watching his mobile face aglow with childlike eagerness and a sourceless, unbookish intelligence, I began to think of him as someone greater: someone who, despite the untreatable wounds inflicted on him, was passing his time on earth better than most of us.

When I went again to the Buddhist Centre on Caledonian Road, this time to request a private meeting with Sonam as well as to hear him speak, it no longer mattered that he scarcely seemed to take in his audience while he was talking. To me that was part of his unique virtue: his refusal to project, and his ability to stem, while listening, the flow of unconsidered speech.

He spoke this time of how our desires make us who we are. Fully existing only in the interval between desire and fulfilment, we swell with the illusion of our distinctive self. But fulfilment brings little or no satisfaction; lack of satisfaction makes us desire again, extending into the future the original illusion of the desiring self, and its discontents.

Nineteen

All around me, the sense of an ending seemed to be gaining ground. People, you said, people we knew were moving away from London amid heightened political and economic uncertainty; and their imminent flight from what they had long seen as the centre of the world seemed to diminish the parties we went to, making the liveliest expatriates there look like they were hiding a nervousness about their future.

Amid multiple crises, and half-news and rumours about deals and no-deals, the expectation of a dénouement heightened the most banal headlines in the *Evening Standard* about Britain and the European Union – what the vendor at the Tube exit near your apartment cried out in abrupt throaty bursts as people surged up the stairs thick and black to showery afternoons, unfurling their umbrellas as they hunched away, outpacing the black cabs with glistening tops creeping through the rain.

I was, however, waiting for a different climax, waiting to end a relationship, and in my last few days in London, I often found myself playing with these words, as though starting a book: *One morning, while she was sleeping . . .*

As it turned out, you *were* sleeping on your stomach, your hair a mass of tangles on the pillow, and the lemongrass-smelling remnants of a Thai takeaway from two evenings ago still scattered around the cold white kitchen, when I stuffed my last pound notes in an envelope and left them on your desk. Slowly tiptoeing across the wooden floor, which creaked just as reproachfully as it did in my first days in London, I crept out with my suitcases, dragged them down the uncarpeted stairway, thumping past the spew of unopened *Hello!* in front of our Russian neighbour's door, out to the empty street where a white cat wove itself in and out of black iron railings, and took an Uber to Heathrow.

I know you have never understood why I couldn't speak to you before leaving. But I just didn't know how to explain myself to you – why I kept waiting for my mother's death to become real to me and was bewildered that it hadn't; why it had suddenly become, after Virendra's death and my discovery of Sonam, impossible for me to stay in London any longer; why I now felt lost in the perfect order and calm of your home that I had so cherished during my early days in the city.

In the morning, with the homeless still slumped in doorways, London looked even more grey and over-used, a city carefully patching up and maintaining its past, and posing endlessly for photographs, paintings and now Instagram. How suddenly had I lost all my pleasure in the city!

And as the car hurtled down a traffic-less stretch, the air suddenly rushing in through the half-open window, I felt a surge of possibility. Perhaps I could now finally set aside this laboured character who had lived in a foreign country, speaking a familiar language that fit him like a second skin without ever being intimately his, still beholden to a past that no one he knew shared or understood.

But the British-Asian woman at the check-in desk said that my flight was delayed by three hours due to 'late arrival of the aircraft'. The news came as a blow, and I stood staring at the inflamed blood vessels around her irises before turning away: for some reason, I had imagined myself airborne, 30,000 feet high, while you lay deep in asleep.

I went to Costa and sat down with a cup of tea I didn't need and a protein bar that I couldn't eat. A tinkle alerted me to pound coins that had yet again fallen out of a trouser pocket. I retrieved them from the grimy floor, feeling slightly foolish as always, my face flushed, and then made the mistake of doing what everyone around me seemed to be doing. I opened my laptop, glanced at the *Guardian*'s home page and its unvarying mix of slow-moving horror and jauntiness.

I noticed a long strand of hair sprawled across my keyboard; it must have come from the teeth of your comb that I had hastily drawn through my hair that morning.

I looked at drafts of my departure note to you – my first attempt to communicate all that I felt incapable of expressing, and whose scope has widened so uncontrollably in the months since.

Nearly all the drafts began with the line, *Dear Alia, I find it nearly impossible to explain why I decided to go back to India, without telling you* . . . And they were all followed with, *These last few months with you have been wonderful* . . .

They then stalled variously at, *But beneath the joy of being with you there was anguish and fear, and lately I have begun to feel them* . . .

One of the drafts attempted a larger self-reckoning: *I have searched and searched but cannot isolate any day or month or incident when I took a wrong turning. All I know is that I did take it* . . .

I closed my drafts and checked your socials.

You were up, probably still in bed, and hectic on Twitter, though you complained often about squandering your most productive hours to it. You had thanked @Malala 'for speaking out on Kashmir'. The first of sixty-two responses to your gratitude was from @proudlyHindu: 'Dream girl, dream on', liked by 243 people. You had retweeted a recent op-ed in the *Washington Post* asking Bill Gates to rescind his foundation's award to Narendra Modi.

*

Finally, I boarded the aircraft. Two Indian girls settled in the seats behind me were discussing their adventures in London clubs.

'So we are talking about tennis, and the skinny Spanish kid says, "Why don't you come visit me in Mallorca and we'll play there?" and I am, like, "OK, sure," and then he goes, "Actually, that's a serious invite," and I am, like, "Yeah, man, I'd love to, whatever," and he gets my vibe and is kinda upset, goes all class struggle on me, starts saying stuff like how Nadal is a true son of the soil or some such shit while Federer is some spoilt Swiss guy . . .'

I had noticed them at the check-in desk, wearing identical outsized earrings, hunched over Facebook, and then at the boarding queue, teetering on high heels, and thumb-pecking their iPhones. One of them stroked her dyed blue hair.

Standing behind them, I espied their fake fingernails and their names on boarding passes. Teenaged daughters of upper-caste rich businessman, I speculated, recently released from a constricted adolescence and now returning home after a heady experience of London.

I could imagine them arriving in Delhi at night. The uniformed driver waiting, bleary-eyed but watchfully obsequious, the swift drive in a Mercedes or Land Rover to Golf Links or Sunder Nagar, restful sleep followed by breakfast – masala omelettes cooked by a maid who got up at 4.30 a.m. and started work at 6 a.m. – with adoring parents on the terrace, as the morning sun dances and parakeets chirp in the neem trees, and servants walk plump Alsatians and Dobermanns on the shaded lanes below.

I sat in the reclined chair, and closed my eyes, waiting for sleep, and distance. I must have dozed for a bit before being woken up by a memory of my toothbrush in a glass at your apartment – I had left it behind.

Other anxieties of domestic life stirred: whether you had cleared the kitchen of its dirty mound of dishes and takeaway bags before Olga arrived? Had I flushed the loo before leaving?

I became aware of the matronly Sikh lady next to me, who had stacked the overhead compartment with bags of duty-free perfumes. A slow, frowning woman, with bristly hair at the corner of her lips, she seemed very unwell, and heavily medicated.

Head thrown back, eyes wide open, she was opening and closing her mouth wordlessly, like a gasping invalid. I twisted the nozzle of the air valve above her and told her to breathe deeply.

She looked at me, blankly, and said nothing.

The dull clunk of ice cubes in the business-class cabin in front began to reach us. The food and drinks trolley presently emerged from behind blue curtains; the cries of 'champagne, please!' rose from an aisle of British men, all thickset, with booming laughs, sunburnt necks and, in one case, a vaguely Australian accent.

Slightly flirty with them –'How about two to get you started?' – the Indian stewardess in a shalwar-kameez was brusque with the Sikh woman, repeating 'Excuse me!' in louder tones to her.

No, it was finally ascertained, she did not want any drinks or nuts.

When food finally appeared on her tray, her thin shrivelled hands shook as they clutched a glass of water, and plastic knives and forks; I had to help her eat, mixing microwaved dal and rice into greater mush.

The Indian stewardess, serving out a third round of champagne to the British men, caught my eye and smirked – *The kind of people who travel these days*, her smirk seemed to say. I was more surprised when she said something to a male colleague, who turned to look at the Sikh woman.

I wanted to scold her. But I saw myself, virtuously outraging, and paused – I could claim no virtue.

When the lights were turned off, window shades drawn, and the voices around me receded, I listlessly surfed through the video channels. I watched half an episode of *Friends*, another half of *Sacred Games*, before finally languishing before the map of the journey, watching the metallic swan inch across borders, obliterating distances that for many millennia had kept the ancestors of modern humans at home, safe within the limits of appeasable desire.

I must have dozed off because when I woke up, roused by the pilot's pre-arrival banter, the stewardesses were coming down the aisles with gaping garbage bags.

Nothing had changed. The Sikh woman was sitting slightly hunched, her blue-veined hands clasped. The British men were heartily consuming their last glasses of free alcohol, the Australian accent amid them now more pronounced. The girls were still chatting.

The seat-belts sign came on. I was almost surprised. I hadn't expected to arrive so soon.

As we descended, ears popping, I inserted my BSNL sim card. 'No Service' the message stood for a few exasperating minutes. And then service kicked in and the emails came pouring in. I scrolled up and down. I checked the spam box. There was nothing from you.

Trapped in my seat by the Sikh woman awaiting a wheelchair, I watched the girls straighten their clothes, cast around in the overhead compartments for their bags.

I saw them again at the carousel sadly looping past, standing with the other calmly impatient passengers, all strangers now, and felt a pang of loneliness: people who had been in my life for hours were about to scatter, attached not to me but to the smiling mouths, waving hands and wide-open arms at the exit.

It was then that the phone throbbed. I swiped down to see a WhatsApp message: *What the fuck, Arun? What happened? Where are you?*

There were also three missed calls from you.

I put the phone back into airplane mode.

Exiting customs, where I heard someone say, 'Do you know who I am?', I walked straight into a milling crowd of thousands, past the kiosks of app-operated cab companies to the old taxi stand, where I was quoted an absurd fare to the nearby airport hotel by a young Haryanvi driver.

I felt an old indignation, always high-minded and now absurd, over my poverty suddenly rise up; I told myself, as I negotiated haltingly in Hindi, a language that felt strangely unfamiliar after being unused for months, that it was a matter of rupees not pounds.

On the airport road, policemen were, with imperious gestures, stopping vehicles and herding them into one lane. A long queue quickly built up; men, women and children in rags began to drift past the stationary cars, a couple vending pirated paperbacks of *The White Tiger* and *The Monk Who Sold his Ferrari*, all the others holding out empty palms.

Outriders presently appeared on motorbikes; a long black Mercedes gleamed past, flanked and trailed by more armed escorts; and the traffic broke loose again, honking at the sluggish and dazed beggars.

At one traffic light, a girl suddenly appeared at the window, smiling as she stretched out both her thin sallow hands into the taxi. But we were moving; the light in her face went out as she drew back empty-handed, and she fell away from the taxi as if she were sinking in water.

I grieved over the girl for a while; and when the taxi stopped in the portico of my hotel, I realised with something like amazement that I had not thought of my own troubles for at least five minutes.

My last night in London had been repeatedly broken by the nagging anxiety that it was time to get up. I hadn't set an alarm for fear of waking you up, and awakened again and again to digits on the bedside radio that told me that I had barely slept half an hour since the last interruption.

I now lay in bed restlessly, the noise of the Boeing's engine still beating at my ears, too exhausted and off-schedule to sleep, and tried to determine the precise moment when you discovered that I had left – perhaps when you came across the envelope of cash, with 'for bills' scribbled on the front, that I left on your desk beside old copies of *Fortune* magazine.

I thought of you waking up and realising that I wasn't lying next to you. The first twenty to thirty minutes of your day were so strictly allotted to news and social media that there wouldn't be a moment for you to think about anything else.

After a while, you would rise from your bed and shake out the duvet right afterwards. You would brew some coffee for both of us in the large cafetière, your eyelashes still stuck with sleep, while still glancing at your phone. Putting out milk and sugar on the counter, you would start to wonder about my absence. But hadn't I resolved, while in Venice, to take more exercise, to go walking in Hyde Park in the mornings if the weather allowed?

Holding your coffee mug, you would go to your study to dally a bit online, and find my envelope of cash.

I woke up in the middle of the night to strange thoughts wafting through my head: could I return to London and resume .

our life? Would you understand that I had got lost for a while? Would you deduce that I had always meant to leave London since I had never tried to convert my visitor's visa despite your urgings and paid my share of the bills to you in cash? Would you try to reach out to me if and when you return to India to attend Aseem's festival in the New Year?

A restless half-night later, much of it spent watching gnats dance in the flickering sulphur yellow light of a broken lamp outside my window, I was on my way again: bleary early-morning flight to Shimla, and a battered Maruti van – the cheapest taxi available outside the toy airport – to the border with Tibet.

The air felt cool outside the small aircraft. My body aching, and mind frozen by jet lag, I looked out of the window occasionally to see giant tin-roofed slums tottering on steep hillsides or collapsing into valleys.

Homes had been nested up high on the hills, with unroofed concrete staircases winding up their sides. There was garish colour everywhere: rocks daubed with Pepsi and Coca-Cola signs, shop signboards with Shah Rukh Khan smiling down, and walls layered with movie posters.

Twenty years ago, I had first taken the road to the Tibetan border, and over several trips, the sensations produced by the stupendously empty landscape had multiplied and re-multiplied. I had brought my mother once. It was the first time she had been in a car for a joyride, and, after the first few moments of fright, when our Maruti 800 nearly collided with a bullock cart full of peasants sitting with legs dangling over the sides, she seemed to have really enjoyed herself, her wrinkled, perpetually anxious face beaming with happiness.

Now, more than a decade later, there were construction sites everywhere for dams and reservoirs, gigantic dynamite-inflicted wounds in the mountains, which rows of labourers, each armed with a shovel, seemed to be scratching all over. And on most corners, there were giant billboards, as big as a house, of Modi promising national uplift, alongside billboards advertising it: condominiums with two-car garages and sparkling fountains, against a background of smooth highways and shiny malls. One of the billboards, dug into mud, and fringed at the bottom with dust, proclaimed an 'Indian Century' together with pictures from a failed space mission to the moon.

You probably have no memory of the promises of national development Aseem and I grew up with. That we, lurching out of our dark huts and fields, were all going to be ushered into sleek bright modernity, that we'd wear suits and ties, and work and live in offices and homes of concrete and glass.

Modi had blown up this relatively modest bubble of collective aspiration: with his 'smart cities' and 'bullet trains' and planned exploration of the other side of the moon, he promised a miracle that would exceed anything in the rest of the world.

The proclamations of unmatched progress had left me cold before. After my months in London, they seemed to radiate pathos: the desire of a small-town tea-seller to project himself as a whizz-kid of modernity, to promise the moon to people as spurned and resentful as he was.

And, in his new plumage, the sleeveless bandhgalla jackets, flamboyantly different in every billboard frame, I saw the vanity that had touched Aseem and me, too, in our flat caps and bomber jackets.

I closed my eyes and tried to sleep, but soon became aware of an empty bottle that was rolling and clinking against the metal legs of my seat. A bus overtook us, revealing a row of men clinging to its steel-framed back, their hair asprawl and trousers flapping hard against their ankles, and disappeared from sight. We then languished behind a loose convoy of military trucks, in which, under roped tarpaulins jabbering loose, sat young soldiers in orderly rows. Wrists and necks squirming in ill-fitting uniforms, they occasionally had humiliated faces like those of prisoners.

Groaning up steep inclines, the trucks sprayed our car with thick black smoke until, slapping the horn with his palm, my driver scurried ahead; and I braced myself: on those twisty and narrow roads a heedless car or truck would be invisible long enough to produce a collision.

For miles the taxi lagged behind a mud-splattered Hilux overloaded with rusty rebars that protruded out of their tarpaulin cover straight into our windscreen. I felt the driver grow impatient to overtake it. When he thought his chance had come on a section of the road that, though flat, was edged by recently dug ditches, he accelerated, but miscalculated the speed of the oncoming vehicle – a massive, ugly truck.

Cutting in front of the Hilux, which braked with spastic squeals, we avoided collision with the truck by an inch – but only to see a motorcyclist trying to overtake it twist his motorcycle out of our path and plunge, rear wheel cartoonishly raised to the sky, into the ditch.

I looked at the driver; he was glaring ahead. I did the same after an initial burst of anger. You might not sympathise with my hard-hearted decision. But the damage to the motorcyclist and his machine could only have been minor – much less than what we would have suffered had we got involved deeper with the accident and the police.

The driver was barely out of his teens, wearing upper-caste marks on his forehead, and knock-off Barbour, Levi's and Nike on the rest of his thin frame. He worked for Sood's taxi company in Ranipur; slowly detaching himself at Shimla airport from the crowd of ogling drivers with fingers hooked on the diamond-mesh wire fence, he had looked vaguely familiar.

He walked with a swagger, always an ominous sign among taxi drivers on narrow mountain roads, and there was something cocky about the way he slid open the door to reveal empty Bisleri bottles, Frooti packs, and oil-stained brown paper bags on the seats – a mess that he then glacially cleared, or not quite: something kept slithering about.

Small and slumped over the steering wheel, the draught combing his hair into a coarse quiff, he chewed on a toothpick; removing it to clear his throat and spit, he sent an alarmingly thick and green glob out of his window.

He kept me tense, loudly playing Bollywood songs stored in a USB stick flickering amber under an altar to Vaishno Devi; he frequently looked at his Xiaomi, checking WhatsApp, and taking a selfie, all the time bringing the screen very close to his face.

At a dhaba, next to a construction site – cement mixer; piles of brick and rebars everywhere, and the air heavy with the smell of petrol and dirt – the driver draped his head with headphones and crouched over a video. Returning from the toilet, I saw a glimpse of his screen: white buttocks rising up and down between splayed knees.

My phone on the resin seat throbbed often: text message from BSNL, and exhortations to buy Baba Ramdev's grains. If there was more from you, I did not know; I could not bear to look.

The road rose and rose, turning this way and that, past the burned tang of fresh-laid asphalt, and the van made its laboured circles up hills sighing gaseously, the empty bottle rolling and clinking. The green veins on his driver's thin arms throbbed as he pulled at the gears with a high whingeing sound. Under the thick sole of his knock-off Nike, the carburettor gasped, the tyres bumped fast on the potholes, and every shift in speed came as a blow.

Debris from bad truck accidents littered the road. Crumpled cabs, shattered glass on the tarmac, wheels splayed at odd angles, and overturned trucks exhibiting their rusty and greasy metal underbellies.

The thought suddenly came to me, shocking in its stark clarity: *New India will never make it.*

Many of us had assumed it would, because it had been too easy for us, those of the old India, to make a heyday out of the world's *fin de siècle* confusion. People from nowhere taught to read and write, crammed with ready-made knowledge that people in other countries, those Loneys and Irodovs, had worked out, and then released into societies that needed their skills just at that moment and which offered in turn a congenial ideology of self-aggrandisement.

Aseem broke through the membrane of lowly, unpromising birth with his ten thousand fucks. And Virendra paid some Russians to go down on him. Perhaps, young men like my driver were so frantic in their appetites because they knew in their bones that, taken out of their ancestral occupations and small businesses, they had been educated for nothing.

Dispossessed of their original homes, their modest but stable livelihoods, their fatalistic but consoling religion, they lacked even my small advantage: a place to run back to, and hide.

I dozed off, and then woke to a flickering memory of our last meal together at Wagamama.

You are sitting very erect with your elbows on the table. The composed party face you had carefully assembled at home, alertly expectant and confident, as though proclaiming that you are exactly where you want to be, has collapsed; there is sadness in your jaw and fatigue in your eyes.

There is a stray little lash on one cheek, just below your eye. I want to, in the way I have so many times before, take you in my arms, hold your face, and then watch your eyes close. Instead, I feel the knot of anguish inside me tighten, and I wonder, yet again, if I should tell you about my imminent departure.

Returning from the toilet a few minutes later, as usual followed by curious glances, you sit upright, crossing your booted legs. The lash is gone from your cheek, and the surface of your face has shifted; I am again looking at the self-assured woman who left her apartment in careful make-up a couple of hours ago.

A fork spooled with noodles leaves a smear of soy sauce at the corner of your mouth. I watch it for a bit, waiters bearing food-crammed plates whirling around us, before offering you a paper napkin. You look at it, uncomprehending.

And then the memory flew past me, like the metal carcasses of cars and trucks.

The road plunged into a series of damp gorges, and immediately deteriorated. With each bump, I helplessly swayed in my seat, I felt emptier in my head and my chest tightened.

I began to breathe easily only as the road emerged from a long tunnel – and great untenanted spaces opened up: a flat valley scored by the white eddies and swirls of a river revealing from that height a fixed, marbled pattern.

The still air seemed to give the valley unalterable shape and unbreakable conviction. As the road descended into the valley, the pattern broke; and the river's movement came to be matched by noise.

No sooner had we descended than we started to climb again. At nearly ten thousand feet, I felt my heart start to pound. The road was now a thin ledge high above a crazily frothing river – more ruts and rocks than road. Enormous mountainsides rose straight from the river, vertigo petrified, and littered with boulders and streaked with lumps of old snow, which, though no longer pure white, was still obdurately firm in shadowed crevices.

Far beyond them, unmoving even when the road twisted, and our car veered away at the last moment from oblivion, loomed some giants of an opaque whiteness.

I felt a humming in my head, the familiar beginning of a high-altitude headache.

How simple my escape had seemed in my mind in London. The plan for it had taken shape very quickly, over a few Google searches, one late evening after my meeting with Sonam. Flight to Delhi; another flight to Shimla and then a car ride.

Unfolded across several mountain ranges, the journey had assumed its proper dimensions of time and distance, and when the road climbed even higher, I began to worry about the remoteness of the place to which I had chosen to run back.

'Do aur ghantey. Two more hours,' the driver unexpectedly said. 'Garam kapde laye ho? Wahan sardi hogi. Do you have warm clothes? It'll be cold there.'

'Yes, yes,' I said. 'I do.'

Actually, I had only two heavy jumpers knitted by my mother, and a warm Uniqlo undershirt.

'Wahan kyon ja rahe ho? Why are you going there?'

I couldn't tell him that.

He said, 'Saal mein ek baar naahte hain, badi gandh aati hai, aur chai main makkhan aur namak daaltey hai. They bathe once a year; they stink, and they put salt and butter in their tea.

'Lekin, building dekhne main acchi hai. But the building looks good,' he added.

I wanted to say that I had been there before, that I had first seen the building years ago. This was soon after I arrived in Ranipur and started to go on treks in the region bordering Tibet. On one of these trips, I noticed a gompa. Crowned by a gilded pavilion, and looming over a complex of stone houses, barley fields and apricot orchards, it had something of the defiant loneliness of an outpost.

Ascending to these highlands, I had felt myself to be in a different country, Hindu shrines giving way to well-worn chortens, with vines snaking around the walled towers, and faded tattered prayer flags snapping in the crisp wind at high passes.

The vermilion and white façade of the monastery, a hovering weight in the blue air, seemed to proclaim that difference over the whole landscape.

The region was inhabited, a trekking guide from Shimla said, by bhotay – a derogatory term, I learned later, for Buddhists of Tibetan origin. I had seen some of them: men with broad faces and polished cheekbones leading buffaloes and mules slung with brushwood and fodder, and women with centrally parted hair, shining pigtails and necklaces of beads and amulets.

Scoffing at their pre-modern lifestyle, the driver didn't get everything wrong. Going up to the village – on a precarious mountain trail that had been partly washed away in landslides, and made treacherous by unmelted snow – and to be among old men and women with cheeks creased by years of exposure to the high-altitude sun, and foreheads by tamp lines, who wore ragged, home-spun wools, wicker baskets on their backs and rounded sickles in their girdles, was to encounter a distinctive odour: the combined smells of smoke from the hearth, yak butter, sweat, and the bovines sheltered under the wooden balconies of their two-storey homes.

I passed a freshly whitewashed chorten, and walked down an uneven, cobbled street, between the high walls of the monastery and houses with astonishingly elegant wooden balconies. Old men, half-crouching under the chilly dark shadow of the walls with their loaded ponies, watched me. A frightened donkey, its ears erect, suddenly dashed past me, followed closely by a panting boy with a huge saucepan.

At the gompa's sunlit courtyard, a trapa unloaded sacks of grains from a pony. I pushed at a massive brass-studded door, and walked through a narrow little room to suddenly find myself in a silent chapel full of tall, gilded statues, masses of finely carved and brilliantly painted wooden pillars, lamps feeding on butter, silk drapes hanging from the ceiling, silver water stoups and peacock feathers.

The smell – of butter, various kinds of incense and human odours – was intense. And standing there in that hot and spiced darkness, I felt my skin prickle, as though in contact with a new element.

I went out. The sun on the cobbled threshold was blinding. In the distance, a Himalayan range crouched against the blue-green sky, and a pale blue river cleaved the valley. I stood there for a while, amid the prayer flags softly fluttering in the wind and the squawking of ravens; and, as often on lonely passes, when I would look back, resting on my stave, one last time at mountains that flanked by mist lay in light like mountains in another world, I irrationally vowed to return.

It was dusk and drizzly when I returned nearly two decades later, the wind twisting the braids of rain, and draping the monastery with thick mist.

I was expected – Sonam had made sure of this. A young Tibetan, wearing a bright yellow plastic poncho over his crimson robes, took me – up endless dark narrow steps, past many doors – to what was to be my room for the night.

Behind the painted door, there was a straight-backed wooden

chair, a small almirah, a cast-iron bed with a mattress and quilt, the smell of old, unremovable dust, and nothing else.

He left, and for several minutes, I just sat on the edge of my bed. I hadn't imagined such blankness. But there it was at the other end of the earth, suspended amid the great tumult of the world; and it seemed the destination to which I had always been, without knowing it, bound.

Later, as I unpacked, feeling a twinge of homesickness as my backpack released the aroma of Olga's preferred washing liquid, long-legged spiders scrambled out from behind wooden beams on the ceiling to watch me.

Inside my notebook, I noticed your Mont Blanc fountain pen, of an old-fashioned design, stout in the middle and tapered at the end, which I must have picked up from your desk and forgotten to return. For several minutes, I sat gawping at it, worrying that I had taken off with a family heirloom, and wondering if I should risk mailing it back to your London address.

Afterwards, I lay on my bed with my phone and looked at the emails that had arrived during the long drive. There was one from you.

Arun, you had written, *I am trying to stay positive and assume you had to leave due to an emergency at home. It's too devastating to think that you decided to leave without a word to me, and that all these months of living together and our happiness meant nothing to you. I know there is little I can do if that's how you feel, but if you did, we could have at least tried to work it out. Please, when you have a moment, reassure me. And come back soon. The flat feels very empty without you. Much love, Alia.*

For an instant, I saw very clearly how it dawned on you as that email went unreplied: that I am paltry and pathetic.

I lay there for a long time, staring at the dark beams on the ceiling, until the naked bulb overhead started to flicker. It finally went out with the parting roar of an old generator somewhere in the bowels of the building.

The noise stopped an hour later, the generator having probably run out of diesel, and in the pitch dark I then heard for the first time in months the sound of rain pattering on the roof.

In my childhood I would run out into a thunderstorm followed by my little sister, who would leap with delight, her pigtails bouncing, and clasp me as the rain soaked us to the bone, and then go hunting with me for the frogs croaking in the undergrowth.

I remembered undoing her plait afterwards and encircling her with her wet hair in my fist, imprisoning her with its locks until my mother, with a little smile, told us to stop shouting.

There came to me, too, a memory of my mother standing on the balcony on our first snow in Ranipur, looking out at the whitening of the twigs and branches of the bare trees and the top of the straggly wooden fence of the apple orchard, her great duffel coat lifting her arms from her sides, her head nearly submerged under woollen mufflers, emitting small, strangled sounds of excitement.

My heart suddenly ached; and when I crept underneath the quilt smelling of mothballs and closed my eyes, the rain still beating on the roof, I found myself surrendering to my childhood vision of my body, heavier than water, sinking slowly into the sea.

PART FOUR

Twenty

During my first few days at that dark and silent room in the gompa, I slept and woke and slept again, surrendering, as rain turned to snow outside, to my fatigue, to an overpowering desire to sink down deep within myself into unending rest.

Three months have passed since, a time blurred by blizzards, snowdrifts and icicles, and I still try to find peace in that submission, that sense of having given up a struggle and of being removed from a world of confusion and pain.

I have a new room. Magnanimously vacated by a young trainee monk, it is even smaller, with no furnishings apart from big square cushions that lie along one wall, a small, low, square table, and a little wooden altar, with offerings of rice and butter. The walls are adorned with thangkas, representations of Sonam Lha-mo, a female divinity, painted in gold and black. Tin flower cans hang from the frame of the door that opens out to a small balcony.

The room is approached through a storeroom for dung and fuel, and my nostrils are never free of the most evocative scents of my childhood – dung from the yard, and the high note from the cans of kerosene.

The monastery is more than a thousand years old, apparently founded by a lama who translated Sanskrit texts into Tibetan. Perched on a steep slope, in defiance of gravity, its three storeys stand guard over a river valley – less a conventional valley than a circle of steep mountains. And I feel in its dark rooms, so perfectly sealed off from all that blinding high-altitude light outside, suspended in mid-air.

In the gompa, where so much seems to have remained there for ever, rising perhaps when a door or window opened, but never getting out, it is spookily still, the tremendous silence occasionally punctuated only by hurried footsteps, and the agitated rustle of robes. I have yet to get used to the complete absence of the noise that accompanied me here from London, the growl and whirr of engines, and the chattering metal and delirious dance of a loose bottle in a taxi.

I try to recreate the thrill of anonymity I felt when I arrived: *no one* knows me here, apart from Sonam, who is on a retreat in a small cave above the monastery. The monks I see on their few sorties out of their cells, but never speak to, seem to conspire in creating a climate of convalescence for me, treating me as if I was recovering from a sickness. And I spend most of my time trying to meditate.

'If you are looking for improvement, you must focus on meditation and only meditation,' Sonam had said in London.

This project of ceasing to perform for anyone, of becoming perpetually vigilant against deadening mental habits – the project that I have come here to pursue single-mindedly – feels directly at odds with intellectual work, anything, in fact, that requires a furious flux of ideas and thoughts. My small successes with it in this half-dreamy place hint that I may not be very far from a solution to whatever has gone wrong with me.

Looking for prolonged periods at a fixed luminous point in the darkness behind my closed eyes, I lose all knowledge of who or where I am. It is a lucidity greater than any reached by my conscious mind.

Opening my eyes, I am, of course, returned to this bare cell in a monastery, and its everyday props of my existence – this low table, that paraffin lamp, those thangkas on the wall, and the tin flower cans on the door that my head often collides with. Everything is where it should be. And I am who I am. Everything seems normal.

But I can't shake off the suspicion that I have just experienced the sheer contingency of what I call my 'self', a truth I perceived only very faintly in the empty landscapes of my childhood; I know then that what I took to be normal life depended too much on a continuous exaggeration of my identity and significance.

I think of all those who have been here over ten centuries, all those who let go of everything that involves getting somewhere and being someone, who abdicated their gifts and talents instead of forging themselves in the image of a doomed society, and who departed with what Aseem called their 'true potential' unrealised, promise squandered, blessedly unaware of the modern obligation to exploit and advertise oneself.

I didn't tell Aseem that I am here. A part of me still cowers before the vital passion and insouciance with which he has lived right into middle age, scorning the passage of time, and taking no cognisance of death. What Sonam might see as uncontrollable vice – desires of every kind, social, sexual and professional ambitions – has been integral to Aseem's life.

I do wonder now if he, too, is exhausted, occasionally, by the venture of being an uncompromisingly secular and modern man, that while he thinks he knows exactly how to pursue satisfaction, something always seems to be missing, and that he, too, wishes to be awakened to another life – his true life.

I shouldn't make this seem the perfect sanatorium for wounded and fatigued men. It is numbingly cold inside my poorly insulated room; the aged grime everywhere keeps my fingertips perennially black, deepening the longing for a hot shower. I haven't shaved since I left London, and it is just as well that there no mirrors here for me to confront a face altered and aged by its long bristly hair.

The salty tea Tibetans drink makes me a bit sick. The food is terrible, even for someone who grew up in a world divided into those who eat and those who don't; my digestive system is unlikely ever to adjust to tsampa. The hole-in-the-ground toilet, with all that it inflicts on the eyes, the nose and the groin muscles, is difficult to adjust to in middle age, even for someone who as a child squatted by the railway tracks each morning.

I have volunteered to drive to Jalori, where the dirt road to the monastery joins the highway to Tibet, and a petrol pump, kirana shack and chai hut stand between half-ruined buildings, to pick up firewood and make phone calls. But the pick-up truck I use, on a rutted dirt road high above a river, always looks as if it is about to break down. And the smell of the rancid butter that Tibetans use profusely seems to confirm a failure that had occurred, in some choice of mine, long ago.

The days pass. I am never short of things to do. I carry firewood up to the monastery, and fetch water in buckets from the village when the pipes freeze. I read a bit, mostly newspapers and magazines left behind by visitors to Sonam, but not for long. I can't now remember where I read that the healthiest form of life is manual labour in a monastery: the most bracing truths of body and mind lie in physical exercise and silent contemplation, and that, with words and thoughts, one starts to slide into harmful untruth.

A part of me still longs for conversation, wishing the monks weren't always so hospitably indifferent.

Twenty-One

After some months, I had started to know a kind of security at the gompa, feeling myself part of an ancient organism with its own life, identity and purpose. The anxiety and anguish that had sent me there had started to ebb away, leaving behind only a vague unease.

I had dreams in which places and peoples I had known appeared more vivid than they had in actuality, clamouring for my attention, suggesting a lost life in which I neglected so much and mourned so little; and I lurched out of this reproachful drowsing into sweaty shame and bewilderment.

On good days, however, the past appeared to be a place where someone else, not I, had lived. And when one day a fresh shirt suddenly rustled with what turned out to be tissue paper interleaved by Hotel Danieli's laundry, I struggled to remember that afternoon on the Lido.

It began to feel as though I had crossed into another life. And then the past – that deep darkness of howling voices – suddenly returned.

One afternoon inside the chai hut at Jalori, where the crackling fire cast a red glow on leathery faces blackened and spectacularly wrinkled by the high-altitude sun, I called Devdutt.

We had previously been in touch to arrange a new fence for my cottage. Towards the end of our conversation, he said he had Naazku by his side. She is still inconsolable with grief, he said, and then without another word passed the phone to her.

There was a short silence, in which Naazku seemed to be drawing a long breath.

'Aapki mata ji ki bahut yaad aati hai. I miss your mother a lot.'

I didn't know what to say.

Naazku had the same declarative telephone manner as my mother, her sentences emerging in a quasi-panicky rush, and demanding no response.

'Bahut kathin jeevan raha. She had such a difficult life. Unko bahut chinta thi aapke baarey mein, kya hoga unkey jaaney ke baad. Voh aapko khush dekhna chahati thi. She was very worried about what would happen to you after her death. She wanted to see you happy like other people.'

From the darkness of the chai shop I could see the silver slab of midday sun on the snowy road. Someone went past on an old bicycle, hunched over the handlebars, the unoiled wheels whining, the underinflated tyres flatly scrunching the snow crystals.

'Voh aapko khud kahna chahti thi marne se pahley. Unhoney kaha tha ki voh phone karengi aapko. Phone kiya? She wanted to say this to you herself before she died. She said she would call you. Did she?

'Aur sabse acchi baat hogi agar aap pasand karein ladki ko. She said that you will need someone to look after you when she is gone. And it will be best if you choose a suitable girl for yourself.'

As though sensing my bewilderment, she added, 'Unko maloom tha badi kothi ki memsahab ke baarey main. She knew about the lady from the big villa.'

She had started speaking in a low voice and had quickly built up to a squeaky crescendo. But I was no longer listening.

A noisy bus had arrived on the road – and found its path blocked by a seething crowd of Gaddis leading a small, unseasonal flock. The shaggy, dirty-white sheep stood with lowered heads, as though pondering something, refusing to give way to a bus. The ancient bus engine snorted, its metal flanks shuddered, and I saw among the frenetically gesturing and shouting shepherds a young woman with quick, birdlike glances flashing from below her heavy scarf.

I looked away, back to the shop, Naazku still speaking, and found myself staring at a pair of red-streaked eyes set into an old face.

And then something gave. My sight became blurred, I began to blink, and I felt the wetness on my cheeks.

So many memories had come to me since my mother's death, of her walking me to school, lying in wait for me, glass of hot milk in hand, as I returned from the nullah. I had known guilt but no real grief nor sense of an irrevocable passing. I had been moving as though in a brightly coloured dream, effortlessly, everything more vivid than ever but more unreal.

Driving back to the monastery, a long unreleased pain now finally pouring out, I felt closer to the reality of what had happened with her death – the end of something not only for my mother but for myself, and the beginning of a long loneliness. And, in the days that followed, I felt full of mourning and a desire to act before it was too late, to find you and somehow cancel the sequence of events that had brought me to this desolate place.

And then the roaring of the world around my ears suddenly became louder when I picked up an issue of *Outlook* that was lying on the table at the entrance to the gompa, left behind by a recent visitor, and saw the headline: 'The Downfall of an Icon: Aseem Thakur accused of sexual misconduct.'

I read the first paragraph of the cover story in a daze: a

young teacher at Delhi University where Aseem had gone to lecture had charged him with sexual assault. Several other women had subsequently come forward to accuse him of molestation and harassment.

I ran to my room, and, once there, opened the badly creased pages to see, among the unfamiliar faces of Aseem's accusers, a large picture of you, wearing your Ray-Ban Aviators, against a banner advertising the Great Minds United festival.

A sound escaped my mouth; the magazine in my hands started to tremble, and I found myself closing my eyes.

And with closed eyes I saw you, abandoned while asleep in a room thousands of miles away, come to life.

I opened my eyes, giddy and fearful, and only then began to register the nature of the fresh offence inflicted on you.

The report in *Outlook* – full of salacious speculation, for the academic at Delhi University had chosen to remain anonymous – said that you, the scion of a famous and distinguished political family, were the first woman to come forward with a charge of molestation against Aseem. It quoted from your brief statement on Twitter mentioning persistent, though swiftly and decisively rebuffed, advances from Aseem in his hotel room during the festival, and expressing solidarity with the victim of sexual assault.

It seemed that, acting on a First Information Report by her, the police moved remarkably fast to file specific charges and arrest Aseem; and that, arrested, bailed and then rearrested, Aseem is contesting all the charges against him. He blames the most serious of them on a conspiracy by his political antagonists, and he is especially vehement in denying that he had done anything you had not consented to.

He claims that it was you who had gone up to his hotel room at the festival, not once but twice: the first time for an interview, the second time for a romantic tryst. He says he has proof that you were very unhappy over a recent break-up, and were seeking consolation.

As I read and reread the magazine article, squinting hard without my reading glasses at the swimming words, and at the picture of you, a whisper in my brain insisted that I must keep my distance from all this.

And yet an animal flutter in my heart and a growing hole in my stomach told me that the spell was broken and the past I had tried to put behind me had returned.

I would still meditate; fetch water from the village; try to bury guilt and shame under a weight of old and new obligations; and I would compel sleep through a daydream of oblivion. But I would awake, my head teeming with images and thoughts, with the night still outside; and I would be afraid to see it go and to face the white morning.

My room suddenly felt very cold, as I lay on my bed, and for a long time, the weight of my blankets and the weight of the wooden beams on the ceiling seemed to make it impossible that I would rise again. For a long time, I could not think of anything at all, as though chilled arteries were no longer conveying blood to the brain.

I kept picking up the magazine to stare at your photo, as though it would reveal something about the horror of being assaulted by someone you knew and trusted – a horror great enough for you to take the immense decision to go public with it, fully aware that what awaited you, a Muslim woman in a country run by Hindu supremacists, was not justice but a relentless and degrading public exposure.

Later that overcast afternoon, I finally emerged from under my heavy blankets and drove five miles through snow to Jalori.

The monks, whose blameless eyes I now tried to avoid, wondered why I was going out in such intemperate weather. I didn't tell them that I wanted to find a mobile signal and download more news, especially about you.

On that rough road, where the truck rattled and side-slipped, stones clattered away from the wheels, into the abyss of the frothing river, and the ruts jolted my spine, I felt inside me a rolling mass of nausea and apprehension.

The short journey seemed a lifetime. At the end, I was almost relieved to read that the press has failed to contact you and that you had 'muted' your social media accounts.

You were last sighted at Delhi airport, by an acquaintance from your days in TV, who was not tactful enough to conceal your trail.

I sat still in the icy cockpit for a while, thinking of you, your suffering, the courage that lay behind your decision to publicly accuse Aseem, and the ordeals that still lay ahead. The image of you I held in my head had started to fade. It has now been obscured completely by this extraordinary new vision of you – one of the flesh-and-blood victims of atrocities committed by my earliest friend.

As you re-enter my life, so changed as to be hardly recognisable, I wonder if I ever knew you; if, confronted with death and decay, I had used you for a short breather, to appease a belated lust for life.

I agonised at length whether I should ring you and then did nothing more than sit in a cold swirl of remorse and indecision and stare at your profile picture on my WhatsApp, until a strange tremor in my arms and legs forced me to put my phone aside, and steady my shaking knees.

I searched for more news and saw photographs of Aseem arriving at the magistrate's office in a police van, and being met by demonstrators outside. Almost all men, they have been clearly hired by the ruling party; and, shouting abuse, shaking their fists and gnashing their teeth, they fill the background of the photos like film extras.

Their feigned fury touched something in me. I was suddenly full of rage, vengefully wanting to see Aseem's face, and the expression he had chosen to wear at this moment of disgrace.

But policemen, who pushed him out of the car with their hands on his neck, had covered his head with a black blanket.

I kept looking at the photo. There are countless versions of it: Aseem has scaled, while completely blinded and propelled by others, the peak of his fame. And in that moment of lucidity that anger creates, I recalled his callous response to Virendra and Siva's arrest.

It is also 'curtains' for him. His trial in court might go on for years, even a decade and more. However, his political enemies, now in power, will not only remove him from public life for a long time but also devise manifold torments for him.

The journalists camping out in front of Aseem's temporary prison have managed to extract all kinds of details, including about his cellmate, a deranged serial murderer, who spends his days loudly cracking his finger joints. Apparently, Aseem screamed at his lawyers, 'Please get me away from him!'

I saw a photo of his wife, expressionless behind dark glasses, and felt grateful that he has no children. I learned that his mother, whom he hadn't seen in decades, had unexpectedly shown up for his bail hearing. Identified by one of his close friends, her sari-clad diminutive figure rather than Aseem's wife became the focus of sketch artists as she sat at the back of the court, muttering the Gayatri mantra, her fingers working a jaapmala.

She did not look in Aseem's direction once amid all the

nudges and significant looks; the frenetic TV reporters shouting into long fluffy microphones outside the court said she was ashamed of him.

But if I know my own mother, from the same generation and background, Aseem's mother was not ashamed of her son – someone she still loves and wants to protect. She was ashamed of being the cynosure of all those eyes; she, who had always felt herself of so little account.

Since the identity of Aseem's main accuser remains unknown, the media has turned to digging up your past. All the images that I once retrieved from multiple and often obscure sources are featured prominently on the internet. There are also many pictures of Aseem and you at the festival.

Small and indistinct on the phone's screen, they continue to shock. In your equivocal face I search for reminders of our brief relationship, and find not a trace.

In one of the photos, you and Aseem perch on the arm of a narrow sofa on which a celebrity cognitive psychologist from Harvard is sitting. In another, you are whispering in his ear as he smiles, a little awkwardly; and I felt a bitter surge of what in the next moment I saw ashamedly as trite masculine jealousy.

The Hindu supremacists, who have long been trying to find Aseem's weak point, seem overjoyed by these pictures. To them, you are not only a Muslim, a special object of hate, but also a woman drinking wine in a short skirt, who, while blamefully asking for it, managed to bring down their enemy.

These reminders of you settle like a heavy stone inside my chest. I wish again that I could talk to you, and that I could do something to rescue you from such humiliation, and to alleviate your pain; and each time I am paralysed by the memory of my own dereliction; each time, I become aware of just how absurdly belated my impulse to virtue is.

My anger and the explosion of malice in the media against Aseem seem equally futile. I see from the press reports that members of the Lutyens elite, who were always dismayed by the success of someone they considered an upstart, are gleeful. But the most ferocious among those raining blows on Aseem's statues are his former flatterers – those who I saw at his parties in Delhi. They had demeaned themselves by raising him onto a pedestal; they now see an opportunity in his downfall to avenge their humiliation.

They say that all his crusading for environmental issues and against political corruption, all his espousing of women's rights and social justice for the historically disadvantaged minorities, and other left-ish causes, were not more than instruments of an exorbitant lust.

I feel more sympathetic to the toilers in Aseem's magazine's open-plan office, who have recounted stories of glamourous women gliding past their laden desks to his chamber. His inexhaustible energy and charisma had once kept them bound to their meagrely and intermittently remunerated jobs.

No more: many have resigned and are speaking out, solidifying a consensus that Aseem was always a fly-by-night speculator, an opportunist, a name-dropper, symptom of toxic masculinity, exemplar of rootless and unscrupulous cosmopolitanism, if not an out-and-out crook.

Twenty-Two

According to reports in the media today, you have 'gone into hiding'. I think you drove to Ranipur from Delhi. I wonder if your estranged mother and her rich husband helped you; I wonder if I should reach out to them for information.

I feel more helpless and inconsequential, wanting desperately to speak to you, but aware, at the same time, that I can't.

I abandoned you and now I am hiding, too, giving light itself the slip in this gompa, where innumerable days seem to have died without penetrating its labyrinth of windowless rooms, and where monks coming up and down narrow stairs with tightly held candles send flocks of shadows flying along the clay walls and stone steps.

Many more people are trying to hide, or so Sonam said when I went to see him in his retreat today.

Snow was gently falling, big, shaggy flakes floating, as though reluctant to meet the ground. Inside his tiny cave, it was dark; my eyes took some time to see the smoke-blackened walls, the clay hearth in one corner, and the thick incense smoke rising tranquilly up in the butter-scented air.

When Sonam appeared, a pile of firewood on his shoulders, little shining specks of snow melting on the coarse bristles of his head, and gestured to me to sit down, I tried to squat on the dirt floor. I stayed crouched in that awkward posture until Sonam pointed to the stained chatai in one corner where he presumably sleeps.

'I am sorry I barged in while you were away,' I say. As Sonam bent before the hearth, carefully arranging some twigs, he raised his hands – and I was struck by his chipped palms, the crazy network of lines gouged by menial work.

I didn't know what to say. 'You look in good health . . .' I started.

Sonam looked back from the hearth and smiled. 'Yes, yes. Thank you very much.'

From the valley below a soft clang of pony bells drifted up. I had walked past a few of these elaborately girthed and belled packhorses on a narrow snowy path, set beside whom their snow-layered drivers looked underdressed.

'How is the monastery?' Sonam asked.

What could I have said? That it is too late for me to abandon habitual ways of perceiving, feeling, thinking and behaving – the whole point of monastic practice.

I can't tell him about you, or my mother, or that I lull myself into oblivion every night by imagining my body sinking into the sea, by imagining a netherworld where I can live without a corporeal cover, without the strain of presenting to others a body and a face.

He might dismiss it all as fake drama. The years at school and IIT, where what I learned by rote I soon forgot, the sham work at the literary review, the isolated existence in a village, remote from the struggles, quests and sufferings of ordinary people, the translation work, another mode of high-minded idleness that served the intellectual vanity of some rich philanthropist and little else, and now this flirting with detachment in a monastery after betraying those closest to me.

Perhaps he would be right: that I possess no reality beyond this too malleable self. And even this attentiveness to oneself, this search for hidden inner depths and mystery, is false and deceptive.

★

'You have got to be ruthless,' Aseem said all those years ago. And that is what I have been in my own way, holding fast to my instinct for self-protection, quick to withdraw from whatever seems inconvenient and uncongenial, and to suppress the damage I inflict on others.

Anyway, I am no longer sure if I have the resources to last the three more weeks I have here before I try to return to Ranipur.

As though anticipating my thoughts, Sonam said, 'You came here at the right time, and you might be here longer than you planned. I hear that people around the world are seeking refuge from a new disease.'

'Really? What kind of disease?'

If only, I found myself wishing, some great devastation would obscure or diminish my own misery.

He seemed not to want to answer me, and I caught the hint of a smile on his face; it reminded me of those talks in London when Sonam smiled and laughed at the people confessing their suffering to him.

And then he added, 'I hear many people are going into isolation, to evade death and suffering, with a surplus of toilet paper.'

Ignoring Sonam's advice, I have been secretly writing in my cell. I began to think, as snow fell outside, shutting down the access road, and I worked late into the nights, that this quiet labour, this attempt at accounting mine and other lives to you, could become an end in itself, a mode of self-anaesthetising, and perhaps one way of achieving immunity from total despair.

I was wrong. Yesterday, the road finally seemed clear after three weeks. My phone started to tremble uncontrollably as I drove to Jalori to pick up more news. I stopped to see a series of text messages; some enterprising journalists, who tracked down my number, have been trying to contact me to discuss Aseem's case.

It turns out that he has uploaded on to his website an audio recording of his conversation with you with the help of his lawyer. Finding himself on trial by public opinion, he has decided to respond with a public defence against the most prominent of his accusers. The recording is not meant to be conclusive proof of his innocence. For one, the conversation it presents occurred during Aseem's first meeting with you in the hotel suite rather than the second.

Introducing it on his website, one of Aseem's still-loyal friends, a playwright he once employed as a reporter at his magazine, asks for a 'sophisticated literary interpretation' of the conversation. With its subtle emotions, the exchange, he argues, builds up to what he insists was a moment of agreed-upon intimacy with you.

It took me, as I sat shivering in the unheated cockpit of the pick-up truck, nearly an hour, and many aborted attempts, to download the audio file on my 2G connection. Fearing that I might lose the connection, I did not dare look at the news of the worldwide shutdown. Instead, I watched the dirt-streaked windscreen steam up with an air of expectancy.

And then I couldn't wait to get back to the gompa to listen to the recording.

Within a few minutes of meeting, you and Aseem start to talk about sex. Gender, actually, local attitudes to homosexuality, and the differences between men and women. Aseem does most of the talking.

A brief discussion of the British election follows. Aseem says he once met Boris Johnson in London at the *Spectator* summer party; Naipaul and one of his Rothschild friends were there, too. You say that London is going to change – for the worse. Most of your friends in London are relocating to Paris, Berlin, Amsterdam and New York.

There is a dullness in your voice, and an eager expectancy in Aseem's. I hear the tones, and wish you were not there.

Aseem speaks of India: Modi has peaked, he says. More people are realising he is a con artist, and even his supporters are waking up to the damage he has inflicted on India's social fabric.

Aseem segues from this to Virendra's fate. You tell him what you told me about your meeting with him in a Massachusetts correctional facility.

'Poor Virendra,' I hear Aseem say. 'I hope you'll be fair to him. I really hope so. I am really glad you are writing this book, and not some clueless white person.'

Aseem goes on to speak, tangentially, about the 'white masters of the universe', Hindu supremacists, the endgame of modernity and much else. I imagine him picking up and putting down this or that worn subject while focusing harder and harder in the privacy of his mind on a proximate object of desire; and I repeatedly press the fast-forward button.

It is only later in the recording, after your questions about your book have been answered – and I imagine you closing your MacBook, as always, with a slow sigh – that you and Aseem talk about what's uppermost in your mind.

I feel afraid of what I am about to learn.

'I woke up one morning and he was gone. Just like that. I have no idea where he went. We came back from Italy; he was a bit quiet. He didn't even want to talk about Virendra's death. He was going on about this Tibetan guy a lot. How emptiness is something to be embraced . . . And then, he was gone.'

You repeat, 'Gone. Just like that. No message, no text, no email. All he left was some cash for the bills we were sharing.'

For an especially excruciating second, I fear that you will bring up the missing Mont Blanc pen.

'What happened to his mother? She was ill, or something? He was asking me for helpers.'

'She died when we were in Pondicherry. Arun didn't tell me at first. He seemed very upset.'

Aseem doesn't even register this.

He says, 'Maybe he gave up the world or some such shit. This is a classic move by us Hindus – to strike a pose of detachment just when the responsibilities of the world grow heavy. I am pretty sure he will resurface somewhere or other.'

'I WhatsApped him. I called him. I emailed him. He didn't reply; didn't even have the guts to send back a single word. This, after living together for months. What an asshole.'

Aseem's tone changes, perhaps in response to your expression.

'I am sorry to hear this. It must have been awful to wake up and find that he had disappeared.'

Aseem seems to pause. My ears prick; and I am tempted to click stop.

It is best not to know what our friends really think of us.

'To be honest,' Aseem starts again, 'I was surprised to hear that the two of you were an item. I mean, I introduced you and then the next thing I knew you were both in London.'

I was surprised, too, at this turn of events.

'I thought it was strange,' Aseem says, 'that he didn't respond to my new novel. Very unlike him.'

He adds, 'To be frank, he was always a bit of a weirdo, an anachronism – a low-energy guy, as Trump would put it.'

Was this an attempt at humour? I do not hear you laugh on the tape.

'Afraid of life.' He continues with his indictment. 'Afraid of the human condition, which is all about striving and hope and changing your circumstances. There was something very fucked-up about him, not sure what. I mean, living in a village with his mother after studying at IIT. Who does that? He had more literary talent than all of us. He could write, better than—'

Aseem stops. But then an old saw of his occurs to him.

'I mean, we all live inside stories, and when one story ends, another begins. The trick is to find what constitutes your story and have the power to confront your fate. Arun never saw this.'

You are silent for a while.

Then, you say, 'He is a loser.'

There is a pause. 'I was so wrong about him,' you continue. 'I thought he was so serious, and smart, and so . . . delicate. But, no, maybe he is just a loser.'

The words hang, dagger-like, in my freezing pick-up truck.

'I should be going,' I hear you say.

'Listen, I am sorry,' Aseem starts, 'really sorry. I feel personally responsible because I introduced you two. You deserve so much better.'

'No, no. Please don't blame yourself,' you say. 'Anyway, it is good to be able to talk about this to you. Thanks so much.'

'You can always reach out to me. I am always here for you. Again, I am really, really sorry.'

There is another pause, before the recording ends. Did Aseem edit out something?

I can see how Aseem, pressing the red button on his iPhone, would have sprung out of his chair and gone over to you.

The close physical proximity and gaze of X-ray intensity and sincere tenor are, I remember from his Delhi parties, how he conveyed his deeper interest in women.

I had seen the way he worked, moving swiftly from affable dispassion to a hunter's tenacity, mesmerised by his own growing degree of power over his victim. And he wouldn't have been discouraged to see you, standing nearly as tall as he in your high-heeled boots, recoil a little.

This morning had a harder, bluer darkness than yesterday, and the air had a new chill to it. Under a sky piled high with clouds, the mountains stood out stark and black. Snowflakes began to blow when I went down to the kitchen to find some stale bread, and came across a monk admiring an icicle nearly five feet long on the porch, a fat drop burning at its tip.

When the weather cleared a bit, I rushed to Jalori. A mile before Jalori, my phone started to vibrate in my jacket pocket; I stopped, dangerously on a sharp turn, to see many more requests from journalists for briefings and interviews.

The fear of a virus, potentially genocidal in India, has not diminished their interest in this case. They say they want my 'side of the story'; they want to give me a 'chance to respond' to what has been said about me.

It is clear they want me to speak ill of Aseem; inflict a few more hammer blows on the shards of his once colossal reputation.

How can I tell the journalists that I don't presume to see myself as different from, and therefore capable of judging, Aseem? I see myself in all his ruthless egotism. My abrupt disappearance from your life was no less an act of aggression than what Aseem inflicted on you. I ended up punishing you for my self-betrayals, my desertion of my sister and mother and of my sequestered life.

And who can I speak to about the shame of being a man, my complicity in so much suffering?

Not even to you: I don't know now if I'll send what I have written to you. Perhaps, the silence of imperfect understanding should lie between us, and I should no longer cast a shadow in your mind.

I imagine you in your villa, behind the vast picture window that one afternoon so disquietingly altered a familiar view. I can return to Ranipur, to the cottage that death invaded, only after you have gone – and who knows how long I'll have to wait? When I try to look ahead, into the future, I can't make out anything, except some more years, insisting on being lived.

One thing seems certain: I won't see you again. Our story has reached its end. It was one story among a great many that begin and end at each moment, in which, contrary to what Aseem always said, we rarely seize the power to confront or change our fate, and though we console ourselves that we can always run and hide, there is no real escape from that farrago of cravings, delusions and regrets we call the self and the trail of devastation this nothing leaves behind.

Late in the evening, the lights went out. Power cuts here can last for up to twenty-four hours and so I saved my file, shut down my laptop and groped my way in the light from the rapidly fading bars of the electric heater to my torch.

Then, wrapping my heavy, shaggy blanket more tightly around myself, I walked out to the balcony, and immediately hit my head, yet again, on one of the tin flower cans hanging from the door frame.

The thud was loud; the empty can squeaked as it oscillated once, and then I caught it mid-swing.

The new moon poured down silence over the valley. The ground was sparkling faintly. It was nearly midnight and the monks, punctual to a fault, were all asleep, each one of them, I imagined, recumbent in shrine-like cells, among tankas, bowls, rugs, lamps, images and manuscripts wrapped in bright yellow and orange cloth, and a little butter lamp burning by the side.

And then I saw a figure trudging up the steep incline to the gompa, bent under the weight of firewood. On the narrow path, all the hard outlines of this world lost in white snow, it would have been like walking in space.